Castle Of Eyes

A Novel Of Dark Fantasy

Other Fiction Available From Chaosium

KING OF SARTAR, Greg Stafford (ISBN# 0-933635-99-0) $14.95

Castle Of Eyes

by

Penelope Love

CHAOSIUM INC.
——— 1993 ———

Cover Art by Mark Wagner

First Edition

Address all correspondence concerning this book as well as requests fo a free catalog of Chaosium book, games, and novelties to Chaosium Inc. 950-A 56th Street, Oakland CA 94608-3129, U.S.A.

Printed in the United States of America, April 1993

ISBN 1-56882-005-4

"This is a love that equals in its power the love of man for woman and reaches inward as deeply. It is the love of a man or a woman for their world, for the world of the centre, where their lives burn genuinely and with a free flame."

Mervyn Peake, *Titus Groan*

This book was written for Mark.

Prologue

R EVEN HAD BEEN YOUNG, handsome, and vital, and now he was a cooling mass of flesh at her feet. She cursed, first in shock, and then in dismay.

"Why . . ." she started to say, before her voice cracked right across. The demon read her glance and interpreted it aright, interjecting its answer before her question was completed.

"He was going to kill you," Slaarngash said. Its voice was the black tone of a cracked brass bell, or a tomb door grating shut, terrible and final. It turned its head, and then its body to fully regard her. In its wake roiled a multitude of ghosts, after-images on the mind's eye too fleeting to be fully understood, and a breath of air, humid, thick and turbulent with unseen thirsts. The blade it held refracted the red of its eyes and sent their glow skidding wildly along the stone walls like so much splintered stained glass. Reven's blood dripped from it and steamed on the stone floor.

"He was cursing me, not murdering me," she said. She knelt, uselessly, beside the corpse, placing her arms upon Reven's back to see if he still breathed. Her sleeves slid back but the pink, smooth, still-healing stumps at their end no longer had the horror they had held for her scant months past. She managed, by sliding her arms under him, and levering him up, to get him on his back so she could apply her ear to his chest, just above the bloody gape of his guts. Equally useless. She had not liked Reven, so she could not say that she was sorry. But she did not want him dead.

"Do you think he would still live?" the demon said.

"No," she snarled, and sat back. Blood swilled everywhere. On the floor, the sword, on her dress where the blow had sprayed over her, and on her skirt where she had knelt. Its stink overwhelmed her senses. "Here, lift him," she snapped. "Carry him. Quickly," she added. Slaarngash took its time, lowering its ears to its ponderous skull, and wrinkling its muzzle as it returned the sword to a scabbard slung across its back. "Even now one runs," it said, sulkily. "Little feet. Swiftly."

She stood, and looked up the passage, towards the distant Courtyard, then down, towards the Castle Proper, then cursed again.

"Will I kill little feet too?" the demon offered, eagerly. It stretched itself up from its haunches, and lifted its wings, absurdly small for the bulk of it. It raised its ears interestedly also, for all the world like a tame dog.

"No," she said firmly, then, "Marre. She'll kill me." Marre's vengeance would undoubtedly follow soon after discovery. To murder the lover of a powerful sorcerer, however unwittingly, was surely to invite retribution of a spectacular and grisly kind. Nothing came to her, least of all an acceptable explanation for her actions, and she could think of no way to avoid retribution, except to hide Reven's body in the hope of hiding with it her guilt in his assassination.

"Or have you killed," the demon said, slowly. A strange look, half glee, half grief came to it.

"Is that what lay behind your blow?" she spat, rage, life, reality, at last resurrecting itself from her horrified stupor. She rounded on it, "Do you think she would spare you? Do you plot to be freed? She raised you from the netherworlds, and she will consign you to worse if she returns you thus."

"No," Slaarngash protested, its wings and jaws twitching spastically. It whimpered, and cowered, hurrying to its task. "No, there was murder in his heart, I tell you."

"Not now," she said. They plugged the wound as best they could, but it was the pull of the earth and not a beating heart that caused the flow, and it was too great to staunch entirely. She stood and brushed futilely at the blood on her clothes. "He has no weapons, no defenses. And he would have arranged for others to do it rather than dirty his hands."

Slaarngash turned its head instead of answering, and sniffed at the breeze coming down the tunnel, wrinkling its leathery nostrils. It was a powerful head, and a muzzle out of some disproportionate hell. Slaarngash's head and chest were all one width. It narrowed to its jaws, which were flat and wide and dripped crooked fangs, and tapered also to its pelvis, absurdly so for the compressed mass of body those small hips upheld. Its sex was undefinable, being a grotesque and shadowed collection of hooks and flat, stubby tentacles shielding something like the plated mouthparts of a crab. It was too vital for this world, too splendid in its brute assurance to be ever fully contained in it. It battered, slouching, through the opposing air and left memories of itself to flicker briefly and die, grasping for it like the impress of the risen sleeper that remains on the long cold bed. When it spoke or chose to breathe, as it did now, an icy mist lifted from it.

"Little feet come," it hissed as it raised the corpse, "And quickly, with others."

"Too late," she moaned, "Too late already. Down, move him down, towards the Castle. We can hide him in the antechambers. Do you think that we can hide here?" This was a rhetorical question. The chambers and corridors between Castle and Courtyard were deserted, and kept fastidiously, deliberately bare, for it was the fashion of the Castle to disdain daylight along with the common folk who had to endure it. She could see already that her attempt was hopeless, but she would not passively wait to be found. Reven did not deserve it.

The demon had crossed a scant dozen chambers, when shadows darted across the distant entrance.

"Hurry," she hissed. A glitter caught her eye. A bejewelled dagger lay in the pool of blood where the dead man had lain. She had been wrong then in her estimation of his character. She bent by reflex to pick it up. Phantom hands grasped at air, and the hurt and shame stung, as if the wounds were open anew. She shifted it sideways with her foot instead, and a sluggish tide of blood filled her slipper. She turned as the long shadows reached and wavered towards her, as their pursuers briefly passed some opening in the myriad of abandoned rooms and corridors. One squat shadow leading another by the hand, a woman in bulky dress. The last was even more unmistakable, tall beyond the normal human measure, and stooped almost double in the low-ceilinged stone.

She ran, and found that Slaarngash had passed through another dozen rooms with its burden. Despite her precautions, the dead man left a wide trail of blood behind him, lessening as it reached the demon, like a pointed finger.

"It is Caerre and her brood," she said, "If we can but reach the antechambers they will surely not dare follow us."

Echoes span a confused web of footsteps and cries behind them.

"As long as they do not know a shorter way," the demon grunted. Supernaturally strong as it was, a corpse is no easy burden to bear alone.

"I have been back and forward a dozen times, and only Iriethe besides myself knows it," she answered.

"You are wrong there," said a voice, breathless but triumphant, from ahead of them. Caerre was before them. Anna peered from behind her, and they could hear their companion's harsh wheeze from some further stair. Slaarngash snarled. It dropped its burden and unsheathed its milky claws, which sprang blurredly into a foot wide fan around its stubby fingers.

"No," she cried, and Slaarngash staggered back as if from a physical blow, turning at bay against her. She ignored it.

"For shame, Anna, for shame after all I have done for you," she cried instead. Anna hid back behind Caerre's skirts.

"Don't you scold her," cried Caerre, and in a louder voice still, so that again the echoes rang, "What have you ever done for her, Alliole, that she could not have done better for herself if she had been allowed?"

"I saved her life," Alliole snapped back, "She was following me, and now she's run to you with the news. She is a good spy."

"Hah," Caerre said, and started to draw herself up, but then laughed again, a genuine cry of delight. "But I'll forgive you. It is true then. Reven is dead."

She loosed Anna's hand and came forward, skipping a little, in her peculiar way, and hitching her bulky and concealing skirts. She stooped beside the corpse, to feel for his heart-beat, and touch the reality, the finality of death. Caerre's gait was between a limp and an extra step, and quite unnerving. It made Alliole feel that she should step back to give Caerre more room.

"Dead, dead, dead," Caerre chanted, and rocked backwards and forwards, "I am so glad." Slaarngash, confronted abruptly by her movement and her words spread wings and claws anew and gaped, dropping the hinge of its jaw as a snake does, baring yellow fangs and sticky strings of saliva around a thrashing tongue. It was a sight to affright the dead, but neither Reven nor Caerre were moved.

"It is not meet to gloat so . . ." Alliole started, dubiously, as stunned now as when the sword had exploded towards her through Reven's body.

Caerre raised her vivid face from the corpse, and the other two their dull ones, to regard her. Anna was dwarfed and their companion was too tall—to call him a giant was to grant him bulk and width which he did not have. A shadow lay on his face, famished and resentful, that was bleached from Caerre's by some commitment that Alliole had yet to determine. Their faces were otherwise strikingly similar, too round of chin and cheek to be long out of childhood, dark-haired and pallid-skinned as were all folk here, and enlivened by their curious, mismatched eyes, the right one being green and the left, blue. Clothes, once rich and of somber hues, now faded and ragged, hung from them, revealing here a skinny arm, or fingers blue with cold, and there concealing, perhaps, more than anyone knew.

Alliole stood her ground beneath their combined regard, but felt uncertainty well within her. Their manner was not of those who were about to sound the alarm.

"I am not gloating over Reven," Caerre protested. She stood and sobered a moment, before her glee overcame her again. She danced in a halting circle, almost a painful movement, and laughed again, then clapped her hands to still her companions' dutiful echo. "I am laughing over you. What care I for my family, if they will not have me?" She kept her hands together and smiled her odd-eyed, malicious smile above them. White skin and black hair framed her radiant gaze, so that she was for a moment like Slaarngash, a force born of no mortal earth, drawing fire from within. As if in recognition, Slaarngash recoiled further and raged again.

"Do not snarl so, demon," Caerre said, sweetly, "I know the First and Middle Seals, and have long studied your summoner. You do not frighten me, and I might just be tempted to find your true name, and cause you long, slow pain. Or I might loose Tiralgon here on you."

"I don't like demons," the wolfish Tiralgon said, and grinned. Slaarngash shut its jaws with an evil toad-snap, and slunk around the corpse to Alliole.

"My hands," Alliole protested. They were more than two flesh. She relied utterly on Slaarngash to tend to her. Its loyalty was bound to her, but loathing crawled just beneath and tainted its motives, whilst Caerre's very youth and impetuosity abruptly rendered the situation ugly. She felt abruptly old—old and weary and unable to fight against this new uncertainty. She knew Caerre only as the outcast daughter. Their single, brief, earlier meeting had not prepared her for this capable and tumultuous person.

"Tiralgon, get rid of that thing," Caerre said, dismissively, "And Anna, get water." The pair immediately obeyed.

"I did not know you were a sorcerer," Alliole said at last, choosing the phrase carefully from several that presented themselves to her.

"There's a lot you do not know," Caerre said, with satisfaction, "Why did you have to move him? That trail makes it harder to clean."

"No one comes here but I," Alliole said, in defence, "Reven was after me. Anna also."

"You have quite a following," Caerre said, cheerfully, and then thoughtfully, "I wonder if you had any others we know not of." Anna came back, and handed Caerre the jewelled dagger, then scurried off again. Caerre turned it over in her hands. The echo of Tiralgon's laden footsteps died away.

Alliole shook back her yellow hair, and sighed then gasped again, a sound heavy in itself, that holds back tears. Doubt and fear of discovery was within her, but no remorse. Not yet. After a long pause, she braced herself, and asked, formally, "What do you wish in return for your aid?"

"You," returned Caerre coolly, "You have my aunt's regard, and my brother's, from what I hear. Do carry me tidings of them. I would value your opinions."

"I will not be your creature," she said, flatly. But in exactly her brother's manner, Caerre took her refusal simply as grounds for further negotiation.

"Why not? Because you owe loyalty to others? I do not ask you to trespass on that. Simply talk to me of Castle matters. It is my right. You know that."

"I know very little," she said, wincing. Caerre had touched assuredly upon a very sore spot.

"You are also in the dark then," Caerre said, and laughed, bitterly this time, "We are all of us so, and groping towards the light. My wants are simple. My proper inheritance. I do not want to be hidden away in the Catacombs as if I was ashamed. It is they who are ashamed, of what they have borne." She turned her face to the wall in her anguish, as if she could stove in the stone with her shout, and crush the facade, the impenetrable mystery of the Castle, with a blow from her small, capable fist.

"Xoon has the passage of power from the Parrar," Alliole said, cautiously, "You could never hope to rival him in your mother's favour." But she saw by Caerre's agony that she could.

Anna was back, with a bundle of rags and a bucket, and she started to clear the floor, making a big circle around the demon, which swung its head to her movements, as to a pendulum, longingly. Anna wrung the rags into the bucket, whose water gradually turned a deeper color, as the stain was transferred from the floor, as though they were making crimson dyes. The two women watched her, as she backed out of sight, following the blood trail. It was not until she was gone that Caerre spoke again.

"We are, as you say," and here she turned back, and malice pooled in her luminous eyes, "good spies. We gather crumbs and shape them into whole loaves. If you want to know anything you should come to us, if raising the cry of murder from your shoulders is not enough to bind your loyalty to me." At this reminder Alliole winced.

"Rest," Caerre continued, "Recover yourself. And then see how you can aid me. Enough of that, Anna," she said, going into the corridor. The pair went away together, holding the bucket between them, leaving Alliole considering the meaning of their complicity, and the likelihood of discovery. Marre was a sorcerer of great power, through whom Slaarngash had been brought into this world. But Alliole had had to pay a price for her services, such that she knew that perhaps only one other in the Castle would be willing or able to contemplate. Would Marre, unaided, work spells of discovery, of prescience? Blood called for blood, that Alliole knew, and a dark deed such as murder would call for darker deeds of magic to bring the truth to light. It might be that Marre would not tamper with such forces, that Caerre would not insist on the full measure of her bargain. In which case she had gained at the very least a further source of knowledge, such as she had so painfully learnt was most valuable in this place; this vast vault of countless chambers, stairs and passage-ways, a myriad halls whose arched entrances lead only to another hall or inter-connecting stair. In this place, where they said she had been born and raised, but which she did not remember. 🗡

PART ONE

Chapter One

THERE WAS A TIME of waking and darkness; of remembering and then determining to forget; of fever, of dreams that were drained as if by fever; of blackness snatched between streaks of sunlight pouring through a high, arched window set in stone. She closed her eyes again, and when she woke, there was someone leaning over her.

"You're awake then," a woman said to her, a small, dark-haired sallow woman with a pock-marked face and a singular expression hovering between kindness and severity. She called out to someone at the door, "Hurry, tell the Neve that Alliole is awake again."

"Again," she said, meaning to question, but her voice was so weak that her words faded into nothing. She was surprised at how small her voice was. Her gaze wandered over the room of her dreams, high, high, she could tell by the swing of the stone beneath her, and the eastern light sweeping through the window. Blue lay beyond, the eye-aching color of the open sky.

"Where am I?" she asked, and felt her vision falter. Dreams, deep and painful, came strong and unreal upon her, the pull of the dark tide threatening to engulf her. She lay buoyed upon its surface, in her tight snug boat of a body, with no knowledge or understanding of why she rose, what kept her afloat, or when she might again sink. The woman leaning above her said something, but she lost it in the renewed swell of the water. She fought as fierce as she could against it for an interminable time, and found herself all at once and totally awake, beached, exhausted.

"Do not worry about such things now, Alliole. You are in your chambers. You remember, you have had them since you were a baby," the woman said, soothingly. Then she drew back as a second woman came towards the bed. This latecomer was taller, better fed, but likewise with a pale face and dark hair held back with a fillet of silver. Her touch was like the fall of winter sun, cool and firm and more real somehow, than anyone could reasonably be expected to be.

"How do you feel, Alliole?" she asked. A hand pressed against her face, so that she felt the cool bluntness of the other's fingers, as if pressing against living stone.

A shadow swept across Alliole with the touch of her hand, and a sharp, strong moment of agony. A voice that ached with sorrow, searching forever, called out, 'Where is it? Where? You must surely know. Answer me!' the Voice cried, in such pain that she pulled away from the touch, and shadow and voice ceased together, along with the faint starting echo of an answer.

The Silver Lady drew back also, and pleasant look changed to a frown. The absurd words danced in Alliole's head with such urgency that they could not be denied. She wanted to weep for the searching, bodiless Voice, and to cry aloud that she did not know, that she would aid her, but her mouth was bound as if by a corpse cloth. When the tears came, the two watching faces furred and lost their shape, becoming shifting pallid thumbnails of light beneath masses of dark hair.

"Alliole, you are still weak from your fever. Rest," the first woman said.

"Who are you?" Alliole screamed, for she could not remember, and she tried to sit up in bed. She could not, and became aware for the first time of her body as something too heavy to lift, "Where am I? Tell me what it is and I will find it. Tell it to stop weeping."

"Alliole, Alliole," the sallow woman said, and turned away, to a bowl that sat by the fire.

"She is Iriethe," the Silver Lady said, firmly, slowly, drawing Alliole back to her with her gaze, and Alliole saw with something of instinctive horror that the Silver Lady had odd-colored eyes, one blue, one green. She knew somewhere deep within her that this was the mark of a sorcerer. "She is not weeping. She is not sorrowful. And I am the Parrar Neve."

"Surely you know us, Alliole," put in the other, Iriethe, from where she stirred the bowl by the fire, "You know us well. You have known us since you were a child. Surely you remember? Alliole, you remember?"

Alliole could not answer, only gasp and turn her head away for fear of sorceries, and try uselessly to lift herself. Iriethe, returned to the bedside. Scented steam rose from the cup in her hands.

"Be still," she said, "You have been ill a long time. Rest. Recover." She raised the bowl to her lips and sipped, once, and then supported Alliole's head to get her also to drink. Alliole tried to push the bowl away, and then shrieked anew, "My hands," for raised in defense were only her arms, with no length in the bandages for hands, no width even for fists, so that she rocked in the bed and screamed, despite all Iriethe's protestations, and her screams turned to sobs, the sobs of such magnitude that they rocked the frail body-boat that alone sustained her on the surface, and she was swamped, sucked down by the black race of the current within her.

As she sank, she heard the Silver Lady say, musingly, "Tell what to stop weeping? There are no tears here. Who was she talking to?"

"It was some remnant of the fever," the other said, nervously, "It is nothing." Their voices flickered in and out on the edge of her consciousness, until Alliole came to believe that she was dreaming them.

"She spoke when I touched her. It is more than fever."

"Some hold-over from the sorceries then. Poor child, she has suffered enough of them, and never cried out until now. Why Alliole?"

"Because she is dead. The name will do as well as any other."

Then there was nothing, but falling deep, deeper into the swirling dark than she would have thought possible to do, and yet remain alive.

When she awoke again, the fever had left her. A girl was in the room, who took flight when she turned her head. Shortly after Iriethe returned.

"Alliole, remember me?" she said, but Alliole shook her head.

"A little," she said, weakly. "From yesterday. Was it yesterday? I have no hands."

"Yes. It was a terrible accident. Do you not remember?" Iriethe said, her eyes averted to the window. Alliole shook her head. Tears came from her eyes, "I want to die," she said. Iriethe moved over and touched her face. They both stilled, but no unanswerable Voice came with her touch, no shadow. Iriethe called to the girl to get water.

"I would rather be dead than useless," Alliole said, and wept anew. Iriethe made no move to soothe her. She sat by her, her eyes on the window, and waited for her to be silent again, when the breath had left her, and she fell back against the bolster and gasped and moaned because she had no strength for tears.

"You could be dead," Iriethe said then and composedly, into the quiet left by absence of grief, as the girl lingered in fascinated horror by the door, "And whilst we are taught of heaven and of the multitude of hells, I choose to put my faith in neither. To live is better."

"Like this," Alliole cried, and a tremor passed through her, of revulsion and sickly terror, horror for her own self.

"I cannot answer for you," Iriethe said, "Because I have only my two eyes to see and my own experience to offer. Nevertheless I say that to live is better. I would rather not have wasted my nursing on someone who thinks to kill herself when she has not the strength to kill a fly. Rest. Heal. Think again on this matter when you are well. I will fetch you some broth." With these words she left, leaving Alliole gasping afresh, a swimmer seeking air, part in hysteria, part in wonder, at the magnitude of the task thus casually thrust upon her.

The room she saw, opened not into the air but into a corridor. The blue was part of a frescoed wall. The winter sunlight was a pale lamp held up by some hook worked into the fresco. None of her dream was real, and that shook her.

"What do you remember?" Iriethe said, on her return.

"I remember yesterday, was it yesterday?" and Iriethe nodded her head again, "then only blackness shot through with red. What is it that I cannot remember?"

"Great shock," Iriethe said, "often wipes the mind clear. Doubtless when you have rested, your memories will return to you." She fed her broth. "You remember your name, don't you, Alliole? You remember who you are? Your character. Are you strong? Do you remember? Such amnesia is sometimes selective. It leaves the important things, character and names."

"I remember my name," she said, and then faltered, as voices came to her mind, as from a dream.

"You remember me?" Iriethe said, "We were always dear to one another." Then she winced as Alliole shook her head, "Are you sure that you do not?" she tried, "Here, remember the color of my eyes," and she shut them.

Alliole laughed, "They are brown, all eyes are brown around here," she said, "Except. . . ."

"Except the Parrar and her family of course," Iriethe said, re-opening her eyes, and wielding the spoon, "Now you remember them. You must. Who are more important to you? Who provide all that we need except for them?"

"I remember," Alliole said, and her mouth dried despite the good broth, for she remembered eyes blue and green, mismatched, cold. She remembered a babble in her ears that was her own voice, begging. She remembered, "They are sorcerers," she said, and broke out all over in cold sweat. But Iriethe was too pleased to notice her reaction.

"Indeed they are," she crowed, "And all glory to them, that we endure here. There see, your memory is returning to you."

Alliole shook again, and this time her kind friend noticed her agitation.

"There, it is too much for you, while you are still unwell," she said, and setting the remnants of the broth aside, she laid her down in the bed, telling her to sleep. This Alliole was glad to do, but after Iriethe had left the room, she murmured over and over to herself the still unfamiliar syllables of her name. She had a sudden terror that in the morning she would awake and fail to recall them, that she would be left as she was on her first morning, and so go on, forgetting and remembering, day by day, night by night, until the end of her days, with never a thread of common memory to bind her life together.

"All buildings sway," Iriethe told her in her dream, "Invisible to the naked eye, in accordance with their height, in memory of the time that they were living stone and beat with the heart of the earth. Thus do we, mere humans, continue to struggle and live, though we see no point in it, and often wish that we were dead. We remember some former time where we were at one with the center of things, and continue on our journey in the hope of finding our way home."

"What nonsense there is in dreams," Alliole told her, but Iriethe smiled sadly, and then turned at once into the Silver Lady, who lectured long on nonsense and truth, until Alliole slept again. But after that night, no more thoughts of suicide entered her head. Something had strengthened her in her sleep, so that when she woke it was to find her name more familiar instead of less, and the soft blackness in her mind where she felt memories should be held less of terror and more of a comfort—that when she chose she could return again to the dark, nameless bosom of the tide.

Memory did not return to her with her strength, and at times it seemed strange. Iriethe would start talking on events that were common gossip of the Castle, forgetting that Alliole would not know them. Or other times she would explain, in exhaustive detail, something Alliole had already been lectured upon. It was in this way that Alliole found out about the Silver Lady, for Iriethe launched on a story, and Alliole had to break in and beg for further information.

"They rule over us and shield us from harm," Iriethe said, willingly enough, "They have ruled always and will endure forever. Some say they can summon even the demons from the hells, and make them work their bidding. Some say they are demons themselves, although wise and kindly ones. I know nothing of such. I hold that they were born from stone, for they have much power over that substance. By these powers did their ancestors raise this Castle from the ruins of the wild world. Powers seen and unseen attend our Parrar. The Neve can hold sway, as I have witnessed, over Spirits of the Air and with Beasts. They also have some power in dreams." Here she cut herself off, abruptly.

"The Neve?" Alliole said.

"She visited you in your sickness," Iriethe said, surprised and offended.

"The Silver Lady," she said.

"Is that how you recollect her?" Iriethe said, and smiled, "The same."

"And she rules here," Alliole pounced.

"No," Iriethe said, "Her Parrar rules above her. You may expect a further visit from her soon—the Neve I mean, not her sister. She cannot attend to you now, for the time is drawing near to the Solstice, and there is much that demands her attention in preparation for the festivals."

It did not seem strange to Alliole then, that she who had lived here always had no friends to inquire after her, or common company other than Iriethe, who had it seemed other tasks, and as Alliole's health improved, allowed them more and more of her attention. Alliole spent much time alone, or with the company of the girl servant, who was afraid of her, and answered most of her questions monosyllabically.

On the day of observance of the Solstice festival Iriethe visited and gossiped for some time, albeit nervously. It seemed to Alliole that the whole structure that encased her shuddered and then thrummed, resonating. Yet when she tried to listen, Iriethe increased her chatter, so that Alliole lost the thread of the heart-heard song, yet learnt nothing of importance from her mentor.

"What is it?" she asked Iriethe.

"The Solstice," Iriethe said, "You remember. It is nothing. The inlay of jasper passes."

"You remember, you remember," Alliole said. "It is a refrain I grow tired of. When will I remember? If ever."

"You are tired," Iriethe said, "And the inlay of freedom passes." She looked sad. But further questions she would not answer.

And after the Solstice Alliole's first lucidity passed. Even as she sank back into lethargy, Iriethe increased her activity, as if taking on the energy for both of them. But she engaged herself in nonsensical tasks, in the mending of tapestries so ancient that the new stitches tore the old cloth; in the polishing of ewers and silver platters so riddled with decay that tarnish flaked onto the ministering cloth. Tasks in short that seemed to have no value but to fill her time, for she worked at them with distracted mind, yet spoke little of value. The severity and tenderness in her face had never been so tried, and Alliole's own feelings about her friend had never been so mixed. She had yet to learn the values and constraints of friendship, and was inclined to believe the character Iriethe presented to her, without pondering further. This was a fault that remained with her for the rest of her life, and whether it was established during in her already, or born of her amnesia, she never knew. For she never remembered much beyond waking from blackness snatched between streaks of sunlight pouring through a high, arched window set in stone, and believing window and sky to be true.

The lack of memory cushioned as well as hindered her, making her forgetful of how people lived. As time went on it seemed to her that she had lived a long while alone, and she asked Iriethe for further companionship. But her friend smiled and shook her head, speaking quickly and distractedly as she had taken to.

"You are not well enough, dear Alliole, for much company. You would be exhausted by it, quicker than you know." The only result of her petition was that Iriethe moved her chambers.

"You are too close to the Courtyard here. I am afraid that as your health improves, the vulgar may disturb your rest."

She moved her away, to where no sounds save her own could be heard, and the air was muffled with sweet smokes from the braziers that alone lit her chambers. For company Iriethe gave her a small, tawny cat with golden eyes.

"When you are lonely, send the cat for me," Iriethe instructed. Such was Alliole's naivety that she did not think to ask that a cat could find one other person in the maze of stairs, chambers and corridors that was the Castle, or that, as soon proved, a cat could communicate by such gestures and facial expressions that she seemed almost to speak, and had such dexterity in her paws as to have hands.

Emotion and curiosity were stifled in this further place, by the soft, amber light and heady fumes of the braziers, whose fuel Iriethe renewed on her visits. Alliole was not unhappy, not with the cat for company, and Iriethe's attendances, although increasingly infrequent. For Iriethe assured her that she was well, and that she had always lived like this. She was not unhappy, but unsettled. And this feeling, as all others were soothed back into sleep, grew more urgent instead of less. Something choked off the words, when she tried to explain this to Iriethe, although Iriethe was always steady and so kind, and so inviting of confidences.

She was unsettled. The light in her would not be quenched, although all forces conspired to urge it inward to the dark. She dreamed of the blue fresco that she had seen only in snatches, and the bright winter light of the lamp hung in the middle of it, and on waking into her placid, quiet new life she would weep, although she knew not why. Fear seemed far away, as far away from her as people were. As her strength improved and she went exploring, she found only empty rooms, dusty corridors and deserted stairs, with abandoned halls, balconies and passages beyond. She explored at first only during the grey, daylight hours, for at night the Castle was as black as pitch. She never discovered a window by which light could enter, and in all her wanderings she never encountered an outside wall. The only change that she could discover was that where she dwelt the cornices and stair wells were decorated with carvings of cats, but when she ventured further, she came to a place where the carvings on the walls changed from cats to birds, birds with long necks, heavy bodies, and wild wings, with grace unspeakable etched into even their graven forms. Bird and cat fought in a carved flutter of fur and feather all up one stair and onto the accompanying balcony, that must have taken a skilled stonemason a lifetime to complete. Touching the stone, so patiently, so uselessly carved, fear utterly overcome her, of being lost in this never ending empty grandeur, and she retreated to the rooms that she knew well, her chambers so warm and companionable in comparison with the cold, enduring stone outside.

Yet this instinct that she did not know she possessed, it persisted. It was curiosity and hunger for the truth, her great and besetting sin, but she could not yet name it. In the end it would not let her rest, but night after night forbade her to sleep in the sweetly scented room, and sent her roaming the corridors again, the fearful vacancy of the rooms and passages, in search of purer air. She could find her way well enough, for apart from her own footsteps, the dust lay thick and undisturbed along the corridors. Iriethe's footsteps she followed once, but they led to a blank wall, and she knew that to unlock the secret of the passage beyond she would need hands. She never found marks of the cat, and surmised that the cat knew her own routes to where people worked and played and rested. Sometimes she wished the cat could speak, so that she might tell her how to reach them. But the gentle cat only purred, and rubbed her face against her own, and brought her dainty morsels on a tray.

One day while exploring she found other tracks in the dust, that she thought at first were children's feet, until she saw they were misshapen. She followed as far as she dared, and had almost caught up when she heard—Them—speaking above her. One, no, two voices, muttering together. Idiot voices. She hid her ears in her phantom hands so as not to hear them, and was appalled to hear them still, until she raised the stumps to cover them, and shrank back into the corner. She heard the scrape of feet, coming down, and then a vile mutter, a scuffle and a retreat, and knew that what she had followed might be human, but was certainly not sane.

"The Castle is large," Iriethe said, when she told her of her encounter, "And in many places deserted, even ruinous. Some say it grows, you know, or that it links to other Castles, other times, where dwell tribes of lost folk who devour strangers. Keep to the places you know, or you may lose your way, and it would take days to find you again. If ever."

For a while she sank obediently back into her lethargy, but again the light within could not be stilled, and again she went further, further than before, until the birds—swans Iriethe said they were called—changed to masks, gaily ribboned and bedecked in ribbons of gilded stone. Sometimes she saw the little misshapen child's tracks in the dust, but she forbore now, to follow them. Furnishings she found here sometimes, standing mute and patient in the empty chambers, rotted, decayed, yet recognizably the remnants of bejewelled chairs, of tables topped with surfaces of mottled gold, and crimson ropes that dropped to powder at a touch, topped with tasselled bells whose amber tongues were flecked with speckled jade. Ancient, yes, but bespeaking a later abandonment than the chambers which she found previously, still retaining, in however poor a shape, these forlorn artifices of wood and cloth. On her return path, she conceived the fancy that the air around her was composed of thousands upon thousands of motes, so thick upon each other that there was scarce enough left to breathe, that was the remnants of all the vanished furniture, gone to dust.

After this venture she dreamt of the Voice again, as if it had been awoken by her coming in contact again with things people had once used. She dreamt that it was calling and searching amidst the drear grandeur, and she woke crying for it.

"All the empty rooms," she heard her own voice saying as she woke, choked and almost unrecognizable as hers. It sounded like someone stronger, older. "And never finding what you want in any of them, poor thing. There must be one room set aside for you."

When Iriethe next came she made a great effort and spoke to her of it. Iriethe could not enlighten her.

"There are many things unexplained in the Castle," Iriethe said, softly, "And this is one of them. I have heard of nothing like this Voice. I cannot aid you."

"But it is so sad," Alliole said, "And it disturbs my sleep. I cannot rest with it looking so, I cannot. I must search and I fear what I will find. I beseech you." Seeing her distress Iriethe agreed to aid her, but all she did was change the herbs in the braziers, whose fumes plunged Alliole into deeper sleep than before, and forbade visions of blue skies and searching Voices, but left her awakening with an ache inside, as if she had wept in her dreams.

Her hair, cropped for the fever, grew again thick and yellow—the only thing to mark the passage of time she spent in those chambers—until she became afraid that perhaps in its growing it would steal her hard won memories, that they would grow out slyly and secretly with the lengthening strands. She got Iriethe, by turns doting and scolding, to crop it again. They were an obsession to her at that time, her memories, and she often sat idle, trying to think on them, poring over the scant few she possessed, hoarding them, and reburying them in slumber.

Yet for all this, she might not have taken the final step, for she could not see how to find her way through the empty halls to where people were. She might have stayed in her chambers, rested from her forgotten labors, and dreamt her days away. Save one day when she was going past a place near to her own, a balustraded walk above an empty hall. She looked down to see a man looking up at her, a slight, ragged figure who carried a sleeping child in his arms. A look, mutual of horror and astonishment passed between them, for she thought that perhaps here she saw one of the lost folk who devour strangers, and those below had reasons enough not to be seen. By the time their essential humanity, their shape, form and reality, had sunk in, by the time she had recovered from her long solitude enough to cry out, the pair had vanished. She returned down the passage to the stair and ran back to find foot-prints normal enough in the dust. She stood a long time looking at them, but she did not dare to follow. She retreated to her chambers and breathed deep of the brazier-born vapors, until she thought that she had dreamt this, seeing another alive in the halls and passage-ways she had so long roamed alone.

Yet when she awoke it was to the sound of voices, whispering and arguing, and to faces peering around the entrance to her apartments. She sat up in her bed, bemused, so unused to seeing any other than Iriethe, and looked at them dully. The cat leapt up and stirred the braziers, which fumed anew, sweet and heady, and then stood between her and the people crowding in the door.

"Greetings, honored one," said the girl at their head, effusively. Behind her gathered a dwarfed girl, comely but afraid, and behind her another, unnaturally tall, dark, and lupine. Behind the tall one, barely visible through the throng, Alliole saw the ragged man of yesterday, with the sleeper still in his arms. She wondered why he carried the child so. They crowded in the doorway, peering in. All were dark of hair and fair of skin, all faces were dominated by one green eye, one blue. But where the look of their leader was gleeful and sardonic, the rest were fearful.

"How do you, lady?" the leader said. "My, what fine chambers. Do you mind being so far from everybody?"

"Careful, Caerre," warned the ragged man from well behind. Of them all, he looked most ready to run, protective perhaps of his charge.

"Nonsense," she tossed over her shoulder, carelessly, "I told you we would find her eventually, no matter how well they had hidden her. You are so clever, Helaf."

"I did nothing," he said, retreating further, abashed, from the girl's bright gaze, from Alliole's uncomprehending one. His face held no color. "But there are so many below now, I came up here to get some peace."

"It will be better when the Remembrance is past," she said, and turned to view Alliole again.

"Look at her hair," whispered the dwarf.

Alliole drew herself up in the bed, watching dully. The grotesque nature of her visitors, the glitter of their talk and laughter, convinced her further.

"You are a dream," she said positively.

"Are we?" said their leader, composedly, "Very well. Then I don't suppose you mind us visiting?"

"I have no choice," Alliole said, puzzled by this answer, "My dreams seem to come and go as they will. Assuredly, enter." Her eyes wandered over them again, and became fixed on those of the dwarf who was staring at her, with the wide wondering gaze of youth.

"What is your name," Alliole asked, for the trust in the girl's mismatched eyes touched her utterly. But she only ducked her head against the other's skirts and hid her face.

"Here," Alliole said, casting around to find something to tempt her. All she could see was one of the artifacts Iriethe brought to repair while they talked, a bright useless thing of brass molded into the shape of a sleeping bird.

"There," she said, "Would you like that? It is pretty. But you will have to pick it up for yourself."

"Why should Anna do that?" said the leader truculently. She came into the room herself. It was her step that first alerted Alliole to the reality of her visitors, for it was between a bound and a skip, entirely unnatural, and it seemed another walked when she did. It was too real a sound for dreams. Nevertheless, she raised her arms from the bed in mute explanation, looking over them, into their shocked faces.

"Or would you like a lock of my hair," Alliole whispered. For she had lost the sure thread of the vision, when she saw her reality reflected in their eyes. The gentle cat hissed and arched her back.

"Ware," warned the tall one. His voice was deeper than the rest, a thick, throaty growl, "It is one of her Beasts."

The girl, Caerre, jumped back immediately, awkwardly, and was out of the doorway. They were all gone from the door, in a confused scamper, and only the sound of running feet came back to her. Alliole dropped her eyes to the cat, and saw that it had grown to twice its size, and seemed to be growing further, its fur rising and falling upon the swell of its back as its skin and flesh undulated about its spiralling bones.

"No," she said. The cat turned her head, and Alliole saw a wealth of alien knowledge in its yellow eyes. It was too much to think about now, too much, and she sank back into slumber again. On waking she tried to think that it had been a dream, but the eyes of the girl, Anna, and the step of the bold Caerre, they had been too real.

When Iriethe came again, she told her of them, and inquired after them, but Iriethe only shook her head. The severity flooded onto her face and darkened it into a scowl.

"They are the outcast of sorcerers. Do you think I would bother my head with them? They were bold to come here, the brats, they are bound to the Catacombs Below. I shall speak to the Neve. They will not bother you again."

"Oh no," Alliole said, begged, "Please do not. They were no trouble, especially not the little one. Please do not hurt her. Give her this. I said that I would give it to her." She caught at the brass bird wildly with the stumps on the end of her arms, and rolled it across the bed, so that the blue and green carbuncles that were its eyes winked and glittered.

"Very well," Iriethe said, still displeased. "But if you think I would give Anna so valuable a thing you are mistaken. Here." And with her small knife, she stabbed into the soft metal, and pried the stones from their bed, collecting them on the foot-stool, "I will give it to her now. It is fitting for her station."

"She will not get in trouble?" Alliole asked again, for reassurance. The severity on Iriethe's face softened. "If you ask it, no," she said.

"You promise?" Alliole asked. Iriethe hesitated, and then sighed, "Yes I promise," she said, then slowly and deliberately, weighing her words, "The Neve will hear no ill of them of my undertaking. What is it in Anna, that makes you so desirous of protection?"

"Her eyes," Alliole said, and hesitated, "There is such trust. . . . No, that's not it. I do not know. Did I know her? Before?"

"No," Iriethe said, and her grimness had returned. "They are an object of much repugnance to proper thinking people."

"But they are offspring of your rulers, you said."

"They are outcast from their kin," Iriethe said, her frown deepening. "The physical taint they bear is but an outward reflection of the moral one within. They are disinherited. If their own family despise them, then those who follow them, and are dependent on them for their livelihood, for their very lives, and everything they own and are—" there was an uncommon emphasis on these words— "it is only meet that such dependents should display double, triple, many times that seemly emotion, parleying displeasure into hate, and shunning even the memory of their company."

"I did not know," Alliole said, meekly, "I don't remember. Why then are such creatures allowed to live?"

"By the will of their mother, the Parrar," Iriethe said, and rose. "It is not for us to question her commandments. If you ever do find out what so uncommonly attracted you in that child, do let me know."

It was not until Iriethe had left that Alliole realized her promise was valueless. It had, like much of Iriethe's speech, been too carefully weighted to be relied upon. On deciding this, she struggled to her feet, wrapping herself as best she could in her bedcovers, and went out, with some obscure urge of warning. It was not until she was in the corridor that she realized that she needed only to follow the tracks that her unexpected visitors had made, to come again to a place where people were. That was when she realized that she was free.

She had taken but two steps when the cat skipped in front of her, standing in her path. She took a third and the cat growled. A fourth, and the cat rippled and started to swell, as a drop of oil shaken in water is separated into the surrounding fluid but then coalesces whole again. But now the cat was larger. Her growl was deeper.

"I am not afraid of you," she said, and walked around, and continued.

"Do not go, mistress," the cat said.

"I always thought you could talk," Alliole said, and kept walking.

"I wish you well," the cat said. Her voice was deep and pleasant and slightly mad. "Do not step further on this path. It leads to grief."

"I will go where I choose," Alliole said, "To grief or no. I will make my own path." It freed her further to say that. The enervating stupor of the drugged rooms fell from her.

"I have tried to stop you as gently as I might," the cat said, "Because we children of the night see further than those whose eyes are accustomed only to the clear day. Because of what I see I will not hinder you further, save to say that I wish you would not. I wish you would not."

Alliole turned back to face the cat, whose head hung now between great sweeping tawny shoulders on level with her own, and whose breath swept warm and stinking across her bare shoulders. She looked deep into her alien, yellow condescending eyes, and saw the tears, huge beyond all measure, that welled in them.

"What is it that you see?" she asked evenly.

"I see the death of the old ways, and the birth of the new," the cat said, "I see many deaths. One birth. I see you. I would say you held the new world in your hands, save that you have none. Is it wise to create something you cannot hold? What if you drop it, and it shatters? I cannot see beyond the birth, I cannot tell if what is new survives to become the old. The new is a terrible thing, too terrible to know." The cat raised one monstrous taloned paw and rubbed it across her eyes. The golden color smeared across her fur like glue, and other colors came up from underneath, so, so that one eye became green, the other blue. Alliole turned her back, and walked away.

Later she would say she had dreamt it also. But at the time the stink of the cat's breath was, like Caerre's step and Anna's eyes, too real to be denied. It bore her up on her last venture across the precincts of cats, of swans, of masks, following the trail in the dust until they descended a final stair. Here the dust ceased, because she had come to the parts of the Castle where people were.

Nevertheless she walked down this last stair, to where it plunged underground, to where carved into stone, the dead danced in frozen animation around the entrance to a necropolis. From this entrance blew a tomb-wind, as if a steady sigh of the plundered depths. Down there, she knew, her quarry had gone. But at this stair she turned sharply aside, keeping her feet on the saner earth. She could see in the distance a thumbnail of white light, and knew without thinking, although it was so long since she had seen it, that beyond the glitter at the end of the passage was the sun. 🐾

Chapter Two

ALLIOLE CAME TO THE END of the corridor, and stood in its entrance. She saw a small paved courtyard dwarfed by the towering walls of blank stone that surrounded it, unpierced by any window. The courtyard was completely engulfed in shadow, and bitterly cold, colder even than the passage she had passed through. The building resented the light, and wrung all warmth from it. She looked up, and saw the blue of the sky, saw far in the distance, the wholesome light of day. She could see the sunlight striking paving at the end of the last short passage beyond, but the arch held the light in tight embrace, as if begrudging its entrance to the further reaches of the Castle. Even at this distance the light snarled at her eyes, so long accustomed only to the muted tones of grey washed day, and the amber flickering flames. She could hear shouts, and the stir of a large number of people beyond this short passage.

She crossed the courtyard, the paving cold to her bare feet, and the length of the short passage. She could scarcely breathe, so laden she was with the portent of her soul, and dizzy with the exhaustion of the long exertion and excitement that had brought her here. A herd of piglets abruptly charged around the corner from the courtyard in front, squealing, dodging about her feet, pursued by a ragged boy. Their stench and their sound were all around her, but for a moment, and the absorbed attention of the boy failed to take her in entirely, for he dodged around her with a muttered word that could have been a curse or an apology, and continued his pursuit.

She reached the further entrance and turned her face to the sun. And here she knew that Iriethe was wrong, for if she had always lived without it, why did she turn so thirstily to the light now? It was not until silence spread, in great ripples around her, that she opened her eyes and looked around. Before her was a larger courtyard than the first, also paved, but also dwarfed by the sheer mass of masonry that surrounded it, and hemmed it in from all sides by forbidding walls, many storeys high, on whose faces were carved fantastic likenesses of giant beasts, cats, swans and boars, in the company of graven images of people, heroic in their vast stature. The sunlight was allowed to play, grudgingly, in the fall of water in a large fountain in the center of the courtyard, and it seemed to feel the gross nature of its trespass, for it was a timid and sickly light, a pall rather than an illumination. A wind blew from at her back, not altogether sapped of its vigour by the surrounding acres of stone.

At first she had heard the sounds of people, bustling and haranguing each other, and the shouts of children, but by the time she wrenched her eyes from the sun, the only sound were the old constant ones, the hush of the wind through the stone walls, and the fall of water from the fountain. There were many people in the courtyard, and all were stopped, looking at her. Children were there also, dark, sickly and fey as their parents, frozen in their play.

She straightened her shoulders before them, and shrugged the covers closer over her shoulders. For the first time, their bright colors could be appreciated. The counterpane was brocaded with golden threads depicting gambolling cats, whose eyes were tiny flecks of amber, and whose claws and teeth were flakes of opalescent shell. It made a rare rich cover, whose colors plucked radiance from the scant sunlight, and dazzled her weak eyes. She raised her chin defiantly, and the wind stirred her cropped yellow hair. Some of the children fled at her movement. Others edged nearer. And in all the staring, frozen faces there was none that she knew, none that she remembered. There was no recognition in them, but fascination and wonder and disgust. This last she recognized reluctantly. And she left her regard of people's faces to stare again at the surrounding walls, the buildings, drenched in the timid, washed color of the open sky.

She could see the Castle from the outside now for the first time, with no remembrance of the times past when she must have viewed it, when surely it had been most dear and memorable to her. It stretched in all directions, into the westering sun, ruinous, secretive and sly, like the stone hide upon some vast, sleeping beast.

A ripple stirred in the crowd, towards her. A large woman and small man forced themselves to the front, the man making better progress as he used the woman's wake to carry him forward with less effort. The woman was wide rather than tall, and her face held an unpleasant expression similar to Iriethe at her worst, a mixture of vexation and pride. She had a fleshy nose, wide lips, and small eyes, which crowded together in the middle of her face as if anxious for company. At her heels trotted a small brown hog, along whose sharp spine was strapped a wicker basket containing earthenware pots of pigments, tally sticks and other oddments.

The man had a sharp smile, which he flashed at Alliole now, though he kept his silence until after the woman spoke. A sharp smile that went with a long nose and large ears. Features made for prying into other people's business, a sleek weasel face, that went with a body long and lean, and a certain sharp convulsive movement of his limbs whenever Alliole spoke, as if grasping for hoarded secrets. The pair were dressed in clothes of better cloth and richer color than the rest. They looked well fed, and had around their necks curious torques of an antique texture, that glinted dully golden in the weak light. The crowd made no protest as they forced their way forward. Having presented themselves to the fore, as it were, the two were silent, inspecting Alliole with greedy eyes.

She greeted them at last, realizing that they were waiting for her to speak. The woman returned her salutation, in a contralto growl. The man, jittered, shoving the upper part of his body forward from the hips, and then tilting himself back on his toes, a sharp convulsive movement that indicated an interest almost excessive in its enthusiasm, but kept him in line, behind the other. He nodded and smiled again, his sharp devouring smile. His eyes shone like the gem eyes of the cats on the counterpane.

"What brings you here, lady?" the woman rumbled, in an evidently familiar litany. "We most humble of the Courtyard exist only to serve those of the Castle. Speak your needs and we will serve them." But her surly fashion flatly denied the courtesy of her words.

Alliole opened her mouth, and then hesitated again, unwilling to claim unfamiliarity with the place enough to inquire as to her way. The hog rooted amongst the stones. The people nearest it skipped back. The woman spoke a sharp word to it, and brought it to heel, where it sat upon its haunches and surveyed Alliole in a companionable fashion. Its large black spotted ears flopped about its snout.

"I am looking for Iriethe," she said at last, "Where is she?" Evidently these words were even less to the woman's taste than her own speech, for she swallowed and seemed to munch on the question whilst debating an answer, thereby allowing the man to slip in. He jumped physically as he spoke, thus putting both words and himself forwards. The hog gazed upon them all with a look of the most lively interest and intelligence.

"Forgive me, lady," the man said. His voice was rich and oily, and somehow indigestible, "It is I, Sleepghast of the Castle who speak—surely you have heard that it is my honor to serve our most gracious master, Xoon—and by rights I should not answer so pressing a business of the Courtyard, but. . . ." Here the woman cut him off with a short growl. He ducked back, but as she made no move to further continue the conversation, after a short period of wrestling with his own limbs in his eagerness to speak he burst forward again, "But Iriethe is absent from her normal duties for this fortnight. At the Neve's command she dwells with those dead. Grielle, chief amongst stewards of the Courtyard excepting always her most noble predecessor, undertakes her duties for this time."

"I wish to speak to her," Alliole said. Her eye caught at a bench inset upon the wall near by, and she sank into it gratefully.

"You speak to Grielle," growled the woman. She settled herself even more firmly on her feet, as if by contrast to the man Sleepghast, whose eager, ingratiating movements did not allow him to stay still.

"To Iriethe," Alliole said, firmly. It seemed to her that to see Iriethe again, to see the one familiar face, would be the most important thing of all, "I have most pressing business with her."

"That is not possible," Grielle said, equally firmly, "Until the Remembrance of those Dead is past. Until then you must deal with me." The hog leant against her adoringly, and she absently caressed its sleek head. The bustle of the courtyard gradually increased, as around the core of onlookers, the business of the Courtyard gradually returned. People drew water from the fountain. Another hog trotted past, drawing a small cart piled high with dung.

"I must," Alliole said, and leant back against the stone, closing her eyes momentarily. To her, used to Iriethe as a comrade, it did not seem so large a task. The cold air had swilled the dream taint of the last weeks from her head, and the unfamiliarity of the people, the building, of everything, frightened her. She shamefacedly wanted Iriethe to be here, to take over explanations, to shield her from the strangeness of it all.

"I'll go and get her," Sleepghast offered, and took two steps before the woman's growl again stopped him, as short and sharp and jerkily as if he were a marionette and her words the strings that controlled him. People gasped and stepped away from him. The outer fringe of spectators—either the most timid or less devoutly interested—vanished entirely.

"Sleepghast, don't be a fool," Grielle said, loudly, "Iriethe attends the Dead. If the ceremonies are not completed aright the dead will rise and destroy us all." The man turned, his thin arms splayed wide, his bright, sly face darkening, "Arrant superstition," he said, sulkily.

"Hush," the woman said, and crooked a finger so that he came back. She whispered, so that the other folk could not hear, and Alliole heard only accidentally, as if the woman Grielle, included her in some casually conspiratorial circle, "That may or may not be true, but the myths of our rulers serve us well, and we—you and I—benefit from them. Let us dissemble well in public." She smiled at him, but he hung his head, his sulkiness unabated.

"The dead do walk," he said, as if to spite her, his speech a curious mixture of flattery and incivility. "Or so I have heard. So mock them not in case they hear of your impiety. But Iriethe plays no important role in these ceremonies. She goes only to impress you with her importance, and promote herself in your absence to our betters. It will be a matter of moments for me to distract her, and tell her of this"—with a discreet nod in Alliole's direction. Grielle frowned to herself, so that the corners of her mouth tucked down into her redoubtable chin, and then nodded, reluctantly, "Very well," she said, "I will send a message."

"A most noble idea," Sleepghast murmured, "I don't know how you came to think of it," and then turned in a flourish of limbs to Alliole, "And what message will I deliver, honored lady?" Grielle raised one meaty hand and slapped at the back of his head, but he ducked neatly, turning the dodge into a gangly bow, and she came near to overbalancing.

"I'll thank you to save your discourtesy for those fools who might not notice it," Grielle said, heavily, "You are in my precinct, Sleepghast, and for all your fine airs, you will achieve none of your ambition here without my support."

"What message will I deliver, lady?" the abjured Sleepghast murmured, keeping both his bow, and his sharp glance to rearward, in case of further attack. The interplay between the two, so finely composed of spite, self-advancement and mutual support, fascinated Alliole, and made her for a moment forget that she was the object of their debate.

"Tell her that Alliole would wish to speak to her, and lead her here," she said after a blank interval, recovering as quickly as she could. "Quickly," she added. The peculiar mixture of exhaustion and exaltation that gripped her buoyed her up, but she could not tell for how long.

"At once," Sleepghast said, and sprang away, down the passage from which she had just come. Grielle remained, loitering heavily.

"So what think you of this matter," Grielle said abruptly, as he vanished. "You are not playing a part in these ceremonies. Think you that the dead walk?"

"I cannot say," Alliole said, without thinking, waiting urgently as she was on the return of Iriethe, of the return of some familiarity of the world. She buried her mutilated hands further into the covers so as to allow no further cause for such gossip as she was sure furnished the chief entertainment of such people, "I have been much removed from the world of late," she said. Then she was inspired, grasping the need to impress from the dialogue between Sleepghast and Grielle. "I have been speaking chiefly with the Parrar's Beasts," which was true enough, from what she had been able to gather. "As for the dead walking, I too have heard of such a thing recently, and from the Neve's lips. I assure you that is no light matter." Grielle made no sound, but her silence grew heavier, from which Alliole supposed her to be impressed. The circle of watchers around them thinned and then thickened again, as word dispersed amongst them. The hog at Grielle's feet lost its air of friendly inquiry. It sniffed at the air, raising its snout, and then lowered it again.

"You are a confidante of the Neve's, then," Grielle said, slowly, to which Alliole could think of no better answer than to say, loftily, "I cannot say. I am sure she has many confidants," such as she was sure was not true for someone so cool and self-possessed. Grielle again seemed to chew her words over, before changing the topic again. Alliole looked desperately for rescue, but it was yet to come.

"You will be sure to know then the latest word of the Parrar's confinement," Grielle said. "We poor people of the Courtyard look so often for word of our rulers, and it is laggard coming. We wish her well, great lady, after so many bereavements." This was news also, to Alliole, but she was starting to feel an obscure pride in her bluff. More to the point she had clearly hit the right mark in the general favor, for the crowd around them was now thick and admiring.

"What have you heard?" she asked.

"Scarcely any news worth repeating," Grielle answered. Her features shrank together formidably into a fierce watchfulness, whilst the intent expression on the boar changed to one of smugness. Clearly it knew, Alliole thought, remembering the cat, and remembering the call of the giant. Another of her Beasts? But sparing Alliole any further answer—in which she might have been tempted to pass from guesswork to outright lies—several of the circle spoke, one after the other, the heels of each speech tripping over the tail of the last,

as if driven to answer her question. Each speaker was distinguished a moment
only, before they became one with the crowd again. As they spoke, their faces
were highlighted by a light that blazed and died within them almost in the
same instant, as if it exhausted their vitality in its quest to sustain itself, and
left their faces ashen, their gaze duller than before.

"I have heard she has been with child for a year," a girl murmured, a girl
with a pinched face, the sharpness of her profile caught in the glare of the
stillborn, inward fire.

"No, she gave birth but the child died," said another, a man carrying water.

"The child was of stone," corrected a third, an old woman with broken teeth.
The crowd hushed, as of children hearing a familiar, beloved, story. "The child
was stone and it could not live," the old woman said, "She has shut herself up
in her chambers, mourning for that child. That is why we never see her, though
we love her and would give anything to console her grief. Anything." A sigh
ran through the crowd. Grielle settled herself further, and snorted, whether in
derision or agreement it was difficult to say.

"What think you of this?" she asked. But Alliole was again spared any
answer, for the crowd stirred again, with meaning this time, as a sleeper
awakened, and Iriethe was coming towards her, stepping into the Courtyard
from the dark corridor, and creasing her eyes against the light. Iriethe wore
black, much darned clothes, with many useless darts and other decorations.
In her left hand, transferred now to her right as she reached out to her charge,
were three black lengths of smoldering material. Sleepghast was right behind
her, as close on her heels as the speeches of the just silenced speakers.

"What have you said?" Iriethe's words were her first. The vexation on her
face was pure and unalloyed.

"Nothing," Alliole said, surprised.

"Come with me," Iriethe said, her left hand catching at Alliole's arm to raise
her. Alliole resisted. She would stand at her own pace or fall over. The
smoldering ribbons sent off a musky, bitter scent, redolent of crypts, and
closed-in places, losing itself in thin threads in the open air.

"Rise, rise," Iriethe hissed, and then stood back and bowed her head,
allowing Alliole to see the one coming behind her.

Where Iriethe had to force her way through the knot of people, the woman
following her cut through the crowd like a hot knife through butter. The Neve
stood there. She had stopped at the uttermost reach of the passage entrance
shadow, so that she stood cloaked in blackness. She wore robes of ebony and
silver that highlighted the utter pallor of her features. In her right hand she
held a cunningly composed ball of many layers of fluted ivory. In her left she
held ribbons such as Iriethe wore. The sunlight fell towards her but did not
touch her, and when she stirred as if to take a step into it, the entire Courtyard
seemed to shudder and fall back. She was like the scent from the ribbons,
something self-enclosed and forsaken, that should not stand the light of day. She

stood and gazed upon Alliole with such a look of terror and bafflement combined across her features, that Alliole was at loss for words with which to greet her.

"I was lonely," Alliole said, at last, her voice faltering before the silence pressing in on her, as cold and forbidding as the masonry, "I was lonely and I walked here. I followed the others. . . ." Then she closed her mouth. She looked away from the Neve, so tall and grand and awful, and stood up herself. The cloth slipped around her. She had to gather it up, and resignedly, she heard further gasps as she loosed her left arm to shrug the slippery material further.

"Allow me," Sleepghast murmured officiously, and he stepped forward and twitched her clothing about her.

She faced the Neve again, and was relieved to notice that it was now she who was taller. For here was the queer thing, and one she felt strongly. There was a feyness common among them, that went with their small, wiry frames, their dark haired sallow faces, even a certain delicacy of features that went with their sickliness and made her seem clumsy, fleshy and unsupple. Even Grielle seemed smaller, for all her formidable bulk.

"Alliole, you must rest," Iriethe said, nervously. She tugged at her arm. Sleepghast busily, but slightly more squeamishly, pushed at her shoulder.

"I will not return to those chambers," Alliole said, firmly. Iriethe was silent.

"Return her to her old chambers," the Neve said. Her voice was cool and remote. She had stepped back from the edge of the shadow, back into the passage entrance, "Those she inhabited before. I must return to my duties." She stepped back further, so that peering as they were from the bright courtyard only the pallid gleam of her face was visible. "Alliole, I would talk with you further," she said, and was gone.

Iriethe and the efficient, obsequious Sleepghast ferried her to her old chambers, away from the thin web of sunlight splashed around the Courtyard, and the distant view. Back to the first room that she remembered, with the doorway opening onto a blue frescoed wall, and a hanging lamp that had with its heat and smoke smudge darkened and cracked it, spoiling the splendid color at its very center.

"None of your fumes," Alliole said, but she allowed herself to be lowered onto the couch, and her covers rearranged about her, "None of your drugged sleep, I have enough honest weariness."

"Alliole, we seek only to aid your recovery," Iriethe said, and touched her arm, meaningfully, "Remember." Alliole sank down on the couch, overcome with her own exertions, with her venture from darkness to light, to a return of what should be familiar.

"Why did none of them recognize me," she said, "did no one look for me, mourn me?"

"Why should they know you, the common people, the vulgar," Iriethe answered gently, "They have never before seen you."

Behind her, busy about a multitude of little tasks, Sleepghast made a derisive sound that he must have learnt from Grielle. Iriethe turned and motioned him from the room, a summons he obeyed laggardly. She spoke no further until he had left the chamber. "This wanderlust is a new thing to you, born perhaps of your illness, your amnesia. You act out in your journeying the search for yourself. Before you were content to live alone, with only cats for company. Now I see your mind has taken a new turn, and this must be accommodated. We will not aid your sleep if that is not your desire. Rest now. When the Remembrance is past, then the Neve will wish to speak with you."

"What is this? How did I come by this injury?" Alliole said, murmured rather, for she was weary and the couch comfortable. Iriethe stroked her hair. The musk from the ribbons lingered about her clothes, and in this place did not seem so foreign as it had in the courtyard air.

"That is for the Neve to say," Iriethe said, pleasantly, "If she judges you well enough."

"Well enough," Alliole said, boasted, "I walked, I walked so far. How could I have gone so far unless I was well?"

"We all journey in our dreams," Iriethe said, softly, "Perhaps your wanderings were not so far, or further, than you remember." Alliole did not answer. Perhaps Ireithe thought she was asleep, for she left the room, and Alliole, hovering on the verge of sleeping, was for the second time unwitting witness to a conversation she was not supposed to overhear.

"A most strange malady infects her," observed the sly, dyspeptic voice of Sleepghast, "Yet she has an auspicious name. Wherefor, why do not our most glorious and beloved rulers forsake her as they have forsaken the others?"

"For you, and of your courtesy, she is to be one of the dead," Iriethe said, imperturbably, "And not to be spoken of, save to her face and with most honor."

"A most uncommon face," ventured Sleepghast.

"Silence," said Iriethe. They moved further away, but Alliole could still hear them, somewhat muffled.

"I am simply interested," Sleepghast said, "To hear what distracted our Neve from her most sacred duties."

"You spoke loudly on purpose, so that she would overhear," Iriethe said, "And if the ceremonies fail it will be on your head."

"I am but a poor tool who trusts utterly in the power of our rulers. How can they, the most august and powerful, fail?" Sleepghast said, in his turn, imperturbable, "And doubtless Xoon will be able to tell me frankly of this matter, for as the most high, he will have been kept informed of this woman's illness."

"You know as well as I that he knows nothing of it, and should he hear of it I would know from whence came his knowledge," Ireithe said, her voice ominously calm and placid, "And as you value your ambition, do not speak of this elsewhere or you will find Grielle no shield."

"There were a hundred who witnessed the scene, and by evening the entire Courtyard will know of it," Sleepghast said, moving further away. Alliole was yet able to follow him as his voice rose in virtuous indignation. "Am I to be held responsible for countless gossiping tongues? Am I to hold them in check myself?

"The limit to your powers only you know," Iriethe said, "Count this as advice, from one who wishes you as yet no active ill. This matter is none of your interest."

"Tell that to the truth-stone," said the other, "It will shatter." This was a sneer, and it ended the conversation.

And into Alliole's dreams another Voice stole, by turns demanding, beseeching and pitiful, in fruitless never ending search amongst the ruined corridors and chambers, through mullioned arches crumbling as if in retreat from the empty sky.

The next few days were spent resting. Her body ached, and sleep did not refresh her. She would have none of Ireithe's soothing offers of potions and fumes, for fear of being entangled in further dreams, dreams that sapped will and vigour. For her tiredness and pain that was real, as real as Anna's eyes, when the young girl crept in one night to thank her for the brass bird clutched tightly in one small hand, as real as the bruises that were about her face, and the shadow in her trusting eyes.

"Who is it," Alliole asked Iriethe indignantly, when the other reappeared, "Who is it who so abused her?"

"Sleepghast," Iriethe said, indifferently. "She was waiting upon his master and dropped something. Sleepghast beat her. What is the matter with you, that you so defend her? I have kept my word." And Alliole, her suspicions for naught, had to swallow her hasty words.

Anna came often, always at night, until she was playing in Alliole's chambers, softly and quietly for fear of discovery, and feeding and washing her. In her turn Alliole lavished praise upon her, to see the trust dislodge the shadow. Anna, for all the mark she bore of her kin, was no more or less than a normal girl saving only her small stature, and the excessive sweetness and docility of her character. Of that Alliole was sure, and wondered that all others so avoided and despised her. Her head and body were of normal size. It was the shortness of her arms and legs that undid her.

Then with a rush, the last days of the Remembrance were over, in a series of torchlit processions through the Catacombs guided by children who learnt, by rote, some of the ways through these silent arid wastes. Iriethe vividly described the ceremonies to her captive and eager audience, She spoke of a deathly procession that strewed gold dust, salt and attar of roses over their path in accordance with an ancient ritual whose origins and reasons were now forgotten, whose lights illuminated one time in the year the mortuary slabs and sarcophagi. Into those age-worn engravings was sifted the bone dust from the countless lesser dead packed generation after generation into vast ossuaries. Necrogenic lights glinted off tombs of beaten copper and gilded bronze, and so the superstitious whispered, gelid, unwinking eyes that watched the laggard hungrily a moment from the deepest recesses and then vanished, bearing their unknown owners with them. Gone too were the last days of incense-scented supplication and prayer, of the living entombed in the depths, and Alliole received other visitors than the ones she knew.

She was sitting idle at this time, as a woman with no hands might often be expected to do. She had discovered after this long interval with herself that she did not much like to sit so and would prefer work to distract her from herself. There was little she could do, as Iriethe discouraged her wandering so close to the Courtyard, until after the Neve had spoken to her. She disliked to be dependent so upon the goodwill of others. So she looked eagerly upon her visitors, thinking they would make haste to inform her of what she most wanted to know.

The Neve walked into her rooms, as quietly and ably as if she owned them. Close on her heels was another visitor, a dark-brooding woman of evident kin and similar age, with the family eyes, but whose black hair was streaked with silver, and on whose countenance some great bitterness was stamped. This had twisted her features all to one side, so that mouth and nose dragged to the left, and scored her face beyond her age, with lines not of defeat but of angry, defiant, reckoning. She looked upon Alliole as she would look upon some disagreeable object that yet exerted a certain revolting fascination.

The pair stood silent a moment, fixing her with their odd colored stare, and Alliole's soul cowered back into itself. To bolster it she spoke, straightening her back, "What is your will?" she asked, making it a colder question than she felt.

"Doubtless you heard some of the gossip of the courtyard, when you were there last," the Neve replied, fixing her gaze first upon Alliole and then on the blue fresco outside the window.

"I heard something of it," Alliole replied.

"And provoked some," the second woman snapped.

"Peace, Marre," the Neve replied, smiling sadly, "Alliole cannot help what she is."

"And what is that?" Alliole asked, eagerly.

"Great of soul," the Neve replied, readily, although not as Alliole expected, "It is an old saw, but true, to say that such is a curse as well as a blessing. You seek more than you know, when you go wandering."

"You did not used to wander so," Marre put in, as if reminding. The Neve started slightly, and then bowed her head in acknowledgement.

"What is that to do . . ." Alliole started, and then stopped herself, resigned to listening.

"There is much gossip amongst the Courtyard," Marre said. Her voice was hoarse and her eyes black and filled with hate, directed not particularly at any one person, but the world, fate, "We have no wish to add to their store with retelling of our deeds and actions. I forbid you to go there."

"That is not what we came here to say," the Neve said, her voice richer, all the quieter, in contrast to the other's bitterness. She smoothed over Alliole's heated reply, "You are not at fault Alliole, for the loss of memory—"

"—And discretion with it," inserted Marre.

"—That robbed you of your sense of fitness," continued the Neve, with admirable persistence, "And we will let the matter rest there. It seems to us that if you had work to do, then your wanderlust, your inquiries, would ease, and we have set our minds to aiding you in this matter."

"In what way," Alliole said, now thoroughly discomfited, "More of Iriethe's drugs, or new ones of your own? Think you I have no choice in this matter?"

"By your courtesy," the Neve said, "Allow us the intelligence not to attempt a second time a cure which failed so signally on its first application." Her forehead creased, and she drew herself up, blocking the lamp-light from the window. Alliole hastily assented.

"It has come to us that if you had hands you would be busy," Marre took up, her grating voice striking bone anew, "Too busy to get into further mischief. Such would be a long drawn out favor but one which I, I and no other, may be able to do you. And look you how you meet our visit, when we come only with these most admirable aims." She too drew herself up haughtily, and between them they looked most forbidding and terrible.

"Well, I did not know your purpose until you stated it," Alliole said, "Save that Iriethe told me it might be something of how I obtained my injury. I never dreamed hope of a cure, and I do apologize for my discourtesy. I am unused—" and here she must bite her tongue and recover—"I do not remember," she corrected herself. "Much of this place or its ways, and into it I must be initiated anew. I do beg you to remember that, also." Marre drew herself up further, but the Neve found some amusement in her speech, for she laughed.

"Come, Marre, that rebuke is warranted," she said, "We forget as well as Alliole." Marre would not be amused but cast about her with a dark scowl, before resuming, "What know—remember—you of sorcery then?"

"Nothing," Alliole said, "Save that you and your kin are most powerful sorcerers, as can be told by your eyes and your—" here she gestured, in a way that must once have been habitual to her when she had hands "—The way you look," she said, stumbled, "The look behind your eyes. You fill the room between the two of you, not in space but in soul? That is not clear," she murmured, almost to herself, vexedly.

"Soul?" the Neve asked. "Do you perceive them, auras? Colors? Have you recollected powers also in your new awakening?"

"No," Alliole said, "Only the voices, the Voice. Did Iriethe tell you?" She could tell by their silence that they knew, for it fell immediately, and Marre looked elaborately away. The Neve maintained her steady gaze and the crease between her eyes. This indicated, Alliole supposed, her displeasure at the turn of the conversation.

"Yes we have heard," Marre said, "And we shall talk of this later, for it is important to the way I would seek to aid you. You know then, and I will remind you," (this last said most carelessly), "that most sorcery is but a trick of eye and mind, whereby the skilled can conjure visions from fumes and neatly rhyming couplets, or work the stuff of dreams to make them seem real, and so coerce the uninitiated into obeying their desires," Her diction galloped through this detailing, scorning it in her hurry, "But that beneath this frippery runs a greater sorcery, that draws its strength from emotion and force of will, from passion I suppose some call it. Thus can those whose character is suited to such activities focus their powers to awaken the voices and intellect of the elements, and obtain their obedience, and some few initiates summon and bind the very demons from the deepest hells."

"And fewer still they are who can send them back," put in the Neve, politely, in what was evidently an old dispute, "Such summonings are fraught with danger, all the more so because they tap the base-root of our being, such as is normally—and best—hidden from the intellect." Marre glared at her. "Nevertheless the initiated, the select," she ground out, and the Neve smiled, seeming to read some meaning in her words of which Alliole was unaware, "May do such, at great cost, and this is what I propose."

"A demon," Alliole said, blankly.

"She is afraid," Marre sneered, "You see, I make the offer and it is refused."

"I merely ask you what you propose," Alliole said, still stunned, "What use would such a thing be to me? What would it look like? What would it do?"

"It would be your hands," the Neve said, quietly. She picked up a small tapestry from the table, and put it down again in random, meaningless, movement, "It would be bound in utter obedience to your will."

"Appearance and usefulness depend on the sacrifice made to obtain it," Marre said, wresting the conversation back into her control. Her baleful eyes flickered from the room to its inhabitants, seeming to find in both causes for contention, "A great sacrifice draws a creature of power, a lesser sacrifice, well such draws perhaps nothing, or even puts sorcerer and subject in danger. The wrath of the slighted otherworld is legendary."

"Sacrifice of what?" Alliole asked. The Neve became quite still, her eyes still focussed upon the tapestry on the table. It showed a beast with three eyes being hunted through a hall dominated by a giant throne, from whose rich threaded darkness could be gleaned tatters of crimson cloth and skillfully picked out rubies.

"The common people," Marre said, "Claim that the summoning of demons involves human sacrifice, because that is the worst that they can imagine. Time

and again I have heard the most wild and vulgar rumor of my experiments."
She brooded on her wrongs a moment, and a malevolent gleam lit in the dull
smoulder of her eyes, "But in your case, the price would be little in the paying
and would save you much grief. Give me your Voice."

Alliole squawked, "Then I would be useless indeed," she said.

"Not your voice, fool," Marre said, "The Voice. The one that troubles your
dreams and makes you weep."

"Why?" Alliole said.

"Because it is something of which I have knowledge. I recognized it when
Iriethe asked me of it. It is of our family, an inheritance that I have long wished
to study but been frustrated for the lack of a suitable vessel." Her stare was
flat and hostile, and her fingers twitched as if to sink them into Alliole's throat,
"As has been remarked—by others—you are great of soul, and by some
singular coincidence you hear it clear enough to make out what it says. I can
render this dream tangible and can remove it from your head, leaving you no
worse, save that you will be able to sleep uninterrupted. What say you to this?"

"I cannot think," Alliole said.

"There is not much to decide. Yes or no," Marre said, "I am not renowned
for my patience."

"Tomorrow," Alliole whispered. She looked for the Neve to guidance but
she was looking elsewhere. Having exhausted the potential of the tapestry, she
was studying the wall.

"Now," Marre said, "I have work to do. I cannot wait on your convenience, for
you to change your mind hither and yon. Answer." The last was a muted shout.

"Yes, yes, all right, anything but this idleness, anything," she said. Anything that would balk such sorrow, she thought, but would not say.

"Good," Marre said, appeased, "I shall send somebody to direct you to my
chambers. I go now to prepare." She left, and the tension in the air left with
her. The Neve lingered only to direct Iriethe to attend Alliole. There was no
pity in them, Alliole realized, no mercy, anywhere.

When they had left, she breathed easier, and realized that the interview had
exhausted her. It seemed outlandish, foolish even, were it not for the certainty
of their vision, and Marre's utter balefulness, that lent weight to her assertion
that emotion and will controlled the deeds of demons.

"What say you of this?" she asked Iriethe.

"I knew nothing of it," Iriethe said, "Marre made no mention to me that
she recognized anything in your dreams. That is her way." She then made some
quiet comment on the advisability of dressing in warmer clothes for her
journey to Marre's chambers.

"Why does she not just return here?" Alliole demanded.

"There are certain conditions she must meet," Iriethe said. She seemed
subdued. 🟊

Chapter Three

ALLIOLE'S JOURNEY to Marre's rooms was the first she had taken into the inhabited parts of the Castle. One of Marre's servants led her there. The man showed the way but otherwise ignored her, and after her first questions were lost in silence, she let them go, assuming he obeyed an order.

He led her through three distinct precincts, a journey of a little less than an hour. In the first, where she dwelt, walls and decorations were carved with the likeness of ivy, so lifelike that she expected the stone leaves to blow in the soft wind that blew ceaseless through the corridors. Second was a place where roses were carved, in a florid flurry of vegetation at corners and over archways and doors, their stone thorns so sharp in some places, as to tear the cloth of a robe carelessly drawn aside. Last the vegetation gave way to representations of small lithe, sharp toothed animals, like furred snakes, who coiled and fought at intersections and wound around door frames in elaborate, stylized patterns. Despite her vow she spoke in wonder when she saw them, "Such work, surely, it must have taken many lifetimes." Her guide did not answer.

It took her time also, in her travels, to accustom herself to the people who lived there. That any dwelt here at all was a great marvel to her, who had lived so long alone. There were few children, and they were wan, pale and careful in their play. She heard no shouts of laughter, nor vulgar calls and loud talk as there was in the Courtyard. Everything was pale and still, stilted even, but the people richly dressed and better fed withal than those without. They gave way before her in corridors. They bowed their heads. There was no open curiosity, but their eyes followed after her, in their silence.

The walls became patterned with tapestries and lustrous furs, with rusted weapons of ancient and cumbrous make, with suits of antique armor whose grotesque ornaments showed them, even dust covered and obsolete, to be the product of dynasties of skilled smiths. The last of their kind, she wondered, for she saw no recently forged weapons or chattels. Some great disaster, that forbade the study of such crafts, or destroyed all those knowledgeable? Or a succession of slow decays, of insidious forgetting, of wrongly recalled instructions and the loss of inquisitiveness and inventiveness amongst the inheritors of so splendid an armory.

Within the precinct of the furred snakes, the servant took her to a series of apartments, up stairs whose graven ornaments were kept as all must once have been, painted with fresh colors and worn carvings re-ground to fresh depth and decisiveness. Servants worked quietly and purposefully, and forbore to raise their eyes until after she had passed by. The deep chill of the Castle was muted by fires so great that the heated draft they raised roared and shook the chimneys, rattling at the walls with angry fists of flame.

The furniture continued the antique cast of the armor and weaponry that bedecked the hallways. The only new things Alliole saw were some of the clothes. Everything was rich and old and fine. She saw chests whose polished lids bore inlaid patterns of onyx and ivory, lamps of strangely worked bronze that ignited on command, and tapestries that shewed wondrous beasts posturing against a background of stone ruin and darkness. Imposing chairs stood about a table whose gilded polish had sunk into the wood, leaving it with a muted luminosity which seemed to gulp down rather than reflect the light. A black bureau's clawed feet beat an impatient stamp as a servant laid linen within.

They climbed a further stair, leaving the scene of bustle behind them, and passed through a room frescoed to artfully mimic a larger hall, pillared and somber, whose roof was inset with constellations of diamonds. Within could be made out the painted shadow of a large wheel, and a perfectly real pedestal supporting an artifact whose metal yet shone, almost swallowed in the gloom, a tilted globe picked out with a pattern of pierced holes of some unknown portent, circled by several rings of similar metal. When she looked down she saw that, save where it was worn by the passage of servants near the doors, the floor was polished to so fine a finish that the ceiling and the stand and what it held up was reflected in it. She saw the drowned stars reflected in its surface, and herself, bright and bold, her two feet planted firmly on the ground. The servant had ushered her through it before her eyes had had time to entirely accustom themselves to the dark, and she saw that it was useless to inquire further.

Beyond was a corridor leading to a brightly lit room, and from it came the squabble of children, a girl and younger boy from the sound. The servant was past the landing there, and up the last and furthest stair, before she had time to look. But as she was about to climb she heard a deep hail behind her, and a loud, impatient step. She turned to see a heavy-set man approaching her, with one hand outstretched to stop her.

"Go," he said, to the servant, who wavered and fled. Then he turned his attention to her. She could pick at once his resemblance to Marre, for his brows were heavy, his gaze hot and hard, and his mismatched eyes swept up and down her in a contemptuous glare. Yet for all that hate had yet to twist his face, which was still young and fresh and fair.

"Who are you," he said, his voice breaking in his choler, "Who are you to so distract her? What business have you here?" A girl's voice called for him, urgently, from the bright room, but he ignored it, his furious eyes focussed on Alliole.

"My name and my business is my own, if Marre does not choose to tell it," she said, standing her ground.

"You dare rebuke me?" he said, and she saw him raising a hand to strike her. She raised one arm to parry the blow but was saved by Marre's voice.

"Enough, Reven," she said. They both turned to see her standing on the stair, tall and dark and silver, "Mind your business, which is my children. I will talk with you later." He gave Alliole a last furious glare and turned on his heel.

"Reven," Marre said, again. He turned back. She gave him a long communing look. And Alliole saw that they understood each other. Two people rooted in such similar feeling could scarcely live together, so she dubbed Reven the reflection of the other.

"Enter," Marre said to her, "Do not dally. I have other work to do. Do not mind Reven. He is jealous of all business that directs my attention from our family."

"Indeed," Alliole said, politely, "He has a hot temper."

"He has yet to kill anybody," Marre said, with what could be a smile. "Important," she added, softly, as Alliole passed her by. But Alliole had reached the head of the stair, and the sight made her forget the tart retort forming on her lips. Marre shut the door behind her, and locked it, "Remove your outer garments," she said briskly, "For it will get a trifle warm. Do not mind the servant, he is utterly loyal, and in any case deaf and blind. A useful creature. Hurry," she snapped again, when Alliole showed a tendency to linger. Even her good humor had a short fuse.

Beyond spread a large chamber, whose vaulted roofs were separated from each other by stone arches that formed three lowered recesses. The arches were no more or less than giant flues, admitting heat into the room. It was for this that the fires roared below. The first chamber was a study, for books were packed carelessly along the shelves, shielded from the heat by sheets of crystal of a lambent and opaque verdancy. Ledgers, papers and book-binding equipment were scattered carelessly on the shelving, and upon a large bureau, dark of wood and clawed of foot as the one below. This one seemed quiescent, for it made no move that Alliole could see and for that she was thankful. It was laden with a clutter of odd-sized bottles and retorts, a scatter of parchment, several ink bottles of red and green hues, quills, an ugly statuette of what Alliole presumed was some denizen of the netherworlds, and a large pot of glue from which a stiff brush protruded gluggily. Several large gems glinted loose amid the litter, also a pestle and mortar, a black candle with a guttered stub, a knife with a jewelled handle whose blade spotted with scrapes of wax from the candelabra beyond bespoke its use, a skull with blackened teeth on whose ivory forehead was painted mystical runes, and an articulated skeletal hand threaded on golden wire. Something blinked at her from behind the skull, and then scurried over the edge of the desk and was gone, a pink and glossy something that left diminutive wet hand prints on the dark wood.

"Is it not warm enough for you?" Marre asked from the second chamber, where she stood before a reading stand carved into the shape of a spreading tree, whose branches upbore the book whose pages she leafed through.

"How am I supposed to undress," Alliole asked smartly, "Without hands?" The chamber where Marre stood was bare apart from stand and book. The floor was covered with intricate geometrical shapes, some in chalk and others in opalescent inlays, tipped with further candles, all black, some fresh but most half or further guttered, to judge from the accumulations of solidified wax around them.

"I had forgotten. Do not bother then. You won't faint, will you?" Giving Alliole no time to answer she continued, "Over there. No, there. There. Fool. Do not stand on any of the inlaid lines. Do not scuff the chalk. Repeat the words I tell you, and only those. Do not speak to anything else that may appear within that circle. Do not listen to them. Do not, for any reason, depart that place until I give you leave, or I will not be held responsible for you. Do not waste my time. Understand?"

"Yes," Alliole said, "But. . . ." Marre raised her hate-filled eyes to strike her down. Alliole relapsed into silence. She did not know anything of sorcery and did not understand the precautions. She thought—too late, such was the trust in her nature—that Marre might plan to do her evil. And now her own intentions and hopes, not to mention pride, held her to the experiment. Besides, despite her dislike of Marre, she did not doubt her ability to deal on equal or superior footing with the hells and all their legions.

The blind servant strode to Marre's side, and Alliole remarked on the nimbleness with which he avoided the marks on the floor, as if he could see, although cataracts beclouded his vision with their milky haze. He held a cup, a knife and a wooden cage in which coiled resentfully and furiously, a small furred snake-like creature with fur the exact color of verdigris and eyes as sharp as its tiny, white teeth.

"Very well," Marre said, smoothing the page beneath her palms, "We begin."

In her panic, Alliole raised her eyes, and looked beyond into the last room. She saw an alchemical laboratory, torts and limbecks and retorts, complex devices of crystal and silver, and rank upon rank of assorted glassware blown into strange shapes, either for simple effect or because the ghastly configurations into which they were worked were necessary to hold their contents. Some were empty, clean or namelessly stained, some filled with curious liquids of varying colors and torpidity, others with pickled cadavers of small animals and birds, and creatures such as Alliole would rather not dwell on in her current predicament. Some of them were still moving. A workbench littered with artifacts and tools obscured further vision of any rooms beyond, but she caught a glimpse of what looked like a giant skeletal snake wound near a bronze head on whose features were stamped arrogance and despair. Something gaudy and insubstantial flitted across her vision and she wrenched her eyes back to the scene before her, remembering Marre's derisive references to those who could work dreams.

Marre was mouthing redolent words in a language Alliole did not know, and malice hung like a veil between them. For a long time nothing further comprehensible happened, save that Marre indicated her several times, in a peremptory fashion, to obediently repeat the nonsense phrases. The dark mist stirred at last, and thinned, spreading throughout the room. Marre caught the snake-creature from within the cage and drew it out by the scruff of its neck, presenting the knife to it. The creature hissed and struck, its fury dwarfing its insubstantial size. It wound about her hand, attempting to bite, and Alliole shut her eyes, not wishing to see the kill.

She heard the animal squeal, but when she dared open her eyes again saw that it was back in the cage, and the cage on the floor between the servant's legs. The knife blade was smeared with black liquid. She saw that it had struck at the blade in its panic and cut its mouth. It sat there licking its lips, and taking no further part or interest in the proceedings, and evidently Marre needed only that, for she drew the stained knife through the air, and where it passed, an unwholesome glow permeated the air. Alliole was seized with paranoia at the lack of wisdom she had displayed in trusting this person. 'Run,' a voice tolled with in her, 'Quickly, before she properly starts. You will be safe, I promise you.' She started, in blind panic, to set foot from the circle, but the word 'promise' dissuaded her. Why should she promise herself? It was some other attempting to thus persuade her. She stood her ground and raised her eyes again.

Marre flourished the knife at each of the room's corners, of which there seemed to be double the normal number, turned pages, and mouthed further phrases, none of which made sense to Alliole, except that they palpably thickened the miasma, until seething horror hung between them. Within the darkness a heat haze simmered, and then boiled. It started to thin further under its impetus, but then regathered itself, and came pouring in from the corners, obscuring her vision, so Alliole was not sure what came after. Chittering voices filled it, and little laughters, that chillingly reminded her of those idiot voices, heard once and never forgotten in her early days of exploring. The voices spoke too fast to be made out fully, and any shapes that moved within the haze did so too fast for her eye to catch and hold them. She covered her ears, and so missed any further conversation. When two dim ocher globes manufactured themselves from the smoke and swung around, so that she could see that they were but the reflections of a pair of vast, lambent, red-smoked eyes (whose surface, stamped utterly upon her memory in the merest instant and repeated in dreams for ever after, was composed of countless ghostly screaming faces packed rank on rank, snuffed in blood-red flame, their numbers perpetually renewed), she shut her own eyes, and like the snake-creature, took no further part in the proceedings.

It was terrible to tell, and terrible to remember, the utter fear and horror that filled her, and the effort of will it took her to stay rooted in the circle rather than flee the chamber. It was a sneaking, sly horror, that alternately stabbed and suggested, as if calculating for the best effect, the best way to obtain its desired end, the removal of its human quarry from the protection of the circle. It played upon her, as a skilled musician, to build thrills and crescendos of terror out of mere fear, disgust and even curiosity. Small, clawed hands seemed to crawl all over her. Marre had not warned her of this, and had Alliole been any less than what she was, she might have succumbed to her fear, and so, not died, but forever departed from all congress with the sane and human world.

At its end it was Marre's harsh and impatient voice that roused her, to view a room cleansed of all horror, save for the fact of its returning so quickly to mundane reality. Marre stood near her, one hand outstretched to shake her. Alliole blinked and shifted her step. Her feet were numb. But she had held. And what promises Marre had made, or what designs forged with the visitor she did not know, nor knew after.

"Why did you not just end all my problems and flee?" Marre asked. "Then I would have been rid of you. But as you remain, here." She gestured, in her abrupt fashion, towards the room's center. Something steamed and shimmered there, that yet moved too rapidly for her to grasp its reality.

"Quickly," Marre said, evidently from habit, for Alliole saw no reason to hurry. She cautiously approached, only to jump back as the viscous-seeming stuff within hissed violently and surged up against an invisible dome that contained it, in a breaking wave that showed here a massive claw and there the gleam of a jagged mouthful of teeth, barred in a evil snarl.

"How many are there?" she said.

"One, one only," Marre said, irritated, "Do you think I would call up more? It has too gross a vitality, it moves too quickly for this world yet. As it stays here longer its vigor will diminish. I will release it."

"No," Alliole said, hastily, and then seeing Marre's face break out into a scowl as awful as the thing contained within the diagram, added "I must know what to do, how to command it. Otherwise I do not know what will happen. It is a dreadful thing. I am too afraid of it."

"Very well, I will give you time to accustom yourself to command," Marre said, glaring keenly at her, "Let me take this Voice. Give it me now."

"How?" Alliole said, abruptly hopeless. Clearly such ignorance would only provoke Marre's wrath, and she had ignored the request for help. She would be happy to shed it, shed this Voice and its burden of useless, wordless grief, even for so doubtful a reward.

"You need not know," Marre said, stemming any emotion, or perhaps turning it to a greater use, "Close your eyes again." Alliole did so, not without a dubious glance towards the thing in the center of the room. Marre held her hand to Alliole's forehead, and murmured a few words. Something scuttered from the desk. She could hear the click of claws, and then Marre's voice, raised in scathing rebuke. The hand was removed from her forehead, hastily and without design. A liquid squall sounded and an unintelligible giggle. Alliole could bear it no more and opened her eyes. The demon had risen in a wave against its invisible restraints, and red shot from its eyes, bounding wildly off the walls in staccato streaks of color that stained Marre's and Alliole's faces as it passed over. A pallid, mewling homunculus scampered for cover.

Marre started to turn back, and Alliole closed her eyes again, in her first act of deceit. There was a long moment when she was sure the sorcerer was grimly contemplating her, but she held steady and innocent beneath the regard. The hand was returned to her forehead and a silence made itself audible to her inner ear, as of a fist closing over a flower. The hand was removed from her, and she opened her eyes.

"Did I give you leave to do so?" Marre asked abrasively, but Alliole was so used to her displeasure that she simply rose and went towards the circle. She stumbled as she did so, and but for Marre's restraining hand would have fallen forward across it. Within was now visible a winged creature, fluid in shape and constantly changing about its axis, from which a pair of devouring eyes poured forth intermittent streams of light. Around these eyes formed and reformed a fanged maw and other organs, some perhaps internal some external, and a barrage of shifting limbs, all different, all formidable with claws and spurs, with sliding muscle and sinew of alien texture now visible, now engulfed in the gelatinous liquid. As it cooled a black crust formed and from this skin, veins and arteries jutted and knotted with the interior, knitting its fabric together.

"How do I control this thing?" Alliole asked. Her voice fell strangely upon her hearing, and she shook her head. A deadness, a lack of weight was within her soul, a numbness that was the result of whatever Marre had done. She felt out of balance, and wondered if the Voice was all that had been taken from her.

"By your will," Marre said, unbending enough to answer, "If you are ever markedly untrue to yourself, then your control will fracture. Such I suspect would be difficult if not impossible for you to do. You do not have the imagination to contemplate so great a change of character. Bend your will towards this creature and it must obey. Use your voice if you are unsure of the efficiency of your thoughts. Here." She went to book-stand and picked up an object there, that had been invisible to Alliole from where she stood. She turned with it, holding it awkwardly. The object was a sheathed sword about five feet long and uncommonly wide at the base. Its hilt was fashioned of gilded wire about a large, blue, gem that picked up and refracted the color of the demon's eyes. She came towards Alliole holding it distastefully, and Alliole for only a moment doubted her motives.

"Here," Marre said, "All demons must have a binding object, something to focus them to this earth. I have bound this one to the gem in the hilt of this sword. I suggest the demon carry it."

"Is that safe?" Alliole asked.

"Perfectly," Marre said. "It does only your will, remember." Perhaps the irony in her voice was unintentional. She dropped the sword at Alliole's feet. It clattered. "Now," she said, and clapped her hands together. The sound snapped around the room, and an all but invisible vapor lifted from around the demon, followed instantly by an uprush of sulphurous steam that caught at Alliole's throat and choked the half-formed protest from her. The demon, with a gush of noise half scream and half shout was instantly on the ceiling and flipped upside down, a dozen ghosts of itself around the room in its wake, in hopeless chase. The movement was so manifestly impossible, and so rapidly done that Alliole's heart reared in panic. Liquid streamed from those parts of its body still unformed, and splashed and steamed on the stone flags. The appalled echoes rang with its sound. Marre turned away indifferently, and the demon launched itself for her back.

"No," shrieked Alliole, and then a dozen mutually contradictory orders, aghast at this thing so created and so casually thrust into her control. The demon was upside down again, pinioned to the floor with one leg thrust through its own abdomen, before either of them had time to think rationally.

"Sorry," she whispered. Yellow ichor flowed from the wound. Marre turned back.

"Its full name I will not trouble you with," she said, "It will answer to Slaarngash." The last words were directed at the demon, which had turned itself the right way around. The lips of its wound came together before their eyes. The torrent of ichor slowed and then stopped as the flesh flowed, and its belly reformed whole.

"It is able to do that only because it is new to this world," Marre observed, "Think through your commands before uttering them, perhaps." Then she went over to the bureau in the other room and rummaged there, manifestly ignoring them.

The demon grinned at Alliole wickedly from the floor, and did not move. Lamplight polished its nefarious hide. To avoid its gaze she glanced down at the sword at her feet. It struck Alliole as peculiar for it was not of the antique cast of the weapons she had seen previously in the Castle, but neither was it new. The well-oiled scabbard had been broken and carefully repaired. The hilt was worn to fit the shape of someone's hand. Evidently some people within the Castle maintained the use of weapons. She risked a glance back at the demon, which had not moved, and realized that it was not a grin but a snarl, for its wrinkled muzzle bared more than its fair share of fangs.

"Well, creature," she said, and took a deep breath, "Pick up this sword." The demon was instantly on its feet. Phantoms followed it up, wavering around its true course and being devoured again in its deep bulk when it stopped. It was half as high as Alliole, and perhaps twice as wide at the shoulder. It swaggered towards her, vapor running from it in small streams at head, throat and belly. It reached one disproportionate arm and monstrous taloned paw, and plucked up the sword. It examined it interestedly, even greedily, its blunt head hovering over it, whilst one glowing eye kept watch on Alliole. She took another deep breath.

"Follow me," she said, and turned her back to it, something which cost her more than she would admit. She walked out past Marre, who was now sitting at the black bureau. Something small but indefensibly mean slipped from the sorcerer's shoulder to lurk in shadows, from which sprang the tiny spark of its eye.

"Is there anything else I should know?" Alliole asked.

"Do not bother me with trifles," Marre snapped, barely raising her head, "My servants will return you to your quarters."

Descending the stair, she was met by the wrathful Reven again. It was cold on the stairs and freezing in the rooms below. She did not realize how hot it had been in Marre's chambers.

"What took you so long?" Reven yelled at her, "What right have you to so uselessly abuse her time and energy? You are worse than Tyall." The sight of the demon beyond evidently enraged him beyond measure for he threw a tirade of curses at it, and her.

To make matters worse the demon took its time in descending the stairs, each step far too narrow for its stubby claws. Its interest in the careful position and placing of each paw for each fresh descent argued for stairs not being native to whatever sphere it had previously inhabited. At the foot of the stairs it drew the sword, whose blade flashed blue in the lamp light. Only its evident unfamiliarity with the weapon slowed its advance towards Reven, so that Alliole was able to guess its—her—motives and order its halt. It scabbarded the weapon slowly and reluctantly. Reven found fresh fury in its display, oblivious, ignorant or contemptuous of any danger.

It had been a long time. Night had drawn on, for the Castle had resumed its customary blackness. The servant came before them with a lamp but was unsurprisingly nervous, and took flight as soon as they were back in the precincts they knew. The demon then had to be made to understand to hold the lamp and show the way, something that Alliole eventually accomplished with a series of mental pictures that surprised her in their lucid dexterity. The demon changed further, solidified perhaps, on the return journey. It seemed to shrink in size a little, without losing its impression of great mass, and scales could be dimly discerned rising and thickening upon its blunt head.

It allowed the sword to scrape along the flags, an intolerable noise, until Alliole managed to get it to slung across its back. Its multitude of shadows roiled ahead of her, made worse by the flickering lamplight, while its baleful presence seemed to reach ahead with its shadows, and taint even her weariness. Its hide blackened, until by the time they had returned to her quarters it was invisible within the engulfing night, save for the stab and glare of its unwinking eyes.

She could not bear the thought of it inhabiting the same room at night, and so told it to stand sentinel in the corridor. She awoke after an interval of dreamless slumber to find it had disobeyed the order—or perhaps obeyed some new one formed unwittingly in her sleep—and crept to the foot of the bed. Over the edge of the counterpane its two unwinking eyes regarded her, causing fresh horror at the thought of the length and ceaselessness of its regard.

She broke down and wept before it, until the instinctive action of raising her hands to her eyes fooled her. If this was the price of regaining her independence, then such was the price she would pay. For she would not, could not, suffer herself to be long dependent on another. Another of her own kind, that was.

"So now," she told her follower, "so now we understand each other." The demon snarled something that might be agreement, as if lips and a tongue to speak with were also forming slowly. Then it reached out, tenderly, and wiped her tears away. ✳

Chapter Four

THE MORNING BROUGHT a further visitor, and one she did not
expect. She heard a light, impatient step outside, and saw the shadow
across the door, and raised her head from her contemplation. The
demon, which had been experimenting with breathing it seemed, for it was
giving off a constant whistling whine, hushed.

"Stand," she said wearily, "It will not harm you, and I am tired of hysterics."

"Indeed," Sleepghast said politely, his entire, greedy attention focused on
the demon crouching at the window. He seemed wary but otherwise purely
interested. Alliole recollected that as personal servant to the ruling family, he
might be more used to such things than the servants whose fearful reactions
had somewhat disrupted her reverie. He licked his lips, and performed a short
antic, between a bow and a dance, to get himself into the room and facing her,
without taking his eyes from Slaarngash, "It is not for me to say, dear lady" he
began, "but unworthy as I am I speak as mouthpiece for my master, who bids
you most gracious greetings, and asks that you join him in his chambers for
the refreshment of conversation."

Slaarngash raised its head mid-way through this speech to focus hungrily on
the speaker. This caused Sleepghast to garble a few words in a message otherwise
delivered with commendable clarity. Alliole still barely understood him.

"You mean visit him?" she asked.

"Assuredly," answered the other, although evidently pained by her bluntness.

"Why can't he come here?" she demanded. Sleepghast grimaced, and then
physically dodged around the question, inciting the demon Slaarngash to
stand and saunter over inquisitively.

"Do you mind?" Sleepghast said, giving ground rapidly but maintaining
his front in a way which commanded Alliole's respect, after the screams she
had endured earlier, "Dear lady, such is not for me, a dutiful servant merely,
to answer, save that as we owe to our rulers our light and our life, and as our
existences are but unending drudgery whose sole reward is to serve their
will—as I would most expediently make clear with numerous proofs if my
lady had not more pressing business at hand—I nevertheless reply that it
would give her nothing but pleasure incarnate to obey his command." The
last part of the speech came from around the corner, and was somewhat
muffled, but Alliole thought she made it out correctly.

"Slaarngash," she called, surprised at her pleasure in the servant's discomfiture.
The demon returned to her, not without a backwards and baleful glance at

Sleepghast, who poured his weasel body watchfully back through the door. It said something, in a suppressed roar mashed into something approaching voice.

"Ah, it speaks," observed Sleepghast, "How delightful." He skipped back nervously into the passageway as she glanced back at him, mindful of the earlier rebuke. It was a new thing to her, this power.

"Why does he not come here, your master?" Alliole demanded, a second time.

"Lady, it would do you good to walk," Sleepghast ventured, the grimace and the dodge coming immediately, and together, "Did I not hear you say that it was your chief pleasure, indeed your delight, to walk so? And I could show you parts of the Castle, sumptuous and rare, such are visited by very few." Slaarngash shook its head irritatedly and then yawned, gaping its sticky, yellow maw. Two of the larger scales from its head unfolded into tattered, elongated ears.

"Why don't you answer my question directly?" she asked.

"Lady, it is not the custom of the family to visit here," he replied at last, pantomiming his distress with his long body, "And it is a singular honor that two such visited already. None other would dream to so demean themselves by venturing close to the Courtyard." When for the moment she made no answer he ventured further, wringing his hands in excited parody of grief, "I go to report with great sadness your decision to decline, which I am sure will cause my master grave displeasure."

"No, do not," she said, rising, "I will go. I merely wanted an answer. I should tell Iriethe, or she will think I have wandered away."

"There is no need," and now he was sly in his forbearance. "I shall tell her myself. Do you need to prepare?"

"No," she said, fairly sure from his face that Iriethe would never hear of this expedition, unless from her, and wondering at the reason, "Come Slaarngash," she added.

"Ah," replied her guide, "Does a creature such as this, so unbefitting to elegant discourse, need accompany us?"

"Slaarngash is my hands," she replied, simply, and the demon underlined her words with a heavy growl. Sleepghast bowed his head. She saw that he was going bald, and mentally added ten years to her estimation of his age.

Sleepghast led her north, confidently negotiating the maze of chambers and corridors. The creator of the precinct of Ivy seemed fond of confusion, for it was a characteristic of its architecture that many of its halls were dead ends with upper balconies running from them, where stairs must be surmounted and passage taken along the balconies to further steps which must be descended to continue progress. It was also the place best known to her, as mental maps to the other precincts where she had spent much time wandering were confused, if not lost, in the drugged stupor of those days. So she did not take long to notice that Sleepghast led her a route even more circuitous than necessary, and took the time to boast of his own importance. He also attempted to impress her with her own insignificance, although always slyly by reference to those rulers he served, implying his standing with them and his knowledge of their secrets was greater than Alliole had observed. She chose not to believe all his boasting, but listened with eager ears for gossip new to her, searching for some clue, some turn of phrase or remark that might recall her earlier, and she assumed untroubled, existence. None came, except that after a long while the lost echo in the center of her soul grew numb, as if with longing, and she missed the Voice and its unceasing, nagging complaint. She looked about to distract herself, and noticed that all decoration on the stonework had ceased. They had entered perhaps even another, older building, from which all others were birthed. The ceilings soared, and the dressed blocks became larger, heavier, with no carvings or wall hangings to distract the eye from their monumental nature. Yet the building grew colder and darker for all its majesty, until even the vitality of the demon seemed quenched. Its atmosphere grew leaden and dismayed, as if shrugging about itself a cloak of icy morbidity. She longed for her cozy quarters in the precinct of Ivy. Who had built this, and what was their nature, she wondered, and her thoughts leant a most forbidding gloom to the atmosphere.

Finally they came to a balcony shielded by ornate traceries of age-rotted and yellowed ivory, fashioned into spreading trees, from which hung yellow monkeys with wise, sad, mocking faces. At its center hung an oval opening, around which the ivory jungle swarmed in static vivacity. Alliole stepped up to this oval, despite Sleepghast's half hearted attempt to stop her, and gasped at what she saw there. The balcony hung, as if suspended in the air, into immensity. A blue light diffused itself about the space, such as could come from no warm and earthly fire. Many storeys below a parquet floor impatiently echoed the stamp of hurrying feet, of a number of servants dwarfed by perspective, and the grandeur of their surroundings. A raised dais crowded with empty chairs waited in its center, too distant to be anything but a glimmer, but surely of impressive and awe-inspiring dimensions to be made out at all. Banners and tapestries of vast size and intricate design, stiff with worked brocade and semi-precious stones, hung from the lowest levels of the balconies to the floor, and, like the servants, were swallowed effortlessly by the hall's infinity.

Golden balconies lined the walls in massive tiers. Peering upwards Alliole made out what she thought was the roof. The balconies, formidable as they were, swept upwards in dizzying multitudes but were first diminished, and then swallowed by the omnipresent gloom.

"Those balconies," she asked, "Are they real or illusion? Surely they cannot be real. Surely stone cannot contain so vast a space?" The hall swallowed her voice also, with no echo. Her guide made no answer save to hurry her along the balcony. This she thought in itself significant, in the light of his earlier verbosity. Servants swarmed around them again, as if purposely appearing to baffle her questioning. They made further confusion as with cries of alarm and surprise, they tripped over her and her guide, and themselves, in various contortions in order to avoid the demon. Sleepghast busied himself with chastising those who fell within his grasp.

Regular doorways along the wall of the balcony gave Alliole glimpses of books and scrolls, packed in heedless confusion. Through these shelves the servants rapidly found interior routes, and as they progressed along the balcony all encounters ceased, with a corresponding increase in the traffic glimpsed within. At last the balcony was empty again, save for they three.

"Here, lady, are the libraries," Sleepghast indicated, as they passed the requisite chambers. "The tally rooms. Here are made ink and parchment, and here books are bound," this comment scarcely necessary for from within came the rich scent of glue and leather. But Alliole suspected they gave him something to say, for he avoided now, more than ever, her eye. "As you remember," he added at the end of this litany, but in a perfunctory manner.

"What is above?" Alliole asked.

"Further libraries," Sleepghast replied, and would not have answered further but she pressed him, "And the Parrar's quarters, as you remember." And this last was said in real earnest, so that she was puzzled. She peered upwards as they passed into the safe confines of corridor at the end of the balcony, as if her eye could pierce stone and make out this person so remarkable, so commented on, yet so persistently invisible.

When she returned her gaze to the present she found herself at a door. It was almost the first that she had seen. After her vision in the hall, she was for a brief while confused, and saw only the absurd, a thin barrier of wood set in stone, such as would endure no longer than a century or two before it must be renewed. Then she shook off the double vision, and it was a door, strong enough, enamelled with a tracery that mimicked the ivory apes on the balcony.

"Dear sir," Sleepghast was saying. He was half within the door, opened and a light so warm and fragrant as to be almost liquid splashed out around him, and the sound of loud voices, stilled only a moment as the servant spoke. She found herself shrinking back, unaccountably timid, before those careless, confident voices.

"Quiet," a voice from within, a man's voice, curiously both brash and thin, a light tenor. A young man, she guessed. "What did you say, Sleepghast? Lyde was talking over you. It is most disrespectful of her."

"I said, sir, that the woman you wished to speak to is here, as commanded and fulfilled by your most expedient servant sir."

"Oh, what woman? I don't remember." And now the voice was most elaborately careless. Alliole, as she had raised the servant's age, further dropped the master's.

"The woman with, er," and Sleepghast glanced back and fidgeted elaborately, "No hands, sir. That caused such a stir in the . . ." he gave a discreet cough, "The Courtyard.

"Oh well, I am sure I do not remember," the voice replied, "You had best send her away."

"So sorry to trouble you sir," Sleepghast replied, and started to close the door, as the youthful voice replied, benignly, "No matter, no matter." It was a game, Alliole realized, carefully planned, between servant and master. She was the toy, no more. Her wishes were of no consequence.

From behind her the demon spoke, a short, vigorous bark which startled her, for it seemed to command entry in its own turn, and succeeded. There was a startled silence from within and then a woman's voice, lone and cordial, "Hullo, they have one of Marre's creatures out there. Enter, enter."

Slaarngash came ahead of her to the doorway and was through it before Alliole had any time to countermand the order. She heard the sound of the woman's laughter. When she followed lamely into the chamber she found Slaarngash fawning upon the pair within.

"Enough," she said, sharply, and it obeyed, not without shooting her a reluctant glare. She automatically made to hide her hands in her voluminous robes, but then sighed and allowed them to stay in plain sight. What did it matter if they saw what they knew already?

There were two people in the room, a man and a woman, who had the mismatched eyes, the dark hair, pallid complexion and regular features of the Neve and her kin. What was lacking in their regard was the power and forcefulness she had experienced with the Neve and Marre, that had made even a brief interview exhausting, and the sorcerous vigil terrifying.

They sat before a dancing fire whose light somewhat dispelled the pervading gloom. Beside the fire was a crystal decanter, tall stemmed glasses of needlessly ornate design, and a tray of foodstuffs of the kind used more to tempt the appetite than fill the stomach. Above it on the mantel were a pair of amber cat statuettes, tall and lean and scornful.

The woman's face was vivid, made the more so for the robes she wore, which where orange and gold, strikingly different from the somber hues of the man. A hair net of golden thread ornamented with seed pearls contained her hair, and a curious ornament, resembling a lax, golden snake, was wound about her neck, its head upon the throat. During the interview that followed Alliole saw the snake several times open its eyes, and once blink, and shift its head a little closer to the steady blue pulse so uncommonly highlighted by the woman's pallor. Alliole guessed her to be the older, which was not much to say, for her eyes were too lively to have spared much time contemplating the world. She must be Lyde, who would not stop talking.

The man rose on her entrance to play the gracious host. Very young, she thought at first glance, but at second she was not so sure, for there were lines about his face that bespoke a maturity beyond his years, and there was a most peculiar cast to his eyes, half certain and half not, that defied his fresh look. But he was young enough that he grew no beard, and his long black hair was gathered, like the Neve's, with a fillet of silver. He greeted her easily and as there were only two chairs, he invited her to take his. Lyde merely sat and stared at her curiously. The man had a bright, doubtful smile. He was the first doubtful person she had met.

"Will you have some wine?" he asked. Alliole shook her head, and sat, like her host, without certainty. He stood with his back to the fire, and Sleepghast leapt forward to attend to them. She looked around her.

Fire and candelabrum lit the room, whose walls were invisible beneath a weight of tapestries, silken hangings, and gilded panels, presumably depicting the great deeds of the glorious dead. The overall impression was of hastily thought out grandeur. The chamber was built to the monumental scale of the rest of this building, and would have looked sufficiently grand, if a little less warm and inviting, had it been less obtrusively or more skillfully decorated. There were evidently further chambers, but she could not see beyond an arched entrance. She became aware that the man was talking.

"I am so disappointed," he was saying, animatedly, "That you do not have horns and a tail. I expected something more outlandish from—"

"Xoon," said Lyde violently. He stared at her, puzzled, a moment, and then resumed, changing tack, "I am so sorry," he said, "I have not introduced you properly."

"Lady, this is my cousin, Lyde. Lyde, this is the. . . . "

"Alliole," Lyde said again, hastily, cutting him off, "Charmed." She held out her hand, then flushed, mortified, and dropped it. The man's puzzlement was now profound.

"Sleepghast, that will be all," he said, abruptly. The servant, who had been attempting to plump cushions unobtrusively in the background, retired.

"Would you mind moving your creature?" Lyde said, "It is stealing all the warmth." Alliole directed Slaarngash away from the fire. It went over and crouched just inside the door.

"What if she needs it to attend to her," the man protested, and then turned to Alliole, "Is it normal for your kind not to have. . . . "

"Xoon, you haven't introduced yourself either," Lyde said sharply. The man, or boy rather, turned on Lyde, exasperated and then went over to the wall and threw himself upon the cushions there. He folded his arms and glared at no one in particular.

"But of course he does not need to," Alliole said, painstakingly, as if surprised, "All the Castle, uh," and she laboriously forged a note of flattery, with no purpose other than to cheer a child. She discarded 'the most glorious and mighty Xoon,' and substituted, "Sings his praises," realizing she knew little of the man but his name and the disposition of his personal servant. Her duplicity worked, for Xoon's scowl lifted immediately, to be replaced by his bright smile. Lyde gazed at her open mouthed. "I have been looking forward to meeting with you," she continued, which was true, "Since meeting other members of your family, who have been most kind and forebearing towards me."

"Yes, well they should be, after what they . . ." Xoon started, almost severely. But he subsided as Lyde stiffened in her chair, and continued with what he evidently thought was a cunning change of tack, "They were well, my aunts, when you met them? Marre I scarcely see at all now, she is so wrapped up in her family, and my most gracious aunt, the Parrar Neve, has gifted me scarcely two words since the Solstice festivities."

"That was because you got drunk and boasted about how important you are," Lyde said, still severely, "She is so busy now with the seclusion of the Parrar, and she feels you do not do enough to aid her." The boy gave her an angelic smile, and lounged back on the cushions.

"My mother is perfectly well," he said, "I see no reason for Marre to lose her temper, and the Neve to be so brusque with everyone. Whenever I offer to aid her she says that I am not old enough, or she does not have the time to teach me. I am a model of patience myself, although my endless round of duties oppresses me so. It is not easy to be heir to so great an inheritance." Lyde's snort was ungracious, and Alliole wondered if she was always so disagreeable a companion.

"They seemed well enough," she said, cautiously.

"Talking of powers and vitality no doubt," the boy said, and gave her a sharp glance when she nodded. "It seems to me the more they talk of such things, the less it is in actuality. When did you get this?" and he waved a hand at Slaarngash, crouching black and baleful in its corner. Its hide glistened, as if to a rebuke, like spilt oil on water.

"Only yesterday," she replied, "We are still getting used to each other."

"Such a marvel," Xoon said artlessly, very much in Sleepghast's manner so that she wondered who was the teacher, who the pupil, "Why. . . ."

At this moment there was a knock on the door, and it was thrown open almost immediately. She could hear Sleepghast's protests, and an angry reply that made her heart sink. Reven walked into the chamber, preceded by an aura of ill will, turned, and slammed the door in Sleepghast's face. Slaarngash moved back out of his way, its head raised sullenly and its new-born ears flattened, but again Reven took no more notice of the demon than if it had been an item of furniture. He was breathing heavily, as if he had just been running.

"That servant of yours was most abominable rude," he said to Xoon. He threw a heavy cloak down upon a satined footstool, then lowered himself, and looked around, feigning to notice Alliole for the first time. Xoon raised his head from the cushions and regarded the newcomer in an elaborately friendly manner.

"Lyde, why don't you pour Reven some wine," he said, and yawned, "See if you can get him in a better temper." Reven snorted but accepted the glass, draining it at a gulp and then threw it into the fire, an act that made the golden snake around Lyde's neck jump, and open one black eye to regard him. Lyde unwound it from her neck and petted it, feeding it crumbs from the tray of delicacies by the fire, until she had soothed it back into slumber again.

"Cousin Reven, this is the honored Al—"

"We've met," Reven said, brushing Alliole over again with an unfriendly eye. He looked tired—more than tired, exhausted—as if he had not slept for days. There were deep black pouches under his eyes, and the skin was stretched around the bones of his face. He had not looked thus yesterday, "I'm famished. I want the tray, Lyde. You pamper your pet whilst we poor mortals starve."

Lyde picked up the tray without comment and brought it over, balancing it on the footstool. But before he had any chance to sample the contents, she raised his chin with her hand and gave him long and steady regard, before kissing him full on the lips, a long, slow, deep, considering caress. During this interval Xoon yawned again, and remarked on how boring the conversation had become.

Lyde then went over to the door, the golden snake now coiled about her wrist and lower arm with its head upon the elbow pulse. She called for Sleepghast, and told him loudly, pointedly, to get some more food and wine—and glasses. She part-closed the door behind her, and had a murmured conversation with the servant, that went on for somewhat longer and which none in the room could catch.

"What brings you here, cousin," Xoon asked politely, after Reven had scooped the dainties from the tray, and taken some more wine.

"I thought that I'd visit," the older man replied, "How goes it?"

"It?" Xoon raised his eyes to the ceiling, "Meaning my life or my office?"

"Both," Reven replied. Food and drink gone he turned his famished glare to Alliole, until the demon behind him started to fidget with the scabbarded blade so as to attract Xoon's comment. Then he dropped his gaze.

"Well enough," Xoon said, "I was complaining of life earlier but now I am determined to be more cheerful." He stretched himself out on the cushions and then relaxed again, blinking into the fire, "How are little whatsisname, and so-and-so?"

"Eh?"

"Your children," Lyde said, returning to the fire, "That is whom he means, brother. How are my niece and nephew?"

"Fine," Reven said, and brightened visibly, "Jeme is taking to her studies splendidly. Marre says she will surely be ready for sorcerous instruction in the new year. Nick is growing up handsome. I have been teaching him sword play."

"They do grow, don't they?" Xoon observed, evidently bored, and cast about for fresh distraction. His eye lit on Alliole, and she thought that for a moment he had forgotten that she was there. Then came another knock on the door. The demon leapt up and snarled, "Go." Its voice was now quite distinct, although still muddied, as if palate and tongue were part-eaten away. Sleepghast poked his head cautiously around the door.

"Most honored master, may I announce a visitor?" he asked.

"Oh what a bore," Xoon said, and rolled his eyes, "Certainly, anything, as long as it is not my sister."

"Caerre would not come here," Reven said, scornfully. Alliole stared at that, because she had heard the name before.

"No, it is your cousin . . ." Sleepghast started.

"Oh let me guess, Tyall," Xoon said, disagreeably. He sat up. "Come in, come in." A young man, somewhere in age between Xoon and Reven, and of almost identical features, sidled into the room. He too looked as if he was out of breath, but had made some effort, or perhaps had the opportunity to do so whilst Sleepghast was announcing him, to regain his composure. He and the demon manoeuvred cautiously around each other, whilst Xoon surveyed the room, now rather full. Sleepghast came in with the visitor, and put down another tray, laden with smoked meats and bread, before discreetly departing.

"My, how delightful," Xoon said, "I am sure I have not seen all my cousins together since the Remembrance, and that ceremony is so overpoweringly formal that there is not really time to get together and chat. I am sure that it is my natural wit and charm that brings you all together. I like," Xoon continued, with a certain tense, weakly aggression, "To be able to do some things on my own without all of my relatives knowing. Just occasionally." He threw himself back onto the cushions, his sulky look renewed. Tyall had the grace to look embarrassed. He sat down by the fire, between Lyde and Xoon. Lyde ran her fingers through his ruffled hair.

"That's not true, Xoon, and you know it," Reven said, with his mouth full, "And I can't help it if I must come here to visit Lyde. She is never in her own chambers now but always over here. I would swear you two were plotting something."

"I? Nothing," Xoon said, but his good humor was somehow restored by the rebuke, "Save perhaps a visit to the Hall of Great Masks." There was a universal groan at this, and Reven said, ruthlessly, "Marre says it does not exist. She says that because there is a Hall of Masks someone jumped to conclusions. It's a nice story, but it isn't true." Xoon just smiled.

"What about you, Alliole," Xoon asked, "Do you think it is true?"

"What?" she asked.

"The Hall of Great Masks," Xoon repeated, impatiently, "Do you think it is just a story?"

"I have no idea," she said, honestly, "I have never heard—I mean I do not remember."

"How can you remember? Oh, someone told you?" Xoon said, as the room held its breath around him, "Well then, you can accompany me, and it will all be a most delightful surprise," he continued, cheerfully, "It will be an adventure. You like those."

"I am sure Alliole has better things to do than accompany you on a wild chase," Lyde said immediately, to be followed by Reven, who set his glass down so heavily that he spilt the wine, "And she is an invalid, too. How callous of you Xoon."

"I would like to go," Alliole said, firmly, and was rewarded when Xoon's smile, dimming beneath these further rebukes, became brilliant. She was smitten with a warm sense of fellow feeling. Here was someone else being kept in the dark. "Just we two then?" Xoon challenged, "Or are the rest of you scared?"

"Scared? Can't be bothered more like," Reven said, "You'll walk a long way in circles, while I lounge in comfort here." Lyde bit her lip. "It's just a child's tale," she said, "It's nothing. Why should you care?"

"My aunt is too careful in safeguarding my abilities," Xoon said, cheerfully, "I crave responsibility. Adventure. I would do something. At the very least it will be amusing."

"I still don't know what it is," Alliole said, rather bewildered at the speed the conversation was progressing, as old arguments overlapped new endeavour, whose nature was still unknown to her.

"I'll show you," Xoon said, evidently overtaken either with enthusiasm or a desire to leave his cousins behind.

"Show her a place that doesn't exist, a phantom, a myth," Reven sneered.

"No, the Hall of Masks," Xoon said, on his feet, "That exists sure enough. Have you been there?" he asked her.

"No."

"Let's go now," he said, "I've been wanting to look at it again. And we can set off on our great adventure tomorrow." Xoon bounded to the door and could be heard administering orders to Sleepghast.

Reven sighed in disgust, "Well I'm off then. I see no point in tramping round cold corridors to visit a neglected hall with a disgusting inhabitant." He drained his glass and rose.

"I have been attempting to dissuade him," Lyde said, and Alliole realized the blanket of invisibility had been drawn over her again, for they spoke freely, as if she were not there, or they did not care whether she heard or not, "But he will not listen. It is a fool's plan. He wants to surprise his mother at the Festival."

"Of Masks? He has a few days then. I suppose he shall beg me to go, and I shall unbend," Reven said, "Farewell, sister." He turned to Alliole and bowed, frigidly, his old dislike returning with the break up of the meeting.

"Convey my respects to Marre," Lyde said. "No, wait, I'll go with you. We can walk together." They left the chamber.

Alliole turned back to the fire, to meet the unexpectedly steady and sympathetic gaze of Tyall.

"I'll go with you tomorrow," he said, "If you want me to go." He smiled warmly at her, as if to atone for his previous embarrassment, "They can be rather overbearing, my relations, and Xoon expects everyone to be infected with his enthusiasms."

"Are you ready?" Xoon asked impatiently, returning to her.

"Yes," she replied, gladly, rising and gathering her demon to her with a glance. She could see through the open door that Reven and Lyde had paused by Sleepghast. The trio spoke long, earnestly and low, before brother and sister departed.

"You won't run into any danger with that around, will you?" Tyall said, with a look at Slaarngash that could be doubt or admiration.

"We won't run into any danger at all," Xoon said shortly. His friend frowned thoughtfully, and Alliole was seized with the remembrance of the idiot voices chuckling in the distant corner of the Castle from whence she had come, of Iriethe talking of a lost folk that no one knew.

"Trust to your demon," Tyall said to her, in a low tone, as Xoon vanished again into the corridor, "Today you will be safe. But away from the inhabited parts of the Castle trust no one you do not know. They may be dreams, or phantasms. Or worse." He touched her arm, briefly, and she measured his face as he turned away. It was calm, but it was watchful of which emotions to display, and curiously melancholy. A young man under expert tutelage, she decided, of some old sorrow. Belatedly, she realized that of the four he was the most worth her regard. Then he was gone with a last hail to Xoon, a jocular remark about keeping out of trouble.

"He has run off to my aunt," Xoon said, with a scowl.

"To Marre?"

"No, the Neve. He tells her everything. Here, you'll need some of these." Sleepghast appeared, laden with furs and wraps. "It gets cold, but it is very peaceful. I go there sometimes to be alone. I would go often, but every time I visit I must pay respects to Aubon, and he is such a bore." He and Sleepghast distributed lamps and unlit torches between them, and she realized, that, of course, the confidential servant was accompanying his master. Slaarngash, with the air of a clever person mastering a complex trick after much cunning and patient practice, picked up a lamp also.

"What was Tyall saying to you?" Xoon asked, as if carelessly, "That he would come with us tomorrow?"

"Yes." For some reason that put him first in an ill and then a very good temper. She could see the contrasting emotions chase each other across his face.

"Well I do not know if he will be able to after all," Xoon said, "He walks in his sleep, you know, and there are some places he is not allowed to go because they trespass too heavily on his dreams."

"Let us be gone," Sleepghast said, officiously. 🌠

Chapter Five

THEY PASSED DEEPER into the monumental building, heading west through passages which ceased to have any slabs paved or walled. It was as if they had been molded from living stone that even now, dead and brittle, remembered the shape into which it had been pressed and faithfully retained it through the centuries. They passed through a hall which was filled with fluted plinths, atop which stood life-size statues made out of folded paper, who wafted from one to the other on the slightest breath of wind, strung with an elaborate arrangement of feather counter-weights and wires. Stairs and corridors departed their progress on the south side, but none on the north.

"We are passing the Cross," Xoon told her when she asked. "It goes on and on. Then we must pass through the Wheeled Hall and then we reach the Hall of Masks. Over there is the Musk. That is a hall so large that it engenders its own weather. You are not tired, are you?" This was the first time she had encountered any solicitude.

"No," she said, "Sometimes I think I could walk forever."

"It is not that far," he said. He dropped back beside her, from where he had pressed forward in his eagerness, and took her arm, "What do you think of this place?" he asked. Behind them Sleepghast dropped his bundle of torches, and began picking them up again, noisily apologetic. Xoon spun on his heel and surveyed his servant, making no move to aid him in his gathering.

"You are not normally so clumsy," Xoon remarked. Sleepghast repeated his protestations, and on the heels of an apologetic speech launched into salacious gossip about Grielle and Iriethe, which Xoon clearly enjoyed, professing all the time his abhorrence of idle rumor, and horror at such slander. But when Sleepghast's story was over, and Xoon resumed his chatter, he spoke only of such things as Alliole already knew.

This continued as they passed through another hall where hung great sheets of polished metal, so that they were endlessly reflected in the walls. It had became cooler, so that their breath frosted in the air. Then they passed into another hall, higher, darker and colder even than the rest, whose high pitched and steepled ceiling nevertheless let in light from some far source, for a long streak of sunlight, hazy and streaked with patches of shadow, all the darker for the surrounding light, splashed across the stone at the center of the hall. Alliole stopped and wondered, all annoyance at Sleepghast's gossip and suspicions of its hidden purpose driven from her head. For the hall was filled on all sides with titanic devices of metal, some blackened and green with age, others retaining a paler color, jostling, looming around the patch of sunlit square, as if they wished to annihilate it, but did not dare leave the shelter of the shadows.

Sleepghast and his master plunged into the hall without stopping to look and wonder, leaving Alliole a dozen paces behind before she had a chance to recover. Fierce cold welled up from the body of the hall, a deep chill that penetrated the many thick layers of clothing wrapped around her. Surely here was the very heart of this building, the point furthest from the sunlight and the distant warmth. Surely here the masonry was thickest. Slaarngash withered into itself, become denser in the face of this onslaught, and sluggish vapor flowed in thick streams from its shoulders, the base of its throat, and the half-seen phantoms that flowed in its wake. Snatches of light from its lantern dodged around its reflections, and Alliole felt the floor resonate when it shifted its weight.

"Wait," she called out, "What is this place? Is it safe?"

"The Wheeled Hall," Xoon called back over his shoulder, "I told you." He then saw that she had stopped, and slowed himself, turning to face her. A set of stairs descended from the entrance to the floor of the hall, so he must look up to her. From where she stood she could see a badly illuminated balcony running the length of the wall behind her, pierced by regular entrances that must surely lead back in the direction from which they had come. Ivory trellis similar to those above the grand hall she had seen this morning bedecked the balcony, but were in a dreadful state of repair, black and slick with rot.

"What are all these?" she asked.

"Nothing," he said. Then shrugged his shoulders and elaborated, rattling out the words, "Nothing that anybody can make out. They just sit here. They don't do anything. They've always been here. Some relic I suppose of our glorious ancestors"—of them all, Xoon managed to press the most irony, almost to the point of bitterness, into those two simple words. "Make haste," he finished, "Lest we awaken the hall's keeper." Beneath his voice, as if mocking his meaningless bustle, tolled another noise, a mellow, liquid, mechanical sound like the slow dripping of water.

She started down the narrow aisle that threaded through the devices, wondering at their size and their grandeur. Plated bodies of nickel and copper sprouted reaching arms sequinned with pearls and emeralds, as if beseeching forgiveness from the stone heavens. They stood in every conceivable position, frozen into countless contortions expressive of their desertion, for dust coated the lower segments of many a device, and ice rimed the upper parts and let down icicles to join the highest spokes together, further heightening the mockery of their prayer. The mellow regular sound continued, tickling her hearing, as if someone was breathing close to her ear. It grew louder as they descended further into the body of the hall, so that the entrance by which they had come was blocked from sight by the devices, but no new exit presented itself.

They came at last to the most impressive device, a vast Wheel whose spokes and rim were enamelled and heavily bejewelled, yet seemed nevertheless to snare the gloom about it, especially at its base, which immediately abutted the patch of sunlight. Here shadow gathered thick and malevolent, contemplating attack on this errant trespasser from the outer world, and yet not quite daring to provoke it, fearful of this new and untried power.

"This one works," Xoon said, turning to face her. His breath bloomed white in the frigid air, "It is our calendar. We hold the festival of the New Year here. The devices sing together."

"Oh, so they do have a purpose then," Alliole said.

"Oh no, my aunts make them sing by their powers," Xoon said, "There is nothing here." Slaarngash, who had lingered at the entrance while they made their way forward, came forward now. It came clumsily and seemingly slowly, testing each step before it took it, yet far faster than was comfortable. It took the stairs at a controlled scramble, moving now on three limbs, now on four, in a way difficult to make out through the shadows, ghosts and white vapor that engulfed it, but altogether disconcerting. It reached them and stood upright. Its unsheathed sword gleamed in the ice-ridden air. It snarled, and its ghosts spewed companion vapors, until it was all but invisible again.

"There is nothing here," Alliole repeated, to the demon as much as herself, for Slaarngash, unconvinced, snarled again, a harsh bark whose echoes spoke volumes of pain. She saw that it was glaring at the shadow at the base of the Wheel, and followed the line of its sight. A red-eyed white oval stirred there, hovering mid-air.

"It is but your own reflection," she said, as a man stepped forth as if conjured by her words from the frozen air, a raggedly dressed, hunch backed, albino reflection, with mad red-flooded eyes, one green, one blue.

"I thank you for your solicitude, cousin," the reflection boomed, in a harsh voice of irregular pitch and volume, the voice, as Alliole knew from painful experience, of one used to living long alone. Xoon, who had his back to it, started and whirled around, evidently startled. "But," the shade, if such it was, continued, "My slumbers are uninterrupted by your visitation. As you can see I am already awake. Or am I dreaming? If so, depart my dream at once, vile trespasser." He spread his arms wide and theatrically on his last words, and the ragged sleeves of his poor clothes fell wildly around him.

Slaarngash made a sound altogether horrible, and for a few moments it took Alliole all her mental exertion to keep the demon still, for it not to use its weapon. Her mind filled with whirling visions of the war of hatred against cold, of the ragged mannikin that capered and jeered before her, until she almost believed them. In the pause while the demon raged within and without her, words must have passed between the others, for when she emerged, victorious, from this battle, they were speaking together.

"I sought only not to disturb your work or your slumber," Xoon was saying, courteously.

"Or evade meeting with me," the other corrected, "Ha, think you I care on the matter, save that discourtesy to the keeper is discourtesy to what I guard?" He jumped, agilely enough, on to the frame of the great wheel, winding one arm around a spoke of dark wood patterned with diamonds that bled light into the darkness, as blue as Slaarngash's sword. The ragged man caressed the wood, "Think you I care?" he repeated, "There are nine here, diamonds (as you see), opal, topaz, ruby, sapphire, emerald—now that is an easy one to replace, but—jasper—where are we to get another? It is so often useful in alleviating the disorders of childbirth that it is never returned to this shelter—and onyx."

"That is eight," Xoon said querulously, "You always miscount. You of all people should know the number." He shifted from one foot to another and glanced at Alliole, then away. He had covered his initial shock with a mask of boredom and disbelief. She looked curiously over to Sleepghast to make out what he thought of the matter, but the servant was simply standing, with his head slightly bent, on the fringes of the sun-square, so that his deep eyes were engulfed in shadow and could not be read. The unusual nature of this unaccustomed silence and stillness only struck her as important later.

"There are nine," Aubon repeated, and rattled them off again, ticking them off on his splayed fingers, "Diamond, opal, topaz, ruby, sapphire, emerald, jasper, onyx. And one other," he concluded, when he found he had not reached the end of his digits, and was compelled to admit their number. He climbed higher, as if examining the Wheel from another angle would permit him to find the additional gem, "The one that must be here, that permits us to read futures."

"I'm not arguing with you Aubon," Xoon said, "Fool," he added under his breath then louder, "We must be going now, Alliole has been ill, and must not be allowed to linger long in a place so cold." He started forwards along the aisle, "We will call you again on our return."

"There are colder places than this," Aubon said, and sprang, nimbly to the ground again. Like all his family he showed no fear of the demon, for he all but trod on its lurking inky mass, "And darker too when it comes to that. Any news? And who is this Alliole?"

"A trav—" started Xoon, only for Sleepghast to start up, and wrathfully come forwards, hand raised as if to strike. "Creature," Sleepghast roared, "Who are you to ask such a question of so honorable a lady? Go back to your work, and do not raise your eyes to those who so outrank you." Aubon shrank back at once. "I meant no harm," he whimpered, his white hands outspread as if to shield his tattered body behind their fastness, "I only meant to ask if she would like a glimpse of her future."

"Such impertinence," Sleepghast thundered further.

"Hold, Sleepghast," Alliole said, "Perhaps I would like such a glimpse. Of my past though, can I ask that?" as the thought struck her. And truly in this place it did not seem so great a thing. The past hung close and sorrowful here, and she had seen wonders such that she would believe the word of this man, when he said he could perceive such things. He had his family's eyes.

"This creature," Sleepghast said, all noise and motion now, his thin arms now reaching forward as if to beseech her, and then moving to cuff the unfortunate Aubon, his body seemingly pulled hither and thither at the whim of his eager limbs, "He lies, great lady. He will claim to see such a thing but it his own madness he sees. It is as my master says. The Wheel is a calendar. No more. Upon its jewelled surface fall the sun's rays, and the moon's, and with the turning year the wheel turns, and so we observe its inlays. It is a great and sacred thing this calculation, such as only the most high are honored to know, but it is no sorcerer's trick, no visions of past or future such as this creature cries. He tries to curry your favor."

"That is a lie," cried Aubon, springing forth from the shadows at the base of the wheel where he had crawled to evade Sleepghast's remonstrances, his ire evidently raised not by the criticism of him but of his beloved device, "Why this very night just passed, just passed I tell you, I woke to see the Wheel splashed with moonlight, with silver, and I felt it, I knew it in the air. Great things are afoot, great things I tell you. A birth. A death."

"Be quiet," Sleepghast said. His voice shrank, so that the same threat of force that had been in his shout was compacted into a whisper. He glanced over his shoulder towards Xoon, who had, Alliole saw, gained a tense rigidity of shoulder and arm as a result of the conversation.

"It is true I tell you." Aubon's face was transformed. Alliole saw that he believed his vision, "A birth, a daughter to the Parrar, a healthy daughter," the last said goadingly, as Aubon's face lost its transfiguration, and his vision returned to earth, "Who then will be their mother's delight?"

"That's enough," Sleepghast said, "Let us leave this poor creature. Let us go." He turned theatrically on his heel, but Alliole saw that his own face was transfigured. His face twitched and burned with exultation, and his dancing eyes darted to Xoon.

Xoon's features had darkened and knotted, so that Alliole was hard put to remember the pleasant faced youth she had started to like. "Take that back," he said, in the even, deep voice of extreme anger, the one that skates along the surface until the tension breaks.

"You see, he knows, he knows what I say," Aubon boasted, "I cannot take it back. Can we take back the truth?" Sleepghast whirled back, raised one arm, and before Alliole could move to stop him, had struck the other man such a blow as tumbled him over, back into the shadows of the Wheel.

"Recant," Sleepghast said, standing over him.

"No," Aubon said. Sleepghast kicked him in the head and then the stomach, so he doubled over convulsively, his white hair, and a spatter of blood shining in the sunlit square.

"No," Alliole cried, "Stop that, Sleepghast. Xoon, stop him." Sleepghast raised his head to regard his master, but Xoon crossed his arms and knit his brows sullenly, "Aubon should be punished for telling lies," he said, "And in any case he is ill-bred, built of the stuff of deceit. He does not feel pain as we do. You are too soft-hearted." He turned away, and Sleepghast took that as opportunity to renew his blows with greater vigor than before.

"I forbid it," Alliole cried. Sleepghast drew back his foot and kicked again. Aubon tried to crawl away into the Wheel but the blow knocked his legs from under him, and he fell. Sleepghast looked down, almost disinterestedly, as Aubon choked and tried sobbingly to draw breath.

"Recant your folly," he said, drawing his foot back again.

"How can I recant the truth," Aubon asked again, and tried to fend off the descending blow with his fragile hands. Alliole heard a bone snap.

"Enough," she said, "Slaarngash." The demon lumbered forward, unwillingly enough, its uncommon density seeming to drag it back rather than propel it, as it normally did. Sleepghast jumped back warily. Aubon, drawing his right hand across his face, and so smearing red color across his cheeks that they never had in life, pulled himself back into the shadows.

"What is this, Xoon?" Alliole cried, "He is a man, such as you and I. See, he bleeds. He is rebuked. Have pity, Xoon." She went after him, reaching out to clutch his arm and turn him around, and failed to do so, having no hands. Instead she missed his departing back and had to stand foolishly, and watch him purposefully stride away. Then Slaarngash descended from the devices, from where he had evidently climbed or flown, and barred Xoon's path. Her hands.

"Xoon," she said. The sound of Aubon sobbing and gasping was muted behind them, but when she looked back Sleepghast was still standing alert by the Wheel. He was ready at a word to renew the beating, and evidently disregarded her word except where backed by a demon.

"Get this thing out of my way," Xoon said, softly, and still without turning, "Or I shall ask Marre, as a personal favor, to inflict upon it such pain as it will never stand in my way again."

She could say nothing except repeat his name again, helplessly, and then inspiration came to her, "I do not know much of this matter, and yet surely it is not just for a vigorous man such as your servant to beat someone older, and so frail. Surely there is some person, your steward, before whom you can array your cousin with his insolence, and have some redress?"

"There is," Xoon said, "The Neve, and she will tell me I had no business being here in the first place. Aubon is not much older than I, but his kind age faster. You don't understand, do you?" He shouted, turning around, and she could see the immediate anger dying away and being replaced by some older anger, that had time to fester and turn sour.

"All I understand is that your mother is with child, and this has made you angry," Alliole said, "Please do not discharge your anger on this innocent. Call Sleepghast off."

"Yes, with child," Xoon shouted, and turned away and started walking again, still shouting to the walls, "And what business has she, conceiving, at her age, with her powers, with her history? Oh, come on then, let's go or we shall not be back by dark." The last said in a most vehement tone, either in disgust or to dissuade her from broaching further on the topic, "Come Sleepghast, leave that creature alone. We have better things to do."

Sleepghast came forward willingly enough, and took the chance as he brushed past Alliole, to whisper, "Do not mention this again to him. He is very sensitive."

"So I see," she hissed back, deciding that his familiarity was insolence. He abruptly remembered himself and contorted his face and body into his smile.

In uncomfortable silence, they proceeded through the remainder of the hall, Alliole too wrapped up in her thoughts to take further note of her surroundings, and came to a second hall, through a pillared arch supported by two carven masks, around whose blank faces were wrapped ribbons of giant proportions, whose gilding had long since gone, leaving them with the original grey hue. She recognized the masks, as similar to those she had encountered, etched into doorways and corners of masonry, on her long wanderings in her early days of remembrance, but many times larger, so that now she could see, carved on the faces, that one depicted mockery, the other despair. She wondered how close she had passed to these halls in her earlier time, and marvelled at the irony—or perhaps the design—that had sent her footsteps elsewhere. Xoon passed between these titans without comment, but his face had taken on a better color and she suspected, so little did she know him, that he was in the process of putting Aubon out of his mind.

The hall beyond was in even greater disrepair, and any grandeur was swallowed in its clutter. All but a narrow central aisle was filled with wooden vaults, with worked handles, and countless dividers, rusted into disuse. Wooden balconies ran the length of the room at the second and third floor, although they looked dangerously unstable. Smaller entrances led out towards the south, entrances that struck Alliole somehow as unspeakably threatening and claustrophobic, as if they dared her to enter, and believed devoutly in their capacity to crush her if she was so foolish as to accept the challenge. She counted six entrances from where she stood, so many evil maws down which she had no inclination to venture. Dust and cobwebs were thick everywhere, and the alcoves and slatted shelving that filled them seethed with the scuttlings of thousands of hirsute spiders, pallid in the gloom, whose legs and body together covered the circumference of an outstretched hand.

"And you like coming here?" she said, in a conversational tone, putting her confused feelings for him to one side, until she had had time to dwell on them.

"Oh yes," Xoon said, "At this time of year, the inlay of onyx, there are a lot more spiders. Normally there are only a few." He shrugged his shoulders to indicate his ignorance of any cause, "They ignore you unless you annoy them," he added, "They are more companionable than some humans I know." Sleepghast seemed to find much merriment in this witticism, and seemed in danger of throwing himself onto the floor and rolling around in his amusement, but fortunately remembered the filthy state of the flagstones and desisted with a few last sycophantic titters.

"Here anyway is the Hall of Masks," Xoon said jocularly, theatrically raising his lantern higher, "Behold the great works of my ancestors." Sleepghast recovered from his amusement and proceeded to light torches from the lamps, expertly spinning them until the resinous wood caught fire. The circle of light around them grew, and the surrounding hall grew darker as their eyes were baffled by the shadows.

Masks leered at them from all around, caught here in a leap of light, and there wedged in shadow. Web had been woven beneath them, so that their blank eye sockets threw back a silvery echo from a myriad empty frameworks of leather, wood and metal and other, less identifiable substances, all reduced now to dark shapes in the darker shadow. Slaarngash, a blacker shade, dodged amongst them, stamping on spiders and moaning with delight.

"Over here," said Xoon, who trod the central aisle confidently to the furthest wall, where huddled a great shape. His light bobbed around him, diminishing as he strode away, and sometimes hidden or confused as it crossed his body. It grew again into a pool of radiance as he reached his target and trimmed the wick to make it shine anew.

"See, they have woven their webs again," he said, "It does not matter how often I come here, it is always covered anew on each visit. Sleepghast, a torch." Sleepghast was already hurrying to obey his master, and Alliole reluctantly went with him rather than be left alone. The atmosphere of the hall displeased her, riddled as it was with decay, whose dust, curiously heavy as it was, must surely be composed equally of detritus from the masks, their containers, and sloughed skin of the spiders (for she saw their dry husks everywhere, and guessed that with no other insect life able to bear the weight of their periodic increase in numbers, they must at certain seasons, devour each other), borne on the evil air that seeped from the further passageways. The thought of breathing such air made her cough and choke, and finally arrange with Slaarngash to draw some of her cloak across her face, to shield her from such baleful influences.

Sleepghast raised a torch and ignited the object. The webs flared from silver to gold, then as the smoke cleared, returned to the pale color again. Spiders scurried from the webs. Their low slung bodies popped in the flare, their legs were flung upwards in the intense heat and withered, dropping, causing

Alliole to jump back. Beneath was a great mask indeed, nine feet, she estimated, from chin to forehead and molded, or so it seemed, from silver. The blank eye sockets stared, the neglect and sadness of the smaller masks a thousand times magnified in its size, and a cast of countenance either deliberately melancholy, or an accident of lamp light and shadow, that put her in mind of Tyall.

"The face of my ancestors," Xoon said, simply, "Every year the Festival of Masks honors their descendants. The best masks are kept here. The tenth day of the inlay of onyx, that is the only time this hall is opened."

"Is it a faithful likeness?" she asked.

"As far as I know," he said surprised and perhaps displeased, for he frowned at her, a black half-circle of hair falling across his forehead, and enhancing his essential human-ness in the face of the mask's alien hauteur.

"Oh I can see your inheritance," she said hastily, "But it is so wide across the forehead and cheek, and yet so narrow." There, again she could not put into words what she wished to say, and so was vexed, stumbling over her words when she felt that she should be sure. There was a mould to the mask that marked its maker as a unique artist, or what it depicted as something more or less than human. She remembered the gossip that gifted Xoon's family the blood of demons, shuddered and looked away, only to note something even more disquieting.

Near her foot, planted in the dust, were more of those deformed child-prints recollected from her earlier days with an effort, as if pinning down an elusive vision. There were a dozen or more, or perhaps just one, but one that had moved around a good deal and in a displeasingly random manner. The tracks were clustered together, fresh and unmarred by dust, as if their maker had just a moment before her entrance fled elsewhere. And feeling the chill breath of the six passageways on her cheek, she had no doubt as to the direction of their flight.

"Slaarngash," she whispered, "What think you of this?"

But the demon shuffling reluctantly over from its pursuits in the darkened shelving, only sniffed at the prints, raising the heavy dust, and pondered, lowering its head almost between its knees. It gave no other answer.

"And you think," she asked, recollecting herself and raising her voice, "You think that there is somewhere a whole hall of these masks? Is that what you mean?"

"Oh, well, yes and no," Xoon said, "Why would this mask be here if that was so? Surely it would be with all the others? But it is an excuse for an adventure. I am so tired of the quarters, and the people that I know." And he did now look fed up, sulky, a tired child who threatened a tantrum, "Also there is something that gives me some idea. Tyall, I told you Tyall walks? He had a dream once, of a hall, lined with pillars and these masks, 'in countless numbers' he said, which is a quaint way of putting it. Numbers can't be countless can they? Else the science of numbering things would fail. Tyall related the dream to me, until I was thoroughly bored. Each mask was built of silver, and inhabited by a wise and kindly demon, who gave him learned discourse on many important matters. He sat up with them all night, and in the morning when he awoke he could not remember a single answer." Xoon pulled a face to indicate what he thought of his friend's singular memory. "Sometimes Tyall dreams of things that are true, and he was positive that this was one of them. He might be right. Who's to tell? It is off to the south, Tyall said, and no one has been that way for more than a century, not since the Mad Parrar. . . ." Here Sleepghast who had been quiet enough, cleared his throat. Xoon bent and trimmed the lantern anew. The wick, so uselessly cut down in its prime dipped and almost drowned in its tiny lake of oil. "We had best be going," Xoon said at last, subdued, "You must be tired."

Alliole was glad to leave the hall, and the remote, alien visage washed up and beached on the furthest wall. What did it dream of, she wondered, as darkness veiled it again, in the long years passing, alone in the abandoned hall. Perhaps Xoon did do a kindness more than he knew, visiting it and for a while reviving the life of the hall, before leaving it again to the dark and the spiders, and those—other—visitors. As they passed through the Wheeled Hall she kept a look out for its keeper, but the shadows hid him. With Xoon beside her, she felt that to linger in search of him would only provoke matters further.

Most of the day had gone in their travel. As they returned to Xoon's chambers, servants were lighting lamps and hanging torches in wall niches. Xoon's farewell was perfunctory, so that she feared a return to his brooding on Aubon's sins. He ordered Sleepghast to accompany her to her quarters, but on the way she was seized with the idea of bringing her plaint to the correct authority, discreetly. This made her desirous of inducing her guide to abandon her.

"Take me to the grand hall we saw this morning," she ordered, herself peremptory, "I want to see it from the ground."

When Sleepghast would have demurred, she said only, "You told me you would take me to places in the Castle, 'sumptuous and rare' you said, and all I have seen is a pair of halls, damp, draft-ridden, and unpleasant. Let me see something lovely. Live up to your promise."

"Alright," Sleepghast said, his face turning smooth and sullen, for all his body's fawning demeanor, as he led the way, "You may look, but do not touch anything, you or your creature. It is the Cross, the hall used on our feast days, and I won't have you disturbing anything."

Viewed from the ground, without whatever self-deceiving glamour was laid upon the oval in the ivory traceries, the hall was still immense but believably so, soaring two storeys high at the arms and three in the center over the dias, in the shape of an even armed cross, with a dome in the centre. The balconies and banners shrunk in proportion with the hall, although all retained their majesty. She wondered at the person who had cast such spells, and the kind of person who would stand there, under their influence, who would believe the vision of the hall thus presented to them. She wondered whether they ever descended to the ground to see for themselves whether the vision of the hall was true. She walked towards the dais, despite Sleepghast's whispered protestations. The clack of Slaarngash's claws and the shush of her own slippered feet were the only sounds.

The seats were gilded and bejewelled. The cushions were covered with gold and silver thread, ornately tapestried with animals with diamond eyes, and forests filled with thumbnail fruits of ruby and leaves of jade. They were grouped about a central throne, grander and taller than the rest, but she did not need to touch it to confirm her guess. The whole of the throne was covered with undisturbed dust.

"My lady, I must protest," Sleepghast was at ear, startling her.

"This is the Parrar's seat, is it not?" she said.

"You are not supposed to approach the dais, save on bended knee, and after the three genuflections," he said, pulling her away, and casting anxious looks about.

"But there's no one there," she protested, "Answer my question."

"That doesn't matter," he said, in a well-mastered tone of virtuous indignation. As he touched the high notes for a moment the echoes rang. He caught himself up, and hushed. But this time he seemed to mean it, "We are not supposed to be here. I allow you here as a courtesy and you abuse it."

"Beware, Sleepghast," she said, evenly and placidly, recalling Iriethe's tone when she dealt with him, "I am not your equal, whatever you might think. Loose my arm." He stopped and looked at her, and she saw the flash of fire in his eyes, the curbed ambition, the anger masked by his constant patter and bodily contortions. She must stop that, she thought, or he would be constantly fighting for her position. She must impress him.

"Slaarngash," she called softly. The demon snarled wickedly, "Yessss," or so its seemed, and woke the echoes again, so that the sound came rushing in at them from all around. Sleepghast dropped her arm and his eyes.

"Who told you stand guard over Xoon's tongue," she asked, "Or is that a secret?"

"There are many secrets in this place," he said, then after a pause in which he tried and failed to avoid her level gaze, "My master had no knowledge of your amnesia, and it was feared he would say something, in idle gossip, that would impede your recovery. He has now been informed, and will guard his own tongue most carefully. This way, most august lady, I will return you to your quarters."

"I can find my own way," she said, coldly, and after her rudeness, he was only too glad to leave her, although he watched her from the door out of sight, as if suspicious that she would take the opportunity to return to the hall when he was gone. He need not have bothered, for she had no such ambition. She retraced their route instead, to the ivory balconies, and hailed a passing servant.

"Take me to the Neve," she demanded, "At once," when the woman hesitated. She must have hit the right note, for the servant made no more protest, but led her directly to a place she estimated to be just above Xoon's own quarters. She then dismissed the servant, and knocked on the door. 🎇

Chapter Six

AT HER KNOCK, a pleasant voice bade her enter. She found herself in an architecture similar to that of Xoon's dwelling, a series of chambers radiating around a central room in which a brisk fire burned. The difference lay in the decoration, which was left simple, allowing the massive walls and vaulted ceilings to speak for themselves, and in the squalor—for the room was littered with a variety of objects so varied, so vital and bewildering as to rob her a moment of speech.

Books and papers were crammed into recesses in the walls, and other substances with them, in pouches and containers of a mottled surface, that gave off a heady aroma. Incense sticks burned before some of the recesses, that leant a thin reek to the room as of burning feathers. In one glance Alliole took in a stuffed snake with ruby eyes, a fan of black feathers, several objects of finely carved and fretted ivory whose purpose was to her unknown, and many weapons, bright and well used, stacked along the floor and balancing dangerously on closets. The chairs and bed-curtains showed scenes from the same tapestry, of people singing orisons to a great cat, with eyes of flame, and breath, so Alliole deduced from personal experience, of inimitable foetor.

The Neve was seated at a bureau before the fire, with her back to her. She had a pleasant look on her face. This fled when she saw her visitor. Once again, Slaarngash ambled towards the flames, and this time no one stopped it. It's hide took on an oily cadence as it stepped over the grate and waded into the flames, filling the fire place and somehow promoting the fire, which roared anew around it.

"To what do I owe so precipitous a visit?" the Neve asked, cheerfully enough, although her face betrayed no joy, "I own I expected someone different."

"How do you like my creature?" Alliole said, trying to sort her tangled thoughts, and flustered further by the Neve's steady stare, heavy on her soul after Xoon's easy, fretful one, "Is it not handsome?" Slaarngash glowered at them from the fire.

"Handsome enough," the Neve replied, "Now tell me the true reason. I have not much time to spare."

"It's Xoon— Sleepghast, I mean," she said, her contained anger bursting out of her, disregarding courtesy and the unknown gauge of her host's tolerance and temper, "That man back there. He was badly hurt I am sure. And Xoon did nothing to stop him."

"Which man," the Neve replied, patiently, "And where?" And she listened, also patiently and quietly for all her protestation of business at hand, as Alliole poured out as much of the story as she thought prudent to tell, leaving out, on a last minute impulse of loyalty, Xoon's stated object of exploring further. Doubtless the Neve knew it already, if Tyall did as Xoon said, but why trespass further than was necessary on such a private matter? She concluded, by then coherent enough, with a petition that the Neve send someone to find the injured man, and help him, the snap of the broken bone ringing in her ears. She was surprised beyond measure when the Neve shook her head.

"I would send no servant to him," she said, "He must look to his own kind for aid." Alliole was silent for a moment but could not check her imprudent wrath, "Is this how such matters work here?" she asked, "If I am so injured, may I expect similar aid?"

Slaarngash made the purring noise a well-laid fire makes. The Neve simply turned her eyes to the grate.

"I do not think you need worry about further injury," she said, indicating the demon, "And as you know already, here the injured receive succor, the victim justice. But I repeat, Aubon must look to his own kind for aid. I am sure his injury sounded worse than it was. Cleanse your thoughts of this matter. It does not concern you."

"It does. I was there," Alliole protested, "And I cannot so easily wipe it from my mind, that I stood there and could do nothing."

"Could not, or did not," the Neve remarked, as if idly. She turned back and regarded Alliole again with her clear, undeceiving gaze, "Is it your own conscience you wish to clear?" Alliole was silent. After a pause the Neve continued, meditatively, "I can ask no servant to visit him for fear they would do him further injury. His kind are not loved by the vulgar, who hold certain absurd myths about them, and the only reason he is tolerated there is that only his family go there, and we have kept silent on the matter. Would you have me break this silence, to salve your conscience?"

"Why then is he such a secret," Alliole cried, in frustration, "A poor, deformed fool? What makes him so terrible?" The Neve closed her eyes and leant back in the chair.

"His history is somewhat complicated," she said, "And I would request that you do not ask for it."

"I do ask for it," Alliole said, as if meekly, but hot anger still pulsed terribly in her head, "Otherwise how am I to know how things stand here, how am I to remember, if I am not told?"

The Neve opened her eyes again and regarded her thoughtfully, "How indeed, when I see you learning the tricks of inquiry by the day," she said, "You were, you are an innocent. Did you know that? Innocence is terrible too." After a pause, "What would you like to know?"

"Why did Xoon call Aubon cousin, and then creature," Alliole said promptly. She had had time to debate this matter.

"That is a sensitive matter," the Neve replied, as Sleepghast had. "Bear with me a moment. Xoon's father has been dead these six years, and since then my sister the Parrar has taken no other lover.

"How then is she with child?" Alliole asked, before she could stop herself.

"You know that already?" the Neve asked, but she expected no reply, obviously, for she continued without pausing long enough for Alliole to respond, "Some say by her lover's ghost. Some say, by demons or some Beast-lordling. Others swear that she has been with child for six years, or at least one. This gossip is vulgar." The Neve smiled at her, as if she had answered the question, which she had not, not at all. Alliole did not directly press the matter.

"So shocking a thing," she murmured instead, taking a leaf out of Xoon's book and approaching indirectly, "He was an old man, then?"

"Old enough. He died in a fall," the Neve said, "Although we were much grieved, to tell the truth we thought that she would take another lover, and would have girl children to carry on the proper inheritance, the ceremonies, the leadership. Gaar sired only misbegotten girls, such as are unfit for heir, and Xoon. So Xoon is heir, and I suppose had counted on his mother being past child-bearing to maintain his position. You can understand then, can't you, his anger and his fear?"

"And Caerre?"

There was a long careful silence, until Alliole wondered if she had said the name correctly.

"Where did you hear of her?"

"Xoon spoke of her, once," she said, forebearing to mention the visit she had received.

"Caerre is his sister."

"Misbegotten?"

"She is not as normal people are. I would avoid her. She gathers about her the forsaken of others, and so they prosper as best they may. They do not live long, their kind, and are prone to strange fits. We must keep them in exile, else they would bring great evil upon us. Only the powers of the Parrar saved her daughters, and some others. I am sure they are happier than if dead, poor creatures, if such is the choice. . . ." she said, shrugging her shoulders. She rose. The interview was clearly closing, and yet Alliole was sure she had been only told half of the story, or not quite half. And yet she was also sure she had been told the truth, or at least selected versions of it. Some power or rigorously observed choice, she was sure, forbade her informant from entirely lying.

"Daughters?" she said, desperately.

"I believe that you have met Anna already," the Neve said, "You complained to Iriethe about Sleepghast's treatment of her, if you remember. You seem to make a habit of speaking up for miscreants." Alliole, without truly thinking, raised her arms to exhibit her stumps, and felt within her a great unease, a great sorrow. She remembered Aubon, and a vision of a great cat, a Birth, they both said. A Death.

"I am one of them," she whispered. The Neve stopped with one hand on the door, and turned to face her, so slowly and carefully that she must surely be judging to an exactitude her words.

"You are different," she said.

"Exactly," Alliole said, but her lips could yet bear to form the next question, the right one, to which she had been grasping all along, 'Why?' It took all her strength to simply reach for it, tossed as she was about the undercurrents of conflicting thought.

There was a knock on the door, and the Neve moved away from it. Clearly, the expected visitor. Marre came in, as always, abruptly. Slaarngash exploded from the fire, dripping tongues of flame that splashed on the flagstones, and were instantly extinguished. For a moment Alliole feared mischief, but Slaarngash simply slunk behind her skirts, from whence he peered out at Marre, as if Alliole offered some protection.

"What is this?" Marre demanded, pulling up short.

"A visitor," the Neve said, her own voice quiet and even.

"I was just leaving," Alliole said, feeling her own face flush with the obviousness of her lie, "I came to show her my—your—creature."

Marre's face twisted with wrath and Slaarngash shrank behind Alliole further. Marre's eyes pinned her. But she said, only, "And you expect me to believe that? Very well, if it suits you. Begone. We have work to do."

Relieved but deeply embarrassed, Alliole left the room, Slaarngash slinking behind her. Reven was standing outside, and he first gaped and then snarled something at her, wordless in his anger. His vitality had returned in the space of the afternoon, indeed redoubled, making Alliole wonder at the cause of its quenching. Suppose it was something to do with Marre's sorcery, some form of emotional leeching? It was worth thinking on, for she realized now—obscurely but certainly—that it was knowledge that she needed to live in this place, knowledge and as keen an eye for character as she could muster. Somehow knowledge would buoy her up, keep her safe, keep the darkness at bay, now that her own memories had forsaken her.

Here came what she thought at first was a stroke of luck, for Anna appeared now, laden with a tray and foodstuffs evidently intended for the Neve's office. Reven diverted his glare from Alliole a moment to engulf Anna, who shrank timorously beneath it, and knocked on the door in her turn. Alliole took the opportunity to depart, but lingered around the corner.

"Anna," she whispered, when the child returned. She made sure she had been seen and then stepped sideways into an antechamber, whose walls were all covered with cloth embroidered with a nativity scene, a richly appointed bed-chamber, filled with appalled councilors dressed in cloth of gold and a mother with her hands to her face in dismay, for the child just birthed was a grey and obdurate shape of stone. Anna followed after, lifting the flap of the tapestry that fell across the door (depicting a swine herd with his charges, hunting through ruins for some trifle, and evidently in their idyll unaware of the terrible events at the tapestry's center). Anna's face lit, her squinting, luminous eyes blurred, with her emotion. Alliole knelt, and they embraced each other.

"Shhh," she whispered, stilling Anna's profuse exclamations. She sent Slaarngash back against the furthest wall, to avoid frightening her further, "Anna I must ask a favor of you. I must tell you. Aubon, in the Wheeled Hall, do you know him?" Anna nodded her head.

"He has been hurt, I don't know how badly. Could you tend to him? He—"

At this point the tapestried wall was flung aside from the doorway. Reven stood there. Anna gave a little shriek, and jumped back, covering her mouth with her hands, and looking for all the world like the tapestried mother. She did not look where she was going, and went straight into Slaarngash, who snarled. Faced with two terrors, and in violent recoil from the one unknown to her, she flew across the chamber and into Reven. He cuffed her violently enough to propel her into Alliole who, unable to catch her, at least softened her fall. The mute cloth councilors looked on, their mouths open, their hands raised in silent horror.

"What is this," Reven asked, furiously, "What do you plot with this creature?"

"No business of yours," Alliole cried, smartly enough, and attempted to soothe Anna, who burst instantly into tears before Reven's glare.

"Be silent," Reven said.

"I will not," Alliole cried again, before she realized he meant Anna, who attempted to master her sobs, incoherent with terror.

"You will be silent also," Reven roared at her, his face turning a most unpleasant, mottled color. He stepped forward and seized Anna's arm, dragging her from Alliole's care, "I cannot hear myself think with your squall." He flung her from him, as if he could scarcely bear to touch her, and whether he meant her to go through the door and misjudged the direction, or whether he did not care, Anna hit the wall, and slid down it, huddling on the floor. Her sobbing, momentarily stopped by a scream, renewed, and this evidently Reven could not bear. He strode towards her with the evident intention of doing serious damage, and Anna, stunned or too terrified to move, simply moved her legs up against her chest and lay there. Alliole, with Aubon's plight replaying itself before her mental eye, stepped forward and got between them, summoning Slaarngash. The demon did not obey. Reven, without speaking, but his face suffusing a darker color with his anger, attempted to sidestep her, but she moved before him, this time verbally calling to Slaarngash to intercede between them. The demon came away from the wall as if it had been set there with trowel and mortar, and slid across the floor on its belly, exceeding slow.

"You dare," Reven hissed, between gritted teeth. As if overcome by great emotion he stood there, shaking, the veins in his neck jutting, his face flushed. The demon stepped between them, and elongated its body, somehow, so that its head and wingspread all but blocked Reven's enraged stare. Reven turned on his heel, and stormed out of the room, leaving his rampant ill will seething in the air. Slaarngash relapsed into itself.

Alliole turned to Anna, who lay still.

"Are you alright?" she asked, and touched her head, and cheek.

"Is he gone," Anna whispered, opening one eye.

"Yes."

"Properly?"

"Gone," said Slaarngash, thickly but distinctly. It prowled the chamber, snuffing at the air. The small room still felt filled with Reven's anger.

"I heard him going away towards the Neve's chambers," Alliole said, "You'd best be quick. He may be back. He is impossible. They are impossible. Him and Xoon."

"So it was Xoon who hurt Aubon then?" Anna said. She scrambled to her feet, and shook herself all over, then winced and clutched her leg, and then her head. She seemed otherwise quite composed, and Alliole remembered, sadly, that she must be used to such violence. Alliole bit her lip, but could not bring herself to disabuse her of the notion. It had been Xoon's will that Sleepghast act so. The servant followed the master.

Anna leant up and hugged and kissed Alliole, who still knelt, awkwardly, and was wondering how to get herself to her feet again, "I'll tell Caerre. I'll tell Caerre about you. Thank you for saving me."

"Go," Alliole said, "Quickly."

"Take care, do take care. Why didn't he hit you? Was he scared?" Anna said.

"Go," Alliole repeated. She got laboriously to her feet, leaning on Slaarngash, "I don't think he was scared, just cautious," she said, remembering the anger in Reven's eyes, "We are close to the Neve's quarters still. Perhaps she would intervene in a prolonged argument."

"Serves him right to be scared," Anna said. She limped to the door, stuck her head out cautiously. Then Alliole heard her irregular step moving away.

"You," she said to Slaarngash, "Why did you not obey me? Come now speak. You have a tongue it seems."

"Loyalty is in me," the demon said, sulkily but clearly, "To you and to those who bound me."

"To me," Alliole corrected it, and felt within her a great onrush of will, born of anger at its duplicity, that forged it anew, "To me. Forget the family." The demon bowed its head in assent. Its red orbs glinted ominously.

And yet, she thought, as she hurried back to her chambers, in all this place, she could not afford to make enemies. Reven and Marre seemed intractable in their hate, but Sleepghast could be won over if she took the effort. She was in more doubt as to her standing with his master, for on the one hand a liking for Xoon as strong as to any she had met in this place struggled with her rage at him for Aubon's beating. She was even more uncertain of the rest of Xoon's family, whose varied natures both appalled and encouraged her. She meditated on this failure as she passed through the passageway below her chambers. There were no people there, poised as they were in the deserted precinct of Ivy, between Courtyard and Castle, neither one nor the other. Then she heard a hail behind her, and turned to see Reven, rapidly approaching, his face still flushed with anger. Later she thought she remembered that he was walking rather stiffly, as if to conceal it from her. At the time she was too occupied in trying to gather her wits to notice the way he walked.

"How do you dare to obstruct me?" Reven said, swinging round in front of her, bringing her to a dead stop. His tone was not conciliatory.

"I only sought that you did not injure the child," Alliole said, belatedly trying to smooth over his ferocity, "She is young and small. You might have killed her."

"Does that matter?" Reven said, and evidently using her words to whip himself into fresh temper, "Do you think that you—you—" and the way he spat out the word was worse than any insult—"Have any say in the matter? Do you hold yourself to be an equal? You should be disabused, outsider." Again, a potent venom shot itself through the last word, black and crimson.

"Your own cousin," Alliole cried, losing her own temper when she saw that he would not contain his. "How could you? Just a child, just a child."

"A creature," Reven hissed. "Born of foulness and damnation, of impure blood that poisons body and soul. A worm that should have been stifled at birth, so that we could be rid of her. And you defend that? You would raise yourself up to strike at the most high, and drag them down into the filth you inhabit, with your friends, fellow filth." He was working himself into a state of utter passion, and Alliole, remembering Marre's casual attitude towards manslaughter was for a moment afraid, but then reassured herself. For all his venom, he was Marre's disciple, and she did not believe that he acted without Marre's will. If Marre wanted her dead, she had had the opportunity many times over.

She had a moment to mull over these thoughts, for Reven's speech left her with no answer. She shrugged her shoulders and opened her mouth to defend Anna's honor, only to see, over Reven's shoulder, a dark and demonic shape with bright-litten, frantic eyes, raise blue fire, and bring it swiftly down. ✸

Here follow the events of the Prologue.

PART TWO

Chapter Seven

THE NEXT MORNING she was caught between the twin states of terror and fatigue, so that the nervous hysteria of the one was smoothed over by the deadly weight of the other. Whether Xoon would keep their scheduled meeting she did not know, and she knew not whether Reven's disappearance would be quickly noted, or when and where the alarm would be raised. She was so tired and vexatious that the demon could do nothing right in tending to her, and dressing her, and was in a fair way towards sulking itself, which would have bore hardly on the other servant, when Sleepghast's quick step distracted them from their mutual glares.

Sleepghast's oily face bore no more than its normal share of alarums as he must smooth it over and express it afresh with each new fact or fiction, although there was in his countenance his own fair share of churlishness. She could guess its cause, but chose not to explain herself, only calling on the demon to take up its sword and follow. They travelled west wrapped in an evil and speculative silence.

Alliole endeavoured as she went to wipe from her all guilt, even to stop the knowledge of it lingering in her mind, uncertain as to how keen her friend's eyes were. Certain of the family she would be happier to see than others, and she was glad when she reached Xoon's quarters to find only him there. He was pottering happily around a great mound of objects, some useful, some not, and attempting to select from their number a smaller sample. He greeted her courteously but absent-mindedly. Alliole's intended coldness towards him melted at the sight of his happy absorption. Who was she to judge anyway, who had just visited far greater violence—however unintended—on a fellow creature?

"How much can that demon of yours carry?" Xoon asked, pausing in his deliberations to flick a speck of dust—real or imagined—from his immaculate clothing. She waited a moment to give Slaarngash a chance to answer but it did not, and so she admitted that she did not know. She asked it herself, and this time it gave ready, if obscure, answer.

"Once I carried a city on my back," it rumbled, swinging its head from side to side so that the red light from its eyes blurred together.

"That's useful," Xoon remarked, "What was it, a city of ants?"

"It was so great a weight that I feared I would drop it. But I did not and it broke my back," Slaarngash boasted.

"I wish these creatures would give a clear answer," Xoon said, not really attending, "Sometimes they are worse than my aunts." He knelt down beside the pile and started sorting it rapidly into three.

"Demons are known for their duplicity then?" Alliole asked. "Oh yes, they are devious creatures," Xoon said. He finished his sorting, and stood up, gazing at his handiwork with pride. He straightened the puffed and elaborately darted sleeves on his coat—a heavily embroidered leather jacket of antique hue, that raised itself into gilded metal scales across his shoulders and fell into burnished ring scale that covered his stomach. Alliole doubted that any protective properties it possessed might be lost in the ornate nature of its decoration, but held her tongue.

"They seek to drag their possessor down to the infernal regions. Their true nature is to deceive," Xoon continued. "It depends on the strictures of the bargain struck with them as to how greatly their evil nature is constrained. What is the character of yours?"

"I wasn't listening," Alliole said. This was something of which Marre had not informed her, but after last night she had worked out for herself that Slaarngash's true nature was covered very thin indeed. Xoon clicked his tongue in absent concern, then returned to sorting the goods they must carry. Slaarngash shifted from one clawed and scale stubbled foot to the other.

By the end of the hour they had culled their load to that she considered reasonable, but then they had to wait on Tyall's appearance. Sleepghast was twice ordered to go and fetch their companion, and twice made fresh excuse as to why he should stay and help them. The third time he left, but there was a lengthy delay before he returned. When he did, he came alone, and so excited that he seemed to have contracted a tic, not just of the face but of the body. This caused Alliole to fear the worst, but he said only that Tyall would wake shortly and meet them. Xoon complained but did not seem so disheartened, so Alliole guessed that either this was a regular occurrence, or that the guardians of Tyall's bedchamber were so ferocious as to negate any chance of his being woken.

Although Xoon seemed perfectly at ease, she was thrown into fits of anxiety with every fresh delay, listening for the first word of the news of Reven's disappearance, that she was sure must come, and that still might hinder or even end their embarkation. She wanted to get away, to get time to think with no other distraction on how best to manage the situation. She felt that if she could escape the Castle she could escape for that time the tortures of doubt and trepidation that filled her—from her stomach which sank precipitously into her feet with every new footstep outside and every smirk which crossed Sleepghast's face, to her shaking hands and cold feet, to her head which whirled with speculation and a myriad counter-arguments and second thoughts, on the wisdom of the course she had found herself embarked on. Murder is no easy action to conceal, especially to one by character inclined to be truthful.

Finally there was a stir beyond, the sound of servants scurrying, and Tyall entered. He did not look like one fresh risen from sleep, but tired and ill-used. He wore armor of similar vintage to Xoon's save that his was less gaudy, and perhaps in better repair. He wore it, as if he was used to it, for his body moved freely within it. One hand rested on the hilt of a sword, whose enamelled scabbard was the same blue as the wall beyond her chamber's window. A red gem dangled from his left ear, affixed with golden wire. Xoon scowled when he saw it, but then removed the look from his face in one graceful and fluid movement when the Neve walked in on Tyall's heels. Alliole, with an effort of will as fierce as she could muster, wiped all recollection of the previous night from the surface of her mind, while her stomach clenched and flapped against the wall of her belly in horror. Behind her, Slaarngash writhed its wings and howled, raising a gale that shook the tapestries of chamber and made the gilded and purposeless ornaments clatter.

"Aunt," Xoon said, springing to his feet, and disregarding the demon's disturbance, "I did not expect such an honor, for you to visit my poor quarters. Enter. Enter." The last said sarcastically, as the Neve was already well within its walls. She did not ignore the commotion but gazed first at Slaarngash and then at Alliole, who smiled as sweetly as Xoon did, and met the other's eyes squarely.

"Good day nephew," the Neve said, formally, turning her gaze to him. Alliole could not restrain a small gasp, as her stomach realigned itself with her liver. "It gives me no small honor to attend you. What is this matter? Why must you explore so, and why drag Tyall along? He insists, and yet he has trouble enough sleeping already, without witnessing some fresh horror."

"There are no horrors," Xoon said, dismissively, "They are long gone. They were old even when the first tales were made up about them. There's just corridors and stairs and empty chambers, countless of 'em. The worst Tyall will contract is a bad case of dust fever." The Neve looked as if to counter this argument but then subsided, "As you wish," she said, and looked around, "I wish you would pay more attention to the decoration of your chambers."

"How can I, when I have so few who will readily advise me?" Xoon said, cheerfully.

"Lyde would aid you, gladly," the Neve said.

"Pagh, she would import fire tapestries and braziers. I would die of heat exhaustion," Xoon said, and then as if idly, slyly "If you were to advise me, or my mother. . . ."

"I have too much business to attend to," the Neve said, dismissively. She turned to Tyall, touched his shoulder, and then as Lyde had the previous day, smoothed the lock of hair from his forehead, "Take care," she said, smiling up at him, "Do not let Xoon's impetuosity carry you too far."

"I won't," Tyall said. He bent his head and kissed her. The lock of hair fell forward over his eyes again. He was old enough for his face to have shed the childhood that blurred Xoon's, and had never gained the bitterness that had soured Reven's. His features were pleasant and regular, marred only by the extreme pallor that showed the full effects of his weariness, and the odd look in his eyes. His back was straight, and the width across his shoulders enough for him to be sturdy despite his height. Truly he was young, and fair.

"I wait on your swift return," the Neve said, with a look to Xoon that turned the pleasantly worded farewell into a command. She nodded courteously enough to Alliole, but spoke no further word, leaving the chambers as quietly and quickly as she had come. Alliole heard a rusty miaow greet her in the corridor, and guessed that one of her Beasts was there. She wondered if it was the same one that had attended her, but forbore to go out to the corridor to check.

"Let us be gone," she said, but was disregarded, as the scowl reappeared on Xoon's face.

"What is that?" he said, pointing accusingly at the gem dangling from Tyall's ear, "No wonder there was no rush to accompany me. Some spy I imagine. Some scrying demon? No wonder you were tired and could not be woken." Tyall raised one hand and fingered the gem gingerly.

"Xoon, it is a device to help me sleep, no spy," he protested, "Els—the Neve did not want me to go at all. I had to get down on my knees and beg. You know why. This will give me dreamless sleep, that's all. Believe me."

"Believe you," Xoon shouted, and stamped his foot, then he modulated his voice, turning to face the wall. Alliole was struck instantly by the mannerism, identical as it was to his sister, and by his face when he turned around again. Identical also in its passion, although disfigured by his childishness. She wondered if they were as alike in greater evils of character, as they were in their anger. If so, it took no great art to foresee the chaos that would result if the sister challenged the brother's ascendancy.

"That's spoiled everything," Xoon said, "Your dreams were the only thing we had to go on. They do not want me to succeed, my aunts. They want me to stay in my place, they don't want me to be important. They don't—" here his anger broke into an ugly sob. He turned back to face the wall again.

"Xoon, I didn't know that, forgive me. You did not tell me such was your plan," Tyall said, appalled. He strode over to his friend's side, "Here I will remove it." He fumbled a moment with the wire, and then had it unwound. Blood seeped from the place where the wire had pierced. "Here," Tyall said triumphantly. He pressed the gem into Xoon's hand, and Xoon turned slowly around. Tyall took him by the shoulders, "There, don't get into such a passion," he said, "You fly off at such little things."

"Little things," Xoon said. Tears still threatened behind his voice. He looked into his friend's eyes, and for a moment Alliole could not read the emotions there, as normally was easy for so open a countenance. Then he again displayed his brilliant, selfish, smile, "Thank you, Tyall, I knew I could . . . I mean you would . . . I'll keep it, and give it back when we return. You can have your sleep then." Xoon closed his fist over the gem. Tyall turned around, the blood as bright on his ear as the ruby had been.

"Reven is not with you then," he remarked, casually. Alliole's stomach, which had been gradually relaxing, tightened again, "Marre was complaining last night, that he had not been in."

"Reven has not spent the night here in a long time," Xoon said, picking up his pack, "Not since Marre decided to take a dislike to me." He laughed, good humouredly, "I think my character was thoroughly blackened."

"I didn't mean that," Tyall shrugged, "He is with Lyde then. I thought he said he would come with us, or at least see us off."

"No," Xoon said, "He said the opposite. We could wait a while if you want, or send Sleepghast." Alliole's stomach curdled. She sat down heavily.

"No, he would be bad company, anyway," Tyall said, "In fact, let's hurry and get out of earshot, in case he has decided to come. He has been so ill humored since he took up with Marre that he is no fit companion."

"He has taken color from her," Xoon said still cheerfully, "That is what happens when you spend too much time with sorcerers. Their characters are too strong and they impress them onto you. He did not used to be so ready to fly off into a temper. Are you all right, Alliole?"

"Oh, yes," she heard her voice say, from far away. Her soul was wrenched with a new emotion, shame and guilt, the clutching avarice of secret murder, "I am anxious to be gone, and all you do is linger here and gossip." Tyall broke off whatever remark he was about to say and picked up his own load. "Let us go then," he said.

That was the signal for Xoon's servants, and a large number of others, dressed as if from the libraries, to turn up, as if from nowhere. They shouted, cheered and wept, and although they clustered thickly around them it was amazingly easy to forge a passage through. Trumpeters appeared, whose silver instruments sent ringing blasts shivering through the corridors, and small children dressed in green surcoats and blue hose, carrying baskets of gilded leaves ran ahead a little way, strewing them along their path. The leaves gave off a heady scent when crushed underfoot. Alliole could not repress a smile, for all her emotion, and anxiety to be gone. Clearly this adventure would not embark hurriedly or without as great a fanfare as Xoon—or most likely Sleepghast—could arrange.

Tyall looked embarrassed, and Xoon pretended to be surprised, by the spontaneous outbreak of affection. The procession accompanied them as far as the entrance to the Wheeled Hall and there disbanded, as rapidly as it has formed, as if unwilling to trust its frigid depths. As they stepped through its doors, Alliole's last sight was of Sleepghast herding the crowd away. As he did so, he turned back to look at her. His shadow seemed to fill the corridor, its gloom intermittently pierced by the retreating, bobbing light from the lanterns. It was a crooked and eager shadow, arms outspread, seeking not to shepherd but to bar their return. Yet she was too glad that they were on their own, and heading further away with every step from what she most feared would be found, to take further notice of this omen.

They passed through the Wheeled Hall lightly, almost easily. Xoon even found courage to whistle as they passed beneath the overhang of the Wheel. There was no sign of Aubon. They passed into the Hall of Masks, and Xoon lead the way across the dust and spider littered floor to the ominous doorways of yesterday.

"The galleries," he said, sotto voce. The doleful atmosphere of the deserted hall encouraged whispering. "We have to pass through them to the further parts of the Castle. There is no other way."

"How do you know?" Alliole hissed.

"The Mad Parrar—because I said so," Xoon snapped, evidently changing his mind as to the information he wanted to impart mid-sentence.

"This is the way my dream led me," Tyall said, "It was horrible. I hope I can remember the way."

"Of course you can," Xoon reassured him, "Just pretend you are dreaming again. The path will come to you."

Alliole could well believe that the gaping entrances led to tunnels dark and horrible. She only wondered at what dream had led Tyall there, and why he chose to follow.

"A nightmare more like," she said, almost to herself. Something inside her hesitated to trust these passages, whose dark maws were set within stone pillars that seemed like the paws of a pouncing cat.

"Come on," Xoon said, but yet he hesitated, and in the end it was Tyall who led the way. Slaarngash pattered along briskly at Tyall's heels, now on four legs, now on two, the red light from its eyes illuminating their path. Alliole and Xoon brought up the rear, and were thus able to talk of pleasant matters, when the gloom of the places through which they passed threatened to depress their spirits.

The galleries were a maze of passage-ways, crammed with countless objects, so that sometimes it was difficult to squeeze through the narrow central aisle. The roof remained for the most part low, raising itself at intersections, but they hurried through these parts, for they disliked the look of the shadows that clustered thick on the higher ceilings. Stairs led away at these intersections and also at intervals from the corridors, promising access to further attics packed with their own store of furniture and goods, enticing wonder at the richness of the things found here, even as the emotion gradually died and was replaced by nausea, as if they had glutted their vision and must rest their weary eyes.

"It is not nearly so bad in life as it was in dream," Tyall told her, reassuringly, as he threaded through the passage-ways, keeping his lantern raised high, "And I do remember the way."

Alliole did not want to rest, and constantly urged her companions forward when they would have halted. She was unable to see whether the little, misshapen child's feet continued within, but she greatly feared that they did. She was unwilling to risk a brush with their maker, especially in a place so dark and claustrophobic. Again the interest of the place outweighed its fears, at least until the sheer multitude of chambers through which they passed, laden as they were with ancient and despoiled goods, threatened a new emotion, that sadness, that sensation of impermeance—of the rapidity with which the flame of life is snuffed in soulless, never ending dark—which comes from meditating too long upon the distant past.

"Who was the Mad Parrar?" Alliole asked, when other topics of conversation were exhausted, and she did not want to lapse into silence for the morbid thoughts that this would bring. She feared to dwell overmuch on the meaning of the contents of the galleries, their darkness and yet their evident fitness and preparedness for habitatation despite their long abandonment.

"Oh, one of my great and illustrious ancestors," Xoon said, carelessly, but he shot a sharp glance ahead towards Tyall's back, in a way which belied his words.

"She came this way then, and left records?" Alliole said, to make sure, "That is why you know the path?"

"Oh, yes," Xoon said, hesitating verbally and physically, so that Tyall and Slaarngash forged ahead and the glow from the demon's eyes waxed and waned in the distance, "But she was mad, you know. You cannot trust a thing she said. She would travel in procession from hall to hall, holding court in no one of them for long. She went on many journeys through here, and from one of them she did not come back. No one dared follow her. It was all recorded in her journal I found in the library. Well, that is, Lyde found it and translated it for me. The Mad Parrar several times speaks of the place we are looking for. That is how I first conceived the idea of finding the Great Masks. But I did not really believe until Tyall told me the same thing."

"What if he read the same journal, and dreamt the dream as a result?" Alliole asked, and again Xoon hesitated. "He has not read it," he said at last, "It is one of the books he is not allowed, and he is an obedient soul, as you may have gathered."

"If Tyall is not allowed to read the book, why do you bring him on this journey?" This was first and foremost in her mind, for to tempt Tyall towards madness for the sake of his company struck her as a piece of monstrous selfishness.

"Because what is real can never be as bad as dreams," Xoon said, and looked irritatedly at her, "And can sometimes extinguish their horror. That is one of the first tenets of sorcery. My aunts, they drown Tyall in lights and drugged sleep, and then wonder why their ministrations only send him further into the dark. He is seeking something real. They are afraid of it, and he—and I—do not know what it is. That's why." In his emotion he had quickened his step, and without either of them noticing they were back in earshot of the others again.

"Yet she was mad, this other explorer," Alliole said, again, "Was she born mad or driven to it? Did she come this way often?" She could well believe that such journeys would drive someone to madness.

"She heard a Voice," Tyall said from ahead, unexpectedly, flat and doleful as if reciting ancient history, and they both stopped themselves and raised their heads from their conversation, guiltily, "A Voice calling and entreating, that would not let her rest, and she went mad looking for it."

Alliole gazed at him, open mouthed, struck once again with an unexpected resemblance between her plight and others, where she had thought she was unique, at the gap between what Marre said and did. For evidently Marre recognized the Voice from her description. Perhaps she had read the very book that Xoon spoke of. The silence in her inner ear rang as loud as trumpets.

"As do I," Tyall said, "As do I. Calling and searching, poor thing, and I cannot find it, I cannot help it." He was silent a moment, head bent in sorrow, and then without further word he struck up a quicker pace.

Finally they came out of the galleries and into a lighter area, a series of halls each greater in proportion and more heroically columned than the last. Mosaics covered their walls and floors, but their ceilings had fallen along the south side and admitted the sky. Many of the columns on that side were tumbled also.

"Surely this was some important place," Alliole observed, anxious to provide a reason for further speech, "Perhaps a former seat of power." This did not seem to cheer Xoon.

"Let's rest here then, if you like it," he said, "I am tired of being hurried. And it is my belief that it has always been so. My great and illustrious ancestors, much honor to them forever, and so on and so forth, probably created them ruined, in order to provoke the awe of the common people."

"Surely not, Xoon," Tyall said, evidently shocked at his friend's heresy. He seated himself on a tumbled column and started to sort through his pack, reciting as he did so, in the sing song chant of utter belief, "Els—the Neve says that they had great power, but chose to invest it in the creation of this safe haven, and so left their inheritors the poorer. We cannot know the reasons for the choices they made, but surely they were right and just, else they—the best and fairest of their kind—would not have made them."

"But before that," Xoon interrupted, "Before that, it all gets lost in the mist. Where they came from, why they chose to stay here. There are no firm answers, just myths. Why shouldn't what came after be myth too? Perhaps our ancestors were not so wise and great after all. I suspect that they were much like you or me. Muddling through as best they could, and making mistakes like the rest of us. I bet they lost their powers by mistake. I'll bet anything that it was by accident."

"Xoon, don't speak that way," Tyall begged, "It scares me, and besides we know some things are true. The war happened, I am sure. And I dreamt them, the Masks. I am sure they exist." He finished his foraging, unearthing a wine skin and some food, which proved to be sweet, slightly withered apples, and strips of dried meat.

"Are my aunts sure?" Xoon asked, "You heard Reven yesterday. If they really believed your dreams they would have found some way to prevent us going. Do you think they want a thing of power around, especially if it has been rescued and presented to them by me?" The last said with such uncommon bitterness that Tyall was for a moment lost for words.

"And as for the war," Xoon resumed after a minute, still bitterly, "If they were so wise and great, and I'm not saying that they weren't, how did they come to have enemies?"

"Those who envied their power," Tyall said, again in the ritual chant.

"You are quoting from the Ceremonies," Xoon accused.

"How can there be debate about a war?" Alliole asked, drawn into the debate despite her best intent, "It either happened or it didn't. How can there be any questions?"

"Of course there was a war," Tyall said, with great, almost anxious, firmness in his voice, "The matter for debate is whether it was purely sorcerous, or if it involved an actual clash of arms."

"I think it was probably just a convenient excuse," Xoon said, "That's all. They probably just didn't want—"

"I think we'd better stop talking about this right now," Tyall said. He lay back, as if to emphasize his denial, and closed his eyes.

Alliole sat looking up at the patch of sky visible to her through the roof. There were clouds in it. She knew they were clouds although to her knowledge she had never seen them before. It was a name that came to her when she saw the tumbled masses of white and grey billowing across the gap in the stone. She noticed that her companions had seated themselves with their back to the fallen roof, and at no point looked at it. And here was another thing. She had seen nothing of orchard, vineyard, or pasture, such as would be expected for pigs to forage on, yet surely they existed, or they would not have such provender as Tyall produced. She puzzled as she ate, as to where they would be found, and determined on her return to see them. On the other side of the courtyard perhaps, logic told her, for there had been many swine there, and people to tend to orchards and vegetable gardens. To this puzzle were added the further questions of the Voice and her friend's progenitors, and the war of which they spoke. Would Tyall go mad as his predecessor had? That would surely be of grief to all, for he was young, and seemingly honest. Why did they not do to him as Marre had done to her? Because he forbade it, surely, or because its hold on him was stronger, and could not so easily be detached, for why cling to a thing so redolent of old and purposeless sorrow? Perhaps Caerre would be of help in answering these questions, she decided, and let the matter rest.

"Where to now, then?" she asked, breaking a long silence.

"I don't know," Tyall admitted. He still lay on his back with his eyes half-closed, and his voice came slowly and reluctantly, "Through these halls, I suppose, but then, I don't know. In my dream the Masks seemed to float up out of the walls." Xoon looked around hastily, but his friend reassured him, "No not here, the ruins were older, taller, wider, I don't know. But different, somehow."

"Very well, let us keep on then," she said, and stood. Slaarngash, crouching by the far wall as was its habit, snuffed and growled.

"What is it?" Alliole called, and made her way over.

"Little feet," Slaarngash said, precisely in yesterday's manner, "They run away."

"When?"

"Just now."

"From how far?" she asked, lowering her voice, so the others would not hear.

"Close by," the demon answered, and coughed a laugh, "They are afraid."

"Anna," she asked, "Is it Anna?" It shook its head. Malice and amusement gleamed from it, and she mistrusted it. She turned back and was surprised by Xoon, who had appeared at her shoulder. He hushed her when she made to speak, "Tyall has fallen asleep," he said, "I knew he would, even without a long march. Sorcery has been enacted through him, and it exhausts even the initiated." He unwound the ruby ear-ring from the pouch in which he had wrapped it, and scowled at it, "Can you hear me?" he asked it.

"I do not think it is a scrying device," Alliole pointed out, "Else they would have prohibited our departure when you removed it."

"I suppose so," Xoon agreed. He re-wrapped the gem, and shoved it back into the pouch.

"You had perhaps better wake him," Alliole said, and looked over to the distant clutter that marked their camp, "Slaarngash says—"

"Shhhh," Xoon said again, hastily, "He needs his sleep. Surely he can rest awhile, Alliole?" She mistrusted him as much as the demon, for his face was too gleeful to be simply commiserating with a friend's weariness.

"What about at night?" she asked.

"We have to camp somewhere," Xoon said, "And it may as well be here, unless you would prefer a little further along. And if Tyall is rested he can guard us while we sleep. Surely that is reasonable?"

"How far do we wish to go?" she asked.

"As far as I have to, or can get away with," Xoon said. He grinned wickedly at her, "They do not like people wandering far from the Castle Proper. If you can get a demon to desist your wandering, I am sure to get something special."

"The demon has not stopped my wandering," she said, diverted from her purpose of waking Tyall, "Indeed it has aided me to go further."

"Only at my instigation," Xoon said, complacently, "I am sure otherwise you would find some more fulfilling task to put your mind to." He returned and settled himself comfortably near Tyall, his mind evidently easy on the matter. Alliole was not so sure. She felt that the value of this place, for her, was in the exploration of it, in a manner that those who remembered it for all their lives could not understand. This thought caused her obscure but terrible sorrow.

Tyall lay still for two hours, and in that time, much of the weariness left his face. Then he raised himself, first on his elbow and then to his feet.

"Are you well rested?" she asked, before Xoon was able to hush her, and before she saw, by the way Tyall's eyes were upturned and from his lack of response to her question, that he was still asleep.

Chapter Eight

"TYALL," SHE SAID, ALARMED. She hesitated to order Slaarngash to shake his arm and wake him only because she doubted the prudence of such an action. Slaarngash might not only rouse him, but tear the limb off.

"Don't wake him, don't wake him," Xoon said, behind her, grabbing her arm in his excitement, "Do not wake a sleep-walker until they do so naturally. You may leave his soul in some strange place. I don't think my aunts would be pleased, after all the trouble they have taken to preserve him."

"What?" she said, and then, "Xoon, you knew this would happen. What can we do? What—"

"No, don't you see," Xoon said, grabbing his pack and silencing her again, bundling her forward after the sleeper, who stepping high and strangely, was moving towards the further entrance, "If we leave him asleep he will walk, and show us the way."

"What?" she said again.

"He will walk in his sleep, and show us the way," Xoon repeated, irritated at her denseness.

"Xoon, this is not safe," she said, "I think . . . ."

"Look," he said, "Who's in command here?"

"You are," she said, reluctantly.

"Very well," Xoon said, and nodded his head, pleased, "I say he stays asleep. Better during daylight than the night, eh?" On that point she fully agreed.

"But what if he goes somewhere else? Weren't they afraid of him sleepwalking near here?" she asked, "If they went to the extent of giving him the charm, if they—" But Xoon waved her to be silent. He was confident and cheerful, sure of success. What had she to doubt him? Rumors and vague warnings. And surely Tyall could not come to too much trouble, in their charge.

The following hours, until well after dark, were spent in following the sleep-walker, dodging through chambers, corridors and stairs so numberless that eventually her brain grew numb, wearied with the effort of counting. In any case their tracks were left perfectly plain in the dust, a wide trail from the demon's dragging walk, and the edges of the robes they had thrown about themselves for warmth. She ceased to bother herself with the thought of how they would return, and concentrated on the task of following on. In this place the ceilings were more often fallen than not, so they had to pick their way over the rubble, carefully and slowly. For all her care, Alliole fell twice, and Slaarngash had to lift her. Her helplessness in preventing the fall discomforted her more than the pain to her forearms when she tried to catch herself. The sleep-walker moved confidently and without care, but did not fall.

There were halls whose ruined walls were symphonies framed in stone, soaring to the sky and exquisite even in their decay. Stairs climbed away from the passages, and finished impotent and gap-toothed in empty air. There were walls once plastered and painted in bright colors and scenes whose ghostly outlines still lingered, and others to which the remnants of much weathered frescoes clung. At the sight of one of them, Xoon exclaimed and lingered as long as he dared, and far longer than Alliole liked. She followed the sleep-walker and watched the light Xoon held retreat behind them into the night. When he joined them again, he said only, "That fresco was the same as the one in my chambers, I swear," and seemed wrapped in thought at the finding of something so familiar in so lost and desolate a place. It gave Alliole pause also, as for a moment it seemed that they had returned to the busy halls and passages of the Castle, and found them long abandoned ruins, open to the sky, with weeds forcing their way through the flagstones.

A wind blew and it became cold. Above, in the black roof of the sky, the stars came out, one by one, as somehow, within herself, she knew they would. Xoon hurried along, with his eyes on the ground. As they passed deeper into the ruins, the width of the masonry also increased, and the number of steep stairs—as if they were descending into the catacombs, but nevertheless kept sight of the upper air. Grass grew up between the paving, and vegetation covered the guttered heights. To Alliole's eyes, alert for attack, it seemed like odd glimpses of thick fur. Again and again she thought the fur moved, and then was still. Several times she thought she heard a distant imbecilic mumble, several times she thought that twin pin-pricks of red air—not her demon's— glared at her from the distant dark, and were then snuffed out. It was as if their owner turned and fled, or was approaching with their back to her. This for some reason frightened her, that the owners of those eyes were coming closer, secretively, and taking such care to hide their faces. Nothing launched at them out of the darkness, but she remained fearful.

Just as she was about to suggest, in desperation and fatigue, that they turn back, or at least halt for the night, they came to a massive building whose first floor ceiling was still intact, for they could not see the finish of the stairs. The entrance was wide and tall, an antechamber rather than a passage. The remnants of a door rusted on its hinges at the top of a short flight of stairs, and a corridor narrowed and turned a corner in the distance.

As they stepped within, the light from their lanterns became confusing, no longer diminished by a vast space and pooled around them in an orderly circle, but a morass of light and shadows, reaching ahead towards the corner of the corridor. Tyall was hurrying now—and certainly the place answered his vision—when Alliole heard a definite hissing and scuttling upon the stair, a resurgence of the idiot mumbling as if in chant, as if from many voices, and a sudden well of sound from all around, the more startling for the silence that had preceded it. Besides, the utter pitch of the night and lateness of the hour made all things seem fraught with portent.

"Wait," she called, but Tyall of course did not listen.

Xoon hesitated beside her. Around the corner ahead, and shining with its own necrogenic light, pallid and uncanny, came a creature. It did not walk but, purely horrible, was carried in a large chair that glided through the air. She had a brief glimpse of its face, withered and milky-eyed, she had a brief glimpse of the claws that rested upon the arms of the chair, she had a brief glimpse of the chair itself, which was built of bones bound together with human hair. It was all the more awful for being so quickly seen, for then Tyall still walking and diminishing in perspective, blocked her view. She shrieked. Slaarngash, obedient to she knew not what command formulated in that moment of terror, bowled through the air and hit the creature, the chair. The deathly light was snuffed out instantly, to be replaced by the wholesome light of the lanterns, and the sounds of furious battle from the dark, a cat-like squall, and a renewed sobbing and shouting from everywhere, torn from throats whose owners possessed no human rationality. All sounds ended together.

"Xoon, the lantern," she said, and went forward. He followed, haltingly. It lit Tyall's retreating back, and Slaarngash standing over the ruins of the creature, spitting out bones, and snarling disgustedly, "There is no soul there, nothing." It wailed and threshed its wings again, so that the lantern threatened to go out in the draft it raised, and Alliole called it to order. As if woken by its voice echoes scuttered and flapped from all about, from above, as if countless creatures were scurrying about on the roof.

"After Tyall," she said, "Quickly, before they catch him." In great dread she skirted the creature. Its arm fell across her path, and she saw that it was semi-desiccated, dwarfed and shrunk, twisted about itself as if from some great pain. Its face was upward and seemed to be peering at her. Its mouth was open, and she could see a livid tongue shining within. Its eyes were stones covered with a cataract growth, one green, one blue. Xoon was even more skittish at passing the creature than she was. For a moment she lost the light, and was floundering down a dark passage towards a receding sleeper, caught in nightmare in which she would never catch him, and he would disappear. Then she had caught up and attempted to block his path, but he brushed past her. She could see Xoon coming up the passage behind them. Slaarngash followed after, and whatever made the noise.

"Xoon, the gem," she shrieked, "The gem. Replace it." Again she blocked his path, and called his name, but Tyall did not answer. His eyes were uplifted and faintly luminescent. His lips were moving, as if in conversation or prayer, "They are the uninterred and angry dead," he was saying, "Those for whom the ceremonies are not performed, the rituals are not sung over, each year.

Those who have no place to rest. thereforee they hate the living, and wish us one with them, forever."

Xoon caught up, the red gem snarling the light. He more or less stabbed it in Tyall's direction. He was badly scared, Alliole saw, and was only thankful that he had held onto his courage enough to follow them, and to obey orders. On the second attempt, the wire was more or less attached. Its effect was instantaneous. Tyall stopped speaking and slumped down in a faint. They stood over him in the corridor, expecting attack at any moment, but none came. The voices retreated, and with them the constant scurrying and scratching at the ceiling. Slaarngash snarled anew and rushed out into the night. There was a mass outburst of gibbering. Then it was back, spitting what looked like sand out of its mouth.

It was almost dawn by the time Tyall came to himself, dazed, confused and incapable of guiding them further. Together they carried him back the way they had come, as far as the galleries, where he recovered enough to lead them. He sank down again in the Hall of Masks, and buried his head in his hands. He would not be moved, and remained speechless. Alliole sent Slaarngash with a message to the Neve, to send servants to help them.

"It was a dream-thing," Xoon said, at last, as they rested, "Nothing more."

"Not the unquiet dead?" Alliole asked.

"What?" he said, and she realized he had not been close enough to hear Tyall's words. She related them to him.

"That cannot be," he said, "For the dead are interred in the Catacombs and kept quiet with ceremonies."

"What about the Mad Parrar?" she asked.

"She was only one. There were hundreds of them, did you hear? Out there," Xoon replied, shaken evidently, even by the memory, "There could not be so many lost."

"What about the war?" Alliole asked, "Could they have been lost in the war?" When Xoon was silent, she said, bitterly, "I thought you said there was no danger there."

"I thought there was none," Xoon said, and spread his hands to show his innocence, "Dreams and phantasms, not—" he paused searching for the right word, but was unable to find it, and so settled for "—things."

"I had almost found it," Tyall said, raising his head from his hands, and looking at them, dreadfully, his eyes still with too many dreams in them, his hands shaking, "I was almost upon it and I woke. If I had kept courage, I would have found it for sure. I am sorry, I am so sorry."

"Do you remember what you said," Alliole asked him, urgently, "About the dead? Is that something you know, or is it something from the dream? Tell me."

"I cannot hear you," he said, but he was not answering her. He was not listening to her. He was listening to another voice, a Voice, that only he could hear.

When Alliole arrived back at her chambers, Anna was waiting for her, hiding behind the bed curtains. Alliole was exhausted already, from the sleepless night and the long journey, but most of all from the ferocious questioning the Neve had given her, which had ended with the forbidding of any further such ventures. In her fatigue she felt as if every separate bone ached, and her fresh grazes throbbed and hurt her far more than they should. She was at first delighted to see Anna, and then not so sure, for the girl was too subdued to mean well. She attempted to maintain her normal chatter and fell short.

"What do you want?" Alliole inserted, into one of the silences. Anna flushed and stammered over her answer.

"Caerre wants to talk to you," she managed at last.

"Now," Alliole said.

"Yes," Anna said. "Please," she added. Alliole was fairly sure that had not been in the original message.

"Anna, I have not slept this last night," she whispered, "Do you think Caerre would forgive me if I failed to answer her summons, at least until evening?"

Anna shook her head, timidly. Silence fell, disturbed only by the demon's fidgeting. Alliole debated in her mind whether putting off the visit would be worth the inevitable backlash, and indeed whether such would not be pleasant after the events of the night. She closed her eyes, meaning to do so only for a moment, but it must have been some hours later that Anna woke her.

"Please," Anna said, again. She plucked at Alliole's overlong sleeves. Alliole rose, in a kind of stupor, and followed where she led.

Anna led her as assuredly as Tyall had, down through the precinct of Masks and to the entrance from which a stair descended, around which skeletons carved into stone capered, and from which stair a tomb wind blew. Anna did not hesitate but plunged into the darkness with the surety of someone who had long lived there. Alliole faltered at the entrance.

"Anna, I need a light," she said, "I cannot see in the dark."

"Can't you?" Anna said, as if surprised, but she dutifully returned back to Alliole's chambers and fetched a lantern. This wait gave Alliole further time to admire the decorations of the entrance, to note the exquisite detail in the worm that crawled from a dead man's eye, and the coffin mould that dropped from the grinning jaws of another. It gave her chance to feel the tomb wind blow upon her cheek, and for Slaarngash to descend and ascend the first stair a dozen times.

"I like this place," the demon observed.

"You would," she said. It grinned, like the skeletons itself, and gnashed its teeth together.

Anna returned, "Sometimes they don't like the light," she whispered, "If they don't like it I'll blow it out, but I'll keep you by the sleeve I promise, and I won't let you go until we get to Caerre." With those comforting words, Anna plucked at Alliole's sleeve, and together they descended below, the demon pausing for a while behind them, to snuff at the air, and admire the graven bones that pranced with such vigor over the entrance, as if to mock the slow and deadly entropy of the years.

Alliole was in such a stupor of exhaustion that her first visit to the Catacombs passed in a blur of stumbling through dark, low stone passageways, lined with the dead, until it seemed to be merely a ghastly repeat of her previous journey. She recollected she had escaped alive from the previous nightmare, and thereforee, presumably, she would escape alive from this one. But the nature of the corridors and cenotaphs confused her, until she feared that the halls of the dead were patterned exactly after those of the living, and here they held court and awaited visitors, such as herself, to be entombed alive with them forever. There was nothing of the splendor and richness that Iriethe had once described to her, just an arid wind blowing, and cold and dreary passage-ways going on forever. Then a cross-wind would catch at her, or she would awaken, it seemed, to the renewed touch of Anna's small, warm hand, and for a moment be comforted and remember that it was not a dream but a real journey, and they would shortly reach their destination. She would speak with Caerre and then return to her own chambers, and, she swore to herself, never again leave them, but slumber in peace for all her days hereafter. Then she would sink into lethargy again, so that again the intricacy of the necropolis—sarcophagi, vaulted tomb, gaping crypt, and ossuary alike—passed by unregarded.

Finally she stumbled into a chamber which differed from the others, being lit with a red, warm thing that crouched in the center of the floor on three legs, and housing dead that stirred and spoke to her.

"Get her to the fire. I think she is cold," Anna said. A firm hand in Alliole's back pushed her towards the three legged thing. She hesitated. She saw, with clearing vision, that coals glowed within a brazier shaped in the form of a wild beast, so that heat and color came from its four eyes and its jaws, distorted in its frozen rage. Similarly she saw that those who were there were alive, for she recognized them. Caerre, smiling slyly, the giant Tiralgon, his limbs stretched out along the floor, Helaf, holding his brother to him. Anna, whom she knew.

She could not frame a greeting to them until she had taken enough life herself from the fire to revive her wits. She raised her head and looked around, and saw that mortuary slabs were set about, in the wall, three high and probably originally two deep, but their former occupants were shovelled into a corner.

"Are you not frightened to do that?" was her first speech, indicating the bones with her head.

"They are the lesser dead. They do not rise," Caerre said. She reclined on one of the lower slabs, her head pillowed in her hand, "And in any case that is a myth, a story for children." Alliole shrugged and returned her gaze to the fire. Ragged clothing covered their skinny limbs, and the fire sparked in their eyes, lending them all, but most particularly Tiralgon, a speculative, even vindictive look. The only one who escaped it was Helaf, who for shyness or some other reason, was sitting on the highest of the slabs, near the roof, too far for the fire to reach. The brazier dispelled the arid cold of the crypts, but could not otherwise provide more than a bare minimum of warmth. Alliole could see only a large earthenware pot filled with water by the door. She regretted not bringing some food.

Some effort had been made at decoration even here, for tattered banners of cloth hung from the ceiling, as if in mimicry of the majestic banners of the Cross. Similar rags formed beds on the mortuary slabs, and tapestries, worn to threadbare and in some places stitched across with coarse thread to hold them together, were on the walls and floor. Stolen from some storage place similar to the galleries, Alliole guessed. On the opposite wall to the door, and all but hidden in the shadows, was a large frieze, depicting three beings, blank faced and dressed in long robes that hid their hands and feet. They were seated on graven thrones and looked most grand and awful. Depictions of the ancestors, she wondered, the honored dead? Ghosts or gods?

"What of Reven?" she asked. Her voice jumped as she said it.

"Are you afraid of him?" Caerre asked, "Do not worry. We have placed him down in one of the deeper sepulchers and done him as much honor as he deserves. Besides, I think he would count as lesser dead."

"Will no one find him then?" she asked. Caerre shrugged her shoulders. "No one has found the others," she said.

"We have learnt since Gaar's death," Tiralgon boasted. His eyes were sly and mean, and his hands clenched, cumbersome fists. Alliole could imagine him pushing someone from a height, although she wondered at his reason. Caerre glared at him, and then said, hastily, "I am sorry to keep you from your slumber. But we wanted to know your news. The Castle is talking of your adventure and we wanted to know for certain. They say our cousin Tyall has gone mad. Is that so?"

"Not mad I would say," Alliole said, dubiously, for it also occurred to her, as Tiralgon had undoubtedly intended, that if Gaar had not been safe then she was not either, "But shocked, rather. I think he will recover." Caerre looked disappointed, "Too bad, I thought it might be two down, but it is only one."

"Caerre," Alliole said, and her voice cracked again, "Your own family. You cannot mean. . . ."

Caerre measured her with one disconcerting eye, "You do not understand. They have been so cruel to us, abandoning us here. Why should we not rejoice in their suffering? But we do not mean them harm, not even Reven, whom you slew, remember, and certainly not Gaar. He was my father, after all. Alone among my family he loved us. He cared for me, and for Helaf and baby, when they were little. He was blessed by the Lady of Cats, so I don't see how he could fall. I suppose he was pushed, and although I hope not by Xoon, I am inclined to suspect so. Who else would benefit from his death? Or it was arranged, to pay him back for his protection of us. Tiralgon is trying to make you afraid but he is a fool."

Tiralgon looked stung. His legs jerked, and he lifted his hands, then dropped them again, clenching them in his lap.

"I thought it was your mother who protected you," Alliole said, cautiously.

"At my father's instigation. She would not have raised a hand otherwise," Caerre said, "Why should she care? Have you news of her by the way?"

"I have yet to meet her," Alliole said, still measuring her words, "How is Aubon? Did you tend to him?"

"Anna did," Caerre said.

"His hand was broken," Anna said, flopping her own hand to show her, "But I bound it and it will get better as long as he is careful. And he had some bruises."

"I wish him well with all my heart," Alliole said, "When you next visit him, tell him I hope that he will soon be better."

"I forgot to thank you also, for looking after Anna," Caerre said, abruptly softer, "And for your words for Aubon I thank you also, and your message will be delivered. You are kind, you are the first that has been kind to us since Gaar died, and we would help you if we could. We can help each other. Speaking of which. . . . "

"I am tired," Alliole said, hastily, "As I am sure you can understand. I have journeyed long and had several severe frights. I would beg you to leave any discussion of ways in which we can aid each other to some future encounter." Caerre looked disappointed but held her tongue. "I too have much to ask of you," Alliole continued, "But I am so weary I cannot think straight. May I tell you my story later? I can give you a full record of it, but not now. I am so tired. How large are these catacombs? I feel I have trod their full measure."

"We don't know," someone said softly, dreamily. She thought it was Helaf. "We don't know how far they go."

"Each generation mines for the next," Tiralgon said, loudly, trying to make up his lost face, "And so on, and on, into the far past, into the future."

"You must understand," Caerre said, over-ruling him, "That we only know parts of the Catacombs ourselves, the upper parts. Some of us have explored down lower, but never far. It is too far, to get there and back in a day, and at night you see, they are not safe. The Kings—" there was a peculiar tone in her voice "—you never know what is there."

"Another Castle," chipped in Tiralgon.

"A bone door," said Anna, and her face lit till it sparked like a moth caught in the fire.

"Be quiet," said Caerre, irritatedly.

"I will not," retorted Tiralgon, uncoiling his long length and waving his arms, "Don't give yourself such fine airs, Caerre. Caerre dreamt of it, she told us, there is another Castle down there, all hidden in stone, a secret place where we could go, we could hide, and no one could find us, ever." Caerre rocked back on her heels and wrapped her arms around herself sulkily.

"What would we eat there?" Anna said, obediently.

"Fungus."

"What would we wear?"

"Nothing," Tiralgon said, triumphantly, and Anna shrieked with laughter. It was evidently an old joke.

"And the door," Anna begged. Caerre scowled further, but again Tiralgon readily took up the answer, "Down there, deep down so far no one knows, but me, and I saw it just the once, there is a bone door." He squinted, as if he could still see it, and shaped it before him in the air as he spoke, "A door built all out of one piece of ivory, all yellow and stained, and bound with," here came the final effort and the one that made Alliole believe him, for he spoke of something he could not properly describe, and made great effort to fully define it, as if it were the truth. Besides she did not credit him with that much imagination, "Bound with straps of metal so undisturbed that it has gone green and furred, and so old that water had run down the bolt and taken bits of the green stuff with it, so that the green metal hangs from the bolt as if they were water drops. I drew the bolt but I could not open it. It was too heavy. And by the time I had returned with the others it was gone. What was beyond it, I wonder?"

"Another Castle," Anna cried, showing limited imagination herself.

"I'll tell you what's there," Caerre pounced, her voice betraying her indignation. She leant forward as she spoke and her unbound hair fell across her vivid face, painting it with shadow. She looked truly wicked then, and cruel enough to kill her own father, "I'll tell you what, there's a place all green, with green things stuck in it without any order at all, and no walls anywhere. And most terrible of all, it has no roof, and when you look up you fall up for ever." The atmosphere of good-will built up in the small chamber withered as quickly as it had arisen, destroyed by Caerre's ill humor. Anna wailed in terror, and Helaf spoke for the first time, mildly, "Caerre don't be so cruel. Anna will have nightmares."

"Do you think I care?" Caerre hissed, lowering her terrible face slowly to that of her cowering sister, "Serve her right for telling fool's lies. Who cares what is anywhere, except where it will serve our cause. Do you think that we will get what we deserve by running away? *They* would be glad if we ran away. They would be rid of us forever, and they would laugh and sing, and make merry, and not care at all. Especially Marre." Marre was evidently the bogey, for Anna wailed again at the mention of her name, and Tiralgon sobered, and sat up straight. Helaf descended carefully from his perch, holding his brother's head protectively against him in order to balance them both, and comforted his sister. Alliole saw by the way they moved together, that the pair were joined at the waist. Caerre sat back and surveyed her handiwork with satisfaction.

"And as for my mother, I am sure she is dying. She could not be with child so long. I have heard it has been more than a year. I cannot find out if it is true. And if she is dying, why then Xoon is still her heir. How can I bear that, if he succeeds to her place? How could I bear it?" Caerre said, as if it was a chant, broodingly.

"I'll take you back now," Helaf said to Alliole, quietly, "To spare Anna." When she hesitated, he asked, and smiled sadly as he said it, "Are you afraid?"

"No," she answered, honestly. She said her farewells and then turned her back on the small group, to make the return journey to the surface of the earth.

"You will visit us again soon," Caerre said.

"Tomorrow, when I have slept," she answered, and wondered at the urgency of her summons here. Unless it was that Anna was accustomed to obeying Caerre's commands absolutely, and had feared to let her go, or perhaps Caerre had wanted to be certain of her new ally. Slaarngash reappeared as she left the chamber, bearing a heavy necklace of silver set with large, dark stones. The silver was tarnished but the stones glinted in the light from the brazier, with a thousand rainbow hues swimming in their utter blackness. Shreds of crimson cloth still clung to it. The demon placed the necklace about Alliole's neck before she had time to guess its plan, and recoil, and she could find no way to remove it. When she protested, volubly, it grunted, "Sorcery," and left her side again to forage amongst the gleanings of the necropolis.

Helaf, like Anna, forgot to take a lantern, and looked startled when she reminded him. Anna at least ventured often into the Castle, while she suspected Helaf, out of shyness or shame, dwelt most of his days in the Catacombs. She could see that he must cradle his brother protectively, for the other was lifeless except for his open and sometimes moving eyes, and evidently could barely hold his own weight upright. Helaf looked over at her several times during the first part of the journey, but did not speak, and Alliole was too busy with her own thoughts to notice his silence, or again, her surroundings.

She wondered about the dead man, Gaar, about his devotion to his children. Had they dwelt in the Catacombs even then? It was a good enough place to hide as any. Where could a man fall so far as to be killed by it? Mentally she transversed the journey from necropolis to the central precincts. She realized, with a start, that there was only one place where Gaar could have fallen—the balconies in the great hall, near the chambers of the Parrar, straight down through an infinity of air.

She emerged from her thoughts with this shock, and shivered.

"Are you cold?" Helaf asked.

"No," she said, but Slaarngash came near, and pulled her cloak higher around her. Helaf watched the demon carefully while it did this, and did not look at her again until it had dropped back to its wonted position. He was thin about the face, Caerre's other brother, although any lack of body weight was disguised by the twin he bore. His eyes lacked the intensity and life of his family, as though they were turned inward, as if their fires were smoldering and would soon go out. Although of Tyall's height, he lacked both the width of shoulder and the strength of features, both, Alliole supposed, because of lack of proper food rather than any other reason, for she saw that his eyes were set well apart, his forehead was broad and smooth, and his teeth were regular. Nature had meant well when she first designed him, but too much had marred him since. He flushed miserably, and she abruptly became conscious of the length of her regard.

"Are you Caerre's younger or older brother?" she asked, to break the tension.

"Older," he said, and smiled, a nervous twitch quickly swallowed in the white anxiety of his face, that nevertheless showed his even teeth, "We both are . . . I mean, that is obvious. My brother. He is not very well. He stopped growing when we were four. We had a fall, and he hit his head."

"It must have been a bad fall," Alliole said.

Helaf blushed and looked away, "Yes it was, but we caught some of the banners on the way, and they slowed us down. Uh. Take care here. The flagstones are uneven. Do not catch your feet."

"I won't," she assured him. After a pause, "Have you lived long here?"

"Always," he answered, with his quick grimace, "Always."

When she shuddered anew at the thought, he interpreted her answer correctly, "Oh, I like it here," he said, "Except when it gets crowded, during the festival. I can go anywhere, and no one will stare at me. Uh. I mean. . . ."

"You do not need to make excuses to me," Alliole answered quietly, and lifted her own arms.

"Oh, no, I mean, you are different. You are so bold and bright," he said, admiringly. He reached back, as if to touch her hair, and then recollected himself and dropped his hand, "Anna says that you stood up to Reven. Is that true?"

"Yes, but I had Slaarngash," Alliole pointed out, "Otherwise I am sure I would not have been so brave." His look continued, until she feared he would run into a wall, and she had lost her certainty as to whether it was admiring or as speculative as his sister's. Fortunately he turned back in time to guide her round a fresh obstruction, an ossuary wall built entirely of thigh bones, and topped with a row of skulls.

"Oh, it is hard to know what effect these things have," he said, "And how anybody would have acted, before or after. The fact is that you acted as you did, rather than as you did not. Slaarngash, is that its name?" and now his look was turned, dubiously, to her creature. He dropped back to walk beside her. "Does it always carry that sword?"

"Yes," she said, not meaning to explain further.

"Even after Reven," he asked, "Caerre says it was an accident, but it is a dangerous sort of accident."

"Especially after Reven," Alliole said, unbending. It was a question with a conscience behind it, although she wondered how flexible a one. "Slaarngash is bound to this world by the stone in the hilt. I would not leave it in my chambers for Marre to find while I was not there. Just in case she should suspect." Her voice died away. They both contemplated the prospect a long while.

Without thinking they had fallen into step, but had to break ranks in order to climb a flight of stairs. Helaf hung back, and Alliole saw with surprise that they had reached the last flight, for the Castle was above her, the inhabited part, precincted, defined and known.

"I can go on from here alone," she said, perceiving her companion's hesitation.

"Good-day then," he said, gratefully.

"Good-night rather," she said, "I think it is near evening. Thank you for your company. The homeward journey passed much quicker than the journey there."

"They always do," he said, but he gave her a proper smile this time, as bright as Xoon's. She climbed the stair, her demon skulking after, looking forward to the familiar route to her chambers, to covering the final distance before she could rest. But in the last corridor, Slaarngash stopped and hissed.

"What is it?" she asked it, softly, and took steps enough to look into the room through the window. There was someone there. It was Sleepghast. He had opened one of her chests, and was peering into it.

"What do you want?" she asked, ferociously, totally surprising him. He leapt up and shut the lid with a bang, whirled around to face her.

"My master wants you to attend him immediately," Sleepghast said, making the best of a bad situation by drawing himself up and putting on a look of hurt patience.

"I have had enough orders for today," Alliole said, "Tell him I will visit when I have slept." She had Xoon's measure now, and was not frightened to disobey him. She wondered at what he wanted so urgently, so quickly after their day spent together, but not enough to further forgo her rest. When Sleepghast hesitated, she became peremptory. "Go," she ordered, "And do not spy so carelessly, or who knows what will befall you."

"I go," Sleepghast said, and bowed, snapping back and forwards on his heels with the force of the thrust he applied to his stomach. "But," he added from the door, slyly, "While it is not my business to wonder what takes you from your chambers so long, I shall have to tell my master of your absence in order to excuse my own." He was gone before she could reply, and her drift into slumber was troubled by thoughts on whether he could find out where she had been, and with whom. 🏵

Chapter Nine

ALLIOLE WOKE LATE the following morning. Slaarngash was peering at her over the bedstead in its accustomed disconcerting manner, and Iriethe and Sleepghast waited on her awakening. Iriethe came forward first, as the acknowledged better.

"Alliole, the Neve requires your attendance this fore-noon," she said, "And bid me wait here until the message be delivered."

"Of course," Alliole said, sitting up in the bed, sluggishly, trying to work out where she was. Iriethe was gone from the room before any further elaboration could be demanded, her face fixed in a frown. Sleepghast alone loitered, and on his face was a benevolent smile, as of one equal to another.

"My message is the same as the one previous," he said, but waved his arms about to emphasize the difference, "Save that I was bid to deliver you to the door, by force if necessary. Not (I hasten to add) that I would lift a hand to so obey, but I repeat these words verbatim so that you should know the strength and urgency of my master's wishes."

"Yes, all right," Alliole said, sitting up further, shaking her head, groggy and half awake. First and foremost she wished the other would stop talking and give her a chance to gather her thoughts.

"And furthermore, once you have spoken with him, I can deliver you to your next appointment, with all due speed and courtesy," Sleepghast said, doing a complementary jig to the movement of his arms, as if to mime the rapidity with which she would be removed from the one interview to the other.

"Ugghh," she said, and then the first thing that came to mind, in order to forestall any further prattle, "How is Tyall?" She bid the demon attend her, with all speed. Sleepghast came into the room further, looking out into the passageway to see if any overheard.

"It is strange that you should ask that," he said, and his eyes glittered, "He is as well as could be expected. His mind wanders."

"Why is it strange?" she asked, arrested by his manner. Sleepghast drew back at once, and spread his arms, this time apologetically, retreating to the door, where again he cast a glance about the passageway, "Oh nothing is strange, good lady," he said, in his most hearty tones, "Nothing. His sickness is upon everybody's lips. It is well to hear your concern on the matter. It does my heart good to know that in this day and age the great and the insignificant do not entirely abandon their interest in each other's welfare." She gazed at him suspiciously, but contented herself with, "I do not need you to dress. Wait at the stair."

Sleepghast bowed, his body exerting itself rather more than was necessary, in the way that it did when he was excited, and withdrew. She finished dressing slowly, trying to determine what she had said that would evoke such interest from him, and then, sick with forethought, attempted to grapple with the reasons behind the twin summons. She must work out innocuous answers to any questions, answers which did not exactly lie, for she feared the Castle's ability both to detect and conceal the truth.

Her first interview was the one that least worried her, and seeing that Xoon was alone when Sleepghast ushered her into his chambers eased the worst of her fears.

"Oh, there you are," Xoon said, ungraciously, uncoiling himself from the cushions in front of the fire. His face was set in a deep frown of infinite flexibility, as Alliole soon discovered, for he was able to laugh at his own jokes and then return the sullen look to his face effortlessly when she spoke. With Lyde not there to hinder it, Slaarngash again waded across the grate, periodically emerging to pour the wine, and hand around the sweetmeats, for Xoon would not allow Sleepghast to attend them, and dismissed the servant before seating Alliole by the fire. He sat himself down beside her.

"You realize, don't you," Alliole asked him, loudly because she still sought some way to pay the servant back, and was unschooled in subtle methods of perfidy, "That Sleepghast is probably just listening outside the door." Xoon shrugged. "No matter," he said, "We will talk loudly of the unimportant and low otherwise. You would not come when I told you," he continued, crossly, "And now I have half a mind to leave you out altogether." She realized, wearily, that she would have to work to cheer him before she would learn anything of importance, but could come to no immediate gossip that would answer her purpose.

"How is Tyall?" she asked at last.

"Well enough," Xoon said, "They are all fussing over him, and would not let me speak to him." His scowl deepened.

"Just as well," she said, grasping for straws, "He needs unencumbered sleep surely. You are probably tired also. Have you slept?"

"No, I could not sleep," he said, "Not with all the details that I had to think about." He brightened, "But then you did not come." His face fell again.

"So you need me then," she said, deciding to be brisk and sensible and pay no heed to his temper, "What do you wish that I should do?" Evidently that hit the right note, or he had had enough of his pretence, for he spoke eagerly.

"It is quite simple really. It is the start and end we have to work out. I have quite decided to make another journey, but we must not tell anybody."

"Another . . ." Alliole said, before she lost her voice in her anguish. Slaarngash hissed, sleepily and raised its wings but fortunately did not fan them. The flames nevertheless rose higher, and took on green and blue colors not fit for an ordinary fire. Sparks spattered about its hide. "Xoon, have you so quickly forgotten the last one? It was horrible that thing we saw, and there must have been hundreds of them."

"But they did not attack us, not directly," Xoon said, patiently. "Keep your voice down. I have been thinking. They were afraid of us. And they only seemed to be about at night. It is not so far. If we were to set off early enough, and trace our tracks quickly, I am sure that we could be there and probably most of the way back again, before night fell."

"It is you who are mad, Xoon, not poor Tyall," Alliole said, making a great effort and maintaining her lowered tone, "Remember. He guided us. We do not know where the hall is, or if it exists at all. We did not see it." Xoon was too wrapped up in his plan, or too sure of his own ability to obtain her obedience, to take umbrage at her. "He took us most of the way there I am sure," he said, "Remember what he was saying, in the Hall of Masks? That he had almost reached it."

"I think he was talking about something else," Alliole hissed.

"Well, I don't," Xoon snapped, and his scowl returned at her unwillingness to fall in with him, "I think we were almost there, we were almost upon it, this hall filled with Great Masks, and I say we make a second attempt. Otherwise the first would be in vain. Nothing would come of it, and Tyall's pain would be made worthless." The last was a cunning argument, although not one she was sure had much occupied his mind. There she may have done him another disservice. "And besides," he added, and this Alliole thought was his real reason, "I have been to a deal of bother and received nothing for it except some strong language from my aunt. I deserve better."

"But with only two of us," she said, at last, "And your aunt flatly forbode it." She shuddered at the language which the Neve had chosen to reinforce her command.

"Oh, I will take responsibility for that," Xoon said, easily. He sat back in his chair. The scowl disappeared. "Her words can be only advisory to me remember. I am the heir. And you must obey my command. But I would rather that she did not hear of it before we were gone. Much rather. And we are three with your demon," he added as an afterthought, looking around as if he missed it for the first time. Finding it, he contemplated it in the altered fire. Like most of his family he paid no more heed to it normally that he would a piece of furniture, and Alliole was both surprised at his regard for it, and alarmed because she supposed their fearlessness was born of an assumption that all demons were bound not to hurt them. Alliole seemed to have removed said binding, at least in this particular specimen.

"I think that it is what they were afraid of, anyway, " Xoon admitted, betraying the source of his regard, "That is why I chose not to go without you. Also, I thought we could take Lyde."

"Lyde is not in favor of the expedition either," Alliole said.

"Oh, Lyde takes color to suit her surroundings," Xoon said dismissively, "She kept her chief scorn for this adventure for her brother." This casual reference caused Alliole such a convulsion of guilt that she shuddered. "Do you have a toothache?" Xoon asked courteously, before continuing, "She was all afire for it with me. She is monstrously selfish, you know," he said, contemplative again, stretching his legs out before the flames, "And wants everybody to think well of her. She wants no fuss or trouble. She turned down my position, when everyone thought there would be no more heirs, because it would be too much bother."

"If she thinks that way then she will truly not be willing to come."

"Oh, we will not tell her until we are well enough gone," Xoon said, "Then she will be happier to come than to go, I assure you. And by the time her first enthusiasm is past she will be so far away that it will not be worth her while to return alone."

"And what help will she be?" Alliole asked, thinking of Lyde's disagreeable words and manner.

"She has great powers over fire," Xoon said, "I think our friends out in the ruins wouldn't like that either." He sprang to his feet and smiled at her, and she saw ghosts flitting across his face—Caerre, Tyall, Marre. Echoes as it changed. "You have no choice anyway. I command you. We'll leave first thing tomorrow. And remember, tell no one."

The first interview was clearly over.

It was evening by then. Blackness was seeping into the grey light of day, and torches were spontaneously lighting themselves in wall brackets. She paced deliberately and took many deep breaths as Sleepghast led her to the Neve's quarters. She felt that her choices were narrowing. She by now felt too much remorse not to reconsider her silence over Reven's death, although she would much rather not do so, for fear of Marre's wrath. Perhaps they would understand. Perhaps her punishment would not be so hard. Nevertheless if the Neve asked the right question she would answer, although she hoped the right question would not be asked. And every time she thought of last night's meeting in the Hall of Masks she took another deep breath, as of a swimmer plunging into deep water, to buoy herself, and Sleepghast's quizzical glances grew speculative.

For a start she had not intended the Neve to personally answer the summons, and had not expected her. She remembered too late that they did not like servants in the Wheeled Hall, and so it was doubtless an impulse to protect Aubon that led the Neve to accompany the rescue expedition. It had not been a pleasant encounter. The Neve had ignored them at first, had gone to Tyall and touched him. He lifted his face from his hands, and she had touched his cheek, a gentle caress, before fingering the ear-ring, which had come loose in her fingers. She cupped it in the palm of her hand. Then she had looked at them. Alliole sincerely wished never again to see such anger, all the worse because, when at last she spoke her words were carefully measured, and delivered quietly. It was not as it was with Marre, so quick to wrath that in the end her anger was meaningless because it was habitual. It was an emotion that expressed itself only after all other options had been tried and exhausted. Xoon had hung his head before her. Alliole thought he had been ashamed but now realized he had simply not paid attention, but counterfeited remorse while it was tactful to do so.

Someone called her name, and she returned to the present. Iriethe was approaching, her face warm with welcome.

"I had just come to find what was keeping you," she said, taking Alliole's arm, and dismissing Sleepghast with a glance. "I hope you are not ill?"

"No, no," Alliole said, glad at any rate to escape her thoughts, filled as they were with dozens of plans and contingencies that led nowhere.

"There, you are quite recovered."

"I still cannot remember," Alliole said, and the other laughed, ruefully, recalling that once constant plaint, then passed lightly on to other topics as she led her towards the Neve's chambers. Iriethe took up the thread of their old companionship so deftly that Alliole was hard put to remember how neatly it had been cut, for she had seen naught of Iriethe since her return save in her official capacity, and they had been brief, brusque meetings. It shook her newly awakened sense of distrust to realize the hypocrisy that must be inherent in this, although her soul was warmed by Iriethe's chatter, and she could not treat her as coldly as such false good nature deserved. Instead she turned her head and was relieved to see Sleepghast still trailing them interestedly. There at least was someone whose deviousness could not hurt her, for she had disliked him from the start. An odd feeling of fellowship with the servant sprang up within her, and heartened her to bear with equanimity the pain of Iriethe's feigned camaraderie.

They arrived at the Neve's door to find one there before them, a black spotted hog whose friendly air vanished on beholding Iriethe. He let out a piercing squeal and dodged behind a neighboring pillar, from which he peered out at them with an expression of mingled spite and joy. Grielle immediately appeared at the door. The woman looked fatter still, for she was dressed in layers of brightly colored clothing, such as could conceivably be her formal livery. The layers were so many that she waddled rather than walked, and stood stiffly. Alliole doubted that she could bend over easily. For all that Grielle moved swiftly when she chose to, although it was her immobility that was formidable.

"Do not mistreat my creature," she said to Iriethe, coldly, drawing herself up so that her impressive bulk filled the entrance.

"I did not touch it," Iriethe said, as if indifferent, although her eyes glittered, and her face fixed into disdain. The hog limped, shivering, out from behind the pillar, and up to Grielle, most piteously holding up one foreleg.

Alliole was appalled at the animal's duplicity, until he peered out from behind Grielle's bulk, and winked, slow and deliberate, delighting her. Grielle closed the door behind her, smartly, but otherwise did not move, staring down her fleshly nose at her rival, whose initial disdain rapidly melted into an expression of boredom, "Alliole here will vouch for me," Iriethe said, "Although, and of your courtesy, you have no right to trespass here without my leave."

"I have searched the Courtyard for the missing man, and come to tell the Neve that he is not there," Grielle replied. Alliole caught her breath, but kept her composure.

"Why did you think he should he go there," Iriethe said, impatiently, "Are you robbed of sense as well as diligence? Why waste her time with trifles?"

"It was on her instruction," Grielle said. This was her crushing victory, and she looked for triumph in Iriethe's face. The hog poked its head out from behind her coats, smugly. "She has other trusted servants beside yourself. She does not tell you everything," Grielle goaded, finding no obvious defeat.

"Be on your way, and take your pig with you," Iriethe said, her sharp tone gone so abruptly that it must be with deliberate effort, "I have other tasks to attend, and so must you. Toad," she added beneath her breath, as Grielle left them. Alliole cast a last wondering look after the hog, and was rewarded with the sight of Sleepghast, who, slinking discreetly out of the stonework, rejoined Grielle. The pair passed in animated conversation from her sight, whilst Iriethe, with a last cordial pat and murmur, ushered her through the door.

Again, she found the Neve seated at the bureau, but this time her surroundings were busier. Servants flowed to and fro, and from some further chamber came the stentorian tones of the invalid, evidently awake and out of humor. Slaarngash stopped at the outer door, and could not be persuaded to enter, which Alliole, on second thoughts, decided was wise. She was unsure how far to trust the demon, and what questions it might decide to answer for her.

"Would you like to see your victim?" the Neve asked, scarcely a propitious welcoming. Alliole nodded and slunk into the other room, a bed-chamber fitted out plainly with martial tapestries, a good deal of antique weaponry, and grotesque and floridly decorated armor. Tyall was sitting in the bed looking flushed and unnaturally well rested. The red gem was firmly wired into his ear with three loops about the outer cartilage. He waved his arm when he saw Alliole, "I am perfectly well but no one will let me out of bed, and they have just forced another sleeping draught down my throat" he said, crossly, "Get your demon here, and it can help me up. At least I can walk around the room until I am tired."

"I'll get you anything you want," Alliole offered, at first relieved and then alarmed to see him so well, "But I do not dare countermand the Neve's order. I am out of favor with her enough as it is."

"I don't want anything except to get up," Tyall said, huffily but then he smiled, and she saw that she had returned him to some form of fretful good temper. She stayed with him talking for a further space of time, happy to be distracted from whatever the Neve required of her. He was irritable and found much trouble in sitting still, even when the soporific drugs began to work on him. He kept waking again, with a start and a demand for further conversation, until Alliole realized that he was simply and understandably afraid to sleep, and that his garrulous irritability was an attempt to stay wakeful. Inwardly she cursed Xoon, her own ignorance and whatever had made her follow Xoon's desires and not her own first impulse to wake Tyall when he fell asleep against the fallen pillar in that distant hall. She gently reminded Tyall of the protection he had gained, so that he reached up and fingered the gem and winced. Then she started talking softly and soothingly, about nothing in particular. If she could have, she would have stroked his pained, wakeful face. He fell asleep at last, with his fingers still wound around the gem. By that time the room was dark, with full night abroad, and the only light came from the other chamber.

"Come away," the Neve said, quietly, from the entrance, "If he wakes again he will call." Her face was softer. She ushered Alliole from the chamber and closed the communicating door, and Alliole felt all the weight of her unbearable tension fasten itself anew around her shoulders.

"I suppose you know why I have called you here," the Neve asked. She returned to her seat at the bureau and indicated to Alliole another by the fire. The seat was worn and sagged comfortably. The wood of its arms had gouges taken out of it, and a systemic series of cuts. Alliole turned her head to follow them. They were pictures of swords, and other things, such as a growing boy might be interested in. She sank into the seat, engulfed by ghosts and misery at what her presence had brought about. "No," she said, "Why did you let me see Tyall, and forbid Xoon?"

"Xoon has been hugging secrets to himself all day," the Neve replied, "I mistrusted his discretion if I allowed them to speak together. He may have involved Tyall in some fresh misery."

"Oh," Alliole said, slowly.

"I have asked Marre to be here, for we have important matters to discuss concerning your hands. So, of your courtesy, we shall wait to discuss these once Reven allows himself to be found," the Neve continued. Alliole was so torn in two by prayer for both the right and wrong questions that she no longer knew where to stand. "The first matter is the most obvious. Has it come to your attention that Xoon plans any fresh venture?"

"Yes," Alliole said.

"Are you free to speak of it?"

"I have been asked not to," she said. The Neve tapped her hand upon the arm-rest of her chair. "In your opinion does it involve undue danger to Xoon or some other person?" she asked.

"Yes," Alliole said.

"Will you be there?"

"Yes," Alliole said. The tension knotting inside her was unbearable. She wanted to scream, 'Yes, yes, I did it please. Just ask me the right question.'

"Then I will leave it with you," the Neve said, unexpectedly, "I can respect confidences, and besides if I were to turn Xoon from this course he would only find some other route by which to assert his independence. Perhaps worse." Her hand kept tapping on the arm-rest. Her eyes were drowned in shadow, "And I have other matters to occupy my attention."

Alliole was too surprised to thank her, or otherwise consider the implications of this singular and unwelcome honor.

"I think," she said, as boldly as she could, "That is part of Xoon's dilemma. He feels that you are always too busy to instruct him in his duties, and perhaps he dreams up such ventures to force your attention. If you were to spend more time with him, perhaps his fears would go away."

"There is, as you say, a dilemma," the other said, "But it is by no means certain that Xoon will be the heir. He is so currently because of his mother's wish and Lyde's indifference. But my sister is also with child, and if the babe is a girl, well—" she stood up and paced about the room, "—And then there is Caerre."

Alliole took a very deep breath indeed, and then started, timidly, it is true, but she at least and honorably made the attempt. "Caerre," her voice was too soft, and fluttered, and she made the effort to bolster it, for even though the Neve terrified her yet she felt strongly that her regard was something to value, "Caerre, she has been too long cast aside. Surely it is only just that she receive some portion of her inheritance? Just and wise."

The other stopped pacing and stared at her, "Wise?" she asked.

"Wise," Alliole repeated, and again her voice jumped before the other's disconcerting gaze, and again she steadied it, "Because she feels that she has the right. She is her mother's oldest daughter."

The Neve resumed her seat, "So you have been talking to her, then, even her." This was a statement, not an answer. "Is there no place you will not go? This prying will be the death of you. Very well then, do you know why she does not have her right?" she asked.

"Because she is malformed," Alliole said, "In spirit as well in body so they say, but I say that if her spirit is darkened it is because of the treatment she has received, not a result of whatever force wronged her at birth."

"You have been listening to Marre," the Neve said, dryly, "There is nothing wrong with Caerre's soul. This may yet prove disastrous if she remains unlearned, for if she takes after her mother she has considerable powers. I say that her misfortunes can be traced to the waning of our powers, but not to a corruption of them. What would you do for her?"

"Why," Alliole cried in her surprise at this answer, before the Neve hushed her, and she lowered her voice, remembering the sleeper in the other chamber, "I would place her in Xoon's position, and give Xoon some other, for I believe that he is capable enough, if given the right direction."

"Well, it is so easy then," the Neve said, and laughed at her. "To what do you think we owe our power?" she asked.

"I don't know," Alliole said, bewildered at the turn of the conversation.

"I do not know either," the Neve said, "But, as I said earlier, it wanes. It is less with each generation, until shortly, I believe, it will be no longer. Marre and I have had much discussion on the matter. She holds that as our birthright wanes so we must turn to others, even if they be infernal. I hold that for all the more reason we must cling to what we have, and supplicate them anew. Yet our earthly power is based in our traditions, our rituals and ceremonies that maintain our fields, that keep our wells filled with water. The life of the Parrar must be filled with such observances, almost to the exclusion of all else, or our stronghold would fail. And most of our earthly management depends upon our people. As long as they believe us their protectors, the highest of the high, they do our will. Otherwise all would perish. But they will not have a ruler who is not what they consider right. Do you understand?"

Alliole was silent.

"I am saying that we cannot take Caerre as Parrar because our people will not accept her. They would be afraid. There would be dissent, then war. Sooner or later. Division would disrupt the ceremonies, in fighting we would lose the memory of the rituals, and the hold of tradition that binds us together, when there is nothing else. There would be chaos. That is why."

"Change their minds," Alliole whispered, "Or perhaps they are more generous than you believe."

"I could sooner change the nature of the elements themselves than the will of the common people," the Neve said, "It is sure and strong, and turns slowly."

"You must persuade Lyde to change her mind then."

"Lyde was wise to refuse the offer. I doubt that she is inward-looking enough to master the observances."

"There may be a war anyway," Alliole said, and threw her arms up, angry and confused, "Why are you telling me this? What part do I play?"

The fire that had been in the other died, and she slumped back against the seat, "I cannot tell, save that you are the only person to whom I have not advanced the argument a thousand times. Xoon, as you know, will not listen, and Marre insists on turning it into a theoretical argument on the nature of the human soul. My sister follows her own will, and does not inform others of it. How can Caerre provoke a war?"

"I do not know," Alliole said, "But give her enough time, down there in the cold and the dark, and she will think of a way." She was dismayed at the turn of the conversation now, and could only think and attempt to avoid dwelling on, the one question from the Neve that could now bring her whole life tumbling down—if Caerre knew anything of Reven's disappearance. But the question did not come.

"What part do I play?" she repeated, wearily.

"I want you to know my position," the Neve said, "And also the way the inheritance of my family plays itself out. I am asking you to look after Xoon as he appears to have taken a fancy to you, and to take up no other of my sister's issue, although I see I am too late." She rose abruptly, "I wish you the joy of having a foot in both camps, but suggest you may find the position uncomfortable when maintained for too long."

"You have given me no firm answer to my petition," Alliole said.

"I cannot."

Alliole rose also, and left shortly after, only once she was gone realizing that again the Neve had given her no clear answers. She was exhausted and shaking with the effort of the interview and the thought of tomorrow venturing into the ruins again. She wondered how much her interlocutor had chosen not to explain, and a thousand questions swarmed in her mind that whilst in the chamber, she had not dared utter. It was not until Sleepghast had returned her to her chambers that she recollected that she had promised to visit Caerre.

She arranged for the servants to bring her some food, and for Slaarngash to carry it, and a lantern. Then she waited a few hours for the Castle to be still and set out on what she hoped would be a final journey. She would speak with Caerre, acknowledge her sympathy for her cause and explain that she had tried her best and failed. Surely that was all Caerre could demand. Then she could return to Xoon's side with a clear conscience, and attempt to persuade him to desist in his foolish endeavors. Her head ached at the thought of the conflicting interests to which she had found herself bound.

When she reached the Catacomb entrance she hesitated whilst Slaarngash lit the lantern. As it did so, a pair of pallid ovals made themselves visible in the murk at the foot of the stair, and turned themselves into faces. Helaf and Anna were waiting for her there. Alliole was struck with despair at their jokes and whispers as they led her down the stairs. They were children. Helaf was the oldest but she would wager that he was not yet twenty. He was in any case too gentle a soul to constrain Caerre. What hope did Caerre hold, that enabled her to pursue her cause?

Together they guided her through the Catacombs, and she was caught up in the maze of their nervous chatter.

"We have been waiting here forever," Anna said, reproachfully, "We thought you had forgotten."

"You should not come at night," Helaf said, "The Kings come out at night, and although Caerre has barred them from the upper catacombs, to get home we must pass through some of the lower places."

"The Kings?" she asked, but Helaf pulled a gloomy face, "Let us not talk of them here, or Anna will be seeing them for the next quarter mile."

"Did you have any nightmares?" she asked Anna, before remembering that that comment too might be tactless. Anna nodded her head, and her laughter stilled. She started to dart anxious glances around. "Do not worry," Alliole boasted to her, "We have Slaarngash here. He is worse than any nightmare." Anna brightened, although dubiously. "And we have brought some supper," she added. Anna brightened considerably, taking her by the sleeve, and forging ahead. Helaf brought up the rear, behind Slaarngash, and was rather quiet. 🗡

Chapter Ten

TOGETHER THEY REACHED the chamber of the previous night's journey, with no discomfort other than the usual one of treading the cold stone paving, of breathing the corpse-dust, and turning sideways at various passages to fit through a cramped space, the earliest being that intruded upon by the ossuary Alliole had noted earlier. She felt soon that she would know this particular journey as well as she knew others.

"Alliole," Caerre called, joyfully, when they were still out of sight of her. Alliole heard a stagger and a rustle and realized that Caerre had stood up. She wished that Caerre's walk was not so disconcerting. In its own way it was as bad as Slaarngash's eyes. "Tiralgon has just been telling me, listen you others, Alliole has been busy on our cause." Tiralgon, again sitting on the floor, his legs outstretched, his face lumpy, grinned sheepishly.

Alliole stopped, momentarily distracted from her pressing business, "You mean he overheard my conversation with the Neve?" she asked, for that was all she could think of to spark such joy, "How can he get so close without being discovered?"

"These crypts continue up into the Castle walls," Tiralgon explained.

"Perhaps they thought the dead would lie easier if they slept side by side with the living," Caerre said, "Or perhaps it was just the fashion of the time. All through the central tower and the precinct of Stone is where we can overhear. A thousand times we thank you, Alliole, for your counsel, even if my aunt did not listen. I knew you would keep your word." Caerre's face shone like mother-of-pearl, and her gaze was as steady and regal as her aunt's. Alliole's doubts and tensions were all swamped in her regard, in her confused affection for both the Neve and her niece—and nephew too, for that matter. She wanted to work great magic, and make it all come right, for everyone. Her resolve to bid Caerre and her cause good day weakened.

"If you heard our conversation, then you heard her answer. Why do you think you could rule, when the people fear you?"

"They don't have to know. No one could see me. No one ever sees my mother, and yet they all adore her." That was no answer.

Anna let go of Alliole and ran to Caerre, and plucked at her sleeve. "She has brought some food with her," she said.

"Not much, just supper," Alliole said, "Caerre, I have to talk to you." She directed Slaarngash to drop its load, and allow Anna to lay out its contents, and then came closer to Caerre, for she wished to talk to her without the others

overhearing. Caerre seized both her arms in a comradely fashion. They were
the same height, and Caerre's eyes searched hers, too close to be avoided,
friendly, even amused. There was in them, and the warmth and strength of
the grasp that contained Alliole's arms, the first flush of growth of the same
power she saw at full maturity in the Neve.

"Caerre, I cannot bear it," she whispered, as behind them Anna exclaimed
over the food, and set it out prettily in the center of the floor, "Reven, Marre
is still looking for him. She will look forever. She will find him in the end, one
way or the other. And I am sure someone will soon suspect foul play."

"They already do," Caerre said quietly, her eyes still searching Alliole's own,
"Has no one told you? But they have no one to suspect. You are too useful a
tool, and besides they believe demons are bound not to harm them. I do not
know how you broke that binding, but they do not suspect you. Peace,
Alliole."

"No, it is the not knowing, it is her not knowing," Alliole whispered, "That
I cannot bear. To think of her searching, and searching, and never finding. . . ."

"You sound like Tyall and his Voice," Caerre said, bluntly, "I think perhaps
a little of it has rubbed off on you. Besides, you just said that she will find him
in the end. You should not hold two contradictory fears at once, or you will
become confused. Hold onto one, and think it through. What if she finds him?
Well, that is bad. But perhaps by then, things will have changed here so that
I will be in a position to better protect you. What if she does not? She has
caused enough misery for others to be entitled to a little of her own. And she
is not so sorry as you might believe. My father, Gaar, was always her favorite.
He is the father of her children, you know. Reven was just their minder. Let
us eat and forget our worries for a while."

As Alliole turned back, absorbing this advice and the light it shed on
Caerre's character, she saw that where Tiralgon was simply watching Anna's
preparations for the meal, Helaf was watching them. He blushed and looked
away as she met his eyes.

"What else did you overhear?" she asked Tiralgon, but Caerre intervened
again, as she limped back and sat, carefully and awkwardly on the floor, "Tell
us of your adventures, Alliole, we are all ears, as you know." Anna sat on the
floor also. Helaf stayed on the mortuary slab to which he had climbed, and
Anna and Tiralgon passed food up to him. Alliole started speaking with much
hesitation, unsure as to when to begin, but picked up pace as she proceeded.
Her audience divided its attention between listening and devouring the food
as if it was the first they had seen in days, as indeed it might have been. To
her surprise, her most disturbing recollection - the withered creature in the
chair—provoked no distress from Anna, and Caerre simply said, with lively
interest, "So the Kings are even there."

"I knew that," Tiralgon said, scornfully.

"The Kings?" Alliole said, breaking off her narrative.

"They are everywhere in the lower Catacombs," Tiralgon said, evidently the authority, "You have to watch out for them. They are weak, but very, very sly, and you do not want to meet them in great numbers."

"They are the dead, then," Alliole surmised. There was a short silence, then Tiralgon said, shortly, "The dead are dead. I have never seen them walk and I have lived here all my life. It is a story made up to scare children and make the common people think our family is special. The Kings are something else." Caerre cried, impatiently, "Go on with the story, just when it was getting exciting."

"No, I am interested," Alliole said, "So you are familiar with these creatures? Xoon said they were some form of phantom." They all looked at her as if puzzled, and she realized that the Kings must be a common item of knowledge amongst them.

"They are a holdover from the war," Caerre chanted in half-litany, "Their souls were drained from them in that disaster, that left them as they are now, hating those who are still alive."

"So you believe in the war, then," Alliole pressed.

"Was there a war, or wasn't there?" Caerre said disconsolately. "Who cares? That is all my aunts talk about sometimes. They sit there and argue and drink wine, and at the end of it, when they seemed to have reached agreement one way or the other, they swop sides and start again. It is a game with them, this argument. It is so boring, yet we must listen to it, for any crumbs of information such that we are interested in."

"I am asking you what you believe," Alliole cried, exasperated.

"Of course there was a war, or the Voice would not come looking for them, and the Kings would not have happened. And they would not have taken such precautions to shield themselves from the world, or be so worried now the shield is broken. There must have been a war," Helaf spoke unexpectedly.

"Oh, that is where Alliole comes in," Caerre said, slyly turning the topic around without properly answering the question, so much in her aunts' manner that she must have purposely studied them, "She must finish her story and then we will tell her ours."

Alliole, about to cry aloud in frustration, was stilled by Helaf's willingness to answer, and finished her own story. There was not much left to tell, for she left out that she would be journeying with Xoon on the morrow, as the Neve had given her leave to keep the secret. She thought she would tell Helaf if he accompanied her again on the return journey, and leave him to judge the timing of the revelation, thereby hopefully maintaining Caerre's confidence without being forced into the unlovely position of spy. Caerre was too busy gloating over Xoon's failure to notice her reticence.

"What have you to say?" Alliole said at last. It seemed that she always had more questions at the end of her interviews than at the start. This was starting to exasperate her unduly.

"Oh, it is simple," Caerre said, "Only what I told you earlier, and you must have guessed. You are not from here, but from outside. Tiralgon overheard it." Tiralgon stuffed a last handful of food into his mouth and looked around hopefully for more, prolonging the suspense for his enjoyment, "Iriethe and Grielle were talking," he said, "They said you had stumbled across the fields when the men were harvesting. Out of nowhere. You were holding your arms up like this—" he demonstrated with a gleeful, grisly dexterity, and Anna squealed—to stop your muscles from slipping out. They could see your bones. You had that sword slung across your back. You couldn't have come far, not like that, and they could not work out whether your hurts were accidental or deliberate."

"So you see, whatever barrier is between us and the outside must have slipped somehow, to allow you through," Caerre said. "My aunts were talking about it, they did not know if it was temporary or permanent at first, and that frightened them terribly. I think that's why they tried to drug you and hide you away. It seems that the barriers are breaking down because no one gives them their full attention. They can repair and maintain them, but they need someone strong, like me, to pay full attention to them, or they will come down permanently, forever. Or," she added reluctantly, "It might be that the sorceries took pity on you when you came up against them, and let you through. They do not really know."

"Oh," Alliole said, and drew a deep hurt breath, "I do not remember." She looked down at herself, seeing herself anew, as someone stumbling across the fields with a bright sword slung across her back, the sword that would kill Reven.

"Of course you don't remember," Helaf said, gently. He was kneeling beside her. She realized that she was weeping. He put an arm around her shoulders, at first tentatively, but then as her sobs continued, more boldly, and even found the courage to stroke her hair. His brother's head knocked against her shoulder as if he too tried to comfort her. "Caerre, you are frightening her worse than you frighten Anna."

"I only told the truth," Caerre said innocently.

"Of course you don't remember," Helaf told her, "They took away your memories. They were frightened, remember. They thought that way you would not try to change things. They could have killed you. That's not so bad of them was it? Marre was the only one who wanted to kill you. "

"But then your memory started to come back," Caerre started to say, cheerfully.

"I think," Helaf said, with more authority than Alliole had given him credit for, "I think Alliole has probably heard enough for tonight. There, are you feeling better?"

"No," said Alliole, shakily, still crying, silently. Anna came around to her other side, and wiped her cheeks for her, then leant against her lovingly, "But I want to know, go on, I'll think about it later."

"It started to come back," Tiralgon said, with a relish equal to Caerre's, "The sorcery had not worked properly. It had got itself caught up with the Voice, and you could hear them both. It would have driven you mad too, I am sure, eventually. Marre was relieved that you so quickly took up her offer to be rid of it."

"If you had waited a little longer your memory might have come back," Anna said, wonderingly.

"But I am sure they would have worked further sorcery first," Helaf said, "Don't listen to them. I am sure you did the right thing. The Voice drove my great-grandmother mad, and it is doing the same to Tyall."

"The Voice?" Alliole gulped, wondering at the undue emphasis, even in the midst of her pain.

"The voice that you heard, that Tyall hears, that is another thing left over from the war. Something they lost back then and have not been able to find. It tries to call them, to come and get it, but they are too scared to go," Caerre said.

"Tyall isn't scared," Alliole said, still gulping. For some reason Helaf and Anna's sympathy was making her tears worse, that and the memory of the bodiless, beseeching thing. Had it been looking for so long then, poor voice, since a war no one could remember.

"He doesn't know what it is, that is calling him," Caerre said, "No one has told him. I've heard that it was something that began and ended the war, so I suppose it would be quite horrible. And anyway, he won't find it. If the Mad Parrar could not find it no one will. She spent a life time looking."

"Caerre," Helaf's gentle, exasperated voice said, above Alliole's head, "Perhaps she did find it. How would anyone know?" Caerre paused, and thought, "Well, if she brought it back, I suppose. But she did not. So she didn't."

"Shh," Helaf said again, "I don't think this is the time to discuss history."

It took Alliole most of the next few hours to collect herself, and the others were surprisingly quiet and respectful. Helaf and Anna stayed by her, and Tiralgon and Caerre went to what were evidently their beds. Tiralgon lay down and slept, his large, skinny frame, ungainly sprawled under his covers. Caerre lit a candle from the brazier, and set it on a shelf beside her bed, where evidently offerings had once been laid. The shelf was covered with the guttered remnants of hundreds of similar candles. She drew a book from beneath the covers and read it. Alliole had her doubts as to whether the tome was of a wholesome nature, but kept her peace. The frieze on the wall was lit from beneath by the candle. The three faceless heads stood out, stern and unwavering and utterly without pity.

When she finally felt enough of herself to depart, Caerre spoke to her, almost absently, "The Festival of Masks commences in a few days. Will you attend?"

"I do not know," Alliole said.

"It may be that they will abandon it if they cannot find Reven," Caerre said, "It is not one of the more important festivals so I am not sure." She shut the book musingly, and turned over, her eyes on the three throned figures that reared into shadow above her.

"Goodnight, Caerre," Alliole said, "Thank you for your counsel."

"I am sorry if it was poorly chosen," Caerre said, with genuine courtesy. When Helaf guided her away, Caerre still lay on her back, looking up at the frieze, and Alliole mistrusted that she was plotting something.

The first part of their return journey was again completed in a thoughtful silence. Slaarngash muttered and scavenged behind them, disappearing for long intervals down passageways, leaving Helaf to attend to her. Once she was fairly sure she heard the demon's wrath-roar, but it was from so great a distance that she did not trust her hearing. Surely it could not have roamed so far.

"Will you be safe on your return journey?" she asked Helaf, at last.

"I will go very quickly," he said, and smiled his quick smile, for the first time that evening.

"It is not fair that you should put yourself to such danger for me," she said, "Soon I will know the way well enough to travel alone. Slaarngash will protect me."

"It is no trouble," he said.

"Perhaps you could sleep at the foot of the last stair," she suggested, and then frowned at the thought of the discomfort he would be in, "Or sleep in my chambers." She wanted to laugh at his look of horror, but winced instead at his answer.

"Somebody might see me," he said, "I would not be comfortable. I would lie awake all night worrying. Besides, Caerre would miss me."

"I am sorry," she said, "So I, instead of your sister, will just have to hold misgivings for you, now that I know the kind of danger you face. Those creatures horrify me." A thought struck her, "Here," she said, and stopped, mid-corridor. Ahead she could see the bone wall of the ossuary, and knew the last stair was almost upon them, "Here, take this necklace," she said, eagerly, "Slaarngash said it was sorcerous, it could protect you. You have it."

"Oh no," he said.

"Then I won't have to worry," she said, and when he still hesitated, "Or is it against your conscience then, to rob the dead?"

"I have never seen that necklace, so I cannot know where it stole it from. Probably a distant relative anyway," Helaf said, "And your creature is uncanny enough that I will believe any pronouncement it makes."

"Well then," she said, "Please take it. Although you will have to take it from me." She bent her head. He put down the lantern and took the heavy silver from her shoulders. He hesitated again a moment as he lifted it, and his hands lay against her throat, against her pulse. She could feel the individual, separate warmth of his fingers.

"Thank you," he said, holding the gleaming thing in his hand.

"It was not mine to give, but I give it to you anyway," she said, glad, for whatever reason—even theft—to finally have a chance to present someone with something, "Thank you also for your understanding." He said only, "Anna is too young often to understand. She is only twelve," thereby mistaking the intent of her compliment.

They resumed progress. Slaarngash did not join her again until they had separated, again at the foot of the stair. It muttered foully to itself, but she did not enquire as to its doings while it was away, having too much else to think about.

To tell the truth, she was glad at the early summons the next morning, to slink quietly away whilst the rest of the Castle slept, to avoid news of any search, of further inquiries after Reven. It was so cold that frost silvered the stone carvings of ivy and rose, so that any living plant would have withered before it, and a light mist lay in the larger halls. Lyde and Xoon were waiting for her in the corridors outside his chambers. Lyde looked bored and irritable. The golden snake, Syl, was wound about her throat, more alert than usual in the cold. Its black eyes glittered. Xoon was impatient, like Alliole, to be gone. They fell into step beside her without word.

They retraced their steps through to the Wheeled Hall, and again threaded their way through the bleak mechanical multitude. Ice coated the bannister of the stair, and some parts of the floor. Mid-way down the aisle, mocking laughter screeched out. Xoon jumped, and looked around wildly, then skidded, losing his footing on a patch of black ice hidden in the Wheel's shadow. The laughter renewed itself at Xoon's expense, and Lyde's vexed look deepened, until she looked uncommonly like Marre. Echoes rebounded throughout the vaulted roof, making it difficult to pin-point the source of the noise.

Ice covered the rim of the Wheel also, adding an extra lustre to the sparkle of its gems, so that the entire device shimmered in the thin thread of daylight that illuminated it, whilst the rest of the hall was quenched in shadow.

"How do you do?" crowed Aubon, and now he was visible. He had wedged himself high in the Wheel, arms and legs akimbo over a spoke inlaid with opals. His pallor had dark patches that were not shadow. When he saw Lyde's scowl, he hastily moved higher, scrambling carelessly across its ice-sheathed surface whilst nursing his injured hand, so that Alliole called out in alarm, "Be careful."

"I do not fear fire, lady, how can I, when water fills this hall. She will quench her flames on the ice," Aubon called, misunderstanding the source of her concern. He settled himself at the highest curve, where rubies and emeralds intermingled, and the sunlight made it seem that gilding replaced the silver plating on the carved wood of the Wheel.

"As if I would waste my power," Lyde muttered, and helped Xoon to haul himself up, "Well then, cousin, you said you would tell. Why have you brought me to this frigid place?"

"All in good time, a little further," Xoon gasped, the breath knocked out of him. He had to hold onto the Wheel to get himself further, as the flags were too slippery to allow traction. Some of the ice, Alliole saw, was curiously discolored. Anna had tended to her cousin but not cleaned the floor. She skirted the area, looking carefully to her footing herself, knowing she would be even worse off if she fell.

"She is afraid, great lady," Aubon taunted, "That if she fired the Wheel the powers unbound would destroy her. Know fear then, you would know fear if you could see your future."

"Oh shut up," Lyde said, under her breath, "Worry more about your own future, cousin, if you persist in this contempt of me." She skidded a little and had to grab at the woodwork to support her, ruining some of the threat of her words. Syl raised its head, so that it curved about in a liquid stream of color, and poured itself down into her breast, clearly deciding to flee the cold. Alliole, who had missed her own creature, saw it standing, hunched, at the foot of the Wheel. It had worked itself into the machinery, and had its head raised, longingly, towards Aubon. As she watched it put one hand upon the lowest spoke, as if to haul itself up, and she called it off, sharply.

"He is thinking evil thoughts of you," it protested, sloping over to her, a mist of shadows obscuring its features.

"He has leave to think what he will," she said, still sharply, "It is of no concern of mine."

"A caution, lady," and Aubon's voice was gentler. She could see him peering down at her, through the spokes of the Wheel, and Slaarngash's miasma, "Do not forsake those you love."

"You will fall in love with a tall, dark stranger," Lyde called at her, from the other end of the hall, her voice booming across the ice, "That is a true enough pronouncement as any that you will get from Aubon."

"Can you truly see futures?" Alliole asked him. His hoarse voice beamed, "In dribs and snatches only, no clear vision."

"Do not forsake those that I love," Alliole asked. It did not seem to her to be advice born of any great wisdom.

"Not in danger," Aubon said. He moved restlessly, so that he almost slipped and gathered himself together again about a spoke, "You, who are so bold, would not abandon them in the face of danger. But you might in the face of ordinary things, of petty, weary fears. Then you must beware."

"No more?" she asked, "What of my past? Is that any clearer?"

"A mist lies across my sight," Aubon said, and grinned, and she knew then that he was joking.

"Come on, Alliole," Lyde called, "I do not know why you waste words with this fool."

"Alliole," Xoon called out after her, crossly, from the entrance to the further hall, "We do not have much time, remember?"

"And as for you," Aubon called out, triumphantly, "A daughter, a daughter." He rocked and crowed, and the spoke he twined around squealed rebelliously. Xoon snarled in fury, his pleasant, aimless face distorted, and then disappeared into the hall beyond, where Lyde had already vanished. Alliole decided it was best to leave, before Aubon could be tempted to further temerity. But the cry rang in her ears, as they closed the doors behind them, blocking out the cold, silver light that filled the Wheeled Hall, and replacing it with the hateful seething dark of the Hall of Masks.

Xoon was nursing his elbow, which he had hurt in his fall. Alliole could not find it in her heart to be sorry for him, but rather to be meanly glad at the justness of the injury. He stormed across the hall, evidently too angered to speak.

"Come on, Xoon," Lyde said, "It's cold and I do not see what is so important that it must be examined. Show it to me, and we can go somewhere warm."

"It's further yet," Xoon said. He vanished into the galleries.

"How much further?" Lyde demanded. She halted in the middle of the floor and crossed her arms.

"A lot," Alliole said, disinclined to lie but unwilling to tell the whole truth, "We have to go through the galleries."

"I don't like the look of them," Lyde replied, "And it is too much bother when Xoon is so cross. Let him go by himself. It will teach him manners."

"Come on," Alliole said, "We should not let him travel through there alone. He might get lost." That was the least of her worries, for she remembered the clear trail their previous journey had laid through the undisturbed dust. But she wondered if perhaps those creatures—the Kings, Tiralgon called them— were in there, how many of them, and whether they would be so afraid, coming up against a lone man. Despite her best intent, she hesitated a moment in the entrance.

"I do not see why he rises to Aubon's taunts so. Aubon only says them to annoy, and is delighted when they have so great an effect," Lyde complained, "It is not as if he has any true vision." Thus leaving Alliole horribly unsure. Nevertheless she followed across the floor, and through the entrance, although something in Alliole's soul squirmed as they crossed the threshold. Slaarngash raised its lamp to light their way. They came across Xoon almost immediately. He had stopped at the first intersection. Alliole was at first relieved that he had seen sense, and then concerned, for he still bristled with hostility. It was only when she came up to him that she saw why he had stopped. In the first passage there had only been their footprints, leading away. But at this intersection something had been busy. In all the corridors beyond was dragged an identical trail, that obscured the original path Tyall had traced for them through the dust.

"This is ludicrous," Lyde complained.

"I'll bet it was Aubon," Xoon said, through his teeth, "That is what he was laughing at."

"No, he would have said," Lyde said, "He has no subtlety."

"He would never come here," Alliole said, soberly. She stared at the trails. That they were here indicated planning and thought, and an extensive knowledge of the galleries, for as they went forward they found at every intersection the paths through the dust met and parted again. And what was worse, to her, was that an intellect must lie behind it, that dwelt in this maze of semi-ruinous corridors and halls, and sought to discourage trespassers. What she had been told, and witnessed, of the Kings did not make her think they were capable of such guile. Was there some other inhabitant whom they had not yet met? A shiver went through her spine as she contemplated this thought.

"Can you remember the way?" Xoon asked her. She hesitated, and then shook her head, "Slaarngash might," she said, and she saw his face turn relieved and hesitant by turns. His nerve, born of their safe return to the places he knew, was rapidly wearing off. He was afraid to progress further, she saw, and his fear grew greater the further they passed from the Castle Proper. What passion was it then, that drove him forward in the face of so terrible a fear?

"Slaarngash," she said, and the demon forged forward, its heavy head hanging between its bulwork shoulders. It kept up a continuous bass whining growl in its throat for the entire time they were in the galleries, that made Alliole first annoyed and then uneasy, wondering at what it thought necessary to warn off so constantly, wondering if the maker of the false paths yet dwelt in the somber corridors, or lurked at the dark head of the myriad staircases.

Yet eventually they won through, guided by the demon's unerring instinct, and into the larger halls. Slaarngash's growl switched off instantly that they were out of the galleries, which gave Alliole no comfort, for through them they must go again, at dusk or beyond, if they were to return to the Castle Proper that evening.

"So what is this about?" Lyde asked, trenchantly, and stopped again as daylight struck her. Her eyes widened at the ruined walls, "I had better to go and look for my brother, than get lost myself."

"He won't be far," Xoon said, impatiently, "He and Marre had a fight, Sleepghast says, and he is in hiding to spite her." Lyde shrugged her shoulders, and her brief look of concern passed.

"Tell me the true purpose of your asking me here," she said.

"We are going after the Great Masks again," Xoon said, taking a deep breath, and looking for certainty towards Alliole, "I thought that you would like to accompany me, but did not know if I could stir you. So I decided not to tell you until we were this far. There, you cannot say that I am not truthful."

Lyde stared, and Alliole feared an explosion. It did not come. Instead, she sighed and looked around again, even seemed to gain some relaxation of her vexed expression with the news.

"So, you have come running to me again?" she said, "It is not enough to drive poor Tyall mad, and my aunt half mad with worry? You must try me as well. Is that your notion?"

"Yes," Xoon said, humbly, but he winked at Alliole.

"Well, I suppose my family will call me a fool, but I see no reason not to accompany you," Lyde said, "If only to keep you out of trouble. We will not stay out long? We have not provision for it." Xoon shook his head, "A day out, no more," he said, "If we have not found it by mid-afternoon, we will turn back. I do not wish to be beyond the galleries at nightfall."

Alliole wanted to say something about the hostile atmosphere of the galleries, to suggest that they may be more dangerous than these halls at night. She disliked their brooding malevolence, that hung almost animate in the air. She disliked the way their trail had been confused.

"Well, you have been clever, haven't you?" Lyde said. She smacked Xoon companionably on the shoulder. "Where now?" She then scrambled forward, over the fallen pillar where they had rested the day before yesterday. Now that she was committed to the expedition she seemed guilelessly cheerful. Xoon looked to Alliole, who motioned the demon forward, and Slaarngash led them, as far as Alliole could tell, a true enough path. She was alert for some new trickery from her sometime ally, but Slaarngash seemed as much in haste to make the journey and return as any. This alarmed her all the more. ✳

Chapter Eleven

THEY RESTED in the early afternoon, about an hour's journey from the hall where they had met and vanquished the king. Lyde spoke of returning then, but Xoon easily dissuaded her. She seemed ready to be thus persuaded, and showed a good deal more interest in their surroundings than Xoon did, marvelling at the ruins, and wondering at how far they continued.

"I hope forever," Xoon said grimly. He kept his eyes on his feet for much of the venture, and stuck close to the walls in the places where the roof was most ruined, as if he feared to see the sky. He took the series of descending stairs particularly badly, for when he looked down he must see space yawning beneath his feet, planted precariously on frail steps, and when he looked up, he must see the sky, an infinity of empty air. At one point where the stair, unseen in the darkness, became precarious and even missing the steps, he sat down and inched his way across them. At their end he seemed ready, riddled with agoraphobia, to stay there and never rise.

"How is Tyall?" Alliole asked, to distract him, when he had sat long enough to regain any breath he might have lost, and then some.

"Much better," Xoon said, cheering almost immediately, "I told him of our journey, and he wanted to accompany us, but I forbade it. I told him he has been in my aunt's care for so long, she would be at her wit's end for what to do if he were long from her."

"Besides, she would forbid it," Lyde added tactlessly, "And forbid you while she was at it." Alliole refrained from saying that his endeavour had at least a tacit blessing from the Neve, but was also struck with another thought, as she followed Xoon down the stairs. If Xoon had spoken of it, at least twice, with her and Tyall, then the chances were doubled that Caerre knew of it, if her talk of their listening posts were true. Had she learnt of it? It occurred to her that she had forgotten to tell Helaf of this venture, as she had intended. Would Caerre think that she kept news of it from her purposely? She also wondered at Xoon's authority when he spoke of Sleepghast's theory about Reven. Was the servant re-telling the gossip currently amongst the common people, to account for Reven's disappearance? Or did the servant suspect?

Such useless fears and suspicions held Alliole's attention during her second journey through the ruins, useless because she had no way of confirming them, and because they did not help her in her current predicament. They occupied her until they reached the complete ruin. Xoon, for all his fears, stepped into it with relief, seeming to straighten and broaden his shoulders once he reached the renewed shelter of roof and walls. Lyde paused at the entrance, muttering charms, and the lantern Slaarngash carried abruptly spewed forth resinous blue flame. It lit the corner, and the rubble on the floor that was all that remained of the creature.

They approached it cautiously, but found only a litter of bones, and a glittering dust. Despite Xoon's hiss of alarm, Lyde bent down and sifted the dust thoughtfully through her fingers. It was the consistency of charcoal ash, with the occasional harder shard, like mica. It was these fragments that flared in the blue lamp light.

"This is it?" she asked. Xoon nodded. She did not seem impressed. Xoon edged carefully around it, Alliole followed him. Lyde gathered another handful, and poured it into a pouch, then walked straight through, kicking at the bones to test their soundness. Alliole debated warning her of her heresy, but decided against it. They continued cautiously down the corridor, which entered a further series of passage and stair and chamber identical to those of the inhabited parts of the Castle save that it seemed of fewer storeys, and that some of the malice of the galleries lingered in the air. The memory of Tyall struck Alliole forcibly, so that his phantom swung ahead of her, getting further and further away despite her best endeavour. She blinked and the shadow vanished. They met no other obstacle.

"I thought you said it was not far," Lyde complained, at last.

"Tyall said it was not far," Xoon corrected. He had been moving along in a taut glide, expectant of danger. He took the opportunity of Lyde's speech to stop and straighten his back.

"Who knows how far 'not far' is in dreams," Lyde said.

"I wish I could remember what the journal of the Mad Parrar said," Xoon said.

"You should have looked it up before you left," Lyde said, rudely.

"I?" Xoon said, stung, "I cannot read her script. It was you who read it."

"Are you saying I should have read it again?" Lyde retorted, with equal vigor, "How was I to do so, when I was not informed of your destination? I would have assumed. . . ." By her tone, Lyde's assumptions would hardly restore harmony to their venture.

Alliole hastily intervened. "Perhaps we have come as far as we should today," she suggested. "We have mapped this far. We can come back tomorrow." She mentally substituted 'you' for 'we.' She would not obey any further order that obliged her to depart the safety of the Castle Proper. She felt exhausted with fear and uncertainty.

"We will go on," Xoon said. He did not say it with much conviction, being as tired as Alliole and probably more scared, she decided. She was however growing skilled at judging her charge. He simply wanted to state the case, that would allow her to persuade him in a little while to relent, and then they could all retire with dignity.

"Xoon," she started, dredging from somewhere an obliging and conciliatory tone, "It must be getting on to late afternoon. I am very tired. We should return, rest and recover our wits."

"I agree with Xoon," Lyde said, unexpectedly, "It seems foolish to come so far, and then turn back tamely." The look Xoon gave her exactly showed his mixed feelings.

"You have not been here after dark," Alliole said, "I have. I think we should turn back in case of some danger. Those creatures. . . ." She could not call them Kings, not say all that she knew of them—which in the end might have persuaded Xoon to turn back, if only on the excuse of safeguarding the honor of his ancestors—because she was reluctant to reveal her source.

"Xoon has," Lyde said, again trenchantly, "Are you afraid, Xoon? Do you want to turn back?" She had, with nicety, struck out at his pride. Xoon swallowed and shook his head. Alliole realized from Lyde's open, gloating look that Lyde judged that this would pay him back for his discourtesy in luring her on this expedition without telling her its real purpose. She was more absorbed in emerging triumphant from the quarrel than assessing the dangers, real or imagined, of the ruins at night. With no choice but to agree, Alliole assented to their continuance.

After a space of time that was undoubtedly much shorter than it seemed, once the hours added by their tension had been accounted for, they came through this further trial, and entered a broad hall, well lit by the late afternoon light. The roof had entirely fallen in, and rubble was strewed across the mosaic'd floor. A tree had seeded itself in one corner, and its yellow fruit bespattered the mosaic, lending a sharp, aromatic odor to the air. Chiefly remarkable about the hall however, and the source of their wonder and excitement were the masks, molded of intricately worked silver that hung upon the walls, each ten feet or more tall. Xoon stopped at the door, within sight of his goal tempted to go no further, and retreated beneath the overhang of the corridor. Slaarngash and Lyde, as ever curious, forged inward. Alliole followed them.

The masks seemed identical to the one in the Hall of Masks, except for one remarkable feature—that where the one in the lesser hall had been fashioned with eye slits empty and open, as if truly for some giant's carnival, these all had their eyes closed, even to lashes molded upon their cheeks. They seemed of all ages, from the puff cheeks and wide foreheads of infants to the thin face and severe line of ascetic middle age, and it was impossible, from the visage presented alone, to determine what sex they were intended to represent. After counting several score, Alliole ceased to care how many of them there were.

"I told you so," Xoon called out from the door, before they were mid-way down the hall. Perhaps he did not want to be left behind. Alliole returned to him. His face was a mix of pride, delight and trepidation.

Each mask had been fashioned so that it fitted snug with the wall, and Lyde, soonest of them all in losing her awe of them, reached out and tried to prize one off, forgetting that if it fell it would surely topple onto her, perhaps crush her if it was truly solid silver. The mask did not move. Alliole then turned her demon to the task, but it did no better. Next, Lyde persuaded Xoon from his refuge, and the three of them tried together. The smoothly molded silver had no ready hold, and in their exertion their hands became slippery with sweat, and so quickly lost any vantage they might otherwise get. At one point Xoon cried out triumphantly that he felt it move, only to find that it was part of the wall that the trio had shifted, and they had to run for cover as rubble came cascading down. The masks ran in seamless line to the wall, so that as evening drew on, Alliole started to imagine that if they looked behind it, they would see the silver bodies to which the masks belonged, which for some reason elected to peer into the building. It was an uncanny feeling, and she shook it off as quickly as she could.

While the others were still occupied in this task, she did a tour of the hall, pausing by a smaller entrance set into the far wall, from which a faint, steady wind blew. Peering in, she could see a flight of stairs descending into the murk from a corridor that continued into further disused chambers, of who knew which vintage, or indeed if they had ever been used. She was about to move on when her attention was arrested by a singular engraving, a bas-relief different from all others she knew. Set in the stone at a little above the height of her head was the outline of a human hand, larger than life and so skillfully graven that it seemed as if it were pressed into the masonry, as if the stone had given way before the impress like butter, leaving the life-line, even the whorls of the finger's ends, wondrously in view.

What of it, she decided eventually, that there were skilful stone-masons at work in the Castle she knew already, and their earliest work should surely be the best, if the Neve's hypothesis of waning powers were true. But as she stood there pondering the bas-relief's peculiarity, she became aware that the breeze that fanned her cheek was one whose exact strength and variance that she knew. She realized that it was the tomb wind that blew, and that the stair descended into the Catacombs. She retreated from it at once, shuddering rather than marvelling at the extent of the necropolis, above and below ground. She returned to the others, whose voices, initially raised in encouragement to each other, now sounded dangerously close to a second squabble.

"We had best leave now," she said, as she reached them. She must have looked more nervous than she knew, for they paused in their umbrage and stared at her.

"Without one of these?" Lyde demanded. "We would look like fools."

"No one would believe us," Xoon said, also mutinously.

"We are very far from the Castle," Alliole said, treacherously striking, as Lyde had a few hours earlier, straight for his weak points, "If we were to leave now, we would not be at the galleries before nightfall. Would you want to set up an encampment here, when so much that is unknown surrounds us?"

"What did you see over there," Lyde demanded, abruptly, "That frightened you so?"

"A hand," she answered, caught out and deciding to give an honest answer, "A hand in stone. And an entrance to the Catacombs below. I do not mind admitting to being scared. I would be a fool not to. I think that we should go, and return another day with a greater force to help us."

"But," Xoon said, swinging indecisively back to the silver mask they had been working on, as unmoved by their attempts to force it as it had been by the previous centuries of weather, or by whatever force had breached the roof. In the gathering gloom it seemed to wear a mocking smile. Alliole glared at it.

"If Slaarngash cannot move it, then I do not see that less than a dozen men could," she said, "Or some enchantment of your aunts'. It would be well to ask that."

"But then," Xoon said, "Why then they would take all the glory, don't you see? There has to be something in it for me."

The last was something of a wail. Lyde snorted derisively, in precisely her old manner, "Well, we cannot move it," she said, "Our strength fails."

"Would any of your charms aid us?" Alliole asked, and Xoon's face a moment brimmed with hope. Lyde's own face clouded, and Alliole wondered abruptly if Lyde wanted Xoon to have the success due to him as planner and initiator of the venture. To have found it, and then turned the final success over to the senior ranks of the Castle Proper, that began to seem more Lyde's intention.

"They are fire spells only," Lyde said, slowly shaking her head, and turning away, in what seemed to Alliole a markedly artificial manner, "They would not aid us here. We need someone who can invoke the element of earth, or stone. You are right Alliole, we need my aunts here."

"No," Xoon shouted, and whirled back to the Mask, with such ferocity that Slaarngash, who lurked beneath it, recoiled in surprise, and had to fan its wings in order to maintain its footing, raising a gust that blew rock dust and flecks of yellow fruit into their faces. Or perhaps not to maintain its footing but in reaction to extreme and violently repressed or expressed emotion, as Alliole had noticed it had a tendency to do. "We will move it," Xoon said, enunciating every word clearly, flying at once into an anger born of exhaustion and frustration, "And if one means won't work we'll try another." He got in underneath, where the demon had been, and tried to brace himself against its chin for greater leverage. He was near tears in his anger, and Alliole supposed to have come so close to the object of his endeavour and return without it was too much for him. Lyde shrugged and turned away, "There is nothing we can do until he recovers his temper," she whispered, "I wish Tyall was here. He is the only one who can calm him in this mood. I will wait you at the entrance to the passage." She moved away.

"No," Xoon shouted at her, seeing her leave. He turned and scrabbled at the mask's smooth face, in a perfect fury of passion, attempting some leverage beyond Alliole's comprehension, and then simply commenced to beat at it, and sob in inarticulate rage.

"Xoon," Alliole said helplessly, and came up to him, drew him away as well as she was able. His shoulders were heaving in wrath and his breath was coming in deep, irregular gulps as he fought with his emotion. She got him away, simmering that Lyde could walk off so heartlessly and leave him, when Xoon simply turned back. The Mask's obdurate smile seemed to broaden further, but that was surely only the effects of the deepening gloom. Xoon commenced to curse at it, deeply impassioned although anatomically impossible actions for so bodiless an entity to undertake. He wrenched himself from Alliole, who could in no way hold him, and threw himself back on it, kicking, punching and yelling at it, "Move! Move! Move!"

And it did.

Alliole at first thought it was only her imagination, and then that the pounding they had given it had finally loosened the wall entirely, and it was falling. Then she realized that it was the Mask that was slipping, as if Xoon's beating had given it the last tiny push into loosening whatever grip held it to the wall. Xoon looked up at her shout, and took two, foolish, faltering steps back, for in no way could he escape the descending shadow, as the Mask fell forward.

"Slaarngash," Alliole screamed, and the demon was moving before, again, she had time to consider whether its summons to action was such a good idea. She deflected her thoughts from pulling Xoon free to deflecting the Masks' fall, and Slaarngash actually sprang in two directions at once. It went one way and its shadows the other, coiling around Xoon, who was thus totally distracted from taking any further action to save himself. By the time the pair of them had attention to spare for the Mask, when it became clear that it would not fall, the demon had lowered it to the floor, and stood beside it, its head flat and appeasingly to the ground. Alliole gave it long observance and its shadows, which had been by their actions disembowelling the one they capered around, fled in a gust of diabolical air to rejoin their creator.

"Let us be thankful that they are only echoes," Xoon said, shaken, "Alliole your demon has a vicious temper."

"It is provoked by great emotion," Alliole explained, "Such as you exhibited." But silently, she agreed with him, and her relief at so close an escape was only tempered by a reminder of how strict a control she must keep on the monster, indeed on her own thoughts, if she was to remain its master.

"I should have known," Lyde observed, walking back and looking at the fallen mask, but not at all as if she was glad to see its fall, "It is the will it obeys, Xoon. Your tantrum broke whatever bindings held it there. It is a thing of power."

"I wasn't in a tantrum," Xoon said, muffledly. He hurriedly wiped the tear tracks from his face, "I was displaying great emotion, like Alliole says. If I was a girl, everyone would say I was a sorcerer."

"It is one of the first strictures of sorcery that the sorcerer keep tight rein on her temper," Lyde observed.

"Says who?" Xoon said, cheekily. His brilliant smile returned to his face, "My aunt Marre? She is such a splendid example of calm and composure." Lyde flicked him a glance, unwilling to allow that he had made a point, then with a gesture made the lamp that Slaarngash had abandoned burn brighter.

"How are we to carry it then?" she said, dousing Xoon's joy with her utter practicality, "When we are only three, and Alliole cannot be expected to carry lantern or Mask?" She folded her arms and awaited Xoon's answer, but he was still too wrapped in his contemplation of the Mask.

"Get your demon to turn it over," he said, and Slaarngash did so.

"Is it heavy?" Xoon asked, feasting his eyes on its upturned countenance. Its eyes were still closed, but now that it was on the floor, it looked less as if it had been molded that way and more as if it was simply asleep, perhaps because it was now in the proper position for a sleeper. No, it was something more than that. Something had risen one step closer to the surface, as Lyde said, some power, that hovered just on the edge of waking. Alliole took a few steps back from it, and was for the first time truly glad of her disfigurement. She did not want to handle the thing, not while it seemed so close to waking. But this seemed not to bother her companions, for Slaarngash lifted it readily enough.

"Not heavy," it said.

"As heavy as that city," Xoon sneered, hefting its weight also, as the demon bore the brunt of it. A peculiar look crossed Slaarngash's muzzled face, "It was a city of ten thousand souls," it said, reproachfully.

"Ten thousand ants," Xoon corrected, and it was perhaps because of his comment that the demon snarled. "It is right, it is not so heavy. Plated, not solid silver," Xoon continued, abstractedly, "I think the demon and I can carry this. Lyde you take the lantern. There, we are ready."

"How will we get it through the corridors?" Lyde said, unmoving.

"We'll manage," Xoon said, "What is eating you, Lyde?"

Slaarngash snarled again, into the gathering dark, and Alliole said, "I see no cause to delay and much reason to hurry. Let us go."

Xoon and the demon needed no further urging but started to haul the Mask across the mosaic, whose faded color had diminished further with the dusk, and past the yellow-fruited tree, whose leaves moved a little in the tomb breeze at their backs. They started to manoeuvre it through the corridors and ante-chambers. Their progress through the first of the intact building was frustratingly slow, for the demon would not obey Xoon's commands directly, but must have them through Alliole. Xoon was unused to gauging the angle and depth of masonry, so consistently found himself running afoul of corners. Lyde made little comment, and that she did make was decidedly unhelpful.

Xoon also tired quickly, not because of the heaviness of the artifact but because of its unwieldiness. He remained cheerful, having won through to his objective, but it was as precarious a mood as his previous temper, and Alliole from her own experience knew how thin the surface tension was, that kept him from plunging into the pit of exhaustion and fear. The mask would only go sideways through the corridors and it would slip, and there was nothing to grab it by, so it constantly fell. By the time they had got to the corridor wherein lay the remnants of the creature, Xoon was so bruised and scraped about the shoulders and shins that he joked about changing hides with the demon, an offer Alliole was quick to refuse. It was full dark by the time they reached the ruined areas, and ascended the stairs. This was not so bad, for with his task to absorb him and clouds to shield most of the sky from his eyes, Xoon made no trouble of getting up them, pausing only once when some rift in the clouds opened up the stars. At the head of the stairs he stopped again, for some length of time, head hanging and breathing deeply, to recoup the strength he had lost in their climb.

"We are all but halfway there," Alliole encouraged him, "Soon we will be back in the known halls. We can wait here a moment to rest." He raised his head briefly, and indicated with his hand that he was too out of breath to speak. While they were standing there, they heard a most terrible and discordant sound from the direction in which they had come, a ululation expressive of rage and dismay, birthed from an unguessable number of throats.

"What was that?" Lyde asked, with comparative calm, whilst the other two exchanged looks of similar dismay as those expressed by the imbecilic voices, but with rather more fear.

"Perhaps we will not rest after all," Alliole whispered at last, when she thought that she could trust her voice not to quiver, "After all, we are almost there."

"Yes, let us continue," Xoon agreed, hysteria-born laughter just beneath his words, "An excellent idea." Judging him close to the end of his energy, Alliole asked Lyde to swap with him. Lyde did but slowly, "What is there to fear?" she asked.

"The creature from the hall," Xoon muttered. He picked up the lantern and his face gleamed pale and unholy in its light.

"A handful of dust," Lyde scoffed.

"They fill me with dread," Alliole said. She at any rate would not be too afraid to say so, and she saw her admittance gave Xoon cheer. If you are to be scared, it is better to be frightened in company than alone. "If you have any preparations to make for your enchantments," Alliole added, "I would like you to make them as we go. We cannot wait, unless absolutely necessary."

They hurried forward, Alliole's previous concerns wiped from her mind by the new ones. Were those creatures mortal? Where they fresh from some tenebrous slumber, or would they tire? Would they discourage trespass as firmly as the unknown lurker in the galleries? She turned her mind sharply from that idea.

Lyde made better progress with the Mask than Xoon had, not necessarily because she had a better sense of perspective, but because she had had time to examine him, and learn from his mistakes. Nevertheless they moved much slower than Alliole would have liked, and she was powerless in any way to hurry them. Again and again the unnerving cries broke out from behind them, until she judged that a large force of the creatures was somewhere behind, and coming rapidly closer.

They reached the halls immediately adjacent to the galleries, before hearing the closest sound yet. It seemed right at their heels, and Slaarngash stopped dead at its outcry. There was no real talk, or any time to make a considered judgement, for things were scaling the further wall, until it was swarming with them, stunted, fiercely pallid things that hopped and crawled.

Desiccated flesh flaked from them, and their limbs, skinny and over-long as if their bodies had shrunk into themselves as corpses do, reached and clutched for foot- and hand-hold. Filmed eyes reflected back the light from the lantern.

Xoon yelled, to encourage himself as much as anything else, and drew his sword. Syl uncoiled itself from Lyde's neck and dropped into her hand. She bent her head over it, and muttered words. Slaarngash surged rather than leapt, its weight, its bulk and its trailing shadows gaining utterly in density, so that it plunged through the first ranks of their followers, and into the thick of them, its black hide disappearing beneath their numbers, its snarls muffled as it took bodies in its mouth and broke them. The terrible outcry again shook the throng as they caught sight of that which they pursued. They wavered back a moment and then surged forwards to meet them. Xoon, with a display of swordsmanship born of desperation, slashed at the foremost of the mob, hacking into its midriff. As it fell, a second leapt over it and Xoon had to dodge back or it would have caught him off-guard. It was too close to strike at with the blade, so he reversed the sword, giving back rapidly and caved in its head with the pommel. It made no effort to defend itself, and there was no blood. It only reached out with its hands, clawed with ragged black fingernails, and came forwards. He struck it again, and it fell. Another came up from behind. Xoon stumbled into Alliole who leaped back herself. She looked behind, at Lyde still standing head bowed, at the Mask, hastily dumped behind her. They would be surrounded soon. There was nothing she could do, except to back up as far as the Mask, beside Lyde. She could barely fend one of them off without Slaarngash beside her, and her soul screamed at the thought of touching such, at the consistency of its flesh.

The light from the lantern, which Lyde set up behind them so it was mirrored in the silver of the Great Mask, swelled, giving her better view. The reflected light outshone the light of the distant moon. Idiot voices chittered and clung together like bats, meaningless echoes took flight and swooped unbearingly through the empty space of the hall. The sight of the mass of withered faces, the blind milky mis-colored eyes, and the sound of their voices, turned Alliole sick.

Lyde had Syl in her hands, coiled about her fingers. She said two words in an unknown tongue, the same tongue that Marre had used, and flung it towards the advancing tide. Syl flew through the air in a golden coil that spiralled out in a ring and then a tongue of greenish fire as high as the walls. Creatures were sucked up in its draft, and whirled within, dancing in its macabre grip, blackening and shrivelling further into it, and flung out at the fire gust's end. The whirlwind dodged amongst the mass, sprouting fresh gusts of flame that touched down everywhere, and then, just as Alliole felt renewed wonder and hope, was abruptly quenched. Alliole blinked, and then realized Syl had returned to Lyde's hand. The wave of attackers fell back, so that Slaarngash was abruptly beached, surrounded by the slain. Alliole called it to her. Xoon fell back to them. Blood was running from his forehead so that he had to shield his eyes, and also along the hilt of the sword, so that he kept shifting his grip to avoid it slipping.

"Those that I burned are still moving," Lyde observed, "We can fight a delaying action only." She looked behind, but the distance to the galleries evidently discouraged her. "How far do they follow?" she asked.

"I do not know," Alliole said.

"That one that I slew," Xoon croaked, "It is up again and moving also." His voice shrivelled in his throat, so that it could be barely heard. He pointed, and Alliole could see the creature, holding its guts together, creeping back towards its fellows, crawling, falling and rising again anew. It was dreadful. But the one with the crushed skull, and all those that Slaarngash killed, they lay still.

The host moved as a wave does, closing over the gap that Lyde had caused in exactly the same way the wound on the new-born Slaarngash had healed, in a moment and leaving no trace of its passing. Now it was in a great wave again towards them. But, as Lyde raised her arms again, it pulled back before it crested and overbore them, leaving only a scattered few that stilled, and then were absorbed again when the mass of their comrades surged anew, and then retreated again. With each mass movement they came closer, until Alliole was sure they must attack, and yet when the moment came the attack was stillborn, and their opponents retreated back, almost to the further wall.

Despite whispered and somewhat frenzied encouragement from both of the others, Lyde withheld further fire. "We may as well use it when we need it," she said, alone among them maintaining her calm, "Than waste it on a large number whom we cannot effect."

"They fear to attack," Xoon whispered, abruptly jubilant, "They won't have it." He stood a little higher, coming out of his defensive crouch. His unsheathed sword rang on the flags as he lowered it. He wiped his forehead with his injured hand, smearing blood across it.

"Or are bound not to," Lyde said. That thought might explain her calmness. Slaarngash crouched at their fore, hissing.

"So if we go slowly, let us retreat," Xoon said. Lyde shook her head, "Are they bound not to follow us?" she asked, "I do not know. I have never heard of these creatures, except in the journal of the Mad Parrar, and she mentions them only sparingly. What if they follow into the Wheeled Hall or further? What is their nature?"

"They are something from the war," Alliole said, hoarsely. The wave swelled again, and inched nearer, this time along the side walls. It was if they feared to confront them directly, "Let us back at least to a wall, so we have one side covered."

"And have them drop on us?" Lyde said, "No thank you. What did you say?" She seemed abstracted rather than frightened. Alliole envied her self possession but doubted its grounds.

"I have heard that they are something left over from the war," she said, trying to remember what Caerre had said, and fall into the pattern of her words, to distract herself from the madness around her, "Their souls were drained from them in that cataclysm, and therefore they hate us and wish us dead."

"Tyall said they were the unquiet dead," Xoon said, "But it came to pretty much the same thing." The longer the creatures refrained from attack, the higher his confidence rose.

"How many are there?"

"Hundreds."

"Surely there could not be so many unburied," Lyde said, bleakly, as Xoon had.

"And more the longer we hesitate," Alliole said. Or was that just her imagination? The further wall seemed furred with their numbers.

"Perhaps it is the light," Lyde said, evidently inspired, "If they are nocturnal. It is the light they fear," She turned back to look at it, and froze. At the same time the air filled with idiot voices. The sound swelled, and then chopped off short, into a silence as terrible as their previous noise. The quantity of light put out by their lantern dipped and then swelled, into a radiance that welled until it filled the hollow of the hall, an increase wholly inexplicable.

A voice hailed from behind them, deep, tender, and rippling with a thousand intricate cadences that no human voice could muster, speaking words that Alliole could not understand, but knew to be of infinite power.

Forgetful a moment of the threat before them, Alliole and Xoon turned together. The mask they had carried so laboriously, its eyes open and bottomlessly black, hung effortless and luminous in the empty air. 🦌

Chapter Twelve

WITHOUT THINKING, Alliole and Xoon together took two steps backwards. Lyde stood before them, blanched in light, haloed in light, drenched in the Mask's power. She raised her arms, and spoke also in the same tongue. But they had not the force or certainty of the Mask's voice. She stumbled here and there, over words, over phrases, and the cadence of her speech was flat and uninspired. When her voice faltered the light from the Mask rippled as if in sympathy. It spoke again, its voice overwhelming. Lyde gave answer, and it returned speech, and then rose higher in the air. Lyde turned, and truly then Alliole could see the family inheritance, from the Mask, to Lyde, to the fawning, senseless faces that crouched en masse at the rim of the light. Pinned or hypnotized, it seemed, for the Kings just stood there as the Mask passed Lyde and went towards them. Its back was too bright to look at.

"I think I said the right thing," Lyde said, stumbling into them from the darkness, "I think I told it they wished us harm, and could it avert it." Even her radiant face was dimmed by the memory of the Mask, whose similar features overlay hers and shadowed them.

As it moved forward, the Mask spoke, effortlessly overwhelming Lyde's voice. Silver flashes came from the Mask's eyes, gouts of power that blasted the ground before it, and crumpled all Kings that it hit into glittering powder, that sifted slowly to the ground, yet retained the outline of that which had animated it.

"What is it?" Xoon said, hushed.

"It told me but I couldn't make it out. Some name I think," Lyde said, "I wish I had paid more attention now when Marre was teaching me. I only ever learnt enough of the old tongue to get what I wanted. It said some things that I couldn't understand."

Those Kings furthest from the Mask had gained enough momentum for collective flight. Those close at hand just stared at it, as if in worship or the utmost fear, and the light from its eyes blasted them to the ground.

"Its first words were a greeting, I think," Lyde said, dubiously.

"I hope it can make a distinction," Xoon whispered, and then straightened his back, for the Kings had melted away before the onslaught of the Mask, and it turned back and floated eerily towards them. Alliole had to admire Lyde's courage, and Xoon's, because he must put more labor into it. She stood her ground but only just, for Slaarngash stood ahead, and she hoped that it could deflect any blow meant for her. Her companions had no such comfort, but neither of them flinched when the light from the Mask's eyes washed their faces. It spoke again, and this time when the others looked to her, Lyde just shrugged. Her face turned sullen in her incomprehension.

The light from the Mask flickered again, and it spoke, urgently this time. Again Lyde shrugged. Its light diminished, and its eyes started to close, as if it were fighting off a terrible weariness. When its voice came for the last time, it was curiously indistinct, as if speaking from a very great distance. Whatever force kept it in the air drained from it, and it sank slowly, face down, inert, to the ground. Xoon gave a cry of anguish and started forward, turning it over before Alliole could warn him of the foolishness of his action. The Mask's eyes were again closed. It slept. Xoon stood up, face set, fists clenched, "Look what you've done," he screamed at Lyde, "You've broken it."

"Don't blame me," Lyde snarled in return, "It sleeps, that's all. We will have to find the right words to invoke it."

"What was it saying? Why couldn't you pay more attention?" Xoon wailed.

"It was speaking from one of the other dimensions," Lyde said, stiffly this time, her voice growing loftier as she progressed, "That's very intricate sorcery, and you do not say anything unless it is going to be absolutely right. Otherwise who knows what could be listening, and take your words as an invitation. It is a complicated business, sorcery, and we who practice it should not be criticized by fools."

Xoon was deprived of speech by her words. He glared at her. She folded her arms and returned his stare.

"Let us take this Mask and go," Alliole intervened, again, "We cannot be sure how long the Kings will stay away." The others ignored her. "Then stand here and squabble until we are overtaken. It is folly that you should act like children when you have just proved in battle that you are heroes."

Xoon dropped his eyes at this, "It is as Alliole says," he said, quietly, and looked, a mixture of pride and remorse, at the wound on his hand.

"Scratched or bitten?" Alliole asked.

"A bite," Xoon said, "Look, a tooth." He worried at the wound a moment, and produced a bloodied, yellow fragment. Then he announced, with great precision, "I am going to be sick."

When he had recovered, Lyde bound his hand and his forehead with strips of cloth, and they continued. The Kings made no further evidence of themselves, although Alliole remained alert and nervous. She was almost glad to plunge into the galleries, and as it happened their journey through them was accompanied by no further mischance. Perhaps the Mask kept the ghosts of the place at bay. They limped into the Hall of Masks sometime towards dawn, and crossed the Wheeled Hall without waking its keeper. They heard no noise save the constant breath, the mechanical heart-beat, that filled the hall at the threshold of hearing. Was it louder than before? It seemed so. Alliole did not know.

Rumor of their return spread like Lyde's gouts of fire. Barely had they returned Xoon to his quarters and broken their fast, that Alliole found herself summoned by Iriethe to the Neve. Lyde too was commanded but chose to ignore the summons, complaining that she was tired, and would only receive a lecture. Then she slipped away on pretext of rejoining the search for her brother.

Alliole left Xoon, who was clearly beginning to enjoy the attention now that the danger was past, in his servant's capable hands. The Mask they left propped up in one of the other chambers, as an afterthought draping one of the bed-curtains to conceal its features. On Alliole's path to the Neve, she was intercepted by Anna, who begged that Caerre wanted to see her also. It was just on dawn.

The Neve had evidently not slept, for the scent of smoke hung heavy in the air from the fire, and the glass of the lanterns were black with use. A litter of parchment covered the bureau before which she sat, and Tyall was curled up asleep in the chair opposite. As Alliole entered he roused himself, yawned hugely and then grinned at her, the red gem winking in his ear. His hair was tousled, showing more curl than she would have given him credit for, and the lines of weariness etched into his face only reinforced his youthfulness. The face of the Neve by contrast was unlined, smooth as stone. Her voice was more tranquil than Alliole had a right to expect.

"So this is what you were holding back the other day."

"I would have told you if you pressed further," Alliole replied. Tyall obligingly uncurled and dashed into the other room to fetch a chair for her.

"But I did not," the Neve observed, "I see that you are unschooled in the subtle nuances of speech. I will require a closer observance of my desires in future. Do you not think that I have worries enough without considering Xoon? Please recollect your journey for me, and then after I have spoken you may depart, for I am sure that you are tired."

Alliole, with the unnerving feeling that she addressed also an unseen audience, did as commanded, concluding with a request that the Neve take no action until Xoon had fulfilled his desire, which was to present the Mask to his mother at the forthcoming feast. The Neve made no comment during her speech, and at this entreaty said only, "It is hard to see that my sister will not hear of it. The gossip is on everybody's lips already, and it is scarce mid-morning. Still, she does not care overmuch for society, and Xoon may yet gain his goal. I will do as you wish. Now what is it that you require, for I see that you have another request to make of me."

"Only," Alliole stammered, caught by surprise for she had paid no thought to her request since she set foot in the chamber, "Only to be allowed admittance to the libraries, and an interpreter. I am afraid of the Kings. I want to find out about them."

"You will find little enough," the Neve observed again, as coolly as Lyde, "And you have already found out their name. You think them a danger?"

"Only that no one knows what they are, what rules they are ordered under. I have heard two versions of their origin already, and they differ. It seems to me that what we do not know we must fear."

The Neve bowed her head as if rebuked, but a smile for the first time thawed her lips.

"You speak well," she said, "I will tell one of my scholars to attend you. By the by, anything that you find there, I would ask that you talk it over with me first, before gossiping on it. There is little profit in fueling idle rumor." There was steel behind that mild remark. Alliole readily assented, "Only bid them attend me quickly," she begged, "I would like to start as soon as I can."

"Without rest?" the Neve asked curiously, and Alliole saw that she was concerned by this desire for haste. She nodded.

"I'll translate for you," Tyall volunteered.

"I see no need in fueling nightmares either," the Neve said.

Tyall sat up straighter in his chair, "I am quite well and it will be very restful," he said firmly. They smiled at each other.

"Very well, if you insist," the Neve said, "I can see that I will have no peace otherwise. Go, the pair of you." But she called Alliole back from the door.

"I will go ahead to the library," Tyall told her, "And find a quiet place and a reading stand and some chairs." He went on.

Alliole, with sinking heart and pounding head, returned to the Neve's side. The other regarded her, still curiously but abstracted now.

"I wish to say, Alliole, that I believe that you are a very dangerous person. Dangerous because you will grasp for the truth, regardless of any difficulty in the way. I do not think that you know the power of truth. It can build up and destroy. It is relative, not concrete. Therefor I indulge your curiosity, because I feel that you will find answers anyway, and I would rather you find them with my knowledge and within my guidance. If you worm your way into versions of the truth without guidance, you bring doom upon all our heads.

"Xoon seeks to get further into his mother's favor, without fully understanding her powers. She is very dangerous, my sister. Gaar could hold her. But not her son. Never. I would ask that you inform me of any further attempts, by Xoon or his sister, to challenge our peace. See this not as spying or disloyalty for I promise not to act on this information unless absolutely necessary to avoid catastrophe. I would rather let these opposing forces play themselves out without intervention, but also without dragging all down in their squabble, Without for example, further harming Tyall, who has suffered a good deal and will suffer further. Do you understand?"

The Neve was silent a moment, not waiting on an answer but allowing her speech to be absorbed, and then continued, "You asked Tyall the other day why there could be a debate about a war. Let me say this. There was most probably a war, but we have little record from that terrible time, and are forced to rely on rumor, guess-work and race memory. The enemy was attracted to our ancestors' power. It was—is—something from outside the normal run of spheres and influences, formless, implacable, and most probably immortal. That is why our ancestors sacrificed their power, to avoid annihilation. That is why they flung the objects of their power so far away. To distil, crudely and without poetry, the essence of countless generations of researches, it is also thought that there is associated with this ancient enemy an ivory door, bound with copper hinges, evidently a sorcerous artifact by which they enter our sphere of existence, and a legend that to explore the ruins around the Castle Proper invites disaster. I am sure you can see now why we discourage such, and why I wish that Mask that you found had not awoken, as you describe it, and certainly that it had never re-entered the Castle Proper. If my sister agrees, we shall return it to its place."

"Why do you speak of this to me?" Alliole asked, her heart stilling at mention of the door, wondering if she should say what Tiralgon said he had found—unless, happy thought, it was a dream inspired by race memory—and wondering what the Neve thought of her grand-mother's journeyings, bringing to mind (and then forcing out of it), Caerre's doubtful philosophies. "I am glad that you see fit to confide in me but puzzled that you should not tell this to Xoon. Surely it is for him to know."

The Neve leant back and closed her eyes, shutting off for a moment her disconcerting regard. "Because it is easier to say this to a woman," she said finally, "And you are, or were, of Xoon's camp, more so than Lyde. You can tell him. I cannot phrase such weighty matters, they will not come to my mind or my lips, when I am speaking to an impetuous boy."

She opened her eyes again. "Go now to your own researches," she said, "And let me know if you find anything. You tell me. You can trust Tyall not to speak of them. Things are stirring, and whether it is for good or ill is uncertain. You are right. We must know."

With more doubts now than before, Alliole repaired to the library, where Tyall awaited her. The Neve's warning in particular puzzled as well as flattered her, for she could not work out how the truth could be dangerous, nor how, within the maze of new and conflicting knowledge through which she must continually sort and remember, which bound as much as it released her, she could ever be a source of harm. Caerre's ability she feared more than Xoon's, and the Neve had just added further to the mystery of their mother.

The most fruitful path to follow, she told Tyall as she seated herself in the book-lined, octagonal chamber in which he had placed himself, was surely to look at the journal of the Mad Parrar that both Lyde and Xoon had spoken of. Tyall assented to this, then vanished for a short while to confirm this new arrangement, leaving her to contemplate the chamber, which was redolent of the scents of leather, dust and old parchment. Books and scrolls filled the shelves in no particular order that she could discern. Dried grasses covered the paving stones, to ease some of the cold, for there was, of course, no fire. The reading stand was of red, deep scented wood, polished and carved into ornate and grotesque faces. She rather wished that Tyall had chosen another, for the faces were an unwelcome reminder of a matter already pressing itself heavily on her mind. The ceiling was low and paved in octagonal blocks. She had just worked out that this was impossible when Tyall returned, and asked where he should begin.

"I can read this old speech, but I cannot speak it," he added, "Els—The Neve taught me."

"At the beginning then," she said, and he opened the book, started to read it to her with the clear steady voice of someone much used to the task, translating as he went. It took them most of the day to read through it in this manner, and at its end Tyall had a list of another half dozen volumes that Alliole wanted to look through. The Mad Parrar spoke very little of the Kings, but there were previous authorities to consult, and cross-indexing to pursue (a matter of which Tyall spoke learnedly but defied Alliole's understanding, so that in the end he gave up and promised only that she would see what he meant on the morrow).

It seemed to Alliole that even this simple task took on ramifications and complications, until it was as complex to figure as everything else was becoming. She was gravely disheartened when she bade Tyall good night, all the more so because she was sure he would report the entire day's understanding to the Neve anyway, despite the other's promise. Slaarngash spent its day hunting the small, white blind mice that haunted the bookshelves, and it proved uncommonly dexterous at this task. Of the two, it was probably the more satisfied with its endeavors.

She went to visit Xoon at the end of the day. He was asleep. Sleepghast gave her a report on the invalid so exhaustive and prolonged that she feared that the retelling would wake him again, and departed, leaving her best wishes. Sleepghast accepted these with his most speculative look.

Upon her return to her chambers she remembered that Caerre had wanted speech with her. She wondered in her weariness whether to ignore the summons and then decided that Caerre would misinterpret it as a slight, and re-directed her path to the Catacomb entrance. In any case, she wished to communicate the same warning to Caerre that she had delivered to her aunt. She thought that if Slaarngash could find its way through the galleries, they could trace their path through the necropolis, but in the end she did not have to do so. As they started down the stair, something stirred in the gloom at its foot. For a moment her heart stopped, thinking it was the Kings, but Slaarngash lifted the lantern, and she saw that it was Helaf. He was sitting on the lowest stair, his brother tucked protectively against his body, head under his chin. He held the ornament she had given him in his hands. He stood as they descended, and lit the Catacombs more than any lantern could, with his smile.

"You are supposed to wear that, not play with it," she said, firmly. His good humor proved infectious, for she was tired and grim with the warning she bore, and had surely not meant to smile in return.

"I am cleaning it," he said, "Look." He showed her, how he had polished the tarnish from most of the wide length of silver, revealing an elaborate pattern of foliage, from which the gems where evidently intended to represent the fruit.

"It is dangerous here," she said, wanting to take his arm and hurry him along. But she could not. "How long did it take to do that?"

"Oh it passed the time while I was waiting. It was not long."

"You've been waiting all day, haven't you? Since Anna gave me the message. I am so sorry. I was working in the libraries."

"And it is not dangerous," he said, taking her arm instead, and leading her, although by this time she knew that she needed no guidance, "The Kings never come here I tell you. They are only a danger lower down."

"That may have changed," she said, "Please take care." He nodded, and led her on.

Caerre and Tiralgon were in their accustomed chamber. Caerre was sitting in front of the frieze. She had lit two sticks of incense, had her doubtful book open in front of her, and was murmuring strange phrases beneath her breath. The very sight made Alliole nervous. Tiralgon was sitting on one of the mortuary slabs regarding Caerre, and when Alliole entered he turned his head. She saw the pride, deep and ferocious, in his eyes. Slaarngash turned away at the door.

"Oh, there you are," Caerre said, as crossly as if she were Xoon, "Why didn't you tell me you were attempting a fresh expedition?"

"Please understand," Alliole said, "I was under a promise of silence from your brother." She looked around for a spare shelf and sat down, "Besides I thought that you would know."

"I don't know everything," Caerre said. She sat with her back to Alliole still, contemplating the three throned figures, the crooked line of her spine mute with resentment.

"Do you know of the result?" Alliole said. Tiralgon answered in the affirmative.

"Then you will know why I say now, take care. Do not trespass on the Kings, for at least a little while, and do not travel alone through their areas, or I will be frightened for you." The apology that had birthed itself spontaneously to Helaf locked up in her throat before Caerre's reproaches, but she could still deliver her warning. "Where is Anna?" she asked, alarmed.

"In attendance on our mother," Caerre said, "She will be there until the festival is over. I will warn her. Is it not typical? We must pay for Xoon's carelessness, and forfeit our rights to travel in the only places where we have freedom."

"I can take care of myself," Tiralgon rumbled. Alliole's concern seemed to amuse him.

"You will remember?" Alliole asked, earnestly, "Do not send anyone out alone, and do not lose sight of them for long."

Caerre whirled around at this, and in her eyes and her next words Alliole read the stab of bitterness, of jealousy, "If they are missing, Helaf and Anna, I know where to find them. They will be somewhere together discussing how deeply they admire you."

Helaf said something indistinct into the following silence, and flushed deeply. Alliole cried, "That is not fair. I do not mean to trespass on their loyalty."

"But you do," Caerre snapped. "And you trespass on mine also. You did not plead our cause very well today, Alliole. I am most displeased."

Alliole, filled with an odd, mixed emotion she did not at that time identify, except to think that she did not want Helaf embarrassed, thought to reply most heatedly, but checked her anger.

"If you seek to provoke a fight with me, Caerre," she said instead, wearily, "Then remember that you risk alienating an ally, who has your interests and affection at heart else she would not be here, but others competing within her, to rob her of the certainty you have. If you heard the rest, Tiralgon," she said, turning the subject, regardless of Caerre's simmering stare, "Then you heard the Neve's warning about the bone door."

"Oh, I left when you and Cousin Tyall did," he said, surprised. He flicked a look at Caerre, as if to acknowledge his failure, "I had to get ahead to the libraries."

Alliole closed her eyes and choked back something between a laugh and a cry of despair, at so remorseless and patient a spy. "The Neve called me back," she said, and then related such of the substance of that conversation as she thought appropriate to the audience. "So you see," she finished, "It is probably just as well that you could not open that door you found, and I would advise you if you see it again, to re-bolt it and leave it there." Tiralgon nodded his head but at the same time said, sullenly, "How long would it take me to open it and look through? If I saw anything approaching, why I could close it again."

"It is an omen," Caerre said, abandoning her moodiness.

"Of what?" Tiralgon said.

"Of great things," Alliole said, slowly, remembering, "A birth. Deaths. Change. Forever. Is that what you want, Caerre?"

When there was no audible answer, she rose, and excused herself, saying that she must return to her chambers and rest. Helaf stood to accompany her, but she insisted that he stayed, saying that she and Slaarngash could find the way without guide, and that she feared for his safety if he returned alone. This he took the wrong way, for he flushed deeply a second time, and mumbled his farewell. As they left she heard Tiralgon's hoarse laugh, and doubted not at what he joked at. She flushed herself, miserably, in the passage, but forgot her discomfort soon enough, in keeping a careful eye on the best route through the countless crypts.

All the next day she kept in the libraries. Books and letters enough soon piled up around them, and Tyall spent half his time fossicking for fresh supply. She took advantage of one of his early absences to hiss at the walls, "Go away. I will tell you all I find out, but I cannot concentrate for the thought of you listening. It is too ridiculous. Go."

There was again no audible reply.

Tyall was an excellent companion, by turns industrious and cheerful, with none of Xoon's mercurial temper, and none of Lyde's idleness and complaints of boredom. Several times when she was ready to give up he kept her at it, throwing her suggestions that opened up fresh lines of search, but mostly following her lead, and bolstering in his commitment, her own belief that there was something to be found. And besides, when there was nothing else to think on she could listen to his voice as he read, and admire his profile. By the end of the day they had pursued some of their avenues of research into the ground. She learnt enough to convince her that Tyall should aid her no further, and talked him into visiting first Xoon, and then Lyde, in search of a fresh translator.

As they crossed the balconies towards Xoon's chambers, Alliole could see servants bustling through the hall beneath, fresh decorations being hung, and numerous braziers being lit along the walls. A woman's voice was lifted in song, a single thread of sound that wound through the ivory traceries as purposefully, as neatly as a needle threaded with golden silk through a rich brocade.

"They have started the invocation," Tyall explained.

Xoon was so restless and excitable that she could get no clear promises out of him, except that he could not read the old text and so was useless for much of the work. His head and hand were healing well, although Sleepghast, at his most unctuous, had evidently instilled in his charge an unwholesome fear of infection.

"You will be in attendance," Xoon said to her, "When I present the Mask to my mother." She hesitated, and then asked, honestly, "Will Marre be there?"

"Of course," Xoon said.

"Then no," she said, "It will only give Marre fresh cause to be angry. Why should I spoil your entertainment? Besides, Xoon," with another attempt at flattery she more than half meant, for she admired his persistence, "It is your endeavour. You should reap the reward."

Xoon did not take her comment well, but scowled. "Very well, if you will miss it then," he said, indifferently, "It is the observance of my mother's birth. She may desire your presence."

"I do not think she even knows of me," Alliole said, although she was nevertheless tempted to attend, for that very reason. But she felt the guilt of seeing Marre again not worth the fulfilling of her long held desire to meet this mysterious woman. "Give me a full report," she said.

"I will be there," Tyall said, loyally, as Xoon's face fell.

Lyde was more malleable, especially when Tyall worked in some subtle flattery that Alliole could only admire, and agreed to meet her the day after the morrow. The observance of Masks commenced late that very night. There was no further time for study before the festival, nor did Lyde seem to think she would be rising the next day. As it was then evening, Alliole had to put aside her urgency to pursue her goal, and after further thought on the matter, turned towards her chambers again, deciding to leave the rest of the Castle to their festivities.

As she crossed the balcony for the last time she could hear snatches of music from below, the viol and the flute playing together, and people sweetly singing. Warm air flooded up to her, colored with threads of smoke and filled with a heady mix of scents, of food, wine, people, and fumes from the braziers, which must be burning intoxicating drugs, for the first breath stung her eyes and nostrils, but the second and subsequent ones seemed pleasant and wholesome. The Festival seemed then to her a marvelous thing, and worth a glimpse, as long as it did not attract Marre's attention.

It occurred to her, as she walked slower to her chambers, that she could slip down to the Catacombs, meet with the others and, as long as Caerre was not still angry with her, they could show her their spying post in the Cross. As long as they kept in towards the center of the Castle they should be safe, for their path there could surely not trespass onto the area inhabited by the Kings. It would just be a question of her travelling quickly through the first necropolis. The more she thought on it, the more enticing seemed the idea. It did not occur to her that the breath she caught from the smoking braziers might cloud her judgement as well as excite her senses, that they might strengthen her own longing to attend until it consumed her common sense.

She waited until full night had fallen and enough time had passed that all attention would be absorbed in the festival, then ordering her demon to keep close, she hurried to the Catacomb entrance, descending the first stair with only a slight, absurd pang that no one waited to greet her.

It was only when she was most of her way there, and thinking that it was odd that she could not see any light from their fire, that she realized the forwardness of her intrusion. Perhaps they would resent her coming without invitation. Perhaps they had had the same idea, and already gone. She would never find them in this vast, arid place. The dark, which she had disregarded in her haste, came pressing in, but she faltered only a moment.

She thought at first the chamber was empty, and was disappointed beyond all measure at the failure of her plan. Again Slaarngash hesitated at the door, and turned back. Something barred the demon entrance, she was certain. She came in, and clumsily stirred up the brazier, so that the heated metal glowed afresh. Someone stirred in the gloom across from her, and gave her heart pause. But it was only Helaf, on his accustomed perch.

"Where is everyone?" she greeted him merrily, "Here I come for a visit, and there is no one to attend me."

"They've gone to look at the festival," he answered, "If they wait towards morning then everyone is too befuddled to notice, and they slip in and join the celebrations."

"Oh I knew it," she cried, "I thought of the same plan, and here I have left it too late." Then she noticed the flatness of his voice, and wondered at it, drawing closer. There was a catch in his breath and a blankness to his eyes. His gaze was turned inward.

"Are you in pain?" she asked, "Why did you not accompany them?" She reached up to touch him in her concern and of course missed, for she had no fingers. Her pain at her own loss, that she had thought long gone, smote her afresh, and from the doorway, Slaarngash howled.

"You ought not to be here alone," she said, her foolish mirth retreating, "Did no one listen to my warning?" Slaarngash's outcry and her own exclamation had brought Helaf out of himself. He cradled his brother against him, and descended, sitting on the lower slab. Silver glinted about his neck, where the rags he wore did not quite conceal the torque.

"Here," he said, and caught her arm, setting her down on the stone beside him, despite her misgivings that she had intruded so needlessly upon some private anguish. He took a deep breath, "No, I do not like to go there. I do not like the Cross. That is where I had my fall. Do you remember being told of it? I uh . . . fell from the balconies there. It hurts when I look upon them." He cradled his brother closer, protectively, and the mute thing turned its head and extended and then retracted its tongue, as if in recognition of their folly.

"Ah," she said, "From where your father fell?

"Yes, it is a little slippery there," Helaf said with some irony. He looked as if he did not want to say any more, but the grief that was in him was so great, it would not let him be still, "It was my fault," he burst out, holding his twin against himself, "I am sure. He was always cleverer than I, when we were small. If we had not, if we had not fallen, why I am sure we would be more Caerre's equal and better able to advise her." He looked away from her, but she did not need to see his face. His voice was hoarse with tears.

"There is nothing you can do now about the fall," she said, gently, "It was so long ago. And I think you are a fine brother for Caerre. You love one another, surely. Do you think one so headstrong would obey any other guidance than her own?" That choked a small laugh out of him, and she felt a little better, but he was twisting his hands together, and still would not look at her. "Ah but it is worse than that," he said, he hurried on, "That is, I have to tell somebody, and I cannot tell Caerre. She is too strong. She would despise me. And the floor. It looked so far, it was as though it dared me to fall. That is, I did not fall. I. . . ."

"You were pushed," she said, trying to help him, "I believe you, that one of these folk could do so cruel a thing. They are not kind."

"I wasn't pushed," Helaf said, dismally, "And I didn't fall. I. . . ." And here she held her tongue, for she saw that he really did want to say it, and that saying it would ease the guilt, the burden he bore, "I jumped. That's all. I was so unhappy. There, and I was sitting here and thinking about it when you walked in and I could not, I'm sorry, with all you have to bear, I . . . sometimes it is all I can think about, first thing in the morning, last thing at night and I cannot bear it. I. . . ."

Here his voice, which had been breaking as he spoke, was lost altogether, and it was her turn now, to comfort him. She could not put her arms around him, not properly, although she tried. She could not stroke his hair. But she could kiss him, first his hair, and then his forehead. "You are worthy," she said, inspired by the memory of her own fears, "You are worthy to live. I won't leave you alone, not now, if that is what makes you afraid." She kissed his tears. Then, gravely, his mouth.

They were both asleep when Tiralgon came plunging in, head and shoulder first through the door, the rest of his awkward body hurried in after any way he could force it through. The noise he made woke them.

"Hurry," he said to Helaf, "Caerre wants you." Then he saw Alliole. "Oh," he said, "Anna has gone to your chambers to fetch you. It is good that you are here. It will save time. Come quickly." Helaf rose quickly, as if used to such summons, his face still raw from his emotion.

"What is the matter?" Alliole said, sleepily.

"Aubon," Tiralgon said, briefly, "We went to get him to come to the festival. Hurry."

She rose at once, chilled and flurried, "He is unwell," she guessed, "His injury." Tiralgon shook his head and even laughed, a guttural snort, finding some jest in her words that she did not intend. Helaf took her arm without comment, taking his accustomed position as guide. Slaarngash fell in behind.

"He has something to impart then," she said, following after Tiralgon. They plunged immediately into a maze of subterranean passages and chambers more severe, more somber and more grotesquely decorated than any she had yet come across. Incense still burned before many tombs from the Remembrance, and its fumes, pungent and sickly, threaded between the mortuary chambers and hovered in pall over many a massive, engraved coffin, lined and soldered and sealed with lead. Helaf's hand tightened on her arm as she spoke, as if to halt her words even as they were said.

"I doubt it," Tiralgon said, turning back briefly to face her, his misproportioned face fixed in a sly, unforgiving grin, "He is dead." ✴

PART THREE

Chapter Thirteen

THE WHEEL WAS POISED cold and silent, frozen in mid-turn. The moonlight that sparkled on its giddy height illuminated striated streaks of the birth-stone jasper, and in the icy shadow at its base blue-frosted diamonds glittered. Diamond, opal, topaz, jasper, onyx, emerald, ruby and sapphire, all glimmered together in the darkness as if spelling out in their mineral light secrets forbidden to mortal humanity. In the shadow at the Wheel's base, little, feeble figures moved around one, blotched on the flagstones, that would never move more.

"He fell," Helaf said, quite steadily, coming to a stop and staring down bleakly at his cousin. Aubon lay face down, quite broken, the useless bandage still wrapped around his hand as if to emphasize his frailty. For a second time blood iced the flags.

"He was pushed," cried Caerre, her face, her vindictiveness, dispelling the gloom. Alliole looked down, briefly, and then up, searching the roof. "It is unlikely that he would fall," she said, and each word smote its echo in the hollow well of the hall, "For he was nimble enough, for all his injury."

"It would not matter," Caerre cried again, and Alliole cursed her for her heartlessness. "It is Xoon who did this, or his creature. What think you brother?" Helaf faltered, "I don't know." Caerre's gaze jumped speculatively from one to the other, "Where is Anna?"

"I found them together," Tiralgon said, dry, boastful, "I brought them here." He moved away and, like the demon the day before, tested the lowest spokes of the Wheel. Then slowly but certainly he moved up them, spread-eagled to prevent his entire weight resting on any one beam. Slaarngash made to overtake him, but then fell back before Alliole's silent rebuke, and made off to the other end of the hall.

"Xoon hates him and Aubon should not have teased him so," Caerre declared, quite certainly, "Anna told us how he boasted. That is why Xoon had him killed. Just like my father."

Helaf drew a deep, ragged breath and looked up. "We have no proof of that either," he said, quietly, so that his voice did not carry and echo as Tiralgon's did, a moment later. Tiralgon's shout carried overbore his words, so that Alliole was unsure who heard him, besides herself.

"There is blood here," Tiralgon cried, almost jubilantly, "In great quantity. He must have clung here a while." He clambered about on the Wheel's utter extremity. Alliole did not call out to him to be careful for she feared that she would break his concentration, the thread of certainty that alone upheld his clumsy limbs there. He was seemingly so unwieldy as to be otherwise in defiance of gravity.

"Such a vile death," Caerre hissed. Helaf shook his head, "I will not believe it," he said, still quietly, still bleakly. Yet Alliole marked this time, how Caerre took his words and considered them. Slaarngash gave voice from the furthest end of the hall, "The door is ajar," it said.

Alliole went over to it, for she was sure that it was closed fast yesterday. Not only ajar, but when the pair cast about amongst the Devices they found marks thick in the hoar-frost, and also upon the stair that led down into the body of the hall. Little misshapen foot-prints, in great host.

"They have come and gone," the demon muttered, "And are now far from here."

"Will they come again?" she asked, but it did not know.

"Here," she called to the others, "It was the Kings that did this." She showed them her proof, and also what they found upon the stair, several hand-prints, small and in their own way as ungainly as Tiralgon, who came slowly down to join them after prising from its silver setting, and pocketing a sliver of jasper. He admitted it, quickly enough, "It took a great number then, to slay just one," he said, "Unless it was some ritual killing."

Caerre clung to her earlier certainty. Helaf took her aside and talked softly to her, but she rebuked him with words Alliole could not hear, and he drew away from her, stiffly. Tiralgon in the meanwhile turned Aubon over, and straightened him out. He placed the fragment of semi-precious stone in his palm and closed the fist over. "Jasper eases the passage out of this world, as well as in," he said, when he saw that Alliole watched him.

"Can you help me close the door?" she asked, and he came over, putting his shoulder to it. Then, with the demon, he propped up as much as he could against it to prohibit easy entry from the other side.

"What know you of these creatures?" she asked him, low, as he rested a moment in this task.

"A little," he jibed her, his brief gleam of humanity over, "I am a good spy."

"You think this was some retaliation?" she asked, pressing, "Do you think they will come again, come further?"

"I have never known them overstep their bounds before," he said, flatly, "I suppose Xoon angered and provoked them."

"What are they?" Useless to ask so directly, for seeing the intensity of her curiosity Tiralgon just grinned. "They are not demons," said he, "I hate demons."

"But it might aid me to know," she cried, "Aid us." He shook his head at her, "Take this as a warning to trespass no further," he said and fell silent. She was caught up in a baffled fury, that he would not tell her when he obviously knew more. But after she had left him and returned to the others, then remorse worked on her. Why should he aid her, Alliole realized. She had caused the death of one friend and the disloyalty of another.

Helaf met her halfway, held her arm a moment and whispered, glancing back at Caerre, "Give me time," he said, "She is very angry but I think I can cool her."

"What did she say to you?" she said, suddenly angry again, and angrier still when he flushed miserably and turned away. "Nothing," he said, but he lied.

"I won't have it," she said to him, in a hissing whisper, "She asks too much of you. I will not have you hurt. I cannot bear it." But she was robbed further speech for they had rejoined Caerre, who—the first shock of fury over—was weeping, and Helaf must comfort her. To Alliole standing, uselessly near, it seemed most terrible of all that Aubon's death should arouse so great a mix of emotions, so fervid, so hopelessly muddied by each other, so that the good was tainted with the bad, the grief with the anger. She scarce knew which way to turn herself and would have been glad if Helaf had comforted her, if he had shown her as much devotion as he showed his sister. And when she did weep, caught under the shadow of the Wheel, she had to admit honestly to herself that she knew not which passion caused her tears, grief, jealousy or fear.

When she at last returned to the Castle Proper it was full day. The music from the festival continued unabated. Anna was waiting in her chambers, poor child, faithful to her direction. She too had obviously spent much time in crying, although now she had fallen asleep on the bed, holding tight in her hand the blind bird. There Alliole left her for much of the day. She bathed her face and ordered the first servant to appear—slovenly and reluctant—to fetch her some of the books from the libraries, and a scholar to interpret them. She spent the day in this fashion. Slaarngash sent any further servants who appeared away, by painless but persuasive methods to which it evidently devoted much thought and ingenuity. What Alliole learnt then was somber and disheartening and added further to her present woes, to her oppressive sense of hurrying to a doubtful conclusion that she would far rather avert, but could not in time. It was hard to concentrate for the distant music was sweet and poignant, and occasionally she heard cadences that thrilled her.

With the lighting of the lamp on the azure wall, she sent the scholar away and closed off her study. At the same time Anna woke, as if summoned by the snap of the clasp on its cover.

"Ai," Anna cried, "What am I doing here? Alliole you must come quickly. Caerre. . . ." Here she burst into fresh tears. Alliole comforted her, and fed her sweetmeats, then explained the course of the day. She would have accompanied her return, but Anna said she must attend to her mother, and departed, still snuffling. It struck Alliole as curious that Anna should be preferred of all the children, but she did not at that time pursue the question. She turned restlessly to the book again, although her distaste and weariness were growing together and impeded even trying to sort through her memories. Then a step alerted her. Slaarngash slithered from its accustomed perch and vanished beneath the bed, in body, if not in spirit, for unquiet air seethed above it. It was Marre.

"Where have you been?" Marre asked, as if it was she who had been waiting.

"Here," Alliole said, hushed and terrified, "All day."

"Last night," Marre said, "When I would have had you attend me."

"In the Catacombs," she said, and then cursed her truth-telling, for she saw that Marre's eye was distracted, and perhaps she would not have noticed a small lie. But Marre did not seem so interested. Marre's face was twisted and sharp as always, but her vision seemed blunted, her eyes blurred, "Reven has been missing these last three days. Have you seen him?"

"No," answered Alliole, honestly.

"Do you know where he is?"

"No," she answered, again honestly, although treading a finer line than ever before. But the other was strangely listless, and evidently could not muster her accustomed vigorous enquiry.

"Strange," Marre mused, "Strange that none have seen him." With an abrupt and terrifying change of topic, "In the Catacombs you say. I would beware of going there."

"Why?" said Alliole, repressing the impulse to say that she would go where she chose, realizing that Marre more than lacked her accustomed manner but had gained a new one. She seemed to speak as if from a dream, as if the observance of the festival had drained her.

"Gaar visited there often and died as a result of it. You cannot trust those children, they are malformed in spirit as well as body. They will destroy us."

"I do not believe they killed him," Alliole said.

"Nevertheless he died," Marre answered, "Ill luck breeds in them." And then she continued, for her lethargy promoted a vision, although at so great a tangent that Alliole took a few moments to follow her reasoning, "The world grows older. Each season that follows is less than the one previous, and so on older and staler until the world ends. Our great and revered ancestors were able to enact marvels, to close and open portals to other spheres, to raise this monument around you within the blink of an eye, and keep it in constant repair. It is said that these miracles were accomplished through an artifact of unknown fashion and antiquity. Until the war, or so the ignorant believe. In a war against some mightier power this artifact was lost. There was no war, I am certain. It was invented to explain our seclusion, to shed some glamor upon mundane reality. This ruin was caused not by war, but by the attrition of decay, neglect, and our own inability to repair. There is no hope, no artifact to retrieve that will restore our pride. Our blood runs to its finish. We cannot work the mighty acts of our ancestors and we abuse our powers to sop our injured pride. The Parrar, she feels this badly, this despair, and contracted the death madness in her youth, although we did not know it. All the men she lay with died, one after the other, of small injuries, of unlikely maladies. She barely recognized it in herself I suppose, and then only when her children were born malformed.

They had suckled on the venom within her. Gaar lasted longer than most, but he had his own patron. He was blessed by the Lady of Cats. Hah! They say he died of a fall, but who would believe it? He was as sure footed as a cat. He could see in the dark, and for those who doubt, why, he bequeathed that sight to his children. But he would not give up his brats, he would run to them, he would succor them, and so he died. And how can we continue, and our children who are whole, how can they maintain our traditions, our heritage? With Caerre waiting in the dark for them. She will undo them. No, we are doomed, within this generation or the next."

"What is this to do with me?" Alliole cried suddenly, in anguish, her already weighted spirits further depressed by this, no longer in fear but rather wishing to break Marre's spell. Marre started as she returned to herself, and her clouded eyes glittered a moment with old suspicions. Alliole regretted her hasty words. But Marre spoke again, slowly, "You can hear—heard—a Voice, calling and beseeching. Some say that this is the voice of the long lost artifact. I recognized your description, and was curious to learn what it really is, although it has to date defied any interpretation. Somehow your absent memories had become tangled with this Voice, and when they returned to you they brought the myth with them. Tyall, among us all only Tyall now hears it, and I cannot help him. That was how he first came to my cousin's attention, when he was a boy and could scarce bear it. At first drugs and fumes would soothe him, but now she says that there are nights at a time she must keep him awake, or he will wander away in his sleep, and never be found." Her voice was barely a murmur. "It is as if the more of us choke it off, so it must concentrate further on those few who can hear, and summon them always, even if it is in the end more than they can bear. . . ." Her gaze fell upon the book on the table.

"That should not be here," she said. She took it up, although the blaze of hostility was all but snuffed, and walked from the chamber, her step slow and lacking its accustomed vigor. It occurred to Alliole to wonder where the guilt for Gaar's murder lay, if both Marre and Caerre so freely accused the other. With Xoon? But that would make him a killer so young that she refused to believe it.

The next day and the next, Alliole kept studiously to herself, shunning all company except Lyde, who visited to aid her but kept in a terrible temper that provoked a quarrel whenever her attention was taken from the books, and always before Alliole could ask on news of the Festival. In the end Alliole guessed that Lyde had an interest in failing to communicate its outcomes and forsook her questions. She had no heart to visit below, not wishing to alienate Caerre, and went no further into the Castle Proper. It seemed to her that a threat lay behind Marre's visit that had not been in her manner. She felt that discovery loomed, that the visit had been to tempt the truth from her and that in failing to admit her secret she had lost her best defence. In her saner moments she knew that this must be impossible, that if Marre learnt of her guilt she would act swiftly, but she could think of no other purpose for the visit, and so looked to her books for company, and sought no other. It was only at the end of these few days that she forsook her chambers, and this was not of her own choosing. Iriethe arrived one evening, and after a short conversation of no matter called her to attend the Neve.

Alliole went reluctantly, for her morbid fears were strong in her. But she could see no other way to avoid the summons save to plead sickness that Iriethe would report as unfounded. If she had but known it, Iriethe would not have reported such, for after Alliole's days of retirement and unhappy study, she looked unwell. Her eyes were tired and puffed, and drained of the boldness that had inhabited them on her recovery from illness. Her cheek was wan, and her hair, now enough again to be tied back, was limp, and no longer of such bright color as it had first had.

"What is it Alliole, that ails you?" the Neve asked in astonishment when she first saw her, checking some other remark.

"A lie," Alliole answered, relieved to be asked, to remove the weight from her soul.

"Go tell it to the truth-stone then," the other answered, "For I may not wish to hear it." She bade her sit, and told the servant to fetch wine. She was alone in her chambers. The fire burned fitfully within its grate. Its light was dim and bad and it did not entirely extinguish the cold. Slaarngash ignored it, crouching in the corner by the book-stand. Tyall was nowhere to be seen. Even the air seemed exhausted, so perhaps that was why the fire burned so ill. But the Neve seemed cheerful enough, for she sat back and regarded Alliole almost playfully.

"Well I too have a question, but so weighty a matter as your face portends takes precedence," she said, "If you wish to speak first."

"I don't know how to say it," Alliole said.

"That is easy enough. Study your phrasing, couch your speech in the most ideal grammar. It is not so hard." Now her cheer seemed mere carelessness, for it seemed that she paid more attention to the wine than Alliole. She dismissed the servant. Upon the mantel a statuette of two amber cats gambolling together seemed to move fluidly a moment as if caught up in their play. Alliole dismissed the vision as something beyond her control. "I mean I would hear your wishes first," she said, "And then attend to my own."

The Neve shrugged, "Very well. It is simple. Who put up the fortifications before the door of the Hall of Masks? It took my servants most of today to remove them so that we could place the masks of this year's festival there."

"Remove them?" Alliole said dully, and then a spasm twitched her guts so that she started, "You did put them back?"

"No," the Neve said, "It would be a great inconvenience. How will we get in to dust?" This last said in jest.

"The Kings came through the door," Alliole said, sinking back again, "They killed Aubon, poor soul."

"Ah," the Neve said. She turned the wine glass with one hand and kept her eyes on it, saying, as if idly, "When did this happen?"

"On the night of the Festival."

"And you did not think to inform me?"

Alliole stared blankly, and then summoned her answer from the depths of a black gulf, "I did not think," she stammered, "I, it seemed so private. Their grief. And we barred the door."

"And we opened it again. I have never heard of such a trespass before," the Neve mused, her eyes still on the turning glass, "What did your researches say on the matter?"

"A Mystery," she said, bitterly, "Deeper than the Kings."

"Ah, and these things trouble you. Or are your words just metaphorical? Out with it."

"Only this," Alliole obeyed her, "It seems that they are the result of sorceries long past that went horribly wrong. Tyall helped me find this, and then I sent him away, once this—other matter—made itself known. . . . An entire generation damned. Records speak of an uprising from the Catacombs of the"—here she recited from memory—"Spontaneously corrupted living dead. That must be the Kings, surely. They were driven beyond the inhabited parts of the Castle, and bound with a pact of non-trespass known as the Remembrance of those Dead. But. But it is also said that a spectral Voice hounded their remorseful creator until she too was dead. And the Mad Parrar. No one said, no one told me the reason why she went mad. I thought it was the Voice, but it seems to me she heard the Voice only after she killed her children."

"You have found that then? It was her right."

"She entombed them alive." Alliole said, indignantly.

"I do not defend her," the Neve said, still not regarding her, "The girl grew malformed and stood in the way of an able heir. The boy would not leave his sister."

Alliole's anger subsided, for her emotion could not last before her exhaustion, and besides she sought further answer. "What is it? Where does it come from? Are you not afraid?"

"This Voice has always been there. It is tied to us, an inheritance of our family, our blood line," the Neve said, "Why should we fear it?"

"Why, the connection with the Kings —and the Mad Parrar. Haunted by that Voice until the end of their days. It would seem that it is the wicked who hear it. What of Tyall?"

"Why should I tell you?" the Neve asked, and looked directly at her, "What guilt throws itself around your shoulders, Alliole, that you seek to fasten it on others?"

"I want to know the truth," she said.

"You know my opinion on that."

"Then what did I do," she asked, "What did I do, that I heard it?"

There the Neve was silent a long while, "I do not know," she said at last, "I believe that behind the Voice is some thing our ancestors made and then deliberately lost. All of us hear it when we are young, but most of us learn to block it, to build barricades in our minds and souls. These barricades break down when we feel a need to atone, hence the historical effects you so describe. Whatever it is, it calls and sobs, and if we are not careful it sends us walking in our sleep to recover it. Those who hear it for too long must die or go mad, or both. I see no connection between it and you. Is that an answer?"

Alliole shook her head. The Neve sighed. She picked up the glass, and poured her untasted wine over onto a mass of papers, quite deliberately, watching while the purple liquid pooled, and the papers turned sodden.

"I suppose you will now ask Tyall," she said. Alliole nodded.

"He has never told me," she said, "Why should he tell you?" But she continued regardless, although after a long enough pause that Alliole thought that she would not answer, "When the children were younger their father, Gaar, used to encourage them to play together. He would bring Caerre and Helaf to the balconies, the two oldest. Reven was the leader then. Xoon and Tyall followed him. Boys can be so cruel. They never got the better of Caerre. She had a quicker tongue, and was a girl, so they did not quite dare to. Also, she was not so clever as Helaf was, although he was younger. She did not brood so. I think they hurt Helaf very badly, here—" she touched her breast, above her heart "—And I think he thought too long on it. Shortly after Anna was born, they were all together on the balconies, unregarded, and Helaf and his brother—fell. No one ever got a clear story, and they were too young to trust with the truth-stone. They closed up as children do. But that very night," she closed her fingers over the sodden pages, and squeezed them together, so that pulpy crimson fluid ran between her fingers, "Tyall's dreams began. I do not blame him. He was young and impressionable, and. . . ." She sighed, and closed without finishing the sentence, as if tired of the topic. Then she tossed the wine-soaked paper into the fire, which blazed tremendously and briefly before again subsiding.

Alliole closed her mouth over Helaf's confidences, wondering only a little. Guilt, guilt and remorse were the common denominators. But that two men should suffer the same shame was absurd.

"Marre talked of the Voice," she said, at last.

"Ah, Marre," the Neve said, broodingly, "Did she visit you?"

"Yes."

"What did she speak of?"

"Matters strange and terrible," Alliole said, "She frightened me."

"It is the return of the Great Mask, that we thought a fable," the Neve said, "It evokes in us wonder if other things we thought myth might also be true."

"She did not think so," Alliole said.

"Marre is not in much position to think now. Did she seem tired, lethargic?" the Neve asked, in an apparent return to her carelessness.

"She seemed drugged," Alliole answered directly, "She spoke of Tyall, and Gaar, and the Parrar. And history."

"Well then she has noticed already," the Neve said. She smiled sourly at Alliole's questioning look. "I would rather she did not go mad searching, and I would rather she did not find what she is looking for. Would you agree?" Alliole agreed, glumly, bracing herself, glad almost to be so close to the revelation. "therefore," the Neve continued smoothly, "I have taken steps to slow her search and placate her mind. Sometimes it is months before one so soothed notices," this said with utmost circumspection, "However Marre is trained to such things and should recover. Shortly."

"How long?"

"A day. A week. Who knows." When Alliole was still and silent as one stricken the Neve leant forward and regarded her, "I am going to ask you a few questions," she said, "And I wish you would give earnest consideration to your answers for I would like to know a little but not overmuch or I would be bound to act, and I would rather still restrain my hand. therefore: are you familiar with the circumstances surrounding Reven's—shall we say—disappearance?"

Alliole nodded.

"Were these circumstances, in your opinion, provoked or exacerbated by Reven's temper?" Alliole nodded again, and swallowed, and stared at the floor. In its corner, Slaarngash skulked most elaborately. The Neve did not regard it.

"Would you want to give names to—those—involved?"

"That depends," she said, because she had to be truthful, "On what the results of this naming would be."

"Anything that I learn, is soon known by Marre. And others I am sure. The only secrets kept here are those unspoken. Marre's vengeance," the Neve replied steadily, "Would be most dire and gruesome, and would doubtless become a by-word in retaliation for several generations. I do not jest."

"Then I would rather not," Alliole said, "But I will if you ask me." There. One question more, and it would be all over. The silence seemed endlessly long. When she looked up, the Neve had sat back in her chair regarding her, awaiting her appraisal. "You see I, unlike you, am not urgent after truth," she said, unkindly.

"What?", Alliole cried, "You cannot press me to this impasse and then abandon me."

"I can and will," the Neve said, "Only do this. Tell me before the final blow, even if only in the last instant, so that I can shelter those I love from its fall."

Alliole gasped and floundered, with the release of pent-up tension and remorse. "I am not worthy of this trust," she said.

"That is for me to judge," the Neve said. She looked as if she would speak more but at that moment the door was flung open and Tyall and Xoon bounded in. Xoon's arm was still in a sling, but this did not dampen his high spirits. They exclaimed at their good fortune in meeting Alliole again, reminisced on the entertainment of the previous few days and drank the remnant of the wine, which only served to heighten their exuberance. By this time Alliole realized that any attempt to further uncover the Neve's design (for design there certainly was, but what she could not figure) was useless. She expected the Neve to withdraw from their clamor, but she seemed to take delight in their zest, even encourage it. Tyall sat at her feet and Xoon, after a fastidious mopping, the bureau. Xoon was brimful of some secret, but whether it was an old or new one Alliole could not fathom, and truth to say, did not care. At the end of it, the pair insisted that they escort her to her chambers. The Neve, in her old manner, called Alliole back a moment from the door, before releasing her.

"One last thing, do not guide Xoon on any further journeys. Let us not provoke your Kings, lest the oft-rumored doom descend upon us from an unexpected direction."

"Never," Alliole said, glad at last to speak the absolute and unqualified truth. She had had her fill of adventuring.

Xoon and Tyall entertained her with further conversation and wine until a very late hour, despite numerous although half-hearted attempts to evict them. Several times she saw Anna peep in, but each time the girl fled before the gale of her companions' clamorous mirth, until Alliole despaired. Most of all she wanted to bury her head in the bolster, and forget, forget everything she had learnt, everything she feared, and to sink back into happy amnesia.

"The festival went well for you, then," she said at last, distracted. Xoon beamed but did not answer. Tyall said slyly, "Oh, he has his sights set on higher things now." This provoked further laughter. Xoon's secret bubbled close to the surface but she did not wish to hear it, and did not press this issue either.

When they had finally departed, she sank back on the bed, but soon rose, determined to find some solace in her misery. Besides, if Caerre wanted her, then Anna would doubtless wake her. She travelled swiftly through the passages, which soon took on their old trance-like aura, so that she felt that she was a figment of someone else's reverie and that nothing could harm her. The rooms and corridors swirled around her, with dream-certainty, and when she found the necropolis stair and descended, it was only right that Helaf was waiting there for her. She had so much to say, yet all she could say was "I am so tired," as she sat down beside him.

Helaf sat very stiffly, even drew himself together, "I see the company Anna saw you with has left," he said, "And you find time for us now." She straightened very slowly. That even gentle Helaf was angry, that was the final blow.

"What do you think of me?" she said. "The Neve asked me about Reven today. I chose not to answer, and she left it there. I believe she thinks that Caerre killed him, and that I cover for you. She looks I think for a war between Xoon and Caerre, and hopes to hold her hand and aid in establishing the victor. Do you think that is a wise choice? She trusts me,"—here her voice caught, as she realized the enormity of this trust, and how terrible it was— "She trusts me to take her part in it".

Helaf still sat stiffly. After an interval of silence she spoke again with less passion, conversationally, "I see that you are disinterested in politics. I have been reading about one of your ancestors, the Mad Parrar, so-called. She killed her two children."

"I know," Helaf said, unbending a little, "Caerre used to tease me about them. She says, would I be so faithful as the boy, Abarrn? He chose not to leave his sister, and was walled up alive with her."

"Would you be?"

"I don't know."

"I think this is a terrible conversation," Alliole said, dismally, staring into the never-ending depths of the catacombs, "I can't see in the dark. I'm blind. What do you see? Is it beautiful, or as horrible as it feels?"

"I see Aubon," he replied, and she jumped and said, "Is he near?"

"No, further down," this was said haughtily, "Only the lesser dead lie here. I am sorry that he is dead. So I see him before me. He has been my companion the last few days, when you would not be."

"Helaf," she said. Her voice cracked right across in the middle of his name, as it had when she had said another name, an infinity of days ago. He looked down at his hands.

"You, you have your sister. What do I have? This—" she said, bitterly, sweeping one arm back to Slaarngash, who glared down from the head of the stair, "Do you think I have wanted to spend the last days alone? With so much guilt, such despair. And the Neve, she will not let me drop this burden, she will make me carry it to the edge of doom. Further. She will not care either."

That brought his head up, sharply. He looked at her again, as if afresh, and then put out one hand to smooth back her hair.

"I do care," he whispered, "I do care." His fingers got caught up and he disentangled them gently, then repeated the gesture, combing the tangled locks with his fingers, drawing nearer so that he could put his arms around her, "I do care," he said again, meaninglessly.

"I feel so ashamed," she said, "But I cannot convict myself. Do you understand?" He did not answer, but his tension eased, until, after a long while, she felt at ease enough to put a long-thought out question to him.

"What did Caerre say to you, back there in the Wheeled Hall?" she asked, a second time, and he hesitated, then answered, "That she did not wish to share me with a lover."

"Why couldn't you tell me?"

"I did not know if that was your intent. I was frightened that you would go away."

"And I did. I am sorry," she said.

"Don't be." He shivered, and then drew them, all three of them, together, joyously.

"They've opened the door," she said distractedly, after a short interval, "From the Hall of Masks. The Kings can get in."

"Tiralgon does not think they will unless we further provoke them."

"The Neve fears Marre may be near discovery of Reven's death."

"So do we all. Caerre has been doing nothing these last two days, except burn incense and chant at the figures on the wall."

A dim sense of crisis, and of her own precipitation of it, welled within her. "What are we going to do?" she asked, miserably.

"Nothing," he said, "What can we do? These forces will play themselves out."

"Save that we are in the middle of them," she said, "And may suffer in the regaining of equilibrium."

He shrugged. "We can wait," he said. He moved back from her, and brushed her hair again, back from her face. He took her by the shoulders, "Hope. Have faith." Then he leant forward and kissed her, giving her confidence back, that she had given him. ✹

Chapter Fourteen

ALLIOLE ARRIVED back in her chambers the following morning to find Sleepghast awaiting her. He looked torn between merriment and viciousness when he saw her, and then both melted into an unaccustomed gravity of expression when the demon at her heels slouched into view. He bid her without ceremony to attend his master, and her sense that some crisis approached quickened.

Xoon was in the same nervous high spirits as when she had last seen him, and Tyall was still at his side. Xoon welcomed her arrival and reproached her tardiness in the same breath, while Sleepghast, at his most unctuous, explained that she had been absent from her chambers when first he attended her. Xoon seemed too abstracted to pay note to this, but Tyall gave her a sharp look.

"I have called you here, Alliole, to help plan my next venture," Xoon said, cheerily, waving his bandaged hand.

"We have been up plotting half the night," said his companion.

"I thought you had abandoned them," Alliole protested, "Were you not sufficiently rewarded for your last?"

Xoon's look grew golden, "Of course," he said, carelessly, "But encouraged also to another, if I can only think out the ways and means. Sit down."

Alliole sat, and was glad to. "I will not pay heed to such plans. Xoon, it is foolish to venture out there, and further stir the Kings. What has got into you?"

"A taste for adventure," Xoon said. He looked about him restlessly. Alliole had from the first noted in him a shadow, that sat ill with his otherwise open countenance, and a character she had first guessed but now knew to be feckless, mercurial and shallow. Looking at him now, she saw that the shadow had deepened. The successful recovery of the Mask had not soothed but rather exacerbated the infection, the passion that drove him forward and outward into the unknown.

"Xoon, I will not aid you," she said firmly, "But I will hear you out if you wish, if only so I can further impress upon you the rashness of your decision."

He dismissed her caution and her rebuttal with another wave of his hand. "I had speech with my mother at the Festival, and also in the days just passed," he said, rattling off what was evidently the proper form of the words, "She is most pleased with my gift, and wishes to express her most generous thanks to you also, for your aid." He reached behind him, and plucked from a miscellaneous pile of objects a golden globe that filled his cupped hands, studded with emeralds and hinged. "Here," he said, "This is for your part in it. It opens, see." Within glowed an artifact of amber, most delightful to look upon, carved so that it seemed to turn ceaselessly into itself. But Alliole had a brief glimpse only before Xoon snapped the clasp shut, carelessly. "Shewing this will gain you admittance to her Solar, at any time, so that you may speak with her also. It is her express wish."

Alliole was so stunned by her moment's scrutiny that her first desire was that Xoon open the globe again, so that she might contemplate the mysterious object within at her leisure. She had to close this request in her throat lest she betray her eagerness, and so she was at loss for words as he continued, "And of course she promises better reward, contingent upon our success in this new venture."

"Do you mean that this plan is at your mother's command?" she asked.

Xoon looked sly. "Not at her command, no," he said, "You cannot understand her subtlety. But I study her to guess her wishes and fulfil them, as is my chief desire, and I believe them to lie so."

"Is it your desire then, to go to your death and lead others to theirs also?" she asked, bleakly. The shadow deepened on his face, affirming this new and dreadful certainty, but then his child's huffiness broke through. "You are no fit companion," he said sulkily, "And if I did not need you, you could stay here for all I care."

"Xoon, I am staying here," Alliole said, slowly and explicitly, "I have said so already. I will not go. Tyall, tell him this."

"Alliole, at least hear him out," Tyall said. She glared at him, not expecting this answer, and he grimaced, attempting, she guessed, to display his concern and his urgency for her attendance, without speaking anything aloud.

"All right," she said.

"It is simple," Xoon said, leaning forward eagerly, in evident anticipation of her surrender, whilst a beaming Sleepghast handed around dainties on a tray and then departed the chamber with conspicuous courtesy, "Why, if this Mask that all thought myth is utter and factual reality, why would not other legends also be true? The Chamber Ultima, for instance, sometime known as the Puzzle Room, or the jewel called the Umber Sea. The Bone Door, even, although that stretches my belief, but most important, the thing that lies behind the Voice that some of my family hear."

"That," Alliole said, without even troubling to hide her despair. "Xoon, do not pick on that, whatever it is. It is not a voice you would wish to hear."

"It is an artifact of unknown fashion and antiquity," Xoon started, determinedly, but she cut him off. "I know, I know," she said, "But it is far away, Xoon. In all her years of searching the Mad Parrar never found it. How could we?"

"Perhaps she did," Xoon said, "She never came back, remember. That is what my mother implied. That she did find it and is bound there. We have only to find her to find success. And we can find her by following dreams."

"Xoon," Alliole wailed, "This is madness. You saw what the last did to Tyall. Everyone will forbid it." She addressed Tyall, "How can you permit it? You, who know best what trials you fell under."

Tyall looked truly uncomfortable, "I cannot," he said, and licked his lips, "I could not go through it again, although I barely remember—Xoon has another plan, I—"

"The plan, is, we do not need Tyall," Xoon cut in, before Tyall could steal his answer, "But there are others we can follow. For example, you."

His audacity again robbed her of speech, but he left her time to recover, "Xoon, I cannot be a guide. I could hear the Voice once but it is gone. Marre took it from me. And I thank her now, from the bottom of my heart, that I can so answer truly. I cannot hear your Voice, Xoon. I am no use to you. That is my answer, and I will go now, so that you can think on it."

Xoon waved her down impatiently. "I have not given you leave to go," he said, coldly, "You do not understand either. Marre took it from you, but she has kept it in her laboratories. I have marked that she is strangely distracted, and now would be a good time to borrow it back from her. I know what she does with the dreams and memories she traps, she keeps them in bottles, and uses them in her alchemy. We must simply select the right memory."

"And I suppose she will allow this?"

"No," he admitted, "We will have to borrow it from her when she is not looking."

"And return it before she notices? It is I she will blame, not you. She likes me little enough already."

"I will shield you," Xoon said, and when she looked entirely unconvinced of his protective powers, "Also my mother will. Do you doubt her capability?"

"Then what?"

"Steal out into the ruins, follow where the Voice leads us. It will be eager enough, I tell you."

"No," she said, firmly, "I will not listen. I am going now, I tell you. With or without your leave."

"Alliole," Xoon called after her, but she was gone. Slaarngash lingered only to scoop up the globe with one taloned paw. She was halfway across the balconies before they caught up with her, together. The servants hurrying about their tasks melted into other chambers, as Xoon impetuously took her aside into a copyist's office for further conference.

"Alliole," Xoon said again, "Why are you so set against me?"

"I am not against you," she said, "I am against your expedition. There are other means to attain power."

"But it is the only thing I can do," Xoon said, dropping his voice, his face like bone in its urgency, "Alliole, I would say this to none other but you. You will aid me in this." The rich stink of ink and leather and parchment, together with the sharp shocked look of the blank pages of a half-finished manuscript spread out at the window confused her senses. The window looked out over the Cross beyond, and its muted radiance supplied the light.

"No," she whispered also, strung out in his urgency, "No, Xoon, this is folly and you would have us killed in over-reaching yourself." She turned away, and would have gone, but Xoon caught her arm again, and played his last card, "If you will not aid me in this, I will tell everyone that you lie with my brother," he said, venomously. She stopped mid-stride, and thought for a moment that her legs would fail with her stomach. "And so you think to coerce my obedience," she whispered.

"Everybody would laugh," Xoon said softly, standing close to her. "Everyone would despise you. You would be thrust into darkness with the others, where you belong, if you do not obey me."

"How did you learn this?" she asked.

"I have my own means," he said, and stood back and frowned, having not instantly secured her compliancy.

"Why should I be ashamed," she asked him, although her heart was shaking, and within her was a dawning horror at herself, that any love she bore could not be free of this taint, should be corrupted by it, but that nevertheless she would bear it, for Helaf's sake, "Of what I do, and who learns of it? Besides I would be shamed rather than dead, which is where your venture leads, Xoon. Good day."

"No," he shouted, forsaking caution. He stamped his foot. "You will obey me," he called after her. But she was already gone.

She hurried to her chambers, and spent several hours there, barely enough to recover from her first agitation, and certainly not long enough to be able to contemplate the events of the last few days with serenity. Then Tyall came rushing in.

"What did you say to him," was all he greeted her with, "He is in such a passion I dared not leave him, for fear he would do himself an injury."

"Why do you attend me?" she asked, fixing him with a glare probably more frightful than she intended, for he stumbled back almost to the doorway before it, then stammered, "Why, to consult you on Xoon. You know his moods as well as I, and have more control over him than I do in the short time that you have known him. What did you say to so distress him?"

"He did not tell you?" she asked, and felt relief, that her fellow feeling with Tyall remained intact. Tyall shook his head, "I told you, he is in a tantrum and nothing can be got from him," he said, "I told him I had to attend the Neve to get away to you. What is to be done?"

"I don't know," she said, mutinously, "I told him I would not accompany him on so foolhardy an expedition, regardless of whatever threats he issued to me."

"I said the same as you," Tyall said to her, fiercely, "But I could not dissuade him, and I saw that he would not listen to you either. His heart is set on this venture, and it is as you said. It is his own death he seeks, I am sure."

"He has contracted the death madness from his mother," she said, slowly.

"Who told you that?" Tyall said, still fiercely.

"Marre," she said, "She did not mean to speak to me, but I was there when she spoke on some vision and I had, perforce, to listen. I would much rather have not done so, for she spoke of dreadful things."

"It is a time of dreadful things," Tyall said, "And we who love him would save him from what he seeks, if we could. I will go with him, Alliole, and I beg you to accompany us also, to save the inheritance of the Castle, and for friendship's sake if that is not enough."

"No," she said, still slowly, for another thought had occurred to her. She thought she knew the father of the Parrar's child, and this appalled her. "I have given a promise to the Neve. As you must have also, for if she knew she would surely forbid your attendance."

"She does not know," Tyall said. "And in any case she believes that old story about doom attending any wandering beyond the Castle Proper. I see no reason to. What of the Mad Parrar? What doom attended her? There are so many old stories. Why she should attach particular weight to that one I do not know."

"Perhaps because she is older and wiser, and knows which stories speak truth. Perhaps you should listen to her."

"And let Xoon set forth undefended as he will do?" Tyall said, bitterly, and then, "Do you think this is easy for me? This is the first time I have withheld the truth from her either, except when she has bidden me suppress it."

"We could not survive in those ruins one hour if the Kings forbid it," Alliole said, "And our trespass may provoke greater ruin on us, perhaps this doom the Neve speaks of, than it has already. No, Tyall, and if you persist in this insistence, I will inform her myself." She sat down, weak and sickly in her emotion, until Tyall must have perceived that to press further would be to invite her to make good her own threat.

"Very well," he said, "I will do as you say." He took his leave, and she felt remorse, that she had left him alone in this battle. She felt remorse for their companionship, which must surely now fail before her desertion, but not that she had failed to accompany them. She would not be dragged on such a venture again, she had vowed it, both to the Neve and to her own conscience. It was too frightful and wild an endeavour to even contemplate, and on thinking on it again she was shaken further, and at once took herself down to the Catacombs. There at least was one source of which she could be sure.

Caerre was alone in the lower chamber when Alliole arrived. It was as Helaf had said, for she sat on the floor, brooding on the wall of the three figures, and incense burned before them. Her book was open at her feet, and its unregarded pages flipped over in the tomb-wind. Shadows flocked about her shoulders, and about the faces of the throned beings.

"You should not arrive unheralded," Caerre said, before Alliole had gathered breath to speak, "You may witness something unpleasant, and I would have to bid you not to speak."

"You have been talking with Xoon," Alliole accused. Caerre maintained her seat and did not turn, "We speak occasionally," she said, "When we have things we wish the other to learn. And what if I have? He is my brother. We have a right to talk."

"You want Helaf for yourself," Alliole said, "That is selfish, Caerre. What of his own happiness?"

"How can he be happy," Caerre asked, "Here? And do you think that you could take him up into the light and have him leave us?"

"No," Alliole said, and she sighed and would have sat, but she feared to do so in case her action was too much for Caerre's forbearance. "I do not know what to think, Caerre, save that Xoon just charged me with it, as if it were some sin."

Caerre turned to her, at that, and her deep-set eyes glittered, "And is it?" she asked, softly, "Are you ashamed, Alliole, of the affection that you have bred?" Alliole opened her mouth and closed it again. "You have your aunt's truth-seeing," she said at last, tiredly.

"I have good spies," Caerre said, and turned back to her idols, "Run along back to Xoon now, Alliole, and keep at his side. I would guess he contemplates further venture, and I would know what he aims at, since he managed to hold his tongue with me."

Alliole returned, slow and disheartened, to her chambers, to find another unwelcome visitor awaiting her.

"I will not speak further with Xoon," she said firmly, to Sleepghast, who was hovering by the door. She sat upon her bed, and looked around. She almost loathed this place, of which she had most remembrance, for the memories that crowded thick after that first awakening. Sleepghast bobbed and bowed, "I am," he began punctiliously, "Your most humble and obedient servant and in all other ways I would instantly leap to your command. Yet I have a message most urgent and—dare I say it—of unnatural import, that I would impart, touching on your decision to withdraw from my master's expedition."

"I do not wish to listen," she said, firmly. The golden globe glimmered at her bedside. Its surface was embellished, she saw, not only with emeralds but with cats, chasing one another across its surface. The pattern and the color drew her eyes, as her attention wandered in her emotional exhaustion.

"Nevertheless," Sleepghast said, and his demeanor was most humble but deeply obstinate, for he jittered up and down on the spot as he spoke, as if to emphasize his inability to leave with the message unspoken, "I would beg leave of you to attend to this matter, and also prior to your listening, to send your demon far enough away so that if you were upset by my words I would not be most immediately slain by its most frightful majesty. For although upon all worlds I have no wish to offend your ears, I fear that some of what I say may have that unfortunate effect."

She raised her head slowly from the globe and regarded him. He was regarding her almost benevolently, arms outspread, with the loving look that a spider must have the moment before it enfolds its prey.

"Slaarngash," she said, "Wait in the corridor, and come not in before I give the word, save if I am in mortal danger." The demon obeyed, and Sleepghast bowed, a short bob, as it departed. "Beware," she told him, "you would make a succulent morsel for my creature."

The bob turned into another, as Sleepghast feigned to take this as a compliment. He smiled at her, and moved further into the room. "Let me tell you a fable, a true fable," he said, "There is in the antechambers of the Parrar a small chamber, the oldest they say, of the Castle. Within this chamber lies the truth-stone, and one who pays a token to the room's keeper may enter and speak their secret to it. The stone will hold this whisper, until the conditions met by its bearer are enacted. Thereupon this secret will be communicated to those specified by the one who spoke to it, in most wondrous fashion, through the Castle walls. I have spoke to this stone, including the whole Castle in this matter, and the breach of the pact, my death. Do you understand?"

"Yes," she said.

"Further," he said, "If anyone touches the stone and says a lie, it will shatter. It used once to be a plinth, but is now little more than a shard, as it is used in trials of any great weight, for example—murder—" and here he tittered, almost apologetically, so that her whole world shuddered, "— and it has been sundered often before. Yet when I spoke my secret to it, it did not shatter. Do you understand this?"

"Yes," she said, and drew herself up. Slaarngash appeared framed at the window, its seething bulk filling it, its red orbs lambent, so that they flung color about the chamber. Unsheathed at its paws were foot long milky claws, and yellow jaws gaped about a thrashing tongue. The blue stone set in the pommel of the sword surmounted its head. It did not look as if it much needed a weapon now. "The corridor," she ordered it. Sleepghast tittered again, "Well I see that we understand each other," he said, "Perhaps I do not need to—"

"Speak," she said, grimly. "You do."

"Oh we do," he said. He had come so far into the room now that he could have touched her, if he would. Instead he reached out and picked up the golden globe chased with cats and ornamented with emeralds, that encased the eternal amber. He turned it in his hands, examining it with scrupulous care.

"It is simply, lady, that you murdered Reven, and concealed his body with the aid of Caerre's people," he said. "To be most blunt and impolite, but sometimes courtesy tests the patience." Slaarngash reappeared at the window, more frightful than before, and she was for long moments constrained to silence while she fought it to a halt. Sleepghast took advantage of this distraction to secrete the globe somewhere about his person, for she saw no more of it thereafter.

"On what do you base this—rumor?" she said.

"This truth? As the test of the stone tells it. To be sure I do not know that I should tell you," Sleepghast replied, "I would not for all the world cause you further distress. Let me hasten to assure you that I would not pain you with this knowledge save at the most urgent requirement—as I said earlier— of my beloved master, in whose service I would die rather than fail to fulfil his least desire. I would not distress others with this news either, unless you persisted in your foolish attempt to thwart his wishes."

"My foolish attempt," she repeated slowly, and then looked at him. "And what do you gain in this?" she asked.

"The satisfaction of my master," Sleepghast said, and smiled.

It was a sullen and disparate group that gathered before Marre's chambers later that night. Xoon was barely out of his tantrum, and showed signs that his recovery was only partial. Tyall was evidently puzzled as to the reasons behind Alliole's return to the endeavour, and less than whole-hearted to it himself. Alliole was held to it only by the memory of Sleepghast's glib smile. She maintained an appearance of calm, but within her surged the most mixed of emotions, that transmitted themselves through the aether to Slaarngash and caused that creature to display the most fiendish and conflicting of tempers, until Xoon ruled that it be left at the door.

Tyall's part in the plan was most simple, being that if Marre was found within to put on a good countenance and endeavour to distract her attention, whilst Xoon and Alliole took the stair to the higher chambers. Therefore he presented himself boldly at the door, whilst the other two waited behind.

The servant that admitted them informed them that Marre was in the children's quarters, and Tyall, at his most friendly, undertook to direct themselves and not trouble the domestic arrangements. Thus they passed through the outer chambers, where fewer fires burned and not so greatly in the hearths as at Alliole's previous visit, and through the room filled with stars. Xoon snatched up a lantern as they went. Tyall, with a last anxious glance, crossed the landing and headed into the further chambers, with a hearty greeting framed to be spoken loud and so cover any stumbles. Xoon led Alliole, all the more reluctant for the foolhardiness of the theft, up the stairs.

Her heart sank further on entering the fateful chamber where Slaarngash had been birthed. Xoon closed and barred the door behind them, but this lent her no security, for it seemed that she was locked in, rather than any enemy locked out. The triple vaulted roof seemed higher as if forbidding their trespass. The arches seemed lower. Even the chill, as opposed to the heat of her previous visit, struck her as forbidding.

She skirted the black bureau most carefully, noting as she did so a decoration missed on her first visit. At each corner of the bureau were carved fanged, grinning mouths with protruding tongues, apt and gleeful for a sorcerer's study. The carelessly packed books were even more spendthrifty distributed about tables and chairs, as if they had been much consulted of late, and many of the sheets of green crystal were laid aside on the floor.

"Xoon, what happens when this theft is discovered?" she asked, as they passed through the second chamber, but he only answered, "Be careful not to touch the lines on the floor. And I would not look at any manuscript."

So she attended to her feet most carefully and avoided even a glance at the book-stand that still stood there, the leaves of the pages it upheld rustling as would the leaves of a live instead of a carved tree, until they entered the third chamber.

The limbecks and such-like devices of the alchemical laboratory were familiar to her after long contemplation during the incantations of her previous visit. She was able to turn her attention to the massed ranks of bottles with hardly a sideways glance at the bronze head and the giant skeletal snake.

"How will I know it?" she asked, in despair.

"You will know it when you see it," Xoon answered, "It is yours, remember."

Her eyes flitted over some of them, unwilling to closely study their contents, and at one point her reluctant attention was attracted by the sight of the chamber beyond, where she could see that a cage of the furred, limbless creatures was set into the belly of the snake. They looped in vigorous, ceaseless activity around each other, but their attention was fixed on her.

"Xoon," she said, in alarm, as Marre's servant appeared.

"Do not worry," Xoon said, "He is blind and deaf, remember. Just stay out of his way." The servant stepped confidently to the cage, where he passed his hand through the bars to pet the animals. They responded by ceasing their disconcerting regard, and vied with each other, hissing and yarring, for his caress. Something gaudy flitted companionably at his shoulder, an insubstantial winged lizard built of greenish-air, with purple crest along its back, that it raised when its vicious eyes darted to them. It hissed, then coiled itself about the man's body so that it seemed to be a body painting, of vibrant hues about his drab reality.

The man seemed to notice nothing amiss, for after removing his hand from the cage, silently he turned towards them, passing within a hand's breadth of Xoon, so that they could see his upturned eyes, glazed with cataracts. Alliole was struck with his resemblance to the Kings, and stepped back herself, straight into a stand holding a retort that was set upon the floor. It crashed and spread its yellow liquid liberally upon the flags. The servant passed into the further chamber without noticing, whence immediately commenced a horrid, spectral, rustling whose source Alliole could not determine through the intervening walls.

"I'll keep an eye on him," Xoon said, and dropped back, leaving Alliole to nervously scan the racks, cursing her clumsiness.

"He cannot see me, he cannot hear me," she muttered to herself, for some reason all the more unnerved by this. Discounting those obviously empty and those containing creatures, dead or alive, she was left still with several score of vessels, and she had to several times look over them, before, as Xoon as said, she recognized one of them. The bottle was at the top-most shelf and filled almost to the brim with a silvery substance. It struck her eye most remarkably.

"Xoon," she called, "It is here."

"Well, fetch it then," he said, re-appearing at the doorway, "The servant is coming back."

"I cannot," she said acidly. That stopped him. He looked at her blankly, "Well I am not," he said, "I would not touch the stuff of sorcerers, not in their own chambers. Who knows what alarm we would raise, or what mark it would leave on the possessor. We will have to fetch Tyall."

"Xoon," she said again, appalled at his duplicity, "You cannot ask Tyall to touch what you will not." He grinned at her, imperturbably, and then stepped back to allow the servant room to pass through. That they should be watching the man when he so manifestly thought that he was alone was almost more than Alliole, in her state of heightened emotion, could bear. The thing that attended him coiled and glared, its substance passing through his body again and again as it turned itself about to look upon them, and Alliole wondered if he was aware even of that. As he trod, she realized that his path was directly towards the broken retort, but before she could sound the alarm herself, he had stepped in the liquid. Again, he did not seem to notice anything amiss, and continued on, leaving damp footprints for a few steps on. The yellow stuff was a little sticky, but did not seriously retard him.

"Quickly," she said to Xoon, "He may notice soon."

Xoon evidently agreed to this, for he carefully gathered himself and climbed onto the bench, reaching precariously for the bottle. He had to pluck it from its resting place, favoring his injured hand. As he did so something dropped from the ceiling. Xoon immediately jumped back, forgetting the distance from the floor, but recovering himself well enough to make a good landing, without unduly disturbing the clutter. The bottle, flung from his hand in this emergency, hurled out in a silver arc, but was caught before it hit the paving.

Something blinked at them from the work-bench, pallid and small and indefensibly mean, then scurried for the edge of the bench, clutching the bottle, a pink and glossy something that left wet hand prints on the dark wood, and mewed as if in pain whenever it moved. Xoon made a grab for it, and deflected its course, so that it jumped instead for the top of the bottle rack. It dangled there a moment, its ridged, glossy, back showing naked muscles moving as it scrabbled for hand-hold without losing its grasp of the bottle, and then it was hidden behind the racks. They could mark its progress by the sight of the neck of their own bottle as it bobbed between its fellows, and by the sound of its unintelligible giggling.

"Give it back," Xoon demanded, "I command you." Alliole stepped around and blocked any run into the further room, hoping the creature had not noticed her inability to catch it. She wished most fervently, then rejected the wish with equal vigor, for Slaarngash.

"You cannot command me," observed the creature, sticking its head out from amongst the bottles. Its red eye glinted. Its voice was cracked and old.

"I can, demon. Obey me," Xoon said, managing to both deepen and impassion his voice simultaneously, so that his fervor reached out and seemed to clutch at the creature. Alliole was impressed.

"You cannot leave these chambers in any case, if you steal something," the creature observed again. It placed the bottle down. The bottle was as large as it was, so carrying it must be no mean feat.

"On my behalf and my mother's give it here," Xoon said, holding out his hand, "You anger me in your delay."

"Get it yourself," the demon said, rudely, "Certainly I will tell Marre." It sprang from the bottle rack to the drapes of the chamber, scurrying from sight. Both were so struck by this exhibit that they were nearly caught by the second pass of the servant, as he came through with a tray, which he set down upon the bench and proceeded to mix substances upon it, locating his ingredients by touch from those about the rack and the room. They had to scatter themselves about the chamber in order to avoid discovery. Xoon had to first scrape up the remnants of the retort and its contents, then hide it. Then he must cautiously recapture the bottle, before the pair of them could retire. All this was under the untiring and vigorous scrutiny of the ghostly lizard.

"We did it," Xoon said jubilantly, as they passed from the laboratory.

"Do not be so sure," Alliole said, remembering the demon's caution, and its wise, wicked eyes. Her words were proved true quicker than she could realize. As they set foot within the second chamber, their path was barred by the spreading canopy of a vast tree. The rustle of leaves and the creak of its limbs against one another was vast and foreboding, and hidden in the shadows, wicked shapes lurked.

"Dreams, it is a dream only," Xoon said, in the voice of one who having had a sudden and nasty shock is endeavoring to calm himself as much as others, "Bound into the book-stand, I imagine." He seized her arm to keep her close and also to halt her further progress.

"What is the remedy?" she asked.

"I do not know," he said. He stopped himself beside her and frowned, "I would say it cannot harm us, except by provoking our own fears as is usual in dream-working. I would also say its purpose is to deceive our eyes, so that we will step by accident upon the markings on the floor. Then all hell would be let loose."

"Did you expect this?" she asked, and he nodded. "Something like," he admitted, "But I did not want to discourage you."

"I thought the demon let us off easy," she said. "Who of us has the better memory?" Oak leaves were thick about them. A tracery of limbs cut off all sight of floor and ceiling. The air was choked with growth and decay.

"You do," Xoon said, querulously, "Why do you think I brought you? I cannot even remember the number of paces to the door." She closed her eyes and mustered her courage to her. The action gave her an idea, for had not the blind servant passed through the chamber several times without fear? She could summon the chamber as it once was in her mind's eye, and the geometric lines of ebony and opal inlaid on the floor. Also the Kings and the events of the previous days between them had taken her to the pitch that she truly believed that nothing born from dreams could scare her. So she paid no heed to the mutterings that, as she stepped deeper into the room, seemed to thicken about her. She paid no heed to the way the stench of rot seemed to congeal the air. But she kept her eyes shut, preferring not to trust to sight of the twined branches and boles, and the multitudinous eyes blinking from the baleful shadows, drawing ever nearer.

"Hurry," Xoon said, nervously at her side.

"Do you wish to pass this chamber or not?" she replied. She took twelve steps to the side wall. When she reached out she could brush against it, although when she opened her eyes again she saw only rank wood. This confused her and she hastily shut her eyes again. They were both gasping for air, and a small panicked voice started to sing in her soul, that she could not breathe, that she would faint and sprawl across the invisible, diabolical geometry of the floor. She shut her eyes again, and took the number of steps required to reach the other side, as she remembered, taking larger steps and directing her charge also, when she thought they would be passing near the lines. Once behind her Xoon choked a yell and stumbled. "One of the candle holders," he said, bending and groping, all but losing hold of her arm until her sharp cry reminded him to take fresh grasp, "It is all right. I have not moved it."

After that it was easy, for she brushed along the far wall until she felt an entrance. She then stepped through. Xoon cried joyously beside her, and she found heart to open her eyes.

"Never do that again," she said, disinterestedly, as she saw the cluttered study beyond, hearteningly normal. She did not really expect him to pay attention to the request. She glanced behind, and saw the second chamber laid out as previous, although her glance skimmed over the oaken carvery of the book-stand without really wanting to take it in. She took several deep breaths. Xoon sprang ahead, the bottle swinging in his hand, and was most of the way across the chamber before the next obstacle became apparent. The dark bureau came sliding across, the click of its claws sounding on the polished flags, and smashing through the opaque crystal sheets set about the floor. Its four mouths were agape and panting. It blocked the door. Its load of mysterious and precious objects shifted and slid. The skull shattered as it hit the flags, the gems rolled. Paper fluttered and swooped about its rapidly moving legs. A pallid homunculus, surprised and uncovered, reared on its hind legs and looked around short-sightedly. On reaching its new position, the bureau commenced to stamp its legs threateningly, swaying from side to side.

As it did so, further objects were shed from it, including the ink bottles, which smashed, splattering color about the walls. By this time Xoon had flung a half dozen curses at it, causing the bureau to bristle. Spikes that had been folded at its side rose, and its back arched malevolently, cat-like, scattering the last of its contents to the floor. The ugly statuette followed the pot of glue to the ground, sticking semi-upright there. Finally only the homunculus remained, balancing on the bucking surface, and now surveying them with interest. Also a skeletal hand had found some fracture in the wood in which to cling, and was observed making obscene gestures during the ensuing fracas.

"I suppose she will have heard that," Alliole said, miserably.

"This place is uncommonly thick-walled," Xoon said, "I have been downstairs when Marre has been summoning the most awful phantasms above, that screamed and howled by the hour I am told, and yet I heard nothing, although I would have thought to, with such giant flues." He pointed to the bulworks in the walls, from which the intense heat of the summonings came. "Out of my way, creature," he directed the bureau, and when it refused to comply he flung himself at it, attempting to wrestle it from the doorway.

"Xoon," Alliole said, nervously, as the multiple wooden mouths gaped and struck at him, emitting sticky sap, but she soon saw that it was as all demons of the family, excepting Slaarngash, for the bureau did not harm him. It did however refuse to yield. After a short tussle, with no ground gained, Xoon came back to her.

"You'll have to help me," he said. "Obstinate furniture," he threatened the bureau, "I'll have you smashed for firewood; and you," he directed the hand, "Will be tied down in that position and used as a cloak stand." This stopped it in mid-caper.

"I think it will have no prohibition against harming me," Alliole said, and looked around, "The fires are down. Perhaps we can climb down the flues."

"I can," Xoon pointed out, nobly, "You cannot." The bureau bristled and prowled, making a short foray from the door as if to taunt them, before resuming its position. Its wooden spines and teeth clicked, most malevolently. Xoon contemplated it, while Alliole looked in dismay at the formerly orderly chamber.

"Then we can wait here and be found," she said, "Either when the servant next enters and discovers this disarray, or when Marre decides to come upstairs."

Xoon shook his head. "No, the matter is to get it away from the door long enough for you to pass through," he said, "I am sure the stair is too narrow for it to follow. Then I can go down the flue, and hope to find the right fireplace."

"It cannot bite off my hands," Alliole pointed out, "But it can do me other mischief. And how will I unbolt the door?"

"Easy," Xoon said, evidently inspired. He leant across the bureau and fumbled with the bolt, drawing it at last, and ignoring the feeble efforts of homunculus and skeletal hand to dissuade him (the hand by ruffling his hair, which irritated him exceedingly). Then he cast about upon the floor, coming up with the broken fragments of the glue-pot, into which he scraped as much of its contents as he could. He took up the already well-pasted statuette also. Then he approached the bureau, and managed, with a deft movement to jam the glue pot in one mouth and the statuette in the other, so that even as its jaws came gnashing down, splintering the crockery into shards, they were as yet too gummed to cause damage.

"Quickly," Xoon said, and he shoved at it. Alliole obeyed and leant her weight to it, not without nervous glances at the furiously working jaws of the thing. The bureau managed other retaliation, stamping at her feet with its wooden paws. Together they managed to get it back against the book-cases, but Alliole turned in time to see that the homunculus had profited by their exertion, and was already disappearing out the door.

"Hurry," she called to Xoon, "We are about to be discovered." She went after it, and just in time. The bureau, with a mighty heave, forced Xoon into a corner and came back-pedalling towards her. She slipped outside, and with a splintering of wood that sounded most baleful, the bureau broad-sided the entrance. Once, twice, and in the pause before the third, she shouldered the door shut. She dashed down the stairs, in time to see the homunculus, evidently uncertain of direction, turn down the further stair, thereby missing Marre entirely. She stamped her foot at it. The demon gave her a flustered look, then vanished behind a tapestry. "If Slaarngash were here it would hunt you like a rat," she whispered to it, "And if you do not stay put there until I am gone, I will summon it."

She stepped back into the corridor, and managed with a movement to catch Tyall's eye. He was sitting with a small boy on his knee, and a slender girl, almost at adolescence, at his side. They must be the pair Reven had spoken of. Marre was not in sight, but the attention of the three was fixed on something beyond her view, so she guessed where she was. Tyall withdrew, gracefully, and joined her in the corridor.

"Quickly," she whispered, "One of her creatures has escaped and will give the alarm soon enough." As they did so, they heard an outcry from the chambers lower down, and shortly after Xoon joined them, laughing breathlessly. He was slightly singed at the edges, although any soot was invisible in his disordered hair. He still held the silver bottle, but the wax stopper had melted slightly, and the glass was smoked.

"Into the kitchens," he sang out, before they had time to hush him. Marre's voice came from the further chamber, "Who is that?" querulous and sickly. The younger of the children peeped out at them, but Tyall saved the day, grinning and winking, so that the boy giggled and reported back only, "Mother, Tyall is making fun of me."

"We'd better be gone then, before there is any discovery," Xoon said—quietly—and swept them both before him, a comradely arm on each shoulder. Both protested but he hushed them by simply reminding them of the outcry that would surely follow. "Better to be safely gone," he said, "And in the celebrations that will attend our return this will be forgiven."

"Or in the doom-saying," Tyall said to Alliole worriedly, as he accompanied her to her chambers, leaving Xoon delighted and hasty, to attend to matters of provisioning and departure.

"I suppose if we spend the night in one of the closer halls it will not be too bad," she said, dismally, "And at least we will be away from discovery, as Xoon says." What worried her most was her unspoken wish, to carry some news to her comrades in the Catacombs, and to Helaf in particular, that she was not deserting them, and that discovery threatened on every side. She wished to warn them most particularly of Sleepghast, but did not know how to announce this without precipitating action perhaps rash and hasty, and as doubtful as the enterprise she now embarked upon.

"You are intent on keeping this a secret?" she asked Tyall, as Slaarngash gathered up items of clothing and such, as she thought would be needful.

"I have to," he said, simply, and his brow creased in his doubt and uncertainty, "Otherwise it would be forbidden."

"I wish it was," she said, and he assented with the same breath, looking most unhappy. It was an ill-favored start to the expedition. ✹

Chapter Fifteen

THEY RETURNED TO XOON, Alliole keeping a vain watch out for Anna. They found that he had gathered up Lyde, and was again refusing to tell her anything but taunts and half truths, managing nevertheless and most cunningly to maintain her interest, so that she tagged along. Tyall slipped to his own chambers to retrieve his weapons and armor. He returned even more out of spirits.

Slaarngash's temper had not improved, and as they set out it turned mutinous, several times refusing direct commands. Alliole abruptly remembered Marre's warning words when she had first invoked it. Had not Marre said that if her character changed, so would Slaarngash's bindings fray, and if she were ever untrue to herself, the bindings would break. Did she stand witness to just such a change? She felt that she barely knew enough of herself to start with to know if any such change occurred. Memory and self were irretrievably precious to her, and even a little lost or altered was too much almost to bear. She felt the return of the terrible uncertainty that had attended her first waking from amnesia. Slaarngash was little enough company at the best of times, but laggard, sullen, and intractable, was worse than Marre. It came to heel only when she attended nothing else, and took the first opportunity of her switching her attention to slink off again into a dead end— a secret passage that went nowhere reached by a trap-door she could not open without its aid, to an antechamber, where she found it devouring centuries-old tapestries from the walls.

"I raised a city once, and brought it here," Slaarngash told her. She disbelieved it.

They made swift journey through the night-Castle, despite Slaarngash. Alliole made feverish protestation that she should be allowed to unseal the bottle before quitting the precincts, but Xoon ignored her until they were before the door of the Hall of Masks. The Wheel swam in a pool of silver radiance behind, and before the bulwarks Tiralgon set up had been put to one side. Alliole examined them carefully and saw that with a little effort they could be propped against the door again. That eased her mind of one misgiving at least. As Xoon laid his hand upon the door, she asked again, "Do we wish to prepare before further journeying?"

"Not until we are past the galleries," Xoon said, starting guiltily.

"Where have I heard that before?" Lyde said, but she followed as they opened the doors and trooped through.

"Are we so certain of our powers," Alliole said again, "As to dare the Kings at night in their own domain?" No-one answered her. Spiders dropped from the lintel of the door and writhed upon the floor. Perforce, they had to tread squirming hordes into the flags as they marched. Echoes scurried through the hall from the seethings and sly scuttlings of its busy insect inhabitants. Without sight, hearing took on redoubled virtue, and Alliole could imagine them slithering through eye holes and stiff-patterned mouths, their small tracks dislodging the dust on the gilding, which pattered onto the myriad further masks below and caused further diminutive but ceaseless echo so that in the dark, the hall took on shifting and infinite life.

Xoon led them through the galleries, at Alliole's direction, and they all took heart—for they did not quite dare to light a lantern—that after his father, he could see in the dark. Alliole was almost relieved to pass through the low mouths of the galleries and so beyond Marre's reach, although she knew not what dweller this evil maze contained. Whatever it was, it did not trouble them, for again they won through to the hall with the fallen roof, and never was Alliole so glad to reach open air.

Xoon dropped down at the fallen column where they had rested at their first memorable journey there. The others followed his example, keeping an uneasy eye out, for the feeling was strong that there were watchers at both thresholds. Alliole set Slaarngash sentry at a recess in the column, where it could view the further entrance and yet remain unseen in the shadows. Xoon pulled the silvery bottle from the pack in which he had placed it, and examined it carefully.

"Do we just unseal it?" Alliole asked. "Is it fume or liquid?"

"You mean, do you inhale or drink it?" Xoon said. "I do not know." He shook the bottle vigorously, and tipped it to examine its wide-bellied base, before Lyde, horrified, snatched it from him.

"Do not treat it so," she said, her eyes wide. "Where did you get it?"

"Marre," Xoon said, his look combining both guilt and shiftiness, yet maintaining an unbelievable innocence.

"She did not give it to you," Lyde said, examining the seal carefully, and pressing back the wax where she saw it was a little broken.

"No," he said. The wax would not reshape properly. Lyde shook Syl free from her neck, and muttered a word, so that a thin blue flame crest licked eerily from the creature's spine. She sealed the wax afresh with this fire. A shiver ran up Alliole's back, for Xoon's eyes reflected the light like a cat's.

"You must take great care with these things," Lyde said, "Even a slight crack or discoloration can taint the containment spell, and if that is spoiled then the magic is untrustworthy." Syl opened its bottomless gaze. Xoon, Alliole and Tyall exchanged furtive glances over Lyde's bent head.

"How do we re-enact it then?" Xoon asked.

"What is it?" Lyde said.

"Alliole's memories."

"I don't think you can." Lyde frowned and bent to her task, "Not without knowledge of the cantrip invoked when it was sealed, and such would be personal to the sorcerer."

"What about the Voice?" Xoon said, "That is what we are really after. Can we sift the Voice from it, from Alliole's memories?"

"Oh, is that it then? That is possible," Lyde admitted, "That is something less integral to the self. We would have to destroy the containment spell to invoke it, that is all."

"And what would that do?" Alliole interjected, her mouth dry.

"Well, everything not caught up in the ritual would be lost," Lyde said, "If we did it here. That is everything not about the Voice. You did steal this, didn't you? The more personal aspects are useless without the proper seals to rebind them to the person concerned. Something general, like the Voice, can be re-enacted without so much loss, assuming the containment spell has held."

"What happens to my memories?" Alliole asked.

"So much smoke," Lyde said, with no pity, drawing her fingers up.

"Then there is no hope," she said blankly. A dry sob wrenched in her throat, for the tenuous memories sifting through her phantom grasp upwards into the air. Xoon frowned furiously, "I did not think it would be so difficult."

"It would not be," Lyde said, "Under normal circumstances."

Tyall shifted, uncomfortably, and then, as Helaf had, came over to Alliole, and drew her close, as though defending her. "We should not go on with this plan," he said quietly, "We seek an echo through a dream, and if we must waste half our answer, then it is not worth the loss, at least not to Alliole."

"We can still do it if Alliole agrees," Lyde said, smoothly.

"So this is your plan," Alliole said, slowly.

"I do not know what you mean," Lyde said, but too sharply after her previous sincerity. "It is Xoon's plan, not mine."

"I do not believe it would be so difficult," Alliole cried, "You seek to rob me of my memory, for once and all." Another sob robbed her of words, for although she did not speak it yet she had to hold it in her throat and it swelled there, blocking speech and almost breath. After all the trials she had undergone, to miss this recovery seemed robbery of half her chance of regaining herself, and plunged her into a very deep pit of self-pity.

"Oh, it is not so bad," Xoon said, urgently, "And it is half my fault for my mishandling of it from the start. You must understand, Alliole, it is for the greater good. Any sacrifice you make will be honored by later generations. You will be a hero."

"Shhh, Xoon," Tyall said, again hopelessly reminding Alliole of Helaf with Caerre, for now he made as if to block her ears against Xoon's railings, a movement that converted into stroking her hair. "It is not fair to ask her to make this sacrifice."

Lyde sat back and surveyed them smugly. "Well, if Alliole and Tyall are set against this expedition we must return," she said, and she had surely not gauged the effect of her words on Xoon before she spoke them, for he flew at once into a very great temper, actually pummelling at the pillar and tearing at his hair. In his first fury he was speechless, or he might have said things that would have turned Alliole from her subsequent course altogether.

Tyall surveyed Xoon hopelessly and then left Alliole to attend to his friend, leaving her to consider. First what was it, this memory that had somehow become detached from her? Surely it was not usual to be so afflicted, and surely most people carried their memories about with them, warm and close in their skulls and would be most aghast at their disappearance. Yet she could survey their loss disinterestedly, for it would be the second time she had been thus bereaved, and although she missed them, paradoxically she could not remember any other way of living. And she had garnered up enough fresh store in these last days, to specifically require none previous to waking in a stone chamber, and mistaking a painted wall for the sky.

Her lack of curiosity towards the cause of her injury both relieved and appalled her, for she realized her appetite for knowledge had been sated. She had no desire for the truth any more. As she spelt this out within herself, Slaarngash, coiled forgotten on the pillar head above them, raised itself up and howled. And no more sense could she get from that creature from then until the day it was no more.

"Xoon," she said, at last, emerging from her thought, and moved it must be said more with the impulse of kindness, of protectiveness towards him, than by any reckoning on the consequences to herself if the expedition failed, "Xoon, it is all right. I have assented. Tell him, Tyall."

Tyall, who had in this interval assuaged the worst of Xoon's temper, looked at her over his friend's head, as dubious and hopeless as he had in her chambers before their embarkation. "Do you hear that?" he said to Xoon nevertheless, gently, "She consents, Xoon if you must have it."

"He is spoiled," Lyde muttered, ill-favouredly. She tossed the bottle in her hand as if weighing it.

"Careful," both Tyall and Alliole said simultaneously, so that Xoon raised his head to see what she was doing.

"Serve you right if I dropped it," Lyde said, "If you will speak so suddenly," and she scowled. But evidently she did not quite dare any injury—or perhaps her desire to retain their regard held her back—for she placed the bottle immediately upon the ground, and began to trace geometric shapes into the dirt around it, mumbling to herself very much in Marre's manner. Syl wound around her arm to take a look, and she pushed it back up beyond her elbow, "Don't you interfere," she admonished it, and then, "Alliole come and sit here. Tyall there. Xoon, if you will not be quiet, sit somewhere out of earshot."

Xoon took several deep breaths, and a beam spread across his tear-stained face, "Thank you, thank you, thank you, Alliole," he said.

"Xoon," Lyde said, chidingly, gesturing for silence.

"I won't forget this ever," Xoon said, ignoring her, his face radiant, although blotched with red, "I promise, I promise I will remember this forever."

"Xoon," Lyde cried again, her voice exasperated. With much mock shushing, and more noise than strictly necessary, Xoon retired.

Lyde's hair fell across her face, her brow furrowed in concentration, and words started spilling not just from herself, but from the air. She took a knife from the belt at her side, and with it made several passes, blade uppermost.

"I'll need blood," she muttered, in careful rhythm so as not to disturb the cadences of that other speech.

"How much?"

"Alliole's will do—not much, but someone else's if that is not possible." She leant again over the bottle, which had begun to shed a faint luminosity.

"What if the Kings interrupt us?" Xoon interjected, but Tyall hushed him. Before Alliole could muster herself, Tyall had held out his hand, which Lyde, eyes unseeing, took and pierced his palm with the tip of the knife, and then turned over the bottle so that the blood splattered upon the seal. Tyall grinned whitely, "Fair's fair," he said, as Lyde dropped her hold. She again made eldritch signs about the bottle with the knife, stabbing its point into the earth, at each of the cardinal points and angles of the geometry she had invoked. The stuff in the bottle seethed.

Then passed an unguessably long period of time, in which Lyde swayed and sang, and occasionally indicated to Alliole her responses. The wind rose, and clouds scurried to cover and uncover the moon, visible through the hole in the roof. It was long enough in any case for Alliole to become bored and her surroundings to establish themselves as thoroughly uncomfortable. Tyall busied himself bandaging his hand, as he had to renew the dressing several times before the blood-flow was staunched. Time wore on and on. Xoon rose and walked a little way, but hastily came back when the wind strengthened, for it started to bell amongst the ruins in a tone most sinister and sorrowful. Then the turn of the night came on, when it is said the dying most easily relinquish their grasp upon the earth. At this time the stuff in the bottle was boiling, and just at the ebb of the night-tide, its seal exploded.

All jumped, all winced alike as the flecks of wax flicked about them. Xoon raised his hands to shield his eyes, and did not for a while lower them. Silver mist coiled out of the bottle's mouth, a most tenacious yet insubstantial aether. It followed the outlines of the geometric shapes in the ground, yet as it flowed, kept all together, a long trail of mist within which scenes from a life—her life or that of the Voice or many memories, for they meant nothing to Alliole thus seen—could be gleaned, in momentary condensations of the vapors, dispersed in an instant and yet seeming to retain the soul of the glimpse that had in them been enacted. Tyall cried out all at once, and she wondered what he had seen.

At the point where the foremost tip of the mist had fully traced the outlines it was fully gathered in the air and the bottle was palpably empty. Lyde sighed with relief and sat back, "Well I timed that right anyway," she said. Her voice was hoarse. The mist seemed to draw itself together, further consolidating the fantastic images that danced within, and to test the boundaries of the space beyond the geometric outlines. Then it poured forward steadily and smoothly, and diffused as it did so, so that it spread irrecoverably. Alliole this time cried out in horror, for it was a dreadful thing to thus witness yourself dissipating into the air. But out of the dissolution one strand remained, that wove itself around the geometric outlines once again, thickening as it did so, as if drawing further remnants to itself. It then turned again outward, this time maintaining its shape.

"What do I do?" Alliole asked in panic.

"Let it go where it will," Lyde said. The mist coiled first around Tyall, nuzzling his face, but then found the ear-ring and fled from him, all but dissipating. It recovered and wound itself around the circle, towards Alliole, who made no effort to elude it, but could not welcome it. Its unnatural movement filled her with horror. It touched at her cheek and throat, and then made an effort to force her lips, but its wisp-strength was no avail.

"Open your mouth," Xoon said, again urgently. She remembered the Voice, wailing feeble and remorseless in an endless maze of chambers, corridors and stairs, and here at the pinch, her courage failed her. She turned her face away. The animate vapor followed her, fanning her face with its cool dewiness.

"Admit it," Lyde advised, more tranquilly, "It will not hold together long, under these conditions."

"Do I have to?" she asked, but as she opened her lips, she felt a rush of air and a whisper go past her, seeking. "Tricked," she said, disgruntled. The whisper receded. The last trace of silver lifted from the air.

Silence.

"What do I do now?" she said, testing the calm. Then swallowed.

"How do you feel?"

"Fine."

"No different?" Xoon said. He sounded disappointed.

"No, should I?" she said.

Silence again.

"Now what?" Lyde asked, testily. Her hoarseness had returned. She coughed, then reached for the wine skin slung on the side of one of the packs.

"Alliole has to go to sleep," Xoon said, seeming to grab an answer from anywhere.

"To sleep?" Alliole said, "Here?"

"Yes, to sleep," Xoon said, recovering his certainty, "And when you wake you can tell us where the Voice was coming from, for it will surely return to you, and we will follow your directions."

"Xoon," she said, "I cannot sleep on command."

"Yes you can," he said, and leapt up. "You must be very tired. It has been a long night," said as if in deep sympathy. He laid out his cloak and borrowed Tyall's, then removed perishable and breakable items from several packs and made cushions of them. Thus made comfortable, Alliole had no choice but to lie down. The three regarded her—Xoon gravely, Lyde blankly and Tyall attempting to hide a smile, and as a result as solemn as Xoon.

"How is your hand?" she asked him.

"Fine," he said, laconically, "Xoon and I, we are a fine pair of cripples."

Xoon scowled at the comparison, and then brightened. "Perhaps you should sleep as well, Tyall," he said, evidently thinking it cunning strategy, "After all the mist touched you, too." Tyall shook his head determinedly, and although Xoon teased, he would not be further drawn. Some merriment returned to the expedition, although Alliole remained sleepless until dawn. In fact, as is the nature of such things, the others fell asleep before her. She felt obliged to maintain some watch other than the unreliable Slaarngash, and so rose again, draping the cloaks over their owners.

Evidently however they had not penetrated far enough into the ruin for the Kings to notice them, for although she heard their ghastly ululations several times in the remainder of the night, they were all distant, and she saw no other sign of them. Tyall woke just before dawn and came over to where she sat, at a distance from the others. She thought that he meant to scold her for not sleeping, but he only said, "Xoon did not used to get out of temper so frequently. It is because he is tired and scared, I suppose."

"This quest becomes more foolish by the hour," she said, recognizing his words as an apology and uncertain as to how to accept them. "It is not your fault." He rubbed at his emerging beard, ruefully, "They will notice us gone by mid-morning, I expect. Did you think to leave a message?"

"No," she said, "But Sleepghast knows. He can allay their worst fears."

"Sleepghast?" Tyall said, "He will fill their ears with lies, and send hordes to the truth-stone to test his veracity."

She stilled at that, "He is known for his lies, then?"

Tyall laughed, "He has a reputation for educated guessing," he said, so glibly that he must surely be quoting the Neve, "The servants think that he has witch-powers but he is just uncommon shrewd."

"Whose ambition does he serve?" she asked, wondering if she had been proved gullible. But he did not understand and only answered, "Xoon's. You should be asleep if you are asking after such obvious answer." He guided her back to her make-shift couch, and sat down beside her to block the worst of the wind and the emerging sun. Although she did not think that she would sleep she soon did, and had no recollection of events for sometime after.

When she awoke she was standing in the hall containing the Great Masks. The shadows of evening were long and thick, streaming from their silver faces as if their eyes cast them. She swayed on her feet in surprise, and because there was no power in her legs, but Tyall caught her before she hit the ground.

"She's just brought us back here. This is no use," Xoon was complaining loudly, when she awoke again, plunging as if from a great height into consciousness from confused and frightening dreams.

"You let me walk in my sleep," she gasped, the world re-consolidating around her as she grasped the situation. This relieved her for the shock of her initial waking had robbed her of all certainty. She shook her head, for there was an unaccustomed weight upon it.

"Yes," Lyde said.

"Tyall would not let us wake you," Xoon said smoothly. Tyall was supporting her back so she could look at him only sideways. "You too," she said, and lifted herself on her elbows by her own efforts. Despite her rejection he helped her to sit and remained kneeling behind her, out of sight.

"Xoon, after the last disaster," she said, and looked around wildly, "It is too late, we cannot get back before dark."

Xoon shrugged, "It is not my fault. You led us here."

She shook her head again, realizing what had happened. Whatever memory had entered with the Voice had obviously settled further, for an intangible substance had returned to her inner ear, that had been absent so long, and the feeling of a counter-weight was strong in her soul. The weight pressed against her skull, so that she shook and gasped and would not make sense for several minutes despite the others' urgings.

"Where is Slaarngash?" she asked at the end, but was met with blank looks and shrugs.

"It did not follow us," Tyall said, quietly from behind, "I suppose your authority slept with you. Alliole, I did not dare wake you, from my own experience, but I several times tried to avert your course. Believe me."

"Did I say anything?" she asked, wishing that she could clutch her head, and also that the weight pressing against her skull had a shape and a purpose. It was trying to tell her something. "Are you sure I am as yet awake?"

"Oh yes, you are much more interesting company," Xoon said, "We thought, Alliole, that before dark we would retire to one of the smaller chambers and fortify it."

"You did not say anything, " Tyall said, then sharply, "Xoon, why do you not attend to that yourself. Can you not see that Alliole is ill?"

"She looks all right to me," Xoon said. Their voices swirled around her, again losing all meaning, for she realized that the weight upon her head was a palm and five fingers, outspread.

"Take your hand off me," she cried to Tyall, but he only raised both his when she turned on him, while the weight remained.

"There is something on my head," she said, futilely trying to brush at it.

"I told you this would happen," Lyde observed.

"Oh that's very helpful," Xoon snarled. Tyall said, merely, "There is nothing there, Alliole, nothing real. What do you feel?"

"A hand," she said, "It is hurting, it is laid so heavy upon me."

"It is some symbol," Xoon guessed. "Responsibility? Perhaps my aunts are angry and have prepared a spectacular sorcery."

"Xoon, I would prepare the room if I were you," Tyall said—for him, icily. "If Alliole comes not to herself, we will not have her demon."

"Why revile me?" Xoon squawked in protest. "Look, she lacks hands, perhaps she summoned it herself from her dream. Oh alright, ignore my suggestions. They are unimportant. I'll do all the work then. Don't mind me." Tyall's concern however was focused purely on Alliole, for he came forward again, and supported her as she shook and shivered in the evening's gloom, and passed and re-passed his hand across her hair, to show her that there was nothing there. Xoon scrambled to his feet, and taking Lyde, departed on their search.

"I can still feel it," she cried, despite Tyall's best endeavors.

"Is it warm or cold?" he asked.

"Cold," she said, "And getting colder."

"A man's hand or a woman's?"

"Neither, it is too large for either." So saying, she scrambled to her feet, awkward and unwieldy herself now. She first staggered, but then forced her feet to support her and made her way to the small entrance she had examined long ago on the far wall. It was in her mind that it was Tiralgon's hand, and she was going to shout down into the Catacombs, through all the inter-linking maze of corridors to reach him, search for him forever if need be, to tell him to cease his tricks. But as she swayed at the entrance she saw the hand-print set into the stone wall there, that she had thought was ornamentation. She knew at once the line of the palm, the individual weight of the fingers. She flailed at Tyall in her fright and said, "See this is it. This is why the dream brought me here." He looked at it and frowned, then scrambled onto a semi-buried block of stone that lay beside it, to stand level with it. He spread his own hand over it, looking down at her a moment and then placing it square. He covered most of the palm, but neither thumb nor fingers of the other hand with his own.

"It must cover half your head," he said.

"What is it?"

"I don't know," he said, "It is not the Kings." He stepped back abstractedly to further examine it, and fell off the block on which he balanced. She did not even smile. He picked himself up and brushed himself off, "Creature," he cried in a loud voice, at it, "Desist in your importunings. We have heard you. Cease this torment." Then in an abrupt change in pitch and tone, to her kindly, "Did that help?"

"No," she said.

"We had better get inside with the others," he said, "Can you call your demon?"

"I do not think it is any longer in my control," she said, "And certainly not with this burden so heavy on me."

"It is terrible," he said, earnestly, as he needlessly took her arm to guide her back, again recalling Helaf's characteristic gesture, "It is terrible when dreams overlap into reality, but you must remember this. It is but a dream. It cannot hurt you, unless under its influence you harm yourself. I know this. I know."

"It is not just a dream," she said, "It is something coming to life through a dream, that we have awoken with our journeying. Is it the Voice do you think? Would it have a body?"

"I do not know," he answered, but he shuddered as he said it, "I think if it did it would a small body, puling and sickly. I do not think the Voice is strong. It is just persistent. It surely would not have a body so large as to create that hand-print?"

"It is weak now," she answered, "Through long denial. Perhaps once it was strong, and now, but now what would we see?"

He left this question unanswered, hurrying through to the chamber where the others waited.

"See," Xoon said, proudly, "We can build up this rubble to block the door, once you are inside of course, and Lyde will cause it to solidify, so that none can get in."

"Or out," Lyde said, dismally.

"Then we can stay here until dawn, and be on our way," Xoon finished. He ushered them both through into the small room and then commenced filling in the entrance, a task in which Tyall aided.

"We could not find an intact chamber on the second floor," Xoon said, as they worked, "For all the roof is open. So although they can come at us from all sides here, nevertheless it is better to be on the ground than above, where they can pour unhindered through the ceiling."

"How will we sleep, if they are all around?" Tyall wondered. All blanched at the thought of being thus surrounded.

"We will manage," Xoon said, nevertheless maintaining his appearance of cheer wonderfully, "And in any case, Alliole will not be allowed to sleep, for we cannot follow her at night and there will be nowhere for her to go but to march around the room. Is that not right?"

"I'll sleep when I can," she answered, but doubted it also.

"She has a phantom hand on her head," Tyall said.

"Also upon my shoulder," Alliole corrected.

"You did not say. . . ."

"It has just now come upon me," she said, "I think the sun has gone down."

Xoon and Lyde gazed upon her, open mouthed, as Tyall hurriedly told her story.

"Ah, I knew you would not fail, Alliole," Xoon cried, jubilantly. "Why this must be why you have brought us here. There is some message for me in it." He had been working on the outside of the barricade, and now that it was more than three quarters risen he scrambled over, and aided Tyall in finishing the remainder.

"If there is I wish it hurry and tell me," Alliole said, "For it is most unpleasant and I would that it were over. Xoon, I am never trusting you again." He grinned, and dodged any proper answer, "I think you are most uncommon brave," he said, instead, "If there were ghostly hands upon me I would be bawling like anything." Alliole gave him a look expressive of her own wish in that direction.

It was several hours before the barricade was finished, for Lyde had to again enact a sorcerous vigil similar to the one of the previous night. They spent the entire interval in wondering if it would be finished in time. It was hard to see what she had done, save when the luminous flash of the knife blade sawed through the air, because the room was as pitch.

"I vote for a light," Xoon said at last, "Lyde, could you. . . ."

"What if they see," Tyall asked, "through a chink or crack?"

"There is no gap. This is a most solid structure," Xoon said, complacently. "And besides, it is comfort to have a light, however unnatural."

"You can talk," Lyde said. She sounded tired.

"Even cats cannot see in total darkness," Xoon said. He sound irritated, and from there it would be but a short slide into petulance.

"A light," Alliole said, "A light please, for there are more hands upon me in the darkness, and I fear that they will drag me under."

Syl flared immediately around Lyde's neck, slithering to first her cupped hand and then the floor, where it flowered in a column, dim and spectral blue, but light nevertheless. The only discomfort Lyde appeared to suffer from this spontaneous combustion was that the draft raised by the fire blew her hair and clothes about. Alliole had not attention or desire to wonder whether this was by design or accident, whether Lyde truly was immune to fire or just her own part of it. In the dark other hands had attached themselves to her, smaller ones, one pair about her waist, and a last grasped at her wrist, as if to lead her, together with the by now oppressive weight of the first pair. With the light, the last pair that had attached itself fled, so that she thought it timid, but the other two remained.

The room thus illuminated showed bare. Dust settled from the ceiling to the floor but it was otherwise intact and unwindowed. The door looked now like a rampart of packed earth, and on its surface was etched a mottled design of unnatural complexity. Lyde was exhausted, Xoon alert and seemingly anxious only as to the success of his expedition, for his gaze was inward and calculating. Tyall's eyes were full of misgivings, and directed at her.

"There is nothing there," Tyall said, and came over to her again. He sat himself next to her, and held her himself. It was a comfort to share his warmth, "And if there is, why we three will be enough to pull you back, if they seek to take you."

"One at my shoulder, wris,t and waist," she cried, in horror, "They are standing there at my shoulder, at my side, in front of me. That is what they wanted me to see."

"They? Who?"

"I do not know, I do not know. I wish I had never seen it, that hand-print. That is what has inspired me."

"If there are three it cannot be the Voice," Tyall said flatly, "It is singular."

"Leave me alone," Alliole cried, in great despair, "Leave me."

"We can't. The door is blocked," Xoon said. Both Tyall and Lyde turned on him, and spared Alliole the labor. ✳

Chapter Sixteen

ALLIOLE BECAME AWARE as the evening progressed of Tyall's own discomfort. Clearly he saw her suffering and apprehended that if she had not been there, the one so under duress would be himself. This thought clearly troubled him, for he attended to her with more than necessary vigor.

Their vigil was further made unpleasant by their discovery by the Kings. About mid-way through the time, a single lurker or possibly a pair snuffled about the room, creaking together with their insane voices, testing, slyly and from each direction, the approaches and the strength of the walls. They were all waiting for it, but nevertheless when the patter from above showed that the Kings were testing the ceiling, nevertheless it was the greatest trial yet, disregarding the unwelcome presence of several pairs of spectral hands.

"Even if they break in," Lyde said, as loosened dust drifted from the ceiling. Tyall coughed and recovered. "Even if they break in," she repeated, "They are bound to go around the course of the sigil. We can slay them as they go past."

"So soon despondent?" Xoon mocked, "The door will hold."

"What about the ceiling?" Tyall asked. No one answered that. The sounds ceased a long while, seeming longer to those straining their ears in the room below.

Then with a rush and a gust, the nightmare was upon them. Kings were evidently outside, in great number, for there were sounds upon the ceiling, and the door, upon the walls. There were scrapings at the corners and for several horrible minutes they were convinced something was digging beneath the floor. Most of the noises were random and meaningless. Sounds were of pattering feet, running about in a purposeless manner, and not so much thumps, as pattings, as falterings. No conversation came, no communication, nothing that would give them any focus. Also the Kings somehow imported their own atmosphere into the room, a feeling of oppressive horror that reminded Alliole of the demonic air that had first accompanied Slaarngash. There was nothing that could be done to fight this feeling, for it simply permeated into the air, and soaked the walls. Spirits and courage failed before it, until they could only sit and wait it out. In her abstraction Lyde allowed Syl to almost reform, until Alliole cried, "The hand is upon my wrist again," and the flame flared anew, driving it away as before.

That was the worst of it. Sometime after the Kings retreated, having made no great effort to breach the walls of the chamber. They listened to the sounds of the departing horde, and knew that they were truly gone when the atmosphere lifted.

"They were afraid to confront us, as usual," Xoon said. He sighed and leant back against the wall, the relief so great that he was instantly asleep.

"And what further consequences will this have?" Alliole asked, of no one. As she asked this, she felt the weight on her shoulder lessen, and the clasp about her waist loosen, and knew, with a stir of excitement, that it was dawn. She held to a faint hope that their invisible touch might vanish altogether, but they remained locked to her, as the others broke down the barrier and then roused Xoon.

"We have to return," Tyall said, taking the lead as they entered the corridor beyond. He took a sharp look around. The Kings had truly gone, although the marks of their claws were everywhere and a vile odor lingered on the air.

"What of Alliole?" Xoon protested.

"Yes, what of her?" Tyall said. "We must get her under Elspeth's protection before nightfall, in case . . . if anything. . . ."

"In case they should return. Very well," Alliole said. She was not anxious to spend such a night again in any case, "We shall have to hurry for it is a full day's journey, and we have lost some time in the barricade."

"Is that my fault, its resilience?" Lyde sniped, "You were glad enough of it last night I am sure."

"I did not mean to find fault with you, Lyde," Alliole explained, "No, the soundness of the barricade was its great virtue. It is just that we have lost time in removing it. We had best erect another at the door to the Hall of Masks also."

"No," Xoon said, and halted as they tried to hurry him forward. "We have to find the Voice, Tyall, you promised me."

"Xoon, if we persist in this search we may well drive Alliole mad, and certainly the Kings would come again upon us. Perhaps they would not be so forebearing next time," Tyall said, "We are in their place, remember. Alliole and I are upon this venture willingly, and have come to our limit. And Lyde here, she has done great sorcery and not slept two nights, besides being lured to accompany us with trickery."

"He's right," Lyde put in, unhelpfully. When Xoon looked as if he would burst, Alliole said with great reluctance, "Xoon, you said yesterday that you would be thankful to me forever. If this promise has any virtue then remember it now."

"But we have got nowhere," Xoon cried, "We have nothing to show for our venture."

"We have come upon a puzzle," Alliole said, "And one that we must uncover if we are to get further. I truly believe, Xoon, that this manifestation that has attached itself to me has something to do with the Voice or I would not suffer it. Let us find out what it is first, and how to alleviate it, before we re-embark on our endeavour."

Her more reasoned words together with Tyall's evident determination against pursuing any course further into the ruins had the required effect. Lyde shortly after said enough to convince Alliole that she had a certain interest in seeing how far she could push the limits of the expedition, but Xoon consented with surprising meekness to their return.

They recovered Slaarngash at about the mid-way point in their journey. The demon came down from its perch but it was recalcitrant. It remained attendant upon Alliole, but would obey her order only when it suited. Fortunately it made no move to exploit any initiative. It seemed sullen and dull. Its vitality had drained from it into its shadows, which flickered and danced mockingly about it.

They pressed their journey further in the afternoon, despite their exhaustion. Not only did they wish to get the journey through galleries over before fully darkness, but with the waning of the light, Alliole felt with full horror the fresh fastening of the first two pairs of spectral hands upon her. They were so tired and footsore that Xoon could not resist raising a cheer at first sight of the gallery entrances, despite their deepening malevolence of structure. But he hushed his careless cry once they were closer, because they could see over the entrance, chiselled in an arch, was a flowing and unintelligible script, in letters about a hand-span in height.

"What is this?" Alliole said, as she limped up to it. "It was not here before."

"Even in death, I do grow," Lyde murmured.

"What?"

"That is what is says."

"Even in death, I do grow," Tyall said, louder than Lyde, almost in disgust.

"Hair and fingernails," Xoon said brightly, and when his cousins rounded on him, "They do, they grow even after you are dead. It is a riddle."

"I cannot figure it," Alliole said, ignoring them and examining the writing as well as she could, "It was not there when we departed I am sure, and see how well it is it carved? It must have been many hours' work, by a skilled mason. And the clearing away of the rubble would have taken hours more."

"This is sorcery," Lyde said, flatly. "There is a curse at work here. We should not enter."

"What other choice have we?" Tyall said.

"This is your fault," Xoon said, "If I had had my way, we would be far from here, recovering the Voice, and it would bear us to safety, I am sure."

"We have woken something," Alliole said, with dread mounting even further into certainty, "Some doom that attends us."

"Some of us more literally than others," Tyall said. "We have no choice. We must enter if we are to get Alliole to safety. Is their grasp weakening?" he asked.

"No," she said, "It is much stronger."

"Perhaps there is some other way," Xoon said, hopefully.

"None that I know of," Lyde said, "In all that I have read."

"Well, what about what you haven't read? Some secret entrance somewhere?"

"The Catacombs," Alliole said, "There might be an entrance through the Catacombs near, like the one back at the hall."

Lyde paused in deep thought several minutes, so that Alliole knew she was giving the matter serious consideration. "None that I know of," she said at its end, reluctantly.

"You should know, Alliole, of all of us," Xoon said crossly. He turned in a tight circle in his agitation, as if constraining the impulse to leave them.

Alliole did not even raise her eyes from her study. She wished she did have some of that knowledge by her, for although Tyall made a good substitute, he was not Helaf. She would have given anything to have Helaf by her side now, or to be able to reach him, if he could somehow be kept from any of the attendant dangers. When she did lower her eyes to the baleful entrance that confronted her, she felt at the same time, the wraith-hands at her waist and shoulder give a forward flex.

"They want me to go in there," she whispered.

"How delightful," Xoon said. He drew his sword, seeming to recover his certainty, "Well then, come on, let us go where they direct us. As you say, perhaps they wish to show us something."

"I'd rather take my chances in the Catacombs," Lyde said, but she fell in behind as Tyall followed Xoon's example. Together they pressed forward, beneath the baleful arch. As she passed into darkness, Alliole felt her wrist clasped again, gently and timorously. A phantom invisible led her forward.

"At least we have left the Kings behind," Tyall observed, but Alliole, beset by these new fears, thought it best to rob him of this false cheer.

"They have penetrated this far before," she said, "They slew Aubon after our last venture."

"Aubon," Tyall said. His face jumped to her, "I did not know," he said, confused, almost stricken, "I did not know." He journeyed on before her a little, then fell back beside her, and said, "He was my brother."

Thus they continued forward, Xoon in the lead, Tyall pressing at Alliole's back as if to convince her that nothing but himself stood at her shoulder, and Lyde behind him. Slaarngash dropped back again. Every now and then Alliole had to raise her flagging attention and draw it forwards with them. They went at first on their way through the well-remembered route through the galleries, but Alliole stopped when she felt the urgings at her wrist, waist and shoulder change.

"Well," she asked, as they stopped around her, "I am given another direction."

"Don't stop," Lyde said, jostling past, "There is something behind us."

"It is Slaarngash."

"No, something behind it," Lyde said, "And a lot of them. I can hear them."

"Do we wish to go forward, or follow where they indicate?" Alliole said.

"Do you wish to stand and be overtaken while we discuss it?" Lyde snapped.

Without further discussion, Alliole was hustled in the direction she indicated, and after that felt that she had been robbed of any initiative or decision. Dream-swiftness and certainty descended on her again, and the loss of any fear that she might be harmed. This shielded her from much of the fearful consequences of what next happened, even given such company, with such guides and such pursuers.

They came, after a time that could have been long or short—for Alliole, entranced, made no distinction of time—to a chamber on the upper storey of the galleries, that showed indisputably that the malevolent maze had once been inhabited. The stair opened into a long room, that had once been divided into two, but the partition had fallen into ruin. The doorway into the second room was arched, and words were graven in stone above it, in the same flowing hand and quite carelessly. Rubble was scattered about the door way and into the entrance.

"Admit me," Lyde read, when she had examined it. She stepped into the second room. "Nothing here but dust," she said.

"Tell me more," Xoon said, sarcastically. Alliole gasped, for the disembodied hands had fled from her, excepting the timid clutch at her wrist, which drew her forward quite gently into the second chamber, and then likewise left.

"They are gone," she said, curiously bereft, for it seemed that whatever it was had reneged on its threat, or promise, and shown her nothing. The second room was very narrow, so much so that she wondered to what use it had been put. A few, very narrow, windows were set high in the wall. Their width was so circumscribed, the thread of thought ran in Alliole's dream, that they would not even admit passage of a fleeing soul.

"What is this?" Tyall said. He was examining the rubble. "This is not the remnants of masonry, "he said. "It is bricks and mortar. This door was once sealed."

"Then who has breached it?" Lyde asked. She came over beside him and started to sift through the fallen stones. Xoon stood at the stair-head, listening. Alliole looked about the room, which might once have been fair, with its high ceilings and closely paved floor. Rays fell in flutes from the windows, filled with dancing motes of dust, and as she walked she passed in and out of moon-light and shadow.

A confused sound came from without, and Xoon jumped back into the room. "Can we re-seal it again?" he asked, "In a hurry."

"The Kings have found us," Alliole said, "I am sorry for this delay."

"No, I think they have abandoned us. It is something large and white," Xoon said. He came back precipitously to her side. Lyde and Tyall deserted the doorway, by common consent making Alliole their standing point, half-way towards the far wall. They could hear something climbing the stair, but not see it, for the tall ruins of the partition blocked their line of sight.

"There are some bones amid the bricks," Tyall said, his voice jumpy, "I did not have time to fully examine them."

Whatever was at the stair-head paused a long moment before it came on again. At the renewed sound of its footstep, Xoon and Tyall drew their swords—both somewhat gingerly, and their grip about the hilt was awkward—and Syl dropped to loop between Lyde's fingers. Their own breath sounded loud and harsh in their ears. And then there was a wondrous thing, for lit by the moon in the dust of the floor were only their own foot prints, but as the foot-steps, still beyond the partition, came on, not one but two trails appeared in the dust and glided about the room, confusing the clear pattern of their tracks from the door.

Alliole still had no fear, but she felt again the strong pull of the night that had accompanied her first awakening. Events raced so swiftly as to be inevitable, so that she must brace all her being or be pulled under. As the unbodied foot-prints ran about the chamber, and the heavy step approached in the room beyond, flowing script appeared upon the wall, in letters a hand-span high. "It is not here," Lyde interpreted. Alliole's dream certainty shattered with this shock, and her footing was all but plucked from under her.

"What?" she whispered, as a woman, naked, white, and taller in death, wider also in shoulder and hip than she must have been in life, appeared at the door. She must duck her head to tread under the lintel, and as she passed the rubble, the phantom foot-prints joined her, and from the ruin rose two children pallid, naked and engorged with death, as their mother. Two came with silent and resistless tread, the third, a wraith-girl swam along the surface of the floor as if through water. These were those who had stood at her side, before and behind her, these were those who had led her here. She was not even able to ask Tyall whether these were the phantasms he had warned her of, for the intent of the ghosts was evident, and their strength tremendous. As they surged forwards, Xoon and Tyall came out to meet them, and were effortlessly flung back, their blades ringing as they hit, as if on stone. The creatures made no move to parry, indeed the eldest grasped at Xoon's weapon as it flayed about her, took it about the blade and broke it. Lyde threw a curse with the ring of fire, but although it burned, the girl-wraith, at whom it was aimed, took no note of it except to change her attention to Lyde, as flames streamed from her side and face. All three had no choice but to give back immediately, leaving Alliole standing alone to face the boy, standing even though she had no weapons and no hope of defence.

"Slaarngash," Alliole said, but even as she named it she knew that it was hopeless. The wraiths were remorseless and terrible. They were stone. Alliole realized that there were tears running down her cheeks as she faced this thing, as she remembered the timorous hold at her wrist that had led her here, as she remembered also the story she had heard, of a sealed room and what lay within. From within this memory welled Helaf's tranquil voice, mentioning a name.

"Abarrn," she whispered, taking it from him, "I remember you." She knelt in the dust to face him. The childish face was set in mineral, his eyes were blank stone. His tread did not falter as he came towards her, "You, you of them all, you chose to be here," she whispered. Shouts rang out behind her, the renewed clatter of weapons and a back-wash of flame. Then a second shout, of pain, and the sound of a body being hurled to the floor. Even they did not have much time. "You chose to come here, for love, remember Abarrn. You would not abandon her," she said, and her tears fell anew, "It was unfair." The stone hand reached out for her throat, but she did not falter either. She had felt its clasp before. His wide eyes, as if carven, showed no emotion. His grasp did not close, but rested there.

"Abarrn," she said again, finding courage in this, in at least being able to name what was before her. Behind the sounds of battle abated. Moonlight bathed the pair, and pooled on the paving stones.

She heard Tyall cry in warning, and heard a tread behind her. She did not turn, so wrapped in contemplation of this boy. She did not turn, even when she felt a cold hand heavy upon her shoulder. The boy dropped his hand to her wrist. The girl rose up through the floor and took her by the waist. She was lame, the books had said. Alliole knelt in silent communion with them, and then the woman turned restlessly, as if in memory of some old pain. Her hand was lifted from Alliole's shoulder, and pointed at the wall. On its surface appeared the likeness of a flowing, careless, script. Alliole did not dare say anything. She did not even dare look at it.

"How did you know his name?" Lyde translated. She sounded as if she was in pain.

"I read it in a book. You were too cruel," Alliole whispered.

"She doesn't mean that," Xoon said, hastily. Tyall hushed him. Again the finger moved, again the writing flowed on the wall.

"I thought we had been forgotten. It has been so long—no, eternity—it has been an eternity here," Lyde said.

"One hundred and five years," Alliole supplied. Under the gaze of the son and daughter, she felt in full the immensity of that century, "It did not help either. Your house is dying." The woman moved towards her as if vindictively, but the boy was between them, and she withheld her blow. Again the hand was raised, again the writing flowed across the wall. There was a long silence.

"I can't read most of that," Lyde said, "I think it means something about despair. Atonement and then despair. And pity. Yours, I think. Something about retribution. Uh . . . 'It will not let me atone, it will not leave me. It will not let my children rest. It steals voices to give voice to its own. It has a heart of stone.'"

"Where, where is it?" Alliole cried, "And what?" The wall being now rather full, the woman raised her hand and it was withal erased. New writing appeared.

"It is not here," Lyde said, "That is all she is saying. Then, um . . . I cannot think, that tense is both past and future perfect and I cannot fully translate it. It means I think that she has looked everywhere and what she is looking for is not in the ruins. It is within, and she cannot go there. There is a very substantive stress upon the negative. Something has forbidden it." Her voice was very faint at the end, so that even had she been fully able to comprehend the script, it was doubtful that she was in a state where her faculties would do her knowledge justice.

The children's hands were cold about Alliole's wrist and waist, and her flesh was iced. She felt that she would faint also before long, before so solemn a regard, and then their questioning would cease. For a last time the hand was raised, all writing was erased as if it had never been, but another line of script appeared, that straggled at its end, as if the writer must fight off some influence that wished to negate it.

"Lyde has fainted," Tyall said, carefully, "Her leg, I think it is broken."

The girl sank back into the floor. The mother turned on her heel and departed. The boy lingered a moment more before Alliole, his hand passing over her face as if he were truly blind, as if he must impress her features upon his sense of touch as well as vision. Then he too turned and walked away, although she cried in sorrow as he did so. At about the place where the rubble lay, his solid form became confused with moonbeams, and vanished.

"What where they?" Xoon asked in wonder himself, "And how did you know to abate them?" Alliole turned to look at them. They had their back to the wall. Lyde was flung up against it, and Tyall was bending over her.

"The Mad Parrar and her children," Alliole said, slowly, "Her son was Abarrn. I never knew the girl's. When I called him by name, he stopped and took my hand. It was they who led us here, and surely they intended to kill us, in malice born of their own despair."

"Why have they approached us, when we sought only the Voice?" Xoon demanded, "What does she mean, it is within? It cannot be, or we would have found it, no matter how well hidden it was. It calls us out, not inward. What does it mean?"

Lyde moaned in Tyall's arms. Xoon ignored her, caught up in this new search for certainty.

"They are tied to it in some way, I suppose," Alliole said wearily, still kneeling, "Did not the Mad Parrar spend her last years searching? Xoon, did you not say your mother thought her bound to it? There is your answer, somewhere."

"That is no help," Xoon snarled. Alliole tried to stand but found she could not. Pain sprang up at the places where the ghosts had grasped. She fell and lay on her side, gasping. She did not wish any more answers, and yet they came hurrying in.

"I am sorry," Tyall said to Lyde, "I am so sorry. You must get up if you can. Can you stand?" It was not broken but dislocated, and they had to bind the leg to aid her, for she was in such shocking pain that she vomited every time she was moved. Alliole found it was almost an hour before she could raise herself. They were a much weakened and woebegone group that prepared to descend the stair, almost at dawn.

"What does it say?" Alliole asked Lyde, as they prepared to depart. Lyde took a long and careful look, squinting against the nausea of her rebellious stomach.

"You must name what you have found to give him rest," she said.

"Is that a hint?" Xoon asked, disgruntled.

"She is bound by some prohibition. It does not really make sense for we have not found it. But she has put it in present tense. Probably as close as she could get," Lyde guessed. She looked as if she gulped bile.

"Poor creatures," Alliole said blankly, "Poor creatures to wait in the galleries here. So close and yet denied entrance to human habitation."

"I would not want them wandering around the Castle at night," Xoon said, suddenly dignified. "If it is a hint, we must worry at it. You must think on it Alliole, you know more than we do."

"I will," she said, "If only for the boy, for I think your great grand-mother a monster of selfishness, and I hope she wanders an eternity for what she did."

"Even she did not deserve this," Lyde said, evenly, "She went mad because of her deed, perhaps that is suffering enough." Alliole limped into the first of the light of the Hall of Masks, and snarled a response. They looked at her in wonder. "You have the most beautiful bruises," Tyall said.

"I have an ache that fills fully half my skull," Alliole answered, "And I think I will die from it."

"Your dream is still trying to tell you something," Xoon guessed, wildly.

"I think it is the aftermath, more like," Tyall said. He was busy with aiding Lyde, or he would have said more, and probably more to the point. Fragments of dreams still whirled around Alliole, despite or perhaps because of her exhaustion. They pieced themselves together with sentences writ by a finger that moved and was still, and past-perfect and future tenses. Something that was perilously close to intuition fought for voice with the pain in her head.

Great havoc had been wrought in the Hall of Masks. Something had struck out at random, here bringing down here entire shelves of masks, and there taking the eye out of a cobweb. The shell of the Great Mask had been ripped from the wall, and cast upon the cobbles. Homeless spiders scurried everywhere.

"Let us hope that this is all they did," Tyall said.

"I think," Alliole said slowly, and actually swayed on her feet, although she did not fall, as enlightenment came to her. Xoon came to support her. "It is all right," she said, abstractedly, "I think I know. It is hard to be sure. My head. What is it that is not hid?" she said, "That we know already. It is not lost, knowledge of it is."

"I knew you would, I knew you would do this," Xoon said, delightedly, "That is why the ghosts came to you. This is where your dream thread led."

"Hush," Alliole said, for she was groping for the enlightenment that had come and gone again, and Xoon's words fell on her like hammer blows, darkening the retreating light and making it difficult to follow. "Follow," she said. It was barely a whisper. But such was her look from that time until she reached their journey's end, of charisma and pain that almost equalled martyrdom, that the others hushed and followed where she led, and would not be drawn from her until her course was finished. Very swift she went, so that Tyall and Lyde had difficulty keeping up and fell behind. Xoon stayed right on her heels.

Straight through the abandoned halls she led them, not even pausing to draw up Tiralgon's barricade against the doors. In and out of the Wheel's shadow she led them, but not out the doors at the end. Instead she turned to the stairs leading into the neglected ivory balconies. Faces distorted by decay peered from foliage black and slick with rot. Stairs groaned beneath their weight, and balustrades splintered. They entered into the back of the libraries on the second floor, and came out onto the balconies above the Cross, directly opposite the oval carved into those ivory traceries still whole and splendid. There Alliole went to the stair she had never before ascended.

"Where are your mother's chambers?" she asked Xoon then, "Up here?" He assented, but then said, startled, "You are not going to see her?"

"Not her, something in her care," Alliole answered, and took the stair. The others exchanged dubious looks. Tyall would have let Lyde down and into the servant's care, but she insisted that they follow, although like Alliole herself, she was now slipping into and out of consciousness, hovering half awake yet caught up in a web of pain that would not entirely let her fall.

Thus they came through into the sole part of the Castle Proper Alliole had not yet visited, although it was familiar enough to the others. Past the first of the seven rooms they went, each simply furnished, and with its walls painted to resemble other chambers and halls, of mystic or ordinary import; past the statutory room, filled with casts of cats in the four precious minerals, amber, onyx, tiger jasper and jade, representing the four cardinal virtues and eight vices of the ruling house, all rumored to come to their defence if roused. Last, before the final stair, is the chamber holding the truth-stone, little more than an antechamber for those who wished to ascend the stairs to the Parrar. Iriethe rose as they gathered before her. This chamber was purposely kept bare.

"So you are here too," Alliole said to her.

"It is one of my duties," Iriethe said, "To wait upon the Parrar at the foot of the stairs."

"And be keeper of the truth-stone," Alliole said.

"That also," Iriethe said, surprised at her, and at the sight of her followers, "It is a superstition of the common people."

"I wish to be certain of something," Alliole said, "So I came here." She limped restlessly towards the further door and looked out, up the stairs. Her sight nearly crippled her, for at the stair's head, a cat, vital, huge and tawny snarled, a rasping rise of sound. Their gaze met, and they recognized each other. It stood and bowed its sleek head, then turned sideways and paced from sight. Its place was immediately taken by a boar, as giant as the cat. It must be of great age, for its tusks twice pierced its lips, and were capped and banded with silver. Its hide hung in ragged strips from its back, as if it were a snake and had not entirely shed it, and its rank stench filled the stair-well. It made no sound but glared at her sideways with one red eye, and scraped its hoof. The cat came back, its movements lilting and deadly, in perfect symmetry, and rubbed its huge head against its companion's, most fond and lovingly, although the boar ignored it. The cat lowered its heavy head again, and snarled at Alliole anew, so that its hoarse rasp came billowing after the stench of the boar, as if warning her that their previous companionship drew heavily on its forbearance. Xoon drew her away. "You cannot pass there without the token I gave you," he whispered, "Her guardians will not allow it."

"I do not need to," she answered, although she had been held spell-bound by the greatness of those creatures. Before their vitality her intuition seemed abruptly to pale, and the desperate chain of logic on which it was built became shaky and unbelievable. "I must pay you a token then," she said to Iriethe, "For the use of this stone." Iriethe nodded her head.

"Of what weight?"

"Sufficient to the truth you wish to entrust to it," Iriethe replied.

"What did Sleepghast offer?" she asked, to have an idea of what she should give.

"He has not been here," Iriethe said, again surprised, "Not in a long time. I do not like him to intrude so, at the heart of my domain."

"It does work," she said, dismayed, "As he said? It will know the truth?"

"Of course," Iriethe said, "But who wants the truth except the common people? The truth is too heavy a weight, even for a stone."

"I have nothing suitable then," Alliole said, "For so great a matter as is in my heart." The others offered, eagerly, but she could not bear a gift less than what she thought her premise was worth. While she hesitated, her idea further spoiled, so that it seemed now muddied and utterly foolish, the product indeed of two sleepless nights and nervous exhaustion. No ordered chain of reasoning had led her here. And yet she held to it. Then she heard Anna's voice on the stair.

"Back, Baarl," she heard Anna say, "I have rubbed your head enough. I know it itches, and I will bring a salve." Anna laughed, a bright, rich and merry sound, "Silly cat," she said.

Alliole went back to the stair. Anna stood at its head. The cat, all malice drained from it, fawned at her feet, though it was so large and Anna so small that as it lay on its back its monstrous paws could bat at her head, so soft, so gently, and its bulk entirely surrounded her. The boar poised just behind, its head lowered, and Anna tugged at one of its fearsome tusks, in play.

"Anna," Alliole said, and her doubts cleared, for surely this was meant to be. If Anna was best regarded of all the daughters, it was surely because she had the gifts of the family, coupled with a clear and unstained character that could attract love so effortlessly because it must love in return, with complete absence of duplicity, "You must help me." The Beasts drew back, the cat snarling furiously again, angry to be caught in frivolity. Anna, with a final caress to both, descended.

"What is it?" she asked, and Alliole knelt before her.

"Anna, I have no hands," she said urgently, "For Slaarngash has abandoned me. Will you be my hands, for me right now? I need you." When Anna assented, and took her wrists in token of her faithfulness, Alliole (feeling the easy tears run down her cheeks) said also urgently, "Anna I must ask the truth-stone something and I have no gift sufficient to entrust it. I know not whether its powers are true, but if they are it is a thing of sorcery, and with all sorcery a greater gift invokes better reply. I would ask you to give me your bird. I cannot replace it, ever, for you and I both know what it means, that it is only an outward token of the love I bear for you in my heart, and that can never be lost, or broken or given away. I ask you this, Anna." She was sobbing, and attempting to clear her voice, for she did not wish to mis-speak her question.

"Of course," Anna said, although she said it slowly, for she loved also the bright blind bird, and had spent many happy hours polishing and regarding it, in company with her brother.

"Come with me then," Alliole said. She started to stand but fell again. Anna had to help her up, and half bear her into the chamber. From some fold in her dress she produced the brass bird, and handed it over to Iriethe, who even in the face of Alliole's distress could not repress a smile that such a little gift would be so valued.

"As keeper of the truth-stone I thank you," she replied, wielding the formula, "In the keeping of the family this stone has been for generations and in that time many secrets held. It has been shattered many times in the course of centuries and as a result I bid you remember that there is a heavy penalty for lies."

"Come into the room with me," Alliole said to Anna, "Where is it, this stone?"

"Here," Iriethe said, and drew aside a silver cover set into the wall. Concealed within was a niche in which sat a very common, rough edged, stone. One half was painted green, the other half blue, but the paint was blotched unevenly into the hollows and spread thin upon the edges. Possibly a child had painted it, for an afternoon's amusement.

"Pick it up," Alliole directed, "And then repeat after me." Anna did so, and for all its foolishness, the lifting gained a certain ceremony by the dignity with which she enacted it. Alliole stood at her shoulder, touching her with the place where her hands had once been. Xoon had come into the room with her. Tyall and Lyde were propped up in the doorway. All exhausted, driven to the pitch of extremity by two days and nights of ceaseless travail, their clothing rent and dirty, muddied and exhausted, with bruises already showing on their faces. All believed, however confusedly. Iriethe, cool, amused and uncomprehending stood alone among them.

"This stone, this is it. This is the source of the Voice," Alliole said. Anna repeated it. All reeled back. The stone did not break. The stone did not shatter. Nothing happened.

"I have found you," Alliole said, "Speak."

Nothing happened again.

"Speak," Alliole cried, as reaction flared around the circle, as Lyde started, hopelessly to laugh. Although Alliole teetered on the verge of the abyss, of the fear of being ludicrous, on the edge of losing her belief, yet she did not. She held firm. She knew it was the truth.

Nothing.

"I know what you are," Alliole cried, "I know it. And if you will not speak unless prompted, I ask you this." Anna ran in obedient echo, although such was the focus of the room that later all swore that only Alliole spoke, "I ask you, why then did you misdirect the search?"

And all spoke, as a sigh, as grief born of the ages, wrenched through them, as a Voice not their own filled their mouths, that spoke with the voice of stones and of demons. "Because I did not wish to be found," it said. ✺

Chapter Seventeen

"HOW CAN THAT BE," Alliole cried again, as exultation not her own filled her, "When you sent searchers mad for it?"

"They must search for me," the Voice, all voices replied, although Lyde was now grasping at her own throat in an effort to choke it, "They must search always, remembering their loss. I must send them far away. O Searchers it is your own yearning given voice that you hear, and the sorrow of your ancestors who flung their powers from them so that their people would live, and bound me into hiding and deceit. This is what troubles your dreams and will not let you sleep."

Alliole was drained of questions. She stood there, staring at the ugly stone in Anna's hands, and Anna herself, very carefully, returned it to its niche, closed the cover and stepped back.

"Release the boy," Alliole whispered to it, "Release them." There was no reply.

Tyall and Lyde vanished from the doorway. Xoon and Iriethe stood rooted in the center of the chamber. Anna tugged Alliole's sleeve. "They have gone to fetch my aunts," she whispered, and fled herself. Alliole realized too late that she had gone to Caerre. She was unsure whether to brace herself or to flee, and hide somewhere until the storm was over. Hide with Helaf at the calm in the storm's center. There was a scent in the air, at first most beautiful and then vile, and Alliole became aware that her companions were looking beyond her. She turned.

The boar stood in the door way, and from him the stench came. The cat was behind, and they flanked a woman between them. The cat head lowered and roared, that most life-giving of sounds, a heraldry. Its muzzle was fixed in a luminous snarl. The boar stood still and silent, but its stillness was a threat, so that a promise of violent action attended on the least danger. The woman was tall. Words cannot describe her. Silver and onyx was her hair. At her throat was a slim, gold torque of sapphire and emerald, but her eyes were as gems of deeper color, and her smile more splendid. At her waist was a girdle inlaid with amber, and in her hand she held a necklace of jade beads. She was with child, and moved awkwardly.

"Anna," she said gently, and looked around, then addressed empty air, "I have to give her this necklace." Alliole swallowed, "She is not here," she said. The woman's regard turned to her, and it was neither sane or kind. "She has gone to fetch Caerre," Alliole said, although she did not mean to. The words jumped out of their own accord, much as the Voice had.

"Give her this then," the woman said, and held out the necklace, "It is to replace what she has lost." Alliole took two steps forward, and held out both hands to accept it, foolishly, for she had none. But the woman touched her shoulder, and she knelt, without thinking, bending her neck. She felt the necklace being fastened at her throat. The woman touched her cheek, then she raised Alliole's bowed head with her hand and regarded her. And Alliole would have done anything for her, anything.

"It is in your keeping," the Parrar said, and in no wise did she just mean the necklace. She turned without backward glance, left the chamber, and ascended the stair. Her guardians followed after. And it was the fragrance of her presence, not the stench of the boar, that lingered upon the air.

Xoon awoke from his trance. He said nothing but smiled at Alliole, brilliantly and in his smile there was nothing selfish. But behind it there was a very great despair.

"How can I ever make her happy?" he asked. Before Alliole could answer, Tyall rushed back into the room. The Neve was close behind, then Lyde, who was supported by two servants. Then Marre, followed by her children. In a matter of moments the chamber was hopelessly crowded. It was of no weight perhaps, but Alliole looked at the Neve and at Marre and saw in both their features reflections of the other, but where one had garnered much of the light, the other only darkness. The light, she realized, would do nothing. It was bound by its own precocity. But things stirred in darkness and were brought to the light. She needed the dark, to act.

"What is this, then?" Marre rasped, "What is this new thing that you have done?" She looked fuddled, but much of the dream trance of her previous visit had fallen from her.

"Peace, Marre," the Neve said, "It is not a new thing. We have always had it." She did not look particularly admiring either. She lifted the cover and took the stone in her hands, turning it over. Marre snatched it from her, "It looks like nothing," she said.

"It has been here always," the Neve said, dully.

"It is not the thing that was lost, knowledge was," Tyall said, eagerly, "Alliole found it."

"The knowledge was not lost but deliberately cast aside," Lyde corrected, "That is what the Voice said." Xoon just smiled. The stone passed hand to hand around the room.

"Yes, cast aside, deliberately, by those whose greater wisdom sought to shield us from harm," Marre snapped, recovering nicely, "And now it has been found again by fools."

"Perhaps it would be well if nobody asked any questions," the Neve intervened, wearily, "Or attempted any great truths."

That was when Caerre appeared at the doorway. She appeared in a halting rush, with Anna at her side, and appalled servants behind. Her hands clutched the door frame, and her unbound hair fell about her face and shoulders. Her face was the color of the trellises. Her vitality as great as the Parrar's twin attendants.

The Neve, to whom the stone had been returned, raised her head from her contemplation of it. Marre actually hissed, and drew back, vindictively. Xoon lost his smile.

"It is mine," Caerre said, "Give it me." The entire room spoke rebuttal, without voice. "It is mine, the only thing I ask," Caerre repeated, so yearningly that Alliole wondered how long it had haunted her sleep. "You never knew you had it. It is nothing to you. Give it me and I will live out my days in the Catacombs, and trouble you no further."

"You will not trouble us at all," Marre said, spitting out her words slowly and clearly in the utter disbelief and hostility of her hatred, "Be silent."

The Neve put the stone aside, as a thing of no regard. Alliole happened to be the person closest by so she received it. She fumbled and almost dropped it, before managing to gather it partly with her skirts.

"You," Xoon squalled outraged, "I found it, I. It was our work. Lyde's leg."

"If it were not for me, you would not have got it," Caerre hissed, "It was I who gave you what you needed to coerce Alliole's loyalty. Reward me."

"Alliole," Tyall said, patiently, "Alliole found it. Perhaps she should. . . ." But his voice was unregarded. Lyde, Xoon, and Caerre spoke without waiting on each other, heatedly. The Neve and then Tyall tried speaking again, but both were drowned. The quarrel raged in its ugly intensity, until lightning flickered about the ceiling, and unseen powers clustered thick and close, as turbulent air rose about them. A mass squalling came from the chamber below, a caterwauling and clanging, as if the cat statuettes turned on each other. Anna hid. Alliole was frightened, frightened until she was so filled with fear that she was inspired.

"And why should I bandy words, let alone powers, with my father's murderer?" Xoon yelled, handing Alliole one last answer. If Xoon was to blame then he would surely not bandy his accusations so glibly. It was then also that she realized how Sleepghast must have guessed her guilt, for she had never once asked after Reven, when surely the whole Castle must have been talking of his disappearance, and then she had not troubled to deny his accusation. Tyall had called Sleepghast uncommon shrewd. She believed him. Answers came tumbling into place, locking themselves within her, when she wanted only to be free of their intolerable burden.

"I," Caerre hissed, "I did not kill him. Others did. I will not say in this room, who. Murderer yourself, you slew Aubon."

"I, I touch that capering ape?" Xoon threw back, "You are mistaken, I—"

"And what of Reven?" Marre inserted, acidly. Lyde, nodding vigorously, backed her up, "Caerre, you will give us answer for him. Why else would he have vanished thus, unless someone slew him. And who had cause but. . . ."

"I killed Reven," Alliole said, seizing the opportunity. This was the time, if ever, to confess, regardless of consequences, because the consequences of laboring under Sleepghast's blackmail were more dire. Besides, within the viewing prism of memory, Reven's death had become little and long ago, not even to be compared to the outrage they had committed in Marre's chambers. "I, I and no other. He came upon me in the passage and spoke heatedly. My demon slew him. He had a knife."

Caerre and Xoon were halted, staring at her. Faces around her blurred into insignificance with the exaltation of ridding herself of this last truth. She fumbled at the stone and held it higher, so all could see that she was not lying, "And none killed Gaar," she said, "He slew himself." The stone did not shatter. "Why should he not? Helaf had tried the same, at the same place, but was too young to fully believe the height of the fall. Gaar had contracted the madness from his lover, and he saw that his children could not be reconciled. Even this last hope was lost to him. Do not quarrel over him now. He loved you."

The truth stone was whole. Silence radiated around her.

"Somebody take this please before I drop it," she said, her voice abruptly diminished in force and intensity. Tyall took it, and the Neve took it from him, ruefully. It was well that he was by her, for with these words the inner force, the feverish certainty, the trance that had filled and upheld her, vanished. She could no longer hold herself. She could no longer even remember herself, or who she was. Not Alliole anyway, for they did not know her proper name. Alliole was just a name that they had given her. She fainted then, as faces, angry, vindictive, and resigned, all alike surprised, whirled around her into nothingness.

She awoke after a passage of further days and nights, how long she was not sure. She remembered only flickering lamp light, and Helaf's face. It was night. Helaf was sleeping by her bed on the floor. She stirred, and he too woke and greeted her. She started to say something, and then halted, for her mouth was dry and words came ill to her.

"Some days," he said, interpreting. He rose and fetched some water, "You have had a fever. The—they—tried to nurse you but you would do nothing but call my name, so they fetched me here. I hope you do not mind."

"No," she said, and drank some water, "I am very glad." She still whispered.

"Caerre and Tiralgon are here also," he said, quietly, busying himself about her. "The Catacombs are not safe anymore. Tiralgon is very angry."

"Caerre," she whispered.

"She is ill," he said, "I have been tending to both of you."

"So I am not even solitary in my sickness," she snapped, and tried to lift herself, falling back as she did so, and rising again. He sat beside her, took her by the shoulders and kissed her. "I am glad to see you whole again," he said, fervently.

"Even in my jealousy?" she asked, and a smile tugged at her mouth when he assented. Yet, truthfully, she could not say the same about him, for whole he was something almost monstrous. It was his mind and soul, his gentleness, that soared above his disfigurement. She felt shame touch her, and turned her gaze away. She was sick of the truth, and yet it must touch on everything she did. Helaf rose hurriedly. Tiralgon stood at the entrance, evidently roused by their talking. He came through the door, having to duck his head and come in shoulder first for the entrance to accommodate him, reminding her terribly of the Mad Parrar's ghost. Tiralgon grinned evilly, and when he stood, leant against the lintel.

She was struck anew by this fresh sight of them, by the likeness Helaf bore to Tyall, yet lacked in robustness of bodily and mental health; by the wolfish ferocity of Tiralgon's countenance, born of hunger and ill-treatment surely, but unsettling nonetheless. That she had paired herself willingly with such as these seemed almost a nightmare, now that they had departed from the Catacombs and come to her. Tiralgon moved and spoke.

"She is awake then," he said. "We will have to move on, more's the pity." Caerre appeared behind him, her movement so unnatural in the half-light that Alliole was sure that she would never be free of fear of her. Caerre's face held a complete absence of color, save around her eyes, which were puffed and red from weeping, so that Alliole was sure whatever decision had been made was not in her favor.

Tiralgon's words came so close to the tone of her contemplation that she decided that he was spying on her thoughts.

"I cannot say that you are welcome visitors," she admitted. She was not strong. She fell back onto the bolster. She hurt Helaf, who recoiled. Tiralgon grinned again. "See how her mind turns," he said, admiringly.

"I only think that my so openly associating with you can do no good to our cause, and a great deal of harm," she said, staring dry eyed at the ceiling, wishing she did not feel so sickly. Her head throbbed in a sly, vindictive, utterly persistent manner. "I will not be able to move, or petition so freely." She heard herself mouth these words, which had no meaning, and wondered at her savage desire to drive them away, but detachedly, as if it were not herself speaking.

"If you think to reject us," Caerre said softly, belaboring a point already decided, "You are only rejecting a part of yourself. You seek to shed your deformity now that you think you can find peace, you seek to shed the companions that remind you of it. It will not work."

"I did not say that," Alliole said, "You did." And then she gasped and cried aloud, then started to weep again. "I cannot bear it," she said, inarticulately, "I cannot bear it. I wish that I were dead."

"Do not wish that," Helaf said, in distress, and limped to her. Caerre and Tiralgon crossed the room, in silence.

"We are leaving since we are not welcome," Caerre said.

"You may yet have your wish," said Tiralgon, "The Kings are very angry. They are gathering in the depths to revenge your trespass."

"Come on, Helaf," Caerre said.

"I will stay here," he said. His face was ghastly. He raised his head to face his sister.

"You still believe," Caerre said, wonderingly.

"It is cowardly to wish for death," Tiralgon said to Alliole, contemptuously, "When the Kings come for me, they will fear me."

"I would be a coward if I ran away," Helaf said, simply to Caerre, their separate conversations touching and then moving on again at cross-purposes, "Perhaps, if I persist, things will come right."

"You are gone from me," Caerre said. She drew her skirts about her, and vanished. Tiralgon followed, pale faces swallowed in the gloom. Alliole started to weep in fresh earnest, "I did not mean," she tried to say, "I do not know why I said," but Helaf only soothed her. But she was glad, glad that the other two had left, at whatever cost. Peril loomed sharp and ominous within her, peril to her frail sense of self, to her soul. And in this extremity she felt rather than knew that she must discard all but the essentials if she was to save herself.

"Go back to sleep," Helaf said, at last, when she had wept herself out.

"I've had enough sleep," she said. She did not ask him for any news of the time while she had been ill. She knew that news would come too soon for her, in any case. She kissed him instead, and raised herself up in his arms, suddenly happy in her ignorance, clamorous for his attention, inspired, tired, defeated, glad.

That night they lay together for the first time, in spite of all troubles and vexations, and this act gave them great joy. Nevertheless, when morning found them together, he must have seen his answer—her shame—in her eyes. He shielded the gaze of his brother, and although they rose together, and he bathed and dressed her, yet they did not speak of that night, then or ever.

Mid-morning brought the Neve to them, but whatever she would have said was silenced by Alliole's indifference. When she was questioned on her state, Alliole said only that the head-ache continued, as was manifestly true. There was a bruise was upon her head in the shape of a hand outspread, and she could get no peace from it. Nevertheless the Neve drew Helaf aside at the door, and said, softly, but loud enough for Alliole to bear unwilling witness.

"It is grief that works in her," the Neve said, "So great that she might die of it. She was not strong enough for the burden I laid on her, and now I most bitterly repent. Take care of her, nephew, and do not let her from your sight."

With the failing of the day, strange rumors worked in the Castle. Whispers passed from place to place with no intervening mouth. Moths fluttered in ominous symmetry from the stairs. Flutes played upon the ivory trellises and balconies, in ill-suited harmonies. Alliole felt this very much, and would have gone from her lover, wandering, but he kept her by him. They drew together as night fell, and she felt anew their remoteness from the main body of the Castle, both its defenses and its surety; their awkward poise between Castle and Courtyard, in the unpeopled gulfs between. Had Helaf not been there she would have been afraid. It was he who told her the meaning of the omens, that the Kings would come tonight, but that the Castle had prepared for their onslaught, and so would be saved. At least so ran the general rumor. Helaf was not so sure, and he knew the strength of the Kings as well as she did.

"They listened to Tyall. He kept warning them," Helaf said, "They barricaded the Wheeled Hall, which is why the army is gathering in the Catacombs. There are more entrances, so many no one knows for sure which they will come up. I wish they had given Caerre the truth-stone. She would have known how to use it."

"Strong words," she said, but she was listening elsewhere, "We wait here?"

"Here is as good a place to wait as any other," he said, "When you are waiting for the end. Do you think any would act to save me?"

"I would," she said, "But I have no defenses."

"Is it selfish then, to keep you by me?"

"I want to be with you," she said, "And this is the first place I remember. It may as well be my last." She rested her aching head against his shoulder. He lifted the silvered torque from his shoulders, that she had given him, and arranged it carefully around her throat. She protested but could not dissuade him. Then he drew her close against him, as close as his brother would allow. They were silent then, listening.

There was a distant explosion. There were shouts and mad echoes. Running. Clash of metal, of claws and knives. There was silence, broken by a long drawn out caterwaul. Then a noise, of rustling, skittering, mumbling of idiot voices, from very near at hand. She gasped and huddled against him, and he covered her ears with his hands, so she did not have to listen.

Then there was a rallying, and human voices, clashing in battle. Tyall was at the doorway, shouting at them, "Quickly, come quickly, while they are gone." There were scratches on his face and across the armor covering his stomach. There was blood in his hair. Valor and vigour sparked from him. When they did not immediately obey but stared at him, he came impatiently into the chamber and dragged Alliole upright, "Do you think we have risked our lives to so release you?" he cried impatiently. He caught up Helaf, and pushed them both for the door, "Come on."

Iriethe was in the corridor, with half a dozen men armed with makeshift pikes and spears. All exuded the same unnatural vigor that flowed from Tyall. Boars ran between their feet gnashing their jaws. "Come on," Iriethe cried, as Tyall, when she saw them. Immediately they started a run towards the Castle's center, the pair hustled along whether they would or not, their rescuers bounding over corpses, smashed furniture and dodging tumbled masonry.

Great sorceries were at work, for the roars of huge cats came from the distance, and unquiet air was thick about them.

"The Kings have breached the first defenses," Tyall called, as they came rushing into the Cross, "But our gracious Parrar and Neve are working magics to save us." The Cross was brilliantly lit and filled with people, milling in confusion apparently meaningless, dwarfed by the hall's immensity. The glamour cast upon it was doubly radiant, so that glowing golden light and furniture drove the shadows into the upper heights, where they lurked, and waited.

"No," Helaf said, stopping dead at the threshold as he saw the great encampment, as the others swept around him, and those at the doors started to close them. Alliole, already swept ahead, turned and saw him, and realized that he feared utterly to face so many people. She called his name, and turned back, struggling against the human tide to reach him, with no hands to force faster passage.

"Wait," she called, "Wait for me," as she saw him at the point of vanishing. His eyes met hers, directly, "I will go to find my sister," he called, and then the closing doors cut him off.

"No," she screamed, and beat uselessly against them, "Open, open them," she directed. When Tyall repeated her order, it was done. But Helaf was gone. She went out into the corridor, "No," she screamed again. She began to run towards the Catacomb entrance, but as she turned the corner came face to face with a mass of the Kings, mute and sightless, groping towards her. Tyall caught her up as she stopped, and carried her bodily, struggling, back to the hall. The entrance was firmly closed behind them.

"Back," he gasped at her, "Back into the hall, to Xoon. You must advise him." A blow was struck upon the door, and his attention switched back to it.

She fell back, seeing the sense of that, and went to the dais, where Xoon stood, and Marre. At Marre's heels lurked a creature that at first Alliole did not recognize, with black, semi-molten features. Xoon held the truth-stone, but lacked any authority.

"Wield it," she said to him, from the depths of her distraction.

"He knows not how," Marre said, acidly.

"Xoon, for the sake of us all," she cried to him, "Your temper is great. Coerce it to your will."

"He cannot," Marre said to her, "He has been trying these last days, and he can in no way master it."

Xoon looked stung.

"Why do you not take it up then?" Alliole said.

"I will stay with the Powers that I know," Marre said, scornfully.

Another blow fell upon the door, and the crowds in the hall shuddered before it, for it promised terrible vengeance, and horror beyond the normal run. And Alliole could only think that Helaf was out there with it and that if she had been whole hearted to him, then he might have found courage to come into the hall with her and been saved.

"Since when, Marre, did you speak for him," she cried, with intrepid, desperate spirit, "Xoon, you do not need to master but to understand it. To know it for what it is. What is it?"

"An artifact of our ancestors," Xoon said, slowly.

A third time the blow fell. The door buckled before it. The noise was insupportable, particularly for Alliole, half whose head was engulfed in torment matching exactly the width of a hand, five fingers spread, till she could barely think for it.

"Yes, but what is it for?" she cried.

"A Voice, a Voice speaks from it," he said, still stupidly, then disconsolately, "My voice. Tyall says that I lie asleep nights, talking to myself. It is foolish."

"Who is the fool is of no matter. What else?" she said.

"It raised this Castle in an eye's blink, in an instant," he said, remembering the old story, "It can create stone and destroy it."

"Make stone then," she said, "The door, the corridor beyond, so that what is in it cannot make way." He looked at her and blinked.

The fourth blow did not fall. The hall held its breath and then released it, as those close to the door cried in wonder.

"It has petrified," Tyall said, coming up to them, "It is the entrance closest to the Catacombs. There are others that they will come through."

Even as he said that a clamoring broke out anew, at every entrance to the hall, as if the Kings had waited on his word to act. Doors burst asunder at the ground, at the first floor, on the balconies they were flung open, and deathless sightless gaze and claws were upon them. Screams, cat and human broke out everywhere.

Xoon blinked again. There was a moment and then the Great Mask burst through the second storey of the balconies, tearing wall and trellises asunder. Great gouts of power fell from its eyes, upon the Kings, so that their massed ranks scattered amongst the people.

"Well done," Tyall cried, in great delight, as the living and disarrayed dead turned on each other.

"That is my mother's doing," Xoon said. He put the stone down on the seat behind him, carelessly, "I did nothing. I could feel it. Come on." He drew his sword and ran down into the fray, and Tyall followed him, leaving Marre and Alliole on the dais together.

There followed a most terrible battle in which living and dead fought together and neither could quite overwhelm the other, so that they were locked in combat. The Mask roamed about the upper air, slaying Kings with bolts from its eyes and speaking in a language Alliole could not understand but to which Marre sometimes gave answer. Cats of beaten metal, of copper, of ivory, jasper, onyx and amber descended in torrents from the balconies and tore the Kings asunder. Yet the dead were strong and could not entirely be overmastered, for it took a direct blow to the head to destroy one, else they rose and fought again. Even thus dispatched the dead limbs twitched and dead hands grasped as if still obeying the will of the creature. It was a horrible battle. Periodically from the Kings rose their battle cry, their ululation, so terrible in the confines and echoes of the hall that it seemed to create a hallucination that the hall was ruined already, and open in parts to the emptiness above, so that those who sought shelter must grasp for foot and hand-hold, else they would fall forever into the sky.

Those who were not fighting mostly managed to flee, back into the towers, some into the precincts, hither and thither with no plan, so that Alliole saw that soon everywhere would be filled with refugees and there would be no rallying point, no order. For soon only the combatants remained, and she and Marre and Slaarngash by the dais.

The lines wavered back and forth, and then both fell back together. The living were first to realize this mutual surrender, and Alliole heard Tyall's voice, abruptly from the ranks, urging his warriors forward to attack. Before them the Kings wavered, they lost direction, the wave of their initiative seeming to founder and give back.

"It is some feint I am sure," Marre observed beside her.

"No, they have won, they have won," Alliole said.

"No, it is a trick. The living can never master the dead," Marre said. And Alliole knew that this was true, and felt great dread rise in her heart, as the Kings gave back further in truth than they needed, out of the hall entirely. Those they fought gave further shout and pursued. Watching as she and Marre were, they saw that the Kings did not need to give back so far, so she could see their plan as those in the thick of the battle might not.

"They will waste their strength in the corridors," Alliole cried in agony, "They will not be able to bring their greater numbers to bear."

"They must be told," Marre agreed, "You must be the messenger. To Tyall not to Xoon, for none listen to him. Take the tiding, quickly, before the Kings muster again."

"I would, gladly," Alliole said, and went down the steps of the dais, calling over her shoulder, "I will be cut down ere I reach him, but know you that I kept my courage." For that finally, was her pride and her answer. Marre called her to a halt.

"Do not be a greater fool than you are already," Marre observed, likewise descending the stair, "Spare me your useless heroics. Do you think I would send you forth undefended? I must join my cousins and prepare against any final assault or I would go myself. Here." They had reached the closest flank of the fallen from the battle, and she directed the demon to haul some of the bodies aside. With the blood upon the polished flags she drew a shape of strange geometry, and spoke words as she tamped down each angle with her heel, firm, vital, incomprehensible words.

"Oh no, not that," Alliole cried, backing.

"Fool," Marre said, "Do not cause me to repent. I am giving you back your hands." That stopped her. The demon squalled, an ugly sound made uglier as Marre forced it into the confines of the pattern. Its body melted entirely into its head. Its trunk, legs and features flowed together until only an ichorous puddle swarming with pestilent life spilled and oozed and bubbled, contained within the geometry. Two arms came from this puddle and flailed upon the floor, two orbs gleamed from it, shedding lambent red. With the army gone the hall's luminosity dimmed, so the light from these orbs raked the gloom. The sword, that had been forgotten upon the demon's back, clattered to the floor, its scabbard lapped in the vile stuff. The arms sank back into the puddle, from which now emerged a liquid and detestable mewling, until only a pair of clawed hands floated upon its surface, still beseeching.

Still speaking words of the old tongue, Marre reached forward and plucked from the puddle first one then the other of its attachments and turned to Alliole, who had backed up as far as the dais and felt that in all honor she could go no further.

"Hold up your arms," Marre directed, and she did so. Still chanting, Marre stepped forward, and touched each hand, first to Alliole's forehead and then to her stumps. Her head-ache immediately redoubled, and the wounds on the ends of her arms opened, so that she cried out in horror as her own blood fountained for an instant before Marre clapped the demon's hands upon them. Alliole shrieked then, for the pain was insupportable, and fell writhing to the floor, clutching at her wrists and only then aware that she had hands with which to clutch. The two flesh knit, and demonic blood flowed into her veins, lessening as it flowed from its source upwards her arm. At her wrists the veins scorched and bulged black from its venom, but at her shoulder was only a feeling of great heat, that coursed into her body, her heart, lights and kidneys, and dissipated. She found her sight had cleared again, and all pain gone. She was lying on her side, her knees drawn up against her. Marre stood over her, looking down dispassionately. Behind her the sorcerous puddle was no more than a stain on the flags.

"Do not thank me," Marre said, when she saw that Alliole had come to herself, "For I do not forgive you, simply acknowledge the necessity. Besides you would not have breached the binding had I instructed you properly. I must acknowledge my own fault in this." She turned away, and then back again, as Alliole scrambled to her feet. Demonic vigor animated her, although she was unsure how long it would last.

"Take better care of this than your last," Marre said, musingly, then seemed to take fresh and uncanny look at her, "You have changed greatly. You will not live long in any case." Then her eyes widened. She took a step back, then recovered herself. "I am sorry," she said, "I would not have done it if . . . oh it is too late now. Be on your way. Hurry." She turned away. Alliole, stumbling, went over and picked up the sword. It came easily to her hands, as if they were used to each other. The hands themselves were blackened, slightly furred on the palms, and clawed like a cat's, so that she put the claws out and then retracted them again. It was a pleasing sensation. She drew the sword from its scabbard and turned it over before her. Her hands, her hands. The thought pulsed and filled her until it was almost ecstasy.

"Do you not wish to question me?" Marre said, very suddenly. Alliole had forgotten her. "No," she said, simply.

"You have so entirely lost your curiosity? Very well then, I will tell you anyway."

"I do not want to know," Alliole said and turned from her, "Whatever it is it will not be pleasant. I have my own business to attend to."

"You have got a child," Marre said, angrily to her back, "Just recently. And now I have mixed you with demon flesh. Who knows what the issue will be, good or ill. I advise you to miscarry." She gathered her skirts about her as stiffly as Caerre had, and walked away towards the stair. Alliole, still filled with a fever that allowed her to pay little heed to Marre's words, caught up the truth-stone from where Xoon had set it, and ran towards the corridor.

The fighting, as she had feared, had got swamped in the corridors, and grown in ferocity, so that small groups of embattled warriors had lost contact with each other. They found the Kings always in ambush, and unsettling, so that a small group would fall back from them in dismay at the first set-back, where a larger group, well led, might have found fresh heart and recovered.

She came upon Grielle leading a group of her people. Grielle with her great bulk and weight had stood fast while the battle ebbed around her, and as others fell back she only stood firmer, and called on all to fight, holding a home-forged pike as large and unwieldy as herself. Her hog lay at her feet, of great size and bulk, but slain, for on it the Kings had ventured their first wrath. Its outline was strangely dim and smoky, as if its firm shape wavered in its hold on the world now that it was dead. It was evidently an otherworldly spirit, this Beast, of less magnitude than those in attendance to the Parrar.

Grielle would have been overborne herself but Alliole came to her rescue. In Alliole's hands her sword flew as well accustomed to the work, and she found that she had a knowledge of the way to hack, stab and parry that argued she had been once well versed in it, for it came back quickly in the heat of battle and did not entirely require her conscious attention. She was able to look around at times, and direct others to their tasks, or to fill a gap and hurry to the defense of a weakening post. She took remembrance of the previous battle to heart, and cut only at their heads, a task most pleasing to her. The Kings alone were not terrible. They were poor fighters, but remorseless. Once overborne, many would attack until the person was torn to pieces, and so the battle continued.

With Grielle at her heels, Alliole pressed on, leading a small band that rapidly swelled as others rallied behind her. Where she could, she held the truth-stone aloft, and cried that she was taking it to its master, and there would great sorcery be worked. She kept as well as she could to the main halls, and followed what she hoped was Tyall and Xoon's course, for in their impetuosity the pair had led a larger host as far as the entrance to the Catacombs. There the Kings had made a stand, recognizing perhaps that to retreat into the necropolis was to acknowledge their defeat.

The press was very thick, so that in some places people could not turn against one another, and the Kings climbed the carven entrance to the Catacombs and threw themselves down onto the packed ranks, to their dismay. Fighting was furious on the stair also. Kings swarmed out of the darkness with the light reflecting in their eyes, for none but Xoon could lead any rally into the dark and maintain their sight.

Alliole forged forwards into this press, for she was reckless of personal danger in her dismay at the turn of events. Besides, she had noticed that the Kings gave way before her, and she trusted to the tomb-found torque of silver that she wore, to provide her with a spectral shield. Grielle kept at her side most valiantly, until some turn in the battle hidden from them forced the press of people forwards and then back. Grielle braced herself and stood. Alliole was brought forwards with the pack, although she managed to avoid its ebb. This brought her to the Catacomb stair, as Xoon came up, trying to draw back the last sortie. He turned to look at her irritatedly as she came up, not really seeing her.

"Here it is," she said, and slapped the stone into his hand, closing his fingers over it, "Use it, for all our sakes."

"That was not me. That was my mother," he repeated. His eye was distracted, his armor bloodied, his hair wild. "What am I to do? Tyall is still down there," he said.

"It was you," she screamed at him, trying to impress him with her urgency, "Use this. Save him." She took him by the shoulders and shook him. "If all others lose faith in you," she said, "Tyall will still be with you, do you understand? Do not let their lack so shake you. This is the time for you to strike boldly, and regain all."

He shook his head, regarding the stone. "I cannot use it," he said, "I am a man. Only women can wield such power. It is no use. Thank you."

She turned and plunged down the stair, for she saw that he had lost heart, if not his courage. Grielle came down behind her, shouting obscenities into the dark, and behind them a rush of people, including Xoon. The dead lay thick upon the stair, where the Kings had rallied, and into the dark, where the clash of fighting continued.

"They were fools to come so far," Alliole yelled, to let those still surviving hear her, "And here we must rescue them."

Echo threw back her words at her, from all around, as if voiced by pit and bottomless chasm, as if in mockery. By ear she could tell the fighting was around the ossuary, a bad place, for there the corridor narrowed, and in no way could they fight more than two abreast. She hoped and trusted that Helaf and his companions were safe in the upper air, and had not retreated to their accustomed chamber, or they would be cut off. As they rounded the corner, running blind, for Alliole was in the lead and trusted the Kings' unsettling eyes to betray them to her, she could see a great fire burned and shed blue light upon the scene. Lyde was there also.

"Back," Alliole cried out, "Back up for fresh fighters to come through."

Then there was a confused and ill lit tussle within the ossuary. Bones and skulls tumbled about underfoot, and crushed in some places to powder. Some of the Kings wielded thigh bones as weapons, and others scrambled onto the walls and rained down their contents pell-mell upon the combat. There seemed an almost limitless number of them coming up the further stair. Alliole's rally drew off some of the wearier, and she and Grielle led her own warriors in, including Xoon, who lay about him furiously and to great effect, now that he had someone to follow. Lyde dropped back to better command her sorceries, and Alliole saw that she moved with a bad limp but otherwise without effort. The fire about the walls grew larger and less tame, its heat and ferocity driving the defenders as well as the Kings back, until the bulk of the two sides regarded each other from across a heated gulf. Only a rear-guard remained within this inferno. Xoon and Tyall were among the laggards, and it seemed to Alliole that Xoon pressed forward even then, as if reluctant to give up the chase. Alliole plunged in, dreading that he would draw Tyall also off in this futile endeavor, calling upon Lyde to momentarily quench the flames. Heat radiated from the charred bones that made up walls and floor. Reeking smoke billowed from them.

"Xoon, we must fall back," she called, "We cannot entirely destroy them, just force them back. Come back." Tyall looked back at her, his face slick with sweat, and seemed to come to his senses from his battle frenzy. Seeing that Xoon would not listen to her, he called also on Xoon to desist, negligently parrying a blow from a bone club as he reached to pull Xoon back.

They came backwards through the ossuary, for with the flames down, the Kings counter-attacked, and forced a path across. Xoon still fought, gripped in his private battle, and again and again Tyall had to lower his guard to pull him back. Claws, blows, and the full horror of the Kings were all about them, and many fell upon Tyall, seeing his distraction. Alliole more than once had to stand over him, so that he could get back onto his feet behind her without being overwhelmed.

"Stand and fight," Grielle called, jeering as the Kings made a last sortie, as the small party negotiated the entrance to the ossuary, and Lyde fanned the flames anew, "You will be torched by my lady." One of the Kings leapt at her and she struck it aside, directly onto Tyall, who in assisting Xoon had not noticed her manoeuvre. It bit and clawed at his head, and he howled and staggered beneath it, dropping his sword. Alliole tore it off and destroyed it, but not before it had bitten her above the eye. Badly shaken, she retreated last but for Grielle, whom she had to haul from the chamber as it became insupportably heated. The bones fell in on each other. Then there was a great rumble, as they retreated, and the super-heated roof fell in. Tyall did not retreat nearly fast enough, as the last blow had started a great flow of blood from his head, and he seemed disoriented. Xoon, recovering from his heedless madness, had to pull him back, crying in alarm and sheltering his friend as slabs of the roof rained around them.

"Alliole, Alliole, quickly," Xoon cried as Tyall fell, and she had to come back to them. She could barely see herself, for the bite over her eye. Together they hauled him up, and got him as far as the final stair, before she stumbled again, and they all three fell.

"Quick," she gasped, "Quickly, we must staunch that wound," for she saw that it was a bad one. Xoon tore at his own clothes to make a bandage. Alliole ran a little way down the corridor, but the fall of the ossuary had blocked the Kings' entrance and there were only a few, that she destroyed, on the Castle side.

"We need only kill those still lurking in the Castle and we have won," she said, returning exhaustedly to where Grielle stood. Xoon had bound Tyall's wounds. He was crying to his friend to keep heart, that he, Xoon, would save him; that he was sorry that he had delayed in the rescue and in the retreat and so endangered him, but that there was no need to be frightened just because of a little cut on his head. But Tyall did not answer. Tyall was dead. 🗲

Chapter Eighteen

THEY MADE a dismal and disheartened return to the Cross. They made a rough bier and on it placed Tyall's body, and brought it back with them, to put on display before the people. Xoon did not weep, but he cast himself down at its foot and would not speak. Alliole herself could not speak on their return from the Catacombs for grief choked in her throat. She lingered by the bier for longer than Xoon, for a servant summoned him away to the balconies. As she did so, crowds passed to and fro in the hall, and rumors passed among them, to which she paid no heed, except to the occasional outbreak of wild sobbing which she directed others to silence, for she deemed them unfitting so close to the dead. Warriors returned, many slashed and bleeding, and gathered, then went again, following rumors of the Kings. Others started to take up the dead, and clear away the ruin, to attempt to return the Cross to some semblance of order. As the night wore on into morning and the danger from their nocturnal enemy seemed past, many dispersed from the hall outward again, to assess the damage, to privately weep, to sleep.

Alliole was herself summoned to the tower, drawn into the antechamber where the truth-stone had so long lain. Grielle followed at her shoulder. Iriethe was there, dead, laid out in the place of her duty. The Neve stood by her.

"Tyall is dead," Alliole said, after a brief search to find some more fitting sentence, but deciding to speak it bluntly. The Neve inclined her head. "I know," she said, "Xoon told me. He blames himself most bitterly." Alliole shrugged. Like Xoon, the Neve showed no open grief, but it could be felt most tangibly, and all the more so that she was close mouthed about it.

"I wish you would wait here, Alliole," the Neve said only, "My sister gives birth. Xoon and Anna attend her, as I will shortly. Then I will attend to Tyall. But such are the portents that I fear for the future. If you will but stand here I am sure the worst can be averted." Alliole assented a second time. The Neve turned from her.

Grielle spoke, "Iriethe's place is mine," she said.

"As is the tradition," the Neve said, without real regard, "Although a show of grief might be seemly."

"We did not love each other," Grielle reasoned, "And I will perform her tasks better." She went and stood at the foot of the stair, in Iriethe's accustomed place. She stood most convincingly. The Neve passed her without further speech. From above came the anxious mew of a cat. Grielle's back was even more redoubtable than her front. The cat would not harm her, and the boar came down and nudged her vast belly, as if to give suck, before it followed the Neve.

Grielle turned her fierce gaze to Alliole. It clung, "You, you, I will follow always," she said, "Now that you have hands. I will spread your fame amongst the people, so all shall honor you. For you led the final assault down the stair, and so saved us all." She closed her mouth over this most remarkable speech, and settled herself firmer still upon the stair.

"I thank you," Alliole said, and turned about the narrow room, its center filled by the corpse. Then she settled herself, wearily. Although the prospect of waiting out a labor here did not please her, for she was tired and filled with aches, yet she was glad to do so, for there was a nervous tension in the air. The crisis was not yet come, it had yet to be averted, she was sure. The Kings were but another omen, and too many omens attended this birth for it to be anything but spectacular. Grief dogged her already, and yet she was filled with obscure certainty that more would die, that events would worsen further. Once she had settled herself, she remembered Marre's words in the Cross, and was filled at once with a flare of horror that settled into her despair and then was lost in her exhaustion. She contemplated the chamber, and then her hands. The sword, that she had slung upon her back, she put before her. Grielle sent servants to attend her wounds, and she found absurd enjoyment in bathing her own face.

Morning wore on, and it was full day by the time anything further happened. Alliole went out onto the balcony for some air, and she saw Caerre beckoning from the further wall. She went to her.

"What do you do here?" Caerre said.

"I attend your mother, who is in labor," Alliole said. Caerre drew herself up further.

"Where is my brother?" Caerre said, haughtily, without deigning to notice any change in Alliole's appearance. "I would speak to him."

"He is not with you?" Alliole said.

"No, as you remember."

"No, I mean, he left me to look for you," Alliole said.

"We had taken shelter in the upper air," Caerre said, "We thought he was with you." The same thought occurred to them both simultaneously.

"He wouldn't," Alliole said.

"He would be a fool," Caerre said, bitterly.

"And yet it would be the most likely place," Alliole said, "And he could not come back. We blocked the stair."

"And you wear his torque," Caerre said, accusingly.

"He gave it to me," Alliole said, realizing that wherever he was, Helaf was truly without defenses. They were of one mind in this matter. She rushed back to the chamber and snatched up her sword.

"Grielle," she said, "I must be absent a short space. Look you to take my place. Admit no one you do not know to the upper chambers. Is that clear?" Grielle folded one of her many chins into her throat to indicate her staunch appliance to the task. Alliole rejoined Caerre in the corridor. Tiralgon also lurked there. He was wounded about the throat, as if something had worried there, and had deep cuts on his arms and back. He stank of rank blood. But their antagonism was a moment set aside. They would have run, but Caerre could not go so fast without limping terribly, and so held them back.

They arrived at the Catacomb stair together, and descended it, Caerre now the faster for she did not slow to pick her path around the dead as Alliole did, but tramped right over them.

She arrived at the roof fall before the others and beat upon it, as if thus to gain admittance.

"We shall have to dig," Alliole said.

"If we have come in time," Caerre said, grimly. She turned from it in despair, "If I had the truth-stone I could make it speak, and it would clear a path in an eye's wink," she said.

"I had it," Alliole said, blankly, "I gave it to Xoon."

Tiralgon got at once to work shifting the rubble, the muscles in his back working through the rent cloth, until they forced the cuts on his back open again. Blood mixed with the dust that they raised in their labor, and coagulated in strips down his flanks.

They breathed the dust they raised, and their hands were soon raw with the work. Their iced breath filled the spaces between them.

"You have hands," Tiralgon speaking, as if surprise, for the first time as they worked.

"Marre gave them me," Alliole gasped, lifting, and of all of them she was best, for the hands were not hers and strong and able, used to lifting cities, "I think they are a mixed blessing." She held back what she also knew, not wishing to further stir their fear and grief and anger.

They had in a short while cleared enough of a space for Alliole to crawl through, and she tore at it from the other side.

"Should I go on?" she asked.

"Wait for me," Caerre said, "There are seals there, that you do not wish to disturb alone. Curse upon me, I never should have tinkered with sorceries."

"If the seals keep the Kings from the chamber then you have done the right thing," Alliole gasped as she worked, remembering Slaarngash's reluctance to venture into it. Caerre's voice came to her, dolefully, "You do not know. I have breached those," she said.

Caerre was through then, and last Tiralgon forced passage, although by then the gaping roof was giving further, causing them fresh fears. Alliole drew her sword, but was forced to stay between them, for she was sightless in the dark, although she found herself sure enough of her way to retrace her steps alone later. They saw none of the Kings.

"They will need to be harried, if we are to use the Catacombs to their proper purpose, for there are many dead," Alliole observed.

"They have retreated with the day," Tiralgon said.

"Perhaps for ever," Caerre said. She muttered occasionally and cast sigils upon the air. Otherwise they hurried without speaking, and breathless, until they came within sight of the reflected glow of the dull embers of the brazier on the wall opposite the door. With her vision gone, Alliole's hearing was supernaturally sharpened, and she could hear within breathing, slow and labored.

"He is here," she cried.

"Something is here," Caerre corrected, and halted her as she went to run forward. Tiralgon behind them pointed, and his dim shadow pointed also, hugely. Little red feet ran from the door of the chamber, away. Slick, wet red feet.

"I breached the seals," Caerre said, in her turn, blankly. Alliole threw off Caerre's restraining hand and ran forward, sword drawn, for Caerre seemed frozen in her dismay. The breathing now filling her ears, as someone in great pain. She stopped at the door, for the glow illuminated only a shadow on the floor, that did not move and was too small. She was afraid. As her eyes adjusted to the light she saw one hand out flung, and that the puddle that oozed upon the floor was crimson not from the firelight but of its own making.

"Helaf," she said. The shape did not move. Sword at ready she stepped forward, gingerly avoiding the pool of blood. The sound of breathing continued, hoarse, so filled with pain that she wanted no more but to put an end to it. She stirred the brazier with her sword, and a little flame leapt from it, and then fell, giving her enough light to glimpse. Caerre and Tiralgon stood at the door. Caerre and Alliole cried aloud at the sight. Tiralgon stood mute, almost pleased, as if finding some fitting resolution to a grim prophecy.

Helaf lay on the floor, but his brother was gone. There was a great wound in his belly where his twin had been. Caerre cried again, a wordless voice of sorrow, and rushed to him, disregarding the blood, turning him, so that the light fell upon his eyes. He winced and moved to raise his hand to shield them but his strength was too little. Alliole stood in front of the brazier instead, and lost all sight of him in her shadow.

"Get some cloth," Caerre screamed at her, "Get something to bind him. Water."

"There is too much blood," Alliole said dully, but nevertheless she dragged bedding from one of the wall niches, and Caerre bound it about him, gulping and trying not to look at the wound or what spilled from it, pushing his guts back into his body as gently as she could. Alliole got other bedding to soak up the mess on the floor, and knelt upon it, pushing more under his body as Caerre lifted him. Helaf's head rolled back in her arms. From the door Tiralgon cursed, thickly and vile, and turned and smote the stone once and then again with his forehead, bringing blood, looking at them sideways. Alliole got water and brought it to Caerre, who wet her brother's lips and supported his head. His eyes opened again and moved from one to the other of them, wonderingly.

"The Kings, it was the Kings who did this," Caerre said, wildly, "It is Xoon's fault, that he brought them upon us." She sobbed.

"The Kings cannot pass the door," Alliole said, and knelt by him on the other side.

"What were the feet then?" Caerre said, and called Helaf's name, as for a moment his gaze passed all of them again, and looked into the eternal. Her voice brought him back.

"That," Alliole said, and touched his body.

"A gruesome jest," Tiralgon said, from the wall, his voice almost overbearing Helaf's as he also spoke.

"They said, they said we would be whole," Helaf whispered, his eyes on his sister, "We wanted it so." He turned his gaze to Alliole, and moved, as if to touch her, but the gesture was too much for him. His head fell back, his eyes closed, and then rolled open again, sightless. Blood came from his mouth and nostrils.

"No," Caerre shrieked, and again she called his name. She would not accept this. She bowed herself over his body calling and weeping, whilst Alliole, smote by such deep and grievous feeling that she was entirely divided within herself, drew back. Anything that she could say, anything that she could do was hopelessly compromised. She opened her mouth only to find Tiralgon beside her, hushing her violently. He took her by the arm, and dragged her to her feet with his giant's strength. He threw her at the entrance.

"Leave," he said, dwarfing her, "There is no place for you here." She stopped herself there, clinging to the door frame, and called out to him in her anguish, "But I loved him, I loved him also. You will not deny me."

"I'll do as I please," he shouted back, although even his voice could not drown out Caerre's weeping, "She who has suffered so much, you have cut her deepest, you who say you would help us. Go."

He came for Alliole, so tall and terrible in his ferocity that she gave back before him, although reason told her he must be close to exhaustion, for he had to hold himself up against the wall as he came for her, and blood still came from his side and now his forehead. Although reason told her that if she was to have any hold on Caerre's regard, to have any aid in alleviating her suffering; if she was to have any to cling to now, it must be them. She could not, she gave way, and fell back into the corridor, then turned and fled before Tiralgon, who shouted and raged down the corridors after her as if he were mad. He did not give up the chase until she was through the roof fall by the ossuary. She heard him, when she was past, building the barricade up anew, and cried out to him to stop, but he would not, not until it was fully formed again. She sprawled in the passage-way, sobbing and fighting for breath, until such time as she had recovered enough to stagger back to her abandoned post.

She was bewildered as to whether she loved or merely needed him, for he was gone at a time when she felt that his living presence might have decided her. And she could not be rid of the idea that his death was the direct result of a last gamble, an attempt to render himself pleasing to her. She did not know if she had mistook an affection for something deeper, or if their union, momentary and joyous, had meant anything at all.

Alliole had got back to her post and relieved Grielle, who went away to sleep, before these thoughts began to greatly oppress her. She took advantage of her solitude to weep, but found shortly that she must stop, for it was necessary for her to be vigilant. She had to keep wiping her eyes and face, and was on the edge of weeping for the rest of the day. Xoon came down to her several times to speak on how events were progressing, but he seemed to take her tears as a right and proper thing and did not inquire further. Sleepghast, whom Alliole had not seen once in the fighting, clung close to Xoon's shoulder as if leashed there. She was unhappy to see him, for she could not forgive him his guesswork, which had driven her in the final search. Yet she could not, as she wished, slay him in Xoon's sight, and so rob the youth of all companionship. The Neve came down late in the day, and made her way across the balconies, not returning, so that Alliole guessed she had taken to Tyall's side. Iriethe still occupied the center of the chamber. The world seemed so full of the dead that she wondered that it was large enough to mourn them all. And Helaf's death, was that an omen only, among the rest of them, had he died to warn them all? This caused her fresh tears, until Xoon descended the stairs one last time, and she must dash them from her eyes, and rise for him. Grielle returned from wherever she had rested, and took up her position as if she had never left it.

Xoon passed her without speaking, his face distracted, across the balconies. Sleepghast paused at the oval in the ivory, and spoke in most measured and mellow tones. Xoon passed from sight without listening, and it occurred to Alliole that now would be the time to strike the blow.

"I speak on behalf of my most beloved master Xoon," Sleepghast announced. His voice filled the Cross. There was a stir below, and curious, Alliole stepped up to the trellises. She saw that many people were below, doubtless gathered by some signal that had escaped her notice immured as she was in the chamber above. Tyall's body had been borne from the hall, so that she and Sleepghast alone represented their rulers. As she stepped forward there were cheers that had not greeted Sleepghast, and she realized too late that Grielle had been good at her word, that her presence must surely give Sleepghast's words greater and perhaps spurious authority. Sleepghast gave her an evil look. She smiled in return and whispered, "I will kill you soon."

He smiled at her most benevolently, and then returned his attention to the people below, clearly judging her intention to withhold the blow. He had courage of a sort, she must give him that. "I must tell you all," Sleepghast said, "As my master's right and proper grief forbids him utterance, of the course of events. This blow against the Castle, this iniquitous assault, has been more grievous than we know, for it has caused our most glorious and beloved Parrar to give birth prematurely, worn out with the task of saving her people from this uprising of the ungrateful dead. The babe, a girl, is sickly, and the mother's health is failing. therefore I urge the most splendid display of mourning, to fortify our souls for the inevitable and supplicate those greater Powers which alone may sway the balance in this battle for her soul." Here Sleepghast shed two oily tears, that glittered like diamonds and greatly reinforced his oratory. A moan trickled through the crowd, as they did most truly mourn, and Alliole's soul, already torn, she thought would sunder entirely with this news.

She turned from the trellis back into the antechamber, repenting most unhappily of all that she had learnt that day, wishing that it could be wiped from her mind, and leave her short of memories, and happy. She returned to stand by Grielle, and only after due interval recovered enough spirits to wonder that, if such was so, why Elspeth and Xoon would leave the Parrar.

"Perhaps she would die alone," Grielle said, stolidly, when Alliole voiced this query, "And Anna is still with her. Perhaps she sent the others away."

Alliole's new disinterest was satisfied with this answer and she sat back, but her misgiving that events still reached for a resolution worried at her. Finally she could bear it no more, and went to the stair. Both cat and boar scrambled to their feet as she mounted the first stair, and both sounded, most dreadfully, when she set foot on the second. She stopped and retreated.

"I must have an answer," she said to Grielle, "It is not right. And why did Sleepghast make this announcement? Surely Xoon cannot be blind to all his duties." Grielle's chins folded in on themselves, "The boar I can manage for his spirit I share," she said, ponderously, "But the cat I cannot without a token to show, and such would not be delivered to me until the ritual mourning be over. Only her family, or those in their company, can otherwise pass her guardians and live."

Alliole stood and paced the chamber. "Then I will go and fetch Xoon to accompany me," she said, "For he owes me several favors. Do as I bid previously," she instructed her charge, as she departed. It was the work of moments to reach Xoon's chambers, but he was not there. She then traced his steps to the Neve's chambers, but this venture cost precious time.

Servants barred her entry to the chamber. "It is the custom," they whispered, "To so mourn together. Leave them." Alliole was by now so filled with ominous feeling that she disregarded them. When one man bodily blocked her entrance to the curtained bed-chamber she drew her sword, and threatened him, but he stood firm, and she had no heart to slay him.

"Where is Sleepghast?" she demanded instead, in a voice loud enough to wake the hells. "I demand entrance."

The curtain was thrust aside, and she was admitted, although no hand touched them. The room was quiet and chill. Tyall was laid out on the bed. Candles were lit about him, and incense was heavy in the air. Xoon sat on the floor at the foot of the bed, knees drawn up against his chin. The Neve sat by Tyall's head. Lyde and Marre stood by, as if idly. They were neither speaking nor weeping but seemed in communion with the dead.

"Where is Sleepghast?" she demanded again, shattering the calm.

"I sent him away," Xoon said, looking up, "He chattered too much." She looked at them, for though they were surely mournful and cast down, exhausted, grim, yet there was none of the sense of tragedy that even now rocked the halls.

"Did you give him leave to stand at the balcony and speak in you name?" she said.

"Why would I do such a thing?" Xoon said, dismissively. He returned his head to his arms, propped up on his knees.

"What are you doing so far from the post I set you?" Elspeth asked. But she asked disinterestedly, as if her mind was on other matters. In her very lethargy, Alliole saw cause for further despair. She crossed the chamber and knelt by Xoon, disregarding the question.

"Is your mother ill, the babe sickly?" she asked urgently.

"They are both perfectly well and sleeping," Xoon said, "Why else would I leave her?"

"What is this?" Marre said, irritatedly, "With wild nonsense you disrupt our mourning?"

"You will have more to mourn of soon," Alliole said, "I have done wrong. Grielle will doubtless admit him." Grielle knew him, and unlike Iriethe, held no suspicion. She turned and ran from the chamber with no further word, realizing she had no time for grief, but cursing her own lack of vigilance. If Sleepghast had ambition then it must be expressed through Xoon, and she could see a perfectly simple plan that in its consequences must raise Xoon most rapidly to a most exalted position, and one he had no hope of filling, save through the capability of his servant. She could see it clear and simple laid out before her, for was not a scapegoat handy, and in this uncertainty and crisis would any listen to pleas of innocence from Caerre, as mourning took those capable of determining the truth from the world, which would surely enact its own justice, and rapidly. And she, who had alone been in a position to perceive this plan in time, had failed them all.

Yet although she ran as fast as she could she was too late. She burst into the antechamber crying to Grielle, "Have any been here?"

"Only Sleepghast, with a message from Xoon," she replied, her phlegmatic nature not allowing her to betray her startlement.

"And you admitted him?"

"He had the token," Grielle said and shrugged her massive shoulders. Alliole ran for the stair, but once again the Powers at their head denied her admittance, the cat screeching most dreadful, as if in pain. She drew her sword and waved it in the air in useless emphasis.

"Hurry," she screamed at them, "He means murder, that man. The Parrar and her child too, hurry." The pair milled in the corridor in confusion, getting in each other's path. She urged them again, trying again to mount the stair, and halted by their enraged squalls.

"Sleepghast," she called instead, "If you think to return I am waiting at the foot of the stair. None other suspect, but I do. Sleepghast hold your hand, or I will slay you."

There was no answer, save suddenly cat and boar gave voice, a most horrible howl, and leapt into the air. Their solid forms writhed and smoked, becoming ethereal.

"No, no," she screamed at them, and another scream, most piercing, outbore hers.

"Murder," shrieked Anna, "Murder most foul."

Alliole, able to bear it no more, ran up the stair. She charged through the forms of the Powers with little hindrance, for they were dissipating, and into a further series of chambers, sparely but beautifully appointed. As she ran, Anna came bolting from the last chamber, a squalling bundle in her arms, almost overwhelming her.

Alliole halted, for she could see through the doorway. She could see a scrap of rich tapestry, a corner of a bed with linen drawn down, and a hand, tapered, delicate and fair, lying limp upon it. Blood ran down the hand, and trickled to the floor.

Anna, with her cry of 'murder,' passed her by, and ran for the stair. She let her go, staring dumb-struck at the fragment of sight thus presented her. Nothing stirred in the chamber, but nevertheless someone must be in hiding for there was no other entrance.

"Your plan has failed, Sleepghast," she said, and then went into the room and destroyed what she found there.

She alone then descended the stair. Xoon came up to the antechamber as she arrived in it.

"Where are your aunts?" she asked.

"None of them will leave him," he said, "What is the matter?"

"Where is Anna?" she asked Grielle.

"Gone, I know not where," she said.

"I do," she said. "Follow me," she said to Xoon.

"What is happening?" he cried, and ran after her. She turned briefly to look at him, at his callow, handsome face already setting into new lines of bleakness, of maturity. If she told, he would surely return to his mother.

"Anna has the babe, and has taken it to her chamber in the Catacombs," she said.

"The beast," Xoon said, indignantly.

"She thinks only of the child's safety, for that is where she feels safe. Helaf thought so too," Alliole said, abandoning all further explanation. Besides Xoon had no weapon, so he could do Anna little harm when they found her, "But the way is blocked so we shall find her there." His eyes set and he followed her, although shortly after he complained of a terrible pain in the heart and wanted to turn back, seeming to guess at its cause. She would not allow it, and he led her one last time down the Catacomb stair.

But when they arrived at the barricade they found that fresh passage had been forced through it. "Surely Anna could not have done that," Alliole cried out in despair, and ran forward. As she did so, she trod in something wet, and Xoon cried, "There are bloody tracks, all over the floor."

"Little or great?" she said to him.

"Small," he said. "The Kings?"

She shook her head, "Another thing," she said, and again forbore to tell him more, although she could guess what it was, and therefore what had forced passage through the fallen roof. "Which way do they go?"

"Toward the Castle," he said, in alarm, "Is it Anna? If she has hurt. . . ."

"No, no, I am sure she would not," Alliole said, and returned to feeling over the roof fall. It would take the amount of work almost equal to their previous attempt to forge passage for both of them, being larger than both that had previously passed through. Anna had evidently just had enough clearance, for shreds of her dress were caught in the stone.

"Anna, Anna," she called, "There is great danger there. It is I, Alliole, who speaks. Can you hear?" Then she clawed in despair at the wall. It would be night soon, and night would bring the Kings. "This should be sealed again," she said.

"I want to know what has gone towards the Castle," Xoon said.

"An evil thing," Alliole said, "We must breach this wall, recover Anna and return to warn the others. We cannot leave her and your sister. Caerre is in very great distress and may do her evil."

"My daughter," Xoon corrected, beside her in the dark. She could hear him fumbling with something. "Here I have the truth-stone," he said, for her benefit. "Move wall, shift stone," glibly and without belief.

Nothing happened.

"I am holding it in my hands," he said, "I cannot use it. Let us return and tell my aunts. They will know what to do."

Alliole leant against the wall, "Think of the babe," she said, "Think on her very urgently. We do not have the time to reach help other than ourselves. We could not save Tyall or Helaf. We can save her." She was begging.

Her words worked, for although Xoon said nothing, the wall stirred at her back, rippling like a live thing. She yelped and stumbled from it. The wall parted. She could hear it grating and stumbling; she could hear the roof starting to roar in its descent, and then desist in its falling, as Xoon's will upbore it. They both yelled in surprise and delight, and the roar of rock saluted them. Xoon moved forwards, clutching the truth-stone, and she caught at his shoulder to guide herself. Once they were passed he still kept to a measured walk, and it took her to drag at him into a run. Some greater power had hold on him, she guessed, and when it ceased its hold, he stumbled and would have fallen but for her support.

"We must keep going," she said, "Xoon, you are my eyes here," and they went on together. She called Anna's name, into the dark, but Xoon's voice did not join hers, for he was wrapped in this wonder. She was in very great fear, for she had remarked on Caerre's long contemplation of the wall with the three beings carved upon it, and on Helaf's dying words. She prayed that Caerre was not so embittered as to turn finally against her own kin.

Nevertheless she knew now that they finally approached the resolution to which they had been hurrying. And whatever shape it would come in, she was glad, glad to meet it. For then it would be over, and she could rest, forever if need be. With these thoughts filling her soul, and determination in her heart, she approached the chamber where Helaf was slain.

"Hullo, the sticky stuff is upon the floor here too," Xoon said to himself, as they approached. She disregarded him, for the unquiet air and stench of sorcery swilled about the approach to the chamber. Caerre's voice, and the sound of a baby crying spilled from the door with the dull light of the brazier.

"Give me the child Anna, do," Caerre said. She sounded brisk and impatient.

"No," Anna said.

Xoon overtook Alliole at the door, but whatever he would have said was choked in his throat as he stopped, and Alliole coming behind him, was stopped also.

The chamber beyond was crowded. Anna cowered half-way within, near her bed, a little way along the wall. Helaf's body was laid out in the room's center, and candles lit about it, in the same manner of Tyall's death chamber above, save that Helaf took up less room than ever before. Caerre perched on the mortuary slab at the far end, her book before her. Tiralgon was half way to the door, also against the wall. All were kept from the center of the chamber because it was filled with the figures once throned, who had now descended from the wall, and milled between Helaf's body and their late frieze. They were of great bulk although not tall, huge and featureless, and as they moved their limbs grated against each other. Their arms were outstretched and groped before them, because, like the Kings, they were blind. Unspeakable evil radiated from them. These were demons given flesh of stone.

When Xoon and then Alliole appeared, all attention diverted from Anna. The blank, malevolent faces of the creatures faced them, and Tiralgon's—near death surely but still merciless. Caerre, who had been simply impatient, now lit up with surprise and spite. Alliole felt the disaster upon her.

"No," she said, feebly, speaking first, "No, Caerre," as if her words could halt such imminent crisis. She had brought Xoon here without even a weapon to defend himself.

"Alliole," Caerre said, broodingly, "How nice of you to bring my brother here."

"Put them back," Alliole pleaded, desperately, "Caerre, please. Not all the grief in the world is worth this."

"And my mother also," Caerre said, goadingly. "We were watching her chambers. We saw. It was a fine blow you struck, Alliole."

Alliole disregarded her, for the demons had found purpose and were making their way towards Anna.

"My mother—dead?" Xoon said, quizzically. He came into the room a little. The demons feinted forward, cutting off Anna, but they went across Helaf's body. Alliole squawked, "No," as one of them trampled him, and another knocked over several of the candles, whose little flames guttered out as they rolled.

"Back," Caerre said, peremptorily, and they retreated again. Her face was split neatly between evil and anguish.

"There is still hope," Alliole pleaded.

"Here," Xoon said. He fumbled with the truth-stone and held it out awkwardly, "Here, Caerre, take this." He knelt and put it upon the floor, before Helaf, "Take this and let the babe go. That is all I ask." Very cautiously now he came forward into the chamber until he was beside Anna. He was defenseless. He held no weapon. Surely Caerre would not kill him.

"Give me her, Anna," he said.

"No," Anna said, clutching the squalling bundle all the tighter, and looking with the wide, wondering eyes of death upon the stone demons, for now they made their approach sideways, around the circle of candles.

"Then run for the door," he said, and turned to face them, with his bare hands. Alliole came forwards now, unsheathing her sword, which caught somber hues from the embered air. Tiralgon had edged forwards a little, she saw, and if they concentrated entirely on the demons, he would be on them.

"Both of you back to the door," she said, "Anna for the love you owe me, Xoon, because you are not a fool. Let us not all die." They both obeyed her. Caerre's expression of malice dissolved into puzzlement, "You do not believe me," she said to Xoon. Xoon hustled Anna backwards. "Why should I? It is not the truth," he said. As he said so, Helaf's brother appeared at the door. He strutted and tittered. He wore around his waist a skirt of ragged flesh. He was as the Kings are, save that his eyes were alert, and they glittered. It was obvious to what he owed his birth, for his kin were before them.

"Give her me," he piped, in mimicry, "Give her here."

Alliole cast a look about the chamber and saw that they were surrounded, but that Caerre, sitting bolt upright on the mortuary slab, was as surprised as they were by this new turn of events.

"You," she said, and other emotions than hatred washed over her face, revulsion and remorse, deep and bitter.

"It was Caerre," Anna cried. "I was asleep. Caerre woke me, calling my name through the peep-hole, or Sleepghast would have killed me too. Caerre," the last was a call for Caerre to save her again, for the creature strutting into the room did not look as if he cared to distinguish between his sisters, and his motives were unmistakably vile.

"It was Sleepghast I slew," Alliole admitted to Xoon, seeing that the end was near. She did not want him to die thinking her false-hearted, "Not your mother." He gave her a look as wondering as Anna's.

"I knew that. You who loved her as much as I did, " he said, then, "Will you accept my gift, Caerre?"

"It is not yours to give," Caerre said, scornfully, "This mockery, this child's toy," but her gaze was abruptly twisted. The demons convulsed and then turned to her. The battle raged within her as much as out.

"I could not save her," Caerre said, wonderingly, "For by the time I had run to the Catacomb entrance and returned it would be too late. And the walls are so thick there they muffle all sound. I called her name and then Anna's again and again. I would have saved her if I could. Why, when I hated her?" Her creatures shared her indecision. One of them span about and smote the wall, which cracked asunder.

"Because you loved her, Caerre," Alliole cried, in anguish, seeing her battle so valiantly with her own darkness, seeing her poised on the brink of turning from her decision, "You loved her and she turned from you, but it was her sickness, Caerre, her own sickness that undid her, her and you. Your father loved you."

"My father died," Caerre barked, and the hopeful flame that had burnt in her was snuffed out, "And my family took what is mine." Her creatures surged forwards. Alliole, with a despairing cry leapt forwards to meet them. Xoon cried out. "Then I'll take what is mine also," he said, and came forward with Alliole, so that she thought he meant his own death. Anna was left undefended by the door.

Alliole parried the maul blow of the first of the creatures, and it was only due to the demon strength in her own hands that she was able to withstand its force. The good sword belled in anguish in her hands. She was driven back across the chamber by its force, whether she would or not. The other two creatures came up behind, one trampling Helaf a second time and going for

Xoon, who knelt before his body. Alliole realized he held the truth stone again in his hands. The third struck at her from the side but she dodged, driven back again.

Xoon fumbled with the stone and looked up hopefully. Nothing happened, save the creature aimed a blow at him, which he rolled from. They moved infernally quickly, these demons, but their blindness robbed them of accuracy in their blows. Alliole struck at the demon facing her, but her sword glanced off, blue sparks flaring where it had touched. There was no mark on the stone. The battle was hopeless. She parried a second blow, but her blade shattered before it, and she flung it from her.

"Caerre," she cried, hopeless, and hoping only to slow their advance and allow Anna time to escape, if she could, "Caerre, I carry your brother's child. If you would save him, save me."

Caerre shrieked in her anger and she stood upright from her crouch on the shelving, "He was gone from me when you got it," she said, and then motioned to her creatures to get the truth-stone from Xoon. The demon fighting Alliole turned back in obedience, and it was only because of that she lived, for another blow such as the first would have destroyed her. Her protective torque was of no matter to such as that.

She turned back to find Tiralgon, Anna, and Helaf's brother all tangled together, rolling about on the floor. She went hopelessly to Anna's aid, but found herself again too late. Tiralgon had killed the thing already and as she came back to them he flung it away into the corridor. He pulled Anna to her feet, scratched and bruised but unbitten. Anna had curled herself protectively around her infant sister, who had thus gained no harm whatsoever.

"I hate demons," Tiralgon repeated, abrupt as always, thrusting them both away into the corridor, "Get out. You cannot harm them."

"What are we to do?" Alliole shrieked at him, but he only smiled, old before his time, mean, grim, and turned back into the chamber. She found Anna clinging to her skirts and both sisters bawling, a great hindrance. She turned back to the chamber, in time to see Xoon stagger, and the chamber shake as a blast rocked it. The flags gaped, and dirt spurted up between them. Xoon was flung from his feet, the brazier overturned and all was disaster. It was not a blast but the masonry that spoke, radiant, guttural. Xoon had got the truth-stone to attend him.

The demon standing immediately before Xoon shattered, its pieces crashing into ruin around the room. The remaining two surged forwards, their hands outstretched before them, and evidently having an uncommon clear idea of where Xoon was, for although he dodged back almost to the door they were upon him. But in the last light as the brazier coals flared as they scattered about the chamber, Alliole saw one of the demons pick up the fallen head of the first and throw it with supernatural force towards them. It would have come through the entrance and hit them, but instead it caught Tiralgon as he turned. It caved his chest in. He fell forwards onto his knees, his blood-barred back still barricading them as the light winked out. Sounds of the most awful battle then ensued, for Xoon evidently had some but not all grasp of the stone, and both sides seemed to take initiatives. Alliole and Anna huddled together, the babe between them, and any noise they made in shrieking was drowned by the ghastly sounds from the chamber.

At last there was an abysmal noise, a grating and echoing as if both floor and roof had given in. They both blocked their ears, and were thrown upon the floor. Rock dust kicked over them, and a body was flung towards them out the door in a flash of white light intermingled with dust, that struck them so hard that they bled from the skin where it ingrained itself. Whomever had been flung from the chamber came ricocheting against Alliole, full length and then away, as the entrance collapsed, and just in time, for she could see in the after-flash a monstrous stone hand grasping at the lintel as if to haul itself through. Utter silence followed this collapse, as they all gasped and blinked at the dust pattering down, and gasped again. Alliole tried to lift herself from the floor and failed and blinked, then blinked some more, for the effects of the flash were lingering, until she was convinced that she could see in the dark, clearly, the fallen entrance, the further wall, Anna lying by her side and the other shape lying ahead of her. It was Xoon, and the truth-stone lay between them. She could see in the dark. Then silence was shattered by a healthy bawl.

"Anna," she said, and reached over, and shook her. Anna had curled herself around her sister again, and cushioned her. Anna sat up, and took her sister in her lap, and looked at the further wall. Every now and again she made a tiny sound, like a hiccup, almost a 'No.'

"Anna," Alliole said again, but could not lift herself. She lay there, and turned her face to one side, blowing at the dirt before her until she could breath clearly again. She could still see in the dark, and wondered if this curse would continue. Xoon stirred, and like her tried to lift himself and then fell. He opened his eyes and stared at her.

"How delightful," he whispered, and grinned, entirely in his old manner, "Here we are lying on the floor, and neither of us can move more than a cats' whisker."

"Do not jest," she said, "You have entombed her." She reached forward, touching the stone, "That was wrong." The stone split in half, neatly, beneath her fingers, along the line between blue and green, and she gasped. Xoon lifted himself a trifle and inched forwards, to take both halves in his hand. He studied them a moment and then looked at her. He was leaning on his elbows, gasping and covered in rock dust as she was. He regarded her. She could see his eyes and their uncommon color, and the new deep lines etched into his face, most clearly in the dark. "Do you think you will miscarry?" he asked her.

"No," she said, "Never." And all the will within her clenched around this small thing, whatever its fortunes at birth would be, part demon, part misbegotten, part her. "Don't you dare, you owe me," she said, for she could see the thought in his uncanny eyes, most clear. She could read him, and he desired not her death but the death of that which she carried, that might be a threat to his own daughter.

He dropped both halves of the stone, and levered himself up, staggered and looked down at her, then moved to collect the babe. Anna shocked and looking only at the wall, making only the small, constant noise, did not halt him, and he took the bundle in his arms. The babe silenced immediately, and slept, having endured more than the normal course of newborns. The lines of Xoon's face relaxed. He touched his forehead to his daughter's.

"I have to take her to her mother aunts," he said, "Perhaps you will look after Anna."

"Caerre," she whispered to him, with no strength to force loud voice into her lungs. She got herself to her knees and reached out to pull herself up with the wall, "You cannot leave her. That is too cruel. We must dig her out."

He turned his regard from his daughter to look at her, and most clearly she saw his new character, the ruthlessness that had been forged into place within him by circumstance. "I did not leave her," he said, "The whole chamber is fallen in. She is dead."

He stooped and picked up the pieces of the truth-stone, then turned and limped away. She could hear him, going through the Catacombs. She could do nothing a long while but sit and gasp, and look back over her actions and her decisions since she had come here. She did not wonder, she did not search for the truth, she simply looked over everything she had said and done, and thought, "Here I could have changed things. Here I perhaps did wrong." And although no creature can change the past, however bitterly they may repent, yet there is no right or wrong, and some healing, in thus thinking. After a long while she got herself to her feet, and gathered up Anna, who made no move of her own, save to gasp and sit. She took the necklace of jade beads from her throat and fastened it around Anna's, murmuring comforting words to her. She then carried Anna back through the Catacombs, the last time in life that she would travel them. She was met by Lyde and Marre at the head of the final stair. A host of servants were clearing away the dead, and warriors stood guard against any further incursion of the Kings. Although this guard was renewed daily, far into the future, until its purpose and origin were forgotten, the Kings never returned. They had stirred once in their vengeance and now were again still and silent and speechless, as befits the dead.

"Xoon has been implying wild things," Lyde said, briskly. When she saw Alliole's face she must have known the truth of it, for she stopped and stared.

"It has been too much for Anna; her mind has gone, I think," Alliole explained, "She is only twelve. There are some things she cannot understand."

"Let me take her," Marre said, unexpectedly. Alliole stepped back warily, but Marre only said, "My servant will tend to her. She will not see me. If she regains her wits he will return her to you."

Alliole remembered the servant and his kindness towards living creatures, and repented of her doubts, surrendering her burden. Marre vanished with her. Lyde stood a while, then strove to say something. Finally she too went away. She had nothing to say. In later days Alliole would seek her out and renew their friendship, for although Lyde would always express even her affection unpleasantly, she was the closest now to Caerre, and to the friendship that might have been.

Alliole, alone, limped back towards her quarters, through precincts where many were busy about tasks of repair and restoration, where people hailed her as she went past as a hero. She passed through these places, and into the doubtful solitudes where she had dwelt for as long as she could remember, between Castle and Courtyard but of neither. As she passed through these deserted places, seeking only her bed and sleep, or forgetfulness if sleep would not come, she heard a creak of hinges, and turned her head.

She saw in the wall, a door, where none had been set before. It was built of ivory, yellowed and spotted with age, and bound with copper hinges, green with verdigris, and rusted almost into disuse. The bolt had been drawn, and she could see that the door sat ajar on its hinges. It did not look so heavy as Tiralgon had described, and it would surely take only a small push to gain admittance. But she had to consider what lay beyond. An alien and implacable hunger? The other, brighter world into which she had been born? Or simply another chamber, with bare stone flags and mystic tapestries bound about with beauty yet lost in a place unvisited and drear? What over all had she learnt since her amnesia, and to what conclusion? Considering this, there was only one thing that she could do. She barred the door anew, and turned away.

As the echo of her foot-step faded, so too did the bright vision of the Door. The Castle returned slowly to its accustomed gloom. ✳

The Family

PREVIOUS GENERATIONS

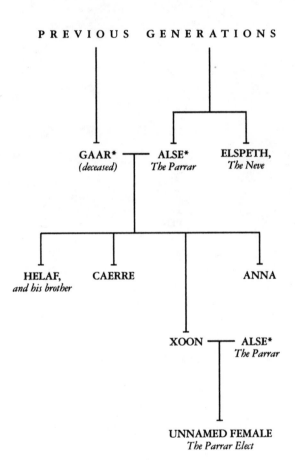

GAAR*
(deceased)

ALSE*
The Parrar

ELSPETH,
The Neve

HELAF,
and his brother

CAERRE

ANNA

XOON

ALSE*
The Parrar

UNNAMED FEMALE
The Parrar Elect

* *appears twice*

PREVIOUS GENERATIONS

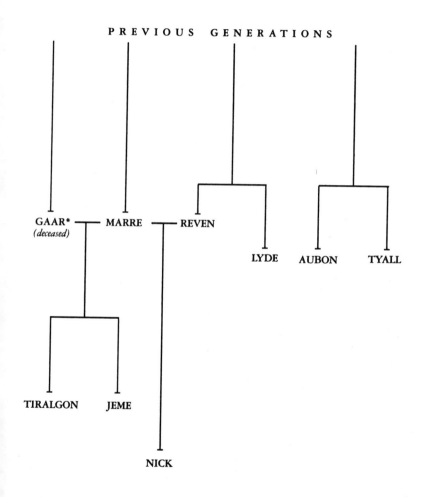

GAAR*
(deceased) — MARRE — REVEN

LYDE   AUBON   TYALL

TIRALGON   JEME

NICK

* appears twice